A *Home*
on Wilder Shores

Susan Posey

PAGE PUBLISHING, INC.
Conneaut Lake, PA

First originally published by Page Publishing 2020

ISBN 978-1-64544-463-3 (pbk)
ISBN 978-1-64544-464-0 (digital)

Printed in the United States of America

This novel is dedicated with love to my family, past and especially present. Bill, Hoyt, and Laurie, you are my world!

CHAPTER 1

The Atlantic, April of 1751
Ardath

THE SHIP WAS FAR into the ocean when the first passenger sickened. Although Liverpool was invaded by the small pox before our departure, the days of endless sun and blue water, the wind filling the sails, the freshness of the air, perhaps made the passenger and crew of the *Gracious Anne,* some 160 souls, feel that we had escaped the contagion. Fortunately, I had convinced Gwyn to take the variolation that Ibrahim, the wise ship's doctor, had offered us before we left, making us immune to the disease.

Father, of course, had refused it, thinking it was the work of the devil, since Ibrahim is of a darker, Moorish complexion. Stupid man! How our mother ever became involved with him is beyond my understanding. Well, here we were, halfway to the New World, being dragged along behind him like donkeys on a rope, for the sake of his wretched religion.

On this April day, as I rocked on my feet in our always-fetid tiny cabin, Gwyn rushed in.

"Ardath, Mrs. Perry is taken ill. I am afraid it is the pox," said Gwyn. "She has fever, and the red spots are appearing on her face and hands. She is with Ibrahim." Gwyn gazed at me and almost fluttered her hands. I admit that my heart sank. This again! But I showed her none of my alarm.

"Roll up your sleeves, Gwyn, and take off your under-petticoat. We'll have work to do," I said. This we did together, bumping arms in our tight space.

Gwyn watched as I bound up my red ringlets with a leather string, then sleeked back her glossy black hair and tied it as I had mine. Her blue eyes were almost black with apprehension, but she would work with me steadily. She took instruction well, being as malleable as I could wish from a younger sister. At fourteen, she was young enough to have a boyish shape still, but she could be more persistent in her accomplishments than many a person twice her age. We tied on our heaviest white aprons, took a quick breath, and got ready to work.

In two steps we were at Ibrahim's quarters. I could hear low groans through the solid oak door. Mrs. Perry was a heavyset woman with a round face who had been kind, almost a mother hen, with Gwyn. Gwyn still missed our mother so much that she was willing to put up with some clucking from Mrs. Perry. At any rate, I knew from Gwyn's description that she definitely had the pox. Ibrahim had isolated her as best he could in his tiny cabin, but the pox would spread anyway. By the time the spots appeared, she could have infected anyone close around her. And on a ship, no one was very far from anyone else.

Ibrahim's pouchy brown eyes met mine as we entered his cabin. I thought I could see the ship's doom written there.

"Ardath, I had hoped you would come," he said simply, handing me the damp cloth with which he had been wiping Mrs. Perry's face. "I must go to talk with Captain Bostwick."

"I hope he will understand what must be done," I said. At that moment, I could hear Mr. Harry Perry next door in the captain's cabin shouting that he must be with his wife in her hour of need. I cocked my head toward the sound. Ibrahim nodded. Being an older man, he had many years of experience in dealing with distressed families.

Gwyn was staring at Mrs. Perry in apparent dismay. Mrs. Perry, though, was lucid at the moment and smiled at Gwyn, gesturing for her to come closer. "Come, dear. It is all right. All will be well," said Mrs. Perry. "It's just this silly sickness. I've been through worse."

I saw Gwyn draw in a deep breath and manage a presentable smile. "Mrs. Perry will respond better to your care than mine, Gwyn," I told her, and went to tell Father the news.

As the only clergy on board, he might be needed, and in a hurry, despite the patient's optimism. I clutched the steps of the grimy ladder to the deck, emerging with gratitude into the fresh salt air. He had his back to me, gazing out to sea. As usual, he wore all black. His cloak flapped in the sunny breeze like a vulture's wing. I had to get close to him to speak only for his hearing. He half-turned to me, staring at his clasped bony hands to avoid my gaze. I sighed.

"Father, Mrs. Perry is taken sick. An epidemic is coming. The pox is with us." He did not reply at all. Instead of doing something useful, he clutched his black cloak close around him and went to his coil of prickly hempen rope to pray.

Standing at the rail of the ship, the wind pushing back the lock of my hair that inevitably sprang from its confinement, I began to count up the possible survivors. Ibrahim and Gwyn and myself, of course. The cabin boy showed the marks of a previous pox, which meant he would survive again. How old could he be? Maybe eleven, and of a slight build, so not made for heavier work, but someone who could scale the rigging. Of the others, a portion would survive. Among these, we would need to have someone who could handle heavy sails and who knew how to get us to a safe landing. Any of the crew should be adequate to man the sails, but setting the course was a different matter. I saw no scars on Captain Bostwick. Ibrahim had told me that the captain refused the variolation, on the grounds that he could not afford to suffer the mild case of pox that sometimes followed, because of his responsibility to be at his post. That meant we could not count on his survival.

I could learn almost anything, having been blessed with a quick mind, but the captain would never reveal his secrets to a woman. I had to have a male whom the captain trusted in order to get more information. His next in command was the first mate. Perhaps Ibrahim could convince the captain to make sure the first mate and at least one other crew member would know the particulars of the journey. Perhaps the first mate already knew the crucial information. I would have to find a way to get close to one of these men and learn more about the ship. Ibrahim could not do it; he would be busy with his patients.

Father would be busy with the burials. That thought made me realize that the extra canvas the ship carried should not be cut into shrouds. The dead would have to go over the side uncovered so that the canvas could be used to provide shade on deck for those still ill. The cabins below would not be sufficient to contain the infected. At least they would be close to the side when they died. Truly these were grim thoughts, but having seen what had happened within a few weeks in Liverpool, I was frantic with the need for preparation. In Liverpool, Ibrahim and I had started a makeshift clinic in an abandoned warehouse on the wharves, so I knew what we would need.

Taking a deep breath of the cool ocean air, I glanced toward Father. He was still bent over in prayer on his rope. I had to give him credit; apparently, he wanted us all to have a better life in Pennsylvania. We were scheduled to meet with his brother Thomas in Philadelphia and to stay with him and his wife, Priscilla, until Father could get a church started.

It certainly took faith for him to go off to the New World with no connection except his brother, or perhaps it was mere foolhardiness. Still, there was nothing left for us but a marginal life of poverty in Wales. And after Mother was gone, he at least took up his responsibilities with us. Since he had never really known us, he might well have left us in the cottage in the woods. Instead, he came for us, a month ago now, and included us in his plans. He actually had some money saved to get us started on the journey, and he carried quite a bit of silver in the money belt under his clothes; he intended to provide.

Still, he was a black-clothed scarecrow of a man, pinched in features, stooped in posture, and mostly silent, a hard man to know and a harder man to like. I suspected he came for us in order to pay for his sins and perhaps to avoid going to the hell he was so fond of ranting about in his sermons.

He seemed to feel that girls and women were generally helpless and had no intellectual abilities, whereas our mother had educated us broadly and always looked to us to show good sense and to take care of ourselves. And she had always looked to me to be in charge in her absence. At least Father made no demands on us except that we be ladylike and not disgrace him.

Gwyn, of course, had wanted to get close to him, claim her long-lost

8

father, tell him all her hopes and dreams. He never looked either of us in the eye, as far as I know, and he always turned away when she approached him. He seemed to tolerate her in his way, though, while he patently hated me, maybe because I looked like our mother and reminded him of his youthful indiscretion. Now what he must regard as his sins of the past were there before him, and he prayed more fervently each day, probably to make up for the fact that we were in the world and it was his fault. This voyage gave us a chance to learn more about him, but I doubted he could do anything to make up for causing our indomitable mother to weep.

Well, my thoughts had made me tired, and there was little I could do yet. I sat down with the mast at my back and drank in the heat of the sun while I could. I should join Gwyn in the medical cabin soon. Meanwhile, I would gather my strength for the work ahead.

I had dozed; the sun was sinking as I woke. I checked to see whether Father was still on his hemp prayer stool. He was, but lying curled up, retching and shivering. I ran to him. His face showed the first of the flat red spots. He had the pox.

CHAPTER 2

April 1751
Gwyn

AFTER MANY HOURS, MRS. Perry lay in a more restful state, a good sign that she might have a milder version of the illness. I felt deeply grateful and found my face wet with tears. I appreciated her kindness to me and had been stricken to think that she was dying. I touched her face lightly; she was definitely cooler, thank God! I longed to stretch out my limbs and breathe fresher air than that of the sickroom. More, I was surprised that Ardath had not returned; she was usually quick to help. Washing my hands and splashing water on my face, I left the cramped room and headed up the wooden ladder to the deck. A gust of sea wind hit my wet face and felt most welcome, as I reached the top and looked for Ardath.

She was bent over a pitiful figure on the deck, a man writhing in his own vomit. He called out to God and some loved one to help him. The sun was setting; its golden light illuminated the scene. I rushed to help; I heard it then. He was calling out our mother's name between his heaves and gasps for breath. Father, then. My heart sank like a stone within me. To lose another parent would be more than I could take. I crept closer.

Despite the sour, greasy remains of dinner that clotted his black clothes, Ardath held him firmly and spoke reassurances in her low voice. He was not just calling our mother's name; he looked at Ardath and thought it was she.

"Carys, I have ever loved you. I am sorry for leaving. Nothing else matters but that we are together. Do not leave me, I beg."

"I will never leave you. I am here," Ardath replied as he turned from her to retch yet again. Her strong features seemed serene in the golden light; her hair fairly shimmered red and gold as it flew in the wind. I loved her for her kindness to him, she who was not often kind. I had never loved her more.

I knelt beside them, careless of slipping in the sour mess. As Father fell into unconsciousness, I turned to hold my sister. As always, her solid body calmed me.

"He is all we have," I said. "How can we lose him too?"

"We will always have each other. I promise you that," she said. I wondered how she could say that, given what we had already lost. But I knew that if anyone could make it so, it was Ardath.

"Help me turn him," she said.

I used a corner of my apron to wipe his face. It was gray, his slack lips hanging open. His limp body weighed more than I thought it could when we turned him slightly to his side. I gagged in sympathy. Ardath reached below his waistcoat, removing a money belt. She tucked it under her apron and belted it down.

"You think he will not live," I said. If Ardath thought that, he was indeed going to die.

"It is best to be safe. We cannot watch all the time."

"But should we…?" I asked.

"We don't know what is coming. We must have funds to survive. I do not trust anyone to hold it for us. They think of us as girls who must be controlled. This is best kept between us. Who would you rather have the power over our lives, some man or us?"

"You, of course."

"No, both of us! If anything happens to me, first you must take the money and don't let *anyone* know that you have it."

"I promise. But you said you would stay with me."

"Of course, I will. Now let us see if we can clean him some more. I believe there is nothing left in him."

Kneeling, we cleaned the vomit up from around him on the deck with a rag and bucket of seawater we found close by. We wiped down his coat as best we could. Ardath went to get Ibrahim. I bathed Father's face and tried for the last time to see if I resembled him. Yes, I had the same dark hair and blue eyes, and others said I resembled him, but I wondered who he was, in his soul, and who I was as well. The slack body seemed to be nobody, now nobody I would ever know, a heavy rag doll propped against me.

"A bad case of seasickness," I told the crew that passed by, never blinking once at my own lie. I doubt that I fooled them, but it was not my place (thank God!) to let out the word of the deadly disease at work on the ship.

CHAPTER 3

April 1751
Ardath

FIRST MATE ALEX WHITSUN was the ugliest man I had ever seen. In fact, he resembled nothing so much as a frog, or, no, with his lumpy, sea-weathered skin, a nice brown toad. Bandy legs stuck out from his squat body. His head was wide and flowed up as a mere extension of his narrow shoulders. When he was pleased, which seemed to be often, his lips split his squashed face in a gruesome parody of a grin. Teeth protruded in all directions, a few of them thrust straight out ahead of him. Ragged squares of brown, they seemed as determined as he was to please and appeal. Normally, those of such disturbing appearance dipped their heads to hide it, but Alex seemed to assume that everyone would like him as much as he liked them, and on first sight. He held his head high.

One might judge him a simpleton for his hopeful attitude, but I had seen the intelligent gleam in his bulging eyes. Beyond that, his most attractive features to me at this moment were the ancient pockmarks on his face and the backs of his hands. Although he would never be a captain because of his appearance, he apparently was a first mate because of his competence. And he would survive. I could use him.

As I hurried down the ladder and turned, I bumped into him. "Oh, Mr. Whitsun, I was just thinking of you a moment ago. Would you teach me a few things about the running of the ship when you have a free moment?"

"Why, I would be pleased to do so, at any moment you suggest," he replied. His accent, like his attitude, was decidedly at odds with his appear-

13

ance. It suggested a background of some gentility. Perhaps some aristocratic mother had loved him anyway. At any rate, he didn't seem to be opposed to a woman who wanted to learn. He stood smiling at me broadly. He hadn't yet heard of the illness, then.

"Thank you!" I said as I edged around him in the narrow passage. "Let us speak in the morning." He made as much of a bow as the corridor permitted and sprang up the ladder.

As I continued on my way again to Ibrahim's room, I smelled the always-pungent odors from the slave area. They were bound below us in the most awful conditions. Ibrahim looked after the three of them as best he could, telling Mr. Padgett, the owner, that they would bring him no price if they were dead of typhoid or other ills. Mr. Padgett appeared as unconcerned about them as if they were not even valuable for profit. I supposed that he was used to losing many of the slaves he traded in. Ibrahim, feeling for them particularly because they were fellow Muslims, had given them the variolation secretly.

Sometimes he took me with him to help clean and feed them. I was learning a few words of their language. It seemed that they were a Mandinka family of mother, father, and son. It was amazing that they were still together, and that fact seemed to give them courage. I admired them for bearing their afflictions stoically.

At this moment, I needed both courage and stoicism myself, dreading to see Gwyn suffer through our father's death. I must curb my tongue; it would do her no good to know that I felt little compassion for this scarecrow man who had deserted his family. In fact, I hated him for it, especially for hurting Mother.

I softly opened the door. Mrs. Perry was asleep, and Ibrahim dozed on his stool at her side, like any good healer. He awoke immediately to see why I came. He lifted his heavy-lidded eyes and bushy eyebrows in a silent question.

"Our father is on the deck. It looks like a bad case," I whispered.

Without a word, he reached for his bag and followed me from the room.

As soon as we were outside, he gripped my shoulders for a moment. "I am sorry," he said.

"Yes, thank you."

Gwyn knelt beside Father still. The moon struck her profile with a silvery grace, glinting off her tears. "Ibrahim," was all she said, but I saw how relieved she was.

He began to examine Father, touching his face and body gently. Though he kept his face calm, I could sense that he found nothing good. Finally, he lifted his head. "I'm sorry," he said again.

Gwyn pressed her lips together. Her chin quivered.

"We can make him more comfortable by loosening his clothing and finding a mat for him to lie on," Ibrahim said. We loosened his clothing while Ibrahim brought a pallet. Then we sisters sat by to wait. I hated to waste the time, but Gwyn needed me. Mother had made clear that Gwyn was my responsibility if anything happened to her, and I meant to live up to my promise to take care of her.

CHAPTER 4

April 1751
Gwyn

THE POX COULD LAST as long as three weeks, but we did not have that long with our father. His face looked gray and cadaverous under the rash after only a night and day. His fever raged higher than I had ever seen in anyone, and nothing we did for him could bring it down. He finally began to choke and convulse, flinging his body all over the deck, rolling as the ship rolled and more. There was to be no dignity to his death, but at least he was insensible for it. It was the most horrible thing I had ever seen. My heart broke over and over again, like the waves relentlessly hitting the ship.

All our effort was spent then on keeping him from throwing himself into the sea. I had little time for the pity that was due in such a case. Ardath was stronger and more able to contain him, crouching down with skirts spread wide and sleeves rolled. Finally, the crew tied his slumped body, sitting, to the mast. Of course, the whole ship was alert now to the disease among us. People murmured among themselves while giving us a wide berth.

"Those poor girls," I heard from one woman, and "Oughta throw him over now, save him from his misery" from one of the crew. "No, throw him over before he infects us all!" said another. Their voices were just part of the blur of my own misery.

Suddenly, Father arched in a violent convulsion that wrenched him against his ropes, then he fell back, limp, his eyes staring sightless, reflecting the blue skies above. God forgive me! I was relieved.

Ardath was immediately with me, her strong arms holding me. She said nothing to me and did not need to. She bent to close his eyes and called for a crew member to send for the captain and Ibrahim.

Captain Bostwick had a shroud with him when he appeared on deck. He gestured to two crew members to roll Father's body into it. They hesitated until he growled at them, then rolled and dumped the body in quickly and laced the strings tightly. The bosun called in a shrill voice for all hands on deck.

The captain addressed the crew and passengers that had gathered. "I am sure it comes as no surprise to you, after seeing the reverend's demise, that we are afflicted with the disease we had hoped to outrun on the sea. You will not panic but will conduct yourselves as proper subjects of our blessed King George." He stopped briefly to wipe sweat from his beefy face.

"At this point, we have only one other case, Mrs. Perry, who will probably recover. Since her case is mild, she can provide serum for the variolation, which our ship's doctor, Ibrahim, can provide to you. I urge you to make use of this to prevent the spread of the disease. I do not order you to do this, as it is not without its own risks of infection." Murmurs of horror passed through the crowd.

"As our only clergy is no longer available, I will read the proper burial service." He immediately brought a Church of England prayer book out of his coat and began the briefest possible service.

I tried to pray along with the rest of the ship members, but it was hopeless. The vision of our father rolling in agony played before my eyes, and then, blackness. I heard and felt nothing until I hit the hard boards of the deck. Several hands picked me up. The captain, when he saw I was conscious, gestured for the shroud to be slid down a plank into the ocean while he said, "God rest his soul."

I clutched the rail. The shroud bobbed twice and sank. The sea rolled on around us, all blue green and heartless in its beauty. Thus ended my hope that we could have a family.

Everyone fled from us as quickly as they could move. Ardath and I held to each other while the setting sun glared across the ocean and into our reddened eyes. In time, she helped me sit and brought fresh water and hard bread. She ordered me to eat. Shamefully, though I felt I should fast in mourning, I was hungry and I ate.

CHAPTER 5

April 1751
Ardath

AT SEA, SAILORS MOST feared two things, fire and the fury of the storm. The contagion that followed swiftly after Father's death resembled both, like a scorching wind that blew down passenger and crew alike, so that the remaining healthy people were hard-pressed to help, running from one scene of disaster to another.

Captain Bostwick had assigned Walt, the cabin boy, to Ibrahim, who had turned him over to Gwyn and me. Walt helped us set up a canvas-covered area on the deck where we laid out pallets, on the port for the more severe cases and on the starboard for those who might recover.

Walter was slight but strong, a redhead with a pale complexion turned blistered and ruddy by the sun. He seemed a truly good-spirited boy and was much help to us. The three of us and Ibrahim worked long days and nights, snatching sleep in staggered intervals.

Mr. Whitsun, too, was working long hours as acting captain. Unfortunately, Captain Bostwick was among those taken ill, though he had a strong constitution and seemed likely to recover from a mild case of the pox.

*****

Day was barely dawning when I dragged myself out of a restless sleep and up the ladder with a pail of fresh water for our patients. At the top, I turned to port and stared in amazement at the empty pallets before me. Every patient on the port side was missing.

A little white hand reached out to me from under a tarp near the pallets. Startled, I knelt to speak with the girl who hid there.

"Watch out!" she whispered. "They threw them all over, even the captain."

"Keep still," I told her, tucking the tarp closer around her.

I rose slowly from my crouch. As I turned, I was staring right into the callous eyes of the four men from the night's watch. They had buckets in hand. Frantic thoughts raced through my head. I had interrupted them as they threw seawater over the deck to make it look like a wave had washed the sick overboard. They meant to mutiny, having killed the captain.

I drew the surgical knife from my apron pocket. They dropped the buckets with a clonk, grabbing their own long knives. The light was still dim, but I made sure they saw my blade, turning it so that the eastern light flashed off it. My heart pounded. I was accomplished at hunting small game with a knife from my life in the woods, but this was very different. I widened my stance as much as the damned petticoats would allow. I did not take my eyes from them.

At this moment, the top of Walt's head appeared at the head of the stairs to my left, where he was not visible to the men ahead of me.

"Get men here quickly!" I hissed at him. Bless him, he did not stop to ask questions. His head dropped from sight, and I was left with the night crew again. I was a witness, and so was the little girl. I couldn't let them get her. Any moment they would rush me and have us both. Fortunately, they could not all rush me at once because of the narrow passage between us, or it would have been over in a hurry, and I needed to stall them until help came.

"I will plead for mercy for you," I said. "I will tell them that you threw over the sick because you feared the contagion. Surely, there are many who would understand that." My throat constricted, but I tried to sound reassuring and calm.

They ignored my speech. They advanced on me, eyeing the knife.

The leader laughed. "You'd gut us all, would you, missy?" Suddenly, he threw his rough body on me, knocking me back, wrenching at the knife. Staggering, I held to my feet. His rotten breath blew foul in my face. He had both my wrists in a steel-hard grip. I jerked my face away, but I did not let go of the knife. I managed to twist and rip at his arm with it. I saw blood sprout there.

This only infuriated him further. His foot lashed out to unbalance me, but I dodged. My breath came in jerking gasps. I couldn't keep this up much longer.

At this moment, Mr. Whitsun and three other men clattered up the ladder from below. They wrestled the night watch to the deck with many a thump and yell. Walt appeared with ropes for binding them. Although they struggled and swore, the mutineers were quickly subdued and bound hand and foot.

"Take them to the empty passenger cabin. It's unused since the pox and will serve as brig," Mr. Whitsun said, shoving his prisoner at a burly seaman.

I drank in deep breaths to stop my trembling. I bent my face to my knees. I vowed never to feel so helpless again.

Mr. Whitsun turned quickly and took my arm. "Are you injured?" he said.

"No, thank you, Mr. Whitsun. You came just in time," I said. "But let us see to Margaret." (For that was the name of the child who had warned me.) "She has been badly shaken." I lifted up the tarp and gestured for her to come out. Her oval face was even whiter than before, but she jumped out quickly.

"You did very well, Margaret. You are a brave girl," I told her as she collapsed into my arms, all bones and sobs. I stroked her hair. "Can you tell Mr. Whitsun what you saw?"

It took her a few minutes to recover, but when she stopped shaking, she told the story. She could not sleep because of her fever. She had heard rough whispering above the usual restless sounds of the sick. Then she was scared by muffled thumps, thuds, and splashes on the port side of the ship, so she had crawled under the tarp and lain very still. Soon, heavy footsteps came to her side of the ship. She began to hear groans and shouts that were cut short, followed by splashes as the bodies of those on the starboard went into the water.

As she told her story, the sun rose higher in the sky. I walked several steps to look at the starboard side, at the pallets that had held those recovering.

21

Every patient was missing there too. The coldheartedness of these men struck me like a blow to the chest.

Mr. Whitsun sent for Mrs. Perry, who had recovered from the pox and gave aid where she could with those who were ill or frightened. This seemed to help her cope with the loss of her beloved husband, Harry, who had died of the pox while she was recovering. She bustled over, immediately taking Margaret under her wing. I breathed a sigh of relief.

Then Mr. Whitsun saw that all the pallets were empty. "The captain?" he said to me.

"All were thrown over," I said.

His face blanched as he realized the extent of our loss and that he was now to be the captain, but he squared his shoulders and said, "Miss Rhys, would you care for a glass of brandy?" I gratefully accepted. He brought two glasses from below. The fiery burn in my throat felt bracing. We looked at each other with sympathy as the sun rose over the horizon.

*****

Mr. Whitsun continued exceptionally attentive to me, though he was very busy as the new captain. I think he truly felt out of his depth, never having had (and probably never expecting to have) such a position of authority thrust upon him. We had this feeling of responsibility in common, as Ibrahim gave me more and more duties in managing the sick.

Mr. Whitsun did not have the crew who killed the captain executed, preferring to keep them in the brig until we could reach port and he could turn them over to the authorities there. He instituted a type of martial law, though, organizing a group of the more able male passengers to watch the rest of the crew, in case there were others who might think of mutiny. An army major, a healthy giant named Booth James, helped in this, quickly organizing the men into squads with proper discipline. Alex confined women and children to the captain's cabin and one other, with guards on each.

Once the prison cell and the civilian guards were well established, Gwyn and I again had the run of the ship. Of course, more people fell ill. A dispro-portionate number had the severe symptoms that Father had suffered. They had burning fevers that seemed to affect their brains, causing convulsions and a swift death, or they had gross infection in their lungs and were unable to breathe, this, too, a quick death. These we put well out of the view of the others that we hoped would survive. There was no way to stop the screams, moans, and sounds of thrashing from them, however.

At least under Ibrahim's care, they were not bled or blistered or given emetics to make their misery worse. Moorish medicine had developed ideas far beyond those of our European doctors, but even so, there was little to be done for those severely ill. They died and died. At first, we had tried to give the dead some services from the prayer book, but we were too hard-pressed to continue that. We slid many of these dead "port" bodies into the ocean our-selves, with, I confess, little ceremony, so many were those that died in those weeks.

While every able person was stretched to work long hours to help out, the most neglected people on the ship were the three slaves way belowdecks, in the dark hold with the baggage. Their condition grew more pitiful by the day, as they lay confined in their tiny squalid quarters, unable to move, on their backs, noses almost touching the rafters above, lying in their own waste. Furthermore, they were well, despite all reason, of typhus or other diseases. They could not get the small pox because of their variolation. We could be using their able hands on deck.

When Ibrahim told me that Mr. Padgett was taken ill, he was helping someone who was dying and asked me to examine the slave trader. He was one of the people I didn't really want to get that close to, but out of duty, I did so anyway. It was easy to see that he had the pox, with a high fever. Fortunately, I had to touch very little of his body to know that. I told him to report to the deck.

Since it was a beautiful day, I went on deck myself to walk and think.

As I paced about, my arms clutched around my body, I determined to ask him if he would sell the Africans to me. I went back to his cabin as he made ready to come out, standing in the open doorway to address him. He straightened from his preparations and turned his face toward me. He had the bulbous red-veined nose of a heavy drinker and small red-rimmed eyes. The cabin smelled of rum-laced vomit. He was widely shunned on the ship, for most people did not like the idea that slaves were aboard this passenger ship, or did not like Mr. Padgett personally. He traveled alone. Mr. Whitsun had told me he had no family and no partners in his business. Obviously, his good and only friend was a never-ending bottle of rum.

"Mr. Padgett, would you sell the Africans to me?" I asked as calmly as possible.

He said, "I intend to give them as a surprise gift to some associates in Maryland."

"But it seems likely that they might not survive this epidemic in the condition they are in. Might you not buy others when you arrive there?"

"Yes, but at a greatly increased price."

"Tell me and I will match it."

"My dear, you cannot afford them," he said with a smirk. I could see that he was thinking, *What a foolish girl!* It made my gorge rise.

He was correct that I could not afford them, but I had heard the fatal rattle in his chest. I brought out all the money Father had had in his belt to prove that I could buy them. He then agreed, saying, "You know they are going to die anyway, don't you?"

"Everyone must die," I said. (In my heart, I added, *But you will die before they do.*) We made the deal and had the papers drawn up officially and signed before his illness worsened. Mr. Whitsun served as witness. He took the money into safekeeping for Mr. Padgett, as he had his other valuables.

I immediately got Ibrahim's help to deliver the Africans out of their confinement. He explained to them in their language what had happened. We stood together with an able seaman, at their heads, trying not to show our disgust at their stink. With muscles straining, we pulled them out of their compartment as if they were logs and slid their bodies onto the platform made by the trunks below them. Ibrahim unlocked the chains on their wrists. The crewman guided them to the floor, propping them up against the trunks, where they clung with trembling arms.

The father took my hands in his, even before Ibrahim could get off the leg chains. He looked into my eyes and gave a long speech in Mandinka, which I did not understand. Ibrahim explained that Omar had called me an angel sent from Allah and pledged that he and his family would guard me forever until the ends of their days. I was hard put to not show the weakness of emotion at this and turned to helping the rest of the family be freed.

We had Gwyn and Walt's help in getting them up the ladder and into our cabin. They were in truly sad condition, dirty and full of sores. We were able to clean them better in the bigger space. We had to shave their heads to get rid of the lice and bathe their bodies in oil of tar to prevent illness. We brought clothes from men and a woman who had no further need of them, having died in earlier days.

With clothes, food, and water, the Africans soon began to look more like humans (albeit bald ones) and less like dirty sacks of chaff. We threw their old garments over the side and washed our hands with rigor.

Mr. Padgett died two days later from the lung fever. Captain Whitsun handed me the ownership papers and the money I had paid. In addition, he said that Mr. Padgett had had a money belt that Alex felt should go to me for the provender of the slaves. I took this because it was indeed needed.

Maybe it would buy Mr. Padgett a way into heaven, although I was skeptical that anything could do that! When I looked into the bulging belt later, I found that it contained a virtual fortune of thickly packed gold coins.

CHAPTER 6

April 1751
Gwyn

AFTER FATHER'S DEATH, I went about in a brown haze of misery and exhaustion. Ardath, as always, continued vigorous, hardly seeming to notice that he was gone. She pitched into the work tending the ill as usual.

"Ardath," I said as we worked on the deck on a day soon after Father's death, "why do you not mourn for our father? You never speak of him and you don't seem to want me to either."

"Sister, I don't want to say ugly things about him when you want to remember him well," she said, rubbing her reddened hands on a rag and gazing out over the railing.

"But it is worse not to speak at all. I feel so alone," I said.

"Well, you didn't see the pain he caused Mother by leaving, because you were only a baby then. Mother, believe it or not, cried for him. I felt I must make it up to her somehow, take responsibility where he did not."

"But you were just three years old," I said.

"I didn't say it was rational," she said in an impatient tone. "He cared only for his 'calling to preach the Gospel', in London. We were nothing to him."

"I don't believe that part. He *did* make sure that his cousins at the Manor House would always help us if we were desperate. And they *did* help us find him. He *did* come for us when Mother was gone."

"These things are true," she said, but in a grudging manner.

*****

Ardath seemed more distracted than usual for other reasons. Her close call with the night watch had sobered both of us. I noticed that she collected knives from the dead sailors' belongings and practiced with them, throwing at a target she had chalked onto a trunk in the baggage hold. It showed the chest of a man, with a bull's-eye at the level of a heart.

*****

Most of our work was both mundane and repetitious. We wiped feverish faces and arms and gave sips of water to those able to drink. We watched the faces and bodies fill with the raised pox that left them looking like monstrous, lumpish creatures. This was especially frequent and pitiful in the children. We comforted the ill as best we could, with stories and ballads, talking with them of their homes and loved ones. And we sent them over the sides in death, with short prayers for God's mercy on their souls. The effort of sliding and hauling the bodies left me weaker and weaker. The despair of the situation exhausted me further.

We would have had more help if so many of the crew had not died, but they did. They had been exposed in the lower seaside inns and taverns of Liverpool, more so than the passengers, who had stayed in the better inns. The captain (or Alex, as we called him in private) needed every man left to run the ship. Walt helped us, but he was often needed to run the rigging, which he did like a scampering monkey. It was a marvel to see him run down the spars as if on a country road, his bare feet flashing, to check ropes or adjust the sails, or to climb to the crow's nest.

We had become special friends, Walt and I. One day as I took a breath from toiling among the patients, I leaned on the railing and looked to the sea and billowing white clouds above it, as I loved to do. I heard creaking and thudding in the sails above me. Suddenly, Walt jumped down from the rigging, landing lightly on his bare feet beside me.

"Miss Gwyn, how do you today?" His grin was delightful, full of boyish mischief.

"It is a fine day, but I admit that I am hot and tired. I must drag around

27

these skirts and petticoats. You are very fortunate to be a male and able to wear seaman's pants!" We were eye to eye in height, so I looked directly into his hazel ones. His pale skin had burned and peeled several times but was starting to take on a browner tone, or perhaps the freckles were merely merging together to give that impression. At any rate, I could see him blush under the brown. Then his eyes lit up, and he grinned broadly.

"You know, I have another pair of these that my mother insisted I bring with me. You could try them on, if you would dare to wear them."

"Why not? I do not think anyone would notice at this point." I looked down at my once-white apron and dark skirt, all splattered with vomit, pus, and filth. "At least I could be cleaner."

We went like conspirators down to the seamen's dark hold, where the dingy hammocks swung from the rafters. We crouched to look into his sea chest. There his mother had lovingly placed clean and folded clothing, both tan canvas pants and a long-sleeved white shirt. It gave me a pang to think of things a mother does to show her caring. He raised them up proudly, like the treasure they were, and offered them to me.

"But, Walt, these are for you."

"Nah, I don't need them. Try them on!"

"Well…" I hugged him quickly and hurried to my cabin. They fit me perfectly. This was one time when I was glad to have the figure of a child still. Ardath had the figure and the stature of a Goddess. I never expected to look like her, but then she would not have been able to wear male clothes!

The canvas pants, though new and stiff, were blousy and quite cool. I rubbed them until they loosened up some. I was tempted to complete the outfit by chopping off my long and increasingly lank black hair, but I just pulled it tighter in its thong. I thought that I must look very much like a boy, a thought that gave me such a sense of freedom that I actually laughed aloud. With some new energy, I began to scrub away with plenty of soap at my filthy apron until it looked almost clean. It would never again be white, though.

*****

Shortly after Ardath freed the Africans, we looked up from our work one day to find that the number of both seamen and passengers was so diminished that the ship seemed almost ghostly. From a vessel of over 160 souls, the *Gracious Anne* now had only a score left.

Ardath spoke with Alex about getting help, within my hearing.

"Alex, we are becoming exhausted. There are not enough men left to help us get the dead overboard and keep up with the ill. Could we please let the Africans help us with this? I fear for Ibrahim's and Gwyn's health. They need more rest."

Alex was too wise about Ardath to say that she needed help too. "I will speak further with Ibrahim about it. It is true that he and Gwyn need more help," he said.

That was how the Africans joined us in our work with the sick. They proved to be both strong and kindly. Omar, the father, had been a carpenter in his native land and was wiry and tough. His son, Ahmed, was taller and had large muscles from blacksmithing. Isa, the wife and mother, was especially compassionate with the ill. Of course, some passengers protested that they did not want black creatures around, and these we tended to ourselves. Most were just grateful for their help, as were we! Their presence gave us a distraction and a new focus that was welcome.

During all this time, no one but Ardath even commented on the fact that I was dressed as a boy. She gave me one glance the first day and nodded approvingly. Father would have been mortified, of course, but he was no longer here to judge.

The Africans began to learn some English, which Ardath and I encouraged as much as we could. Since they were going to the New World, they would need to communicate. At the same time, Ardath learned the Mandinka language at an amazing rate. She had always been a wonderful mimic of voices and accents, but her skill with a totally new language seemed in the realm of magic to me. But then, she always claimed that I had "the sight," so maybe others' abilities always seem miraculous to the ones who don't have them.

With the help of the Africans, our load was lifted. Having a little extra time, Ardath pursued information about the ship from Alex. She had confided in me that obviously, since they were so different in appearance and stations in life, they could never be a couple, so she was relaxed about her friendship with him.

She told me that the most complex aspect of running a ship was the use of the rigging, when to let out or to furl the sails and which ones, for example. How to tack or run with the wind, as needed. These skills could be many years in the making. She quickly mastered the use of the quadrant to measure our latitude, though. She learned how to set the course and loved to pore over the maps of our route that Alex had in his cabin.

She was at ease about her responsibilities toward the ship's company, since Alex was in command. Still, Ardath loved to learn all she could, being the adventurous and inquisitive person she is. I often saw them on the deck, with maps spread on a table, or quadrant in hand. I could rarely hear what they were saying because of sails flapping and waves gushing at the sides of the ship, men shouting in the rigging, and patients calling for help or moaning in pain.

Alex often pointed up into the sails, turning his hands to explain wind direction or turn of a particular sail. At times, his arms reached over hers to show her how to hold the quadrant, or where to look on the map.

I could see by the look in his eyes that Alex was falling in love with her, but I don't think she ever noticed it, so immersed was she in the learning. Perhaps my noticing such things was what made her feel I had "the sight." If so, then probably everyone but Ardath had "the sight." To me, his yearning for her was plain as the nose on my face, and it scared me.

CHAPTER 7

April/May 1751
Ardath

IT WAS MORNING, AND a fine one, but I had been on deck, attending to the sick for long hours already. So far on the journey, though we had been severely cursed with disease, filth, and death on all sides, the skies gleamed blue and cloudless, mocking our miserable state. I stretched my aching back, holding myself upright on the deck for a precious minute, feeling the sea roll and swell beneath my feet. With weary eyes, I gazed upward at the yellow flag of quarantine. It snapped in a fresh breeze on the tallest mast, a triangle bright against the blue sky, to warn away other ships. We were isolated on the wide sea.

Our stores were holding up well, though, for the sad reason that there were very few left to use them and no one with the time or energy to prepare them. Our regular food was the barely adequate salt pork, hard bread, and water; the cook had been among the first of the small pox victims.

The fresh breeze hardly penetrated my skin, sticky and caked with sweat and filth as it was. "Baths" in seawater only made it worse, drying us out with salt. Still, the breeze was welcome and sped us on our way. We hadn't lost any distance on the voyage, thanks to Alex's good management.

I should ask him again how close we were to the end of this journey. To my calculation, we had been at sea for six weeks. I had trouble holding the arrival date in my mind because of the endless days of hard work.

Alex had settled into his role as captain more fully. He had tried to be a fair and good captain, and in this I believe he succeeded. But he was no longer the happy man he had once been. The responsibility of the ship and all lives aboard it had weighed him down. His face grew longer and more serious; he rarely smiled now. He had confided in me his worry that the ship's owners would hold him accountable for the misfortunes that had befallen us on this voyage. He knew them to be hard masters who were famous for taking captains to task, even for acts of God.

Our situation was this: The men in the brig who had dreamed of taking the ship had all died of the pox, making it possible for others to move more freely. Some of the male passengers were pressed into service as seamen. They succeeded at this in varying degrees. We all found out that good hands were hard to create quickly, and we appreciated the skill of the remaining true seamen, though they tended to be a rough lot, as well I should know, and full of superstitions long cast off by most of humanity.

One passenger who did stand out for his hard work and effort, though he knew nothing about sailing ships, was the big army major named Booth James. He did not become ill. He was respected by the men for his work and admired by the women for his handsome features. Even I could spare him a glance at times, though in turn he seemed oblivious to any woman's attentions. I was curious why Booth James traveled to the New World. I doubted it was for religious reasons. Perhaps he saw a chance to make a different life there, or perhaps it was simply an army posting. Rumors of Indian troubles had already reached us in Liverpool.

My thoughts were interrupted by a request from one of those lying on the deck.

As I bent to help, Major James himself passed by our makeshift sickroom, striding somewhere with great purpose. Most people avoided our area, which I could understand, given the stench that arose from the ill and their helpers alike. So I was very surprised to see one of our gentlemen passengers, a Mr. Towler, come to lean on the rail not far from me. He began taking snuff, which perhaps limited his sense of smell. Another gentleman paused beside him.

"Well, Mr. Smythe, our Major James is a busy fellow, isn't he?" asked the well-dressed, diminutive Mr. Towler. He had held himself above the chaos of the ship. I suspected that he would have felt it beneath him to give in to such a bodily nuisance, such a lower-class disease. It certainly seemed beneath him to shed some of his customary well-cut suit of clothes and help out. He stood with one leg cocked as if to dance at court, with his blue silk coat and embroidered waistcoat, his satin breeches. Perhaps, worst of all, he even appeared to be clean! He certainly would not go anywhere near the slop buckets we hauled to throw from the ship's sides. I was tempted to toss one out upwind of him.

He addressed Gregory Smythe, who had likewise not succumbed to the epidemic, but who had the good sense to change to useful clothes and the kindness to help in Booth James's group. He was dressed in plain brown homespun breeches with white shirtsleeves rolled up for ease of work.

"Ah, Towler, the major is certainly busy in a good cause," said Smythe. "Regardless of his father the earl's influence, he seems to have a talent for using his head and for leading the men, though he has no seafaring experience, of course."

"Why is he leaving England, anyway?" asked Towler, wiping his nose with a dainty handkerchief. "He'd have a brilliant career ahead of him, regardless of aptitude. He's not under scandal or family disgrace that I know of."

"True," said Smythe, "but who would not want to be far away from his mother, the Countess Glenmore?"

"She is truly a battle-ax of a woman, I'll warrant!" said Towler. "She is, in fact, the bossiest termagant I've ever had the displeasure of meeting. I don't know how the earl puts up with it."

Smythe smiled as the ocean breeze lifted his limp, fair hair. "He's got the London house, where he spends most of his time, and his club. But the countess rules her sons with an iron fist. Stephen will be the next earl, and if ill befall him, there is Richard, so Booth has no need to stay around the estate. If I were him, I'd put the ocean between myself and the whole family, just as he is doing."

"Hmm," said Towler.

"I'm off now to help Booth's Brigade, as we call ourselves," said Smythe. "Care to join?" he asked with a small smile.

"Oh no, thank you," said Towler, raising his upper lip slightly. He resumed his stance of gazing out to sea, and I moved farther away to continue my work. I really had no time to wonder further about Booth James or any other gentleman this day!

*****

Eventually, the new cases of the pox dropped off and life became easier. On the day in which we had no more new patients to attend, Ibrahim fell onto his cot and slept for two days running. When he awoke, he washed and trimmed his stringy gray beard; he lifted his hands and his pouchy eyes to heaven in thanks.

Poor Gwyn, though, who had taken happily to wearing her boy pants and going barefoot, was ushered by Mrs. Perry into the latter's cabin, washed down and made to return to her shoes and ladylike clothes. She submitted to this meekly, as Gwyn was wont to do. Mrs. Perry was certainly a bastion of civilization! Over the last weeks, though, I had come to respect her no-non-sense and hardworking ways.

As for me, I was able to continue enjoying the ship knowledge that I was learning from Alex. Although I did not expect to need the knowledge, I appreciated his company as a loyal friend. One day, however, as we bent over the charts, I felt his hand on my waist. Before I knew what was happening, he had pulled me around and kissed me. Astonished, it was all I could do not to wipe my mouth in disgust. But he had seen my look. He backed away, drawing in quick breaths.

"So sorry," he mumbled, turning blotchy shades of red. Then his face brightened. "I know that I have not the appearance that you would look for in a man, being someone of such beauty yourself, but I love you. I would always protect you. My life would be devoted to your happiness and nothing else. I would provide you with whatever you want. It would not concern me that you wish to learn and to go about independently. I would never care what others might say. We could continue to be best of friends as well as man and wife."

"Alex, we *are* friends! I don't want to lose that. But I am not ready to marry."

"But I would wait. I would wait until you are ready, however long that might take." His face was earnest, his head cocked to the side, his prominent eyes pleading.

"Alex, I just can't," I said into the awkward silence. His whole body slumped in defeat.

"Then you are most cruel," he said, and left me in the room.

That was the end of our close friendship. He never looked me in the eye again and dodged me whenever we got close to each other at any place on the ship. He took to staying many hours in his cabin. When he did appear, he was sometimes unshaven, with rumpled clothing and red-rimmed eyes. I even thought, once, that I smelled a whiff of the captain's store of rum on him.

Gwyn noticed the changes, of course. "What happened to Alex?" she asked.

"He asked me to marry him," I said.

"Oh, well, I am not surprised," Gwyn said.

I felt my anger rise like boiling oil in my head. "Of course not!" I snapped at her. "You saw it all coming. You see everything! Well! He could be more of a man about it. It annoys me how he slumps about the ship with no self-respect."

"Ardath, don't be in a temper about it."

"Why not? I can't respect a man who doesn't respect himself!" I said.

"But, Ardath," Gwyn began.

"No, I don't want to hear any of your mealymouthed talk of his feelings! And you might have warned me!" I said.

Gwyn said, "But I—"

"No, I won't hear it. This is the end of this subject between us," I told her.

And so it was, because, at that moment, Walt ran by us, headed for the cabins below, shouting for Alex. "Captain, storm's coming!"

CHAPTER 8

May 1751
Gwyn

FIRST, THERE WAS THE heavy sensation, as if a large dog sat on my chest. Then came the rain, sheeting down gray around us, chilling us in its onslaught. In all my life I had never seen such a rain! The quiet blue ocean I had loved turned a somber hue. Peaked white caps began to spring up, stirred by the wind, which began to howl, then to whine, in the rigging. The majesty of nature showed itself, terrifying in its power. Alex had the crew furl all the sails and lash them down extra tightly. The men looked battered as they scurried about in the torrents. As the wind picked up, Alex ordered everyone except essential crew below. I paused long enough to see the ship dangle over a deep trough of water. Ahead a wave rose higher than our tallest mast, a gray mountain for which we headed willy-nilly. I scuttled down the stairs as quickly as my feet would take me.

Below, all was chaos, with people slipping and thrashing as the ship rocked violently from side to side, front and back, first dipping, then shuddering up again. Though the hatches had been battened, the floor sloshed with cold water, so everyone was wet to add to their misery.

Major James took charge, ordering the women to tie themselves and their children into the seamen's hammocks. That was indeed a good course of action. We would be less bruised and spared broken bones.

Amidst the shouting and the roar of the ocean, I found Ardath. She had grabbed a hammock and stumbled back and forth with it in her desperate grip. The icy water swirled around our ankles.

"We have to get into the hammock quickly," she called to me above the din. She held the hammock as still as possible while I crawled up into it, the rough ropes tearing at my hands and slipping and twisting away from me. Finally, I was inside, holding it open for her. She clambered in. We couldn't avoid painful collisions of elbows, knuckles, and heels. Around us, mothers crowded into other hammocks with their children.

In a short lull, the men fastened ropes to the rafters and swung by their arms from them when the ship rolled again and again. The storm made all men equal in their attempts to survive. The African father, Omar, helped Ibrahim, whose elderly arms could not hold after the first hours of jerking in their ropes. The other African man, Ahmed, who had regained his strength over the course of his weeks of liberty, helped others. Above and to all sides, the sounds of the storm roared and wailed so that in time, conversation was impossible. The men communicated with signs and gestures.

I watched from our cocoon as Major James organized the men to man the pumps. Water was spraying in through the boards in the ship's sides at a great rate, and objects of all kinds—a woman's shoe, a dead rat, broken bottles—floated and jerked their way in the waters. The bilge had thrown up its nasty guts, making the stench as lively as the ocean rolls.

The pumps could hardly keep up with the influx, but the men rolled up their sleeves and took turns with them, struggling valiantly. Only two of the crew were with us, the carpenter and a seaman.

I could not help but notice how muscular were the arms of Major James and how pleasant it was to watch his tall, broad-shouldered figure. His plain shirt and waistcoat clung to his body as he worked and encouraged the others at their work. He was graceful even in these conditions, moving about the hold like a giant cat, his usually wavy brown hair sleeked back on a well-formed head, his Roman nose leading the way in his intense face. He seemed a natural leader, which perhaps explained why he had risen to such a high rank as a young man. Ardath had been skeptical and said that his wealthy family probably bought him his commissions, but I did not believe that.

For once, I was happy to have on many layers. I wiggled out of my cold,

37

wet shoes, as well as the rough strings of the hammock would allow and pulled my feet up into my mostly dry petticoats, where they were well covered and somewhat warm. I wore the money belt that had been Father's, as usual; its bulk bit hard against my ribs. Ardath wore Mr. Padgett's, which must be even more uncomfortable. She was tense. I could tell that she hated to be confined when such an emergency was going on, but there was little we could have done.

I rubbed her back and sang into her ear a favorite song that our mother used to sing to us, "Dinogad's coat is speckled, speckled, made from the hide of martens…" When she relaxed, I began to pretend, now speaking into her ear, that we were swinging from a hammock under the green trees of our home woods in Wales. Our mother was in the cottage, making supper; I could almost smell it. Salmon fresh from the river, cakes of the finest flour, greens from the garden. Little birds flitted above our heads in the trees. Red kites soared over the grasslands. The sun warmed us; the wind sang to us. We were safe. In this way, I finally fell asleep, even as the storm raged around us.

I awoke when the ship crashed and shuddered violently. How long I had been asleep, I never knew. Ardath was very alert, shaking me to ensure that I was awake and attempting to cut us out of the hammock with her scissors. Water poured in through a gaping hole in the hull. It must have been at least five feet wide. Frantic men pulled women from their hammocks. Omar got us out and pushed us toward the stairs, where we fled from the waters and onto the deck. The winds had died, but the freezing rain still fell steadily. Through it, we viewed a scene of heartbreaking destruction. The center mast had broken, and its wreckage lay all across the deck. There was no sign of Alex or, I realized with a shock, of Walt. The *Gracious Anne* was perched on a huge gray boulder that had stopped our progress.

Around us there appeared to be a tiny bay of some sort, barren and rocky, but it was land. Major James shouted for the longboat, but it was gone too. The major made his way up to the boulder as the ship listed and threatened to lift off the rocks. He dragged a mooring rope with him. With this, he made a loop and threw it over a point on the rock, tying and coiling the other end to the anvil-shaped object that Walt had called a cleat. To my amazement, this

38

actually halted the listing. The rock that had wrecked us was to be our anchor!

Carefully, I crept down the deck, bending, holding onto the downed mast. I would not believe that we had lost all those seamen who had been on deck. I knew Walt had never appeared in the hold; I had watched for him. I crept back until I found the wheel. Attached to it was a frayed rope, where apparently Alex had tied himself in, but Alex was gone.

As I returned, again bending to clasp the icy mast, I heard a groaning. Searching among the detritus, I found my friend Walt. I felt a great surge of happiness. With renewed energy, I threw wood, canvas, ropes, and other debris from around him. Miraculously, he was alive and did not seem too badly injured. But he was pinned under part of the mast, and I could not move him.

"Walt, can you hear me?"

"Gwyn, is that you? Thank God! Are we finally out of the storm?"

"Yes, and there is land near us. Are you able to move? Are you hurt?"

"I can't get out, but I don't feel any pain."

"Good. I will get help. I will be back very shortly."

I slipped and staggered as best I could on the tilted deck, to Major James, who was organizing people to get onto the rock.

"Major James, can you help me? I have found the cabin boy, but I cannot move him."

From underneath thick brown eyebrows, he turned deep-set but penetrating blue eyes toward me. He had to look down, as from a height, to focus on my face. He was a bird of prey, an eagle, and I was…a mouse.

"Charles and William, help her get her friend out," he said crisply to two able men near him.

We went back to pull out a very bruised, but otherwise whole, Walter. To his great embarrassment, I had to hug him, and I might have kissed him, but he held me away.

The rain lightened enough for us to see that we were almost on the shore. The sea beyond the boulder was very shallow. A grown man could walk in it easily; the shelter of the little cove made the water calmer there. I said a prayer of thanksgiving. We were going to get off the ship!

CHAPTER 9

May 1751

Ardath

MAJOR JAMES QUICKLY BECAME the leader of the ship's people in Alex's absence. He towered over the men on deck, lashed by the wind and rain, throwing his arms in wide gestures to urge the tired men toward their duties and to gather the women and children together to evacuate the ship. He looked magnificent and, more importantly, competent.

Trembling in the biting cold, I had a moment to think. Where in the world was Alex? It seemed impossible to me that he had not survived the storm. It seemed impossible that he would not be here to carry out his duties, as he was a very dutiful man. As to the first, the missing longboat gave me some hope that he had been able to cling to that and might be alive somewhere. As to the second, I might believe it possible that he was so overwhelmed by his captain's duties and worried about being punished by the ship's owners that he would abandon ship when he saw a shipwreck was to happen. I could *not* accept that my rejection might have anything to do with his disappearance. In any case, I did grieve for him, but took care not to show it.

When it became clear that we would be able to get off the ship, Gwyn was busy with Walt, so I sent Mrs. Perry and the African woman, Isa, back to the galley for food. I ran for the medical supplies before anyone could see or stop me, slipping down the dark, wet stairs and feeling my way to the cabins. I also got the documents concerning the Africans and, from the captain's quarters, the quadrant, the maps, and a book, all of which I put in a large oilcloth bag to carry with me off the ship.

The rain had turned into a sharp slanting sleet when I returned to the deck, where the ice was freezing. Major James was red of face from that and the now-whipping wind.

"Where have you been? Get off the ship *now!*" he shouted at me. "You are the very last person!"

"Yes, I'm coming." I hurried to the rock. Three men were standing in the rocky surf as it pounded against the ship and the shore. The major handed me down to them, none too gently, and they handed me in turns across the water. The women were huddled in their shawls, shivering on the shore like a flock of birds in a storm.

"Make your way to the cove!" I shouted and pointed them toward a V-shaped rocky defile that would provide some shelter.

"Major, bring canvas to cover that defile!" I shouted, but he could not hear me. The other men in the water relayed the message. He turned and gathered a large pile of canvas, which he passed over to the men. They brought this to shore, as he slid down the rock and into the surf, the last to leave the ship.

As the men made their way through the bone-chilling surf, I told the women to gather driftwood for an attempt at a fire. There was danger here that we would succumb to the elements unless we took immediate action. Also, moving would help us stay warm. I was grateful that I was wearing wool, including a heavy cloak, as this provided some warmth even when wet.

Gwyn and Walt were on the beach just up from the line of surf. "Gwyn, are you all right?" She was huddled over Walt, who kept pushing her away and saying that he was fine.

"Yes, I'm well," said Gwyn as the wind blew a long strand of her dark hair.

"Good. First, we need to find a way to start a fire," I said.

"Walt may have a flint," said Gwyn.

At this, Walt leaped up. "Yes, I have a flint and an iron. If we could find something dry, I could try to start a spark."

"We have some driftwood that the women are gathering. The rain seems to be slackening again, and I have a dry book," I told him. We made our way up the beach, where a growing pile of driftwood waited to be burned, at the opening of the defile. The women had been fortunate to find some relatively dry wood under a rock overhang.

When Major James saw what we were about, he ordered several of the men, exhausted but willing, to hold the canvas over us. Within this makeshift shelter, I flexed my stiff fingers and took out some pages of the book I had brought from the ship. Walter dried his flint and iron on the underside of his clothes, though they were soaked through, and began to strike flint and iron together repeatedly.

I found that I was holding my breath, so important was it that we get a spark. I let it go in a whoosh. Just then, a spark flashed and caught on the paper I was holding. I dropped it when it blazed up. With shaking hands, I tore out more pages. The tiny fire would not last long, but we began to feed it small pieces of the drier driftwood until it reached a respectable size. A cheer went up from our group. I left Walt to tend to the fire.

I turned to the major, who was helping the men to fold up the canvas.

"Major James, we must get some shelter by placing the canvas over the top of the defile. There seems to be no real wood here, but maybe we can weight it down with rocks."

"Miss Rhys, I am in charge here. I do not need a woman telling me what to do. Kindly tend the fire as is appropriate to your sex," he said. Several of the men chuckled.

I should have known that I could not speak to him so frankly, and in front of others. Nevertheless, I was infuriated. Forced to hide it, I strode farther into the defile. Mrs. Perry was her usual solid presence there, giving every woman some small task to do, keeping them distracted from our situation. She had dug some potatoes and beans out of her bag and put them in a pot with rainwater. Gwyn had taken the medical supplies to Ibrahim, who was sorting through and putting these in order on a flat rock so that he could treat the scrapes and wounds of those who now crowded around. There were surprisingly few of them; I really wasn't needed there.

What was needed next was a source of fresh water. Also, I needed to walk off my irritation! I checked for where the "martinet" was looking, for so I now called the major in my mind. He was busy, pointing and directing the men, so I hurried out of the defile between some tall boulders. There was a pervasive mist, almost a fog, over the area, but the rain had stopped. It was cold here, wherever we were. I hoped for sunshine the next day so that I could take a reading with the quadrant at noon and get some idea of where we had turned up.

When I reached the headland above the beach, I had expected to find forests and meadows. I was sorely disappointed in this. Before me in the swirling mist, nothing could be seen but low-growing grass, moss, and lichen. And of course, rock, everywhere rock. I tried to stay on the rock, as the vegetation was spongy and slippery. I walked through the gray and dull green landscape until my heart was calmer.

As the mist lifted, I spied some vertical shapes ahead and hurried toward them. I saw that they were the timbers of two shelters, unfortunately long abandoned and moss-covered. The timbers leaned in jagged angles on one another and on the rocks and sod that had made up most of the shelters. Wood gave me hope that there could be forests farther inland, until I rubbed at the moss. Underneath it, they were planed wood, ship's timbers. Nearby, I saw a row of weathered crosses falling over in the grass. Beyond the graves lay a single skeleton, curled around itself. Probably the last survivor of a shipwreck like ours. This chilling scene was not one that others needed to see. I quickly set about pulling up the crosses and dragging off the bones, which persisted in clanking and falling apart in a most macabre way. I crunched them together and dumped them in a natural trench, hiding them under some loose rocks. I banged and pinched my cold fingers in the process, sending a fiery pain through them.

While about this task, I found a small stream that could serve as fresh water for us. The water was so frigid that I could hardly believe it still flowed. It seemed to be coming from a bluish cliff off to my right. I followed it upstream. My eyes beheld a most astounding sight. It was not a cliff at all, but a wall of solid ice standing far above my head. Where were we?

This was enough to make me seek companionship and some physical warmth! I hurried back toward the beach. As I carefully descended the boulders, still hidden from view by them, I heard low men's voices above the seething of the surf. They came from a huddle of several men around Major James. One was the ship's carpenter, and another the last remaining crew member. It was the last whom I heard speaking.

"Th' first thing to do is to get us rid of th' witch. She of the red hair has caused us all these maladies, you can be sure! She's had th' ship cursed from th' day we set sail, mark my words, th' sickness, th' storms, all her doing. She tranced Mr. Whitsun. You saw it, and now he's gone!"

"It is true, Major. A woman on the ship is never good, but a red-haired witch is the worst of all. She's not natural. She even tried to give you orders. She'll be after spelling you next. She was seen using our quadrant. She even had a trick at the wheel! She spelled it, and now she's landed us here, on the shores of hell!" said the ship's carpenter.

"Gentlemen, red hair does not make a woman a witch. Miss Rhys is not capable of causing all these calamities. I will indeed be cautious of her counsel, but we need to focus on what can be done to get off this shore, if possible," said the martinet.

I stayed no longer to hear this conversation, but retraced my steps in order to arrive on the other side of the encampment. Bless Walt! He had a nice fire going, which was cheering all spirits. In my absence, the canvas had been spread above the defile, so some shelter helped as well. I warmed myself beside the fire, my freezing hands smarting. I needed to plan what I would be able to do for the ship's company when its obvious leader would not make use of my knowledge. I missed Alex badly; I realized how I had taken his confidence in me for granted. My choices of a male champion were few—Ibrahim, who might be disregarded for his skin color (or even his close association with a witch!), or Walt, who might legitimately know more of seamanship, but could be disregarded for his youth.

Gwyn came over to me at that moment. "Where have you been?" she asked me in such a caring voice, concern for me brimming in her blue eyes.

I touched her shoulder, so little and bony under my hand. "I should have told you that I was going exploring."

"It is all right. What did you find?" she asked.

"We are far north of our planned course. Inland it is icy and barren, but there is fresh water. Come aside with me." We moved away from the fire to a place less populated. I told her of the conversation I had witnessed among the men.

"But, Ardath, if Alex doesn't turn up, we will need all that he taught you about the ship's course, if we are ever to leave here."

"True, but how to let them know that without seeming to be the author of it?" I said.

"You must use Walt, I think. Some things I can tell him, since they know we are friends. Others you may tell him when out of sight, or perhaps you could write them if you have any blank paper," Gwyn said.

"I have to show him how to use the quadrant. It is too much to write. And I have to make sure he turns up in possession of it rather than me. Do you think you could let Walt know of the plan and spy on the men who are suspicious of me?"

Gwyn smiled so that her dimples showed. "I shall love to be your spy. After all, who would suspect such an innocent as I?" she said, with a little moue of her mouth. I smiled, too; her enthusiasm was contagious. The anger about the men's accusations melted away, to be replaced by a certain (probably unwarranted) lightheartedness. Still, I would need all the craftiness of a witch to make this transfer of ship's knowledge happen.

CHAPTER 10

May 1751
Gwyn

OF COURSE, IT WAS absurd. We were in a very precarious position on this cold shore, yet the prospect of helping Ardath excited me, causing me to focus on the adventure more than the danger. First, we huddled around Ibrahim, as if discussing the health of his patients; in this way, we could include Walt, whose injuries Ibrahim pretended to examine. Ardath told us of her discoveries inland and summarized our situation.

"It looks to me that other than fresh water, we will not find any provisions here. We need to get off this piece of land as fast as possible," Ardath said.

"But how can the ship be sailed with so few left of the crew?" asked Walt.

"I can show you how to calculate where we are and plan the direction we must take. Of course, this must be done in secret. The two crew members left, other than you, believe I am a witch, so I cannot be seen to direct anything. You must convince James that you know how to do this. As to the actual sailing, we shall have to do the best we can."

"But what of the gaping hole in the hull?" said Walt, who shivered from more than the cold, I think.

Ibrahim answered this. "Praise Allah that the ship's carpenter still lives! And Omar is a master carpenter, who can assist him if he will permit it. I will speak to Major James about this."

"There are extra timbers in the hold," Walt said.

"A very good thing, as there seems to be no wood growing near here," said Ardath. "Ibrahim, if you can distract the major with this information in

46

the morning, I will take Walt to the cliff above and show him how to use the quadrant."

"I already know how to use the seaman's compass," Walt said with some pride.

"All the better!" said Ardath.

"I will keep watch on the crew members," I said. "And maybe I can find some small reason to distract the major if needed. Right now," I continued, carefully looking down the shore to my left, "he is surveying the cliffs, as if wishing to journey up there."

"We will indeed have to be careful of his whereabouts in the morning. Gwyn, why don't you relay this information to Mrs. Perry as well? If there are no other immediate concerns, let us try to get some food and rest now," Ardath concluded. We nodded and dispersed ourselves discreetly.

I turned back to Major James. The night was coming on fast, and I could see that he hesitated to go up the hill in the dark; indeed, he approached the fire soon after. The sailors and passengers had already crowded around the fire, where Mrs. Perry had prepared the soup. Though most people carried their spoons in their pockets, there were no bowls from which to eat the soup, so all were slowly taking turns around the pot. Though the beans were hard and the potatoes a mush, it was the best meal we had had in many weeks. Its warmth sank down into my bones.

I took Mrs. Perry aside and brought her into our conspiracy. She resolved to be a campfire spy among the women for us. She also gave me her cloak with a jolly wink, saying that she was fat and therefore always warm. We tried to make ourselves as comfortable as possible on the beach. Ardath snuggled up close; we covered ourselves with the cloak and scrunched around in the smooth pebbles until we had something of a depression to lie in. Nevertheless, I was sure I'd never sleep in a bowl of rocks!

*****

I awoke in the morning feeling an energy I had not expected. Ardath was already about, assisting in building up the fire. The best news yet was that the day had broken clear, with a promise of sun already touching the pearly clouds above us. My toilette was brief, a rearranging of my skirts and pulling my hair back into its confines. I chanced to see Walt and had to suppress a grin. He stood, yawning and stretching, his hair standing straight up. His cheek was dented by marks of the pebbles. Well, none of us were at our society best these days!

Mrs. Perry was at the fire, watering down the remains of the soup for breakfast. She reported that Major James had already taken some men up the hill to scout, so we were relieved that the first part of our plan, to get Ardath and Walt up there later, would probably not be disturbed. Also, I remembered to thank God that the ship was still there. In fact, it was low tide, so it rested above the water's edge. The ship's carpenter was surveying the hole in it carefully. Nearby, the older African, Omar, was quietly gazing at it also. His expression was hard to read—so black was his face in the early light—but he did not seem afraid, and from that I took some reassurance.

Ardath soon took Walt aside and commenced talking to him intently. I assumed my duties as chief spy. James had taken the other crew member with him up the hill, and the carpenter was too engrossed in inspecting the ship to notice anything happening farther up in the defile. We were safe for now.

I ventured down to the ocean's edge. There I could keep an eye on the hill above and on our witch-hunting carpenter as well. I could see Ardath and Walt in the defile, where they conferred. She had transferred the oilskin sack to him, and he was poring over the maps. I hoped that he was a very quick learner. When I saw Major James returning, I jumped back and shouted loudly, "Oh, Major, you startled me," hoping that Walt and Ardath could hear me.

"Miss Rhys, do stay back from the edge there. The water is freezing," he said in an irritable tone. Probably, he had not been pleased with what he found on the cliffs above.

"Oh, yes, sir. Sorry, sir. Of course, sir," I tittered in my best silly-girl voice, fluttering my hands. He frowned at me, and for that moment, I knew that I had distracted him.

I followed him back to the defile, where he warmed his hands at the fire. Walt was far on one side of the defile, and Ardath on the other. After the other men came in, he called for order and addressed the group.

"We have scouted the hill above us," he said. "This is not a hospitable land we find ourselves in. We must try to repair the ship and sail away as soon as possible."

"But there is a huge hole in the ship and not enough men to sail it!" exclaimed an older woman.

"Madam, we must all be patient and make the best of our situation. The ship's carpenter is looking at the damage now. We must have faith that it can be repaired."

The people of our small camp looked doubtful at that. Some began to move their lips in prayer, when suddenly the remaining sailor, on the edge of the group, bent down, hawked, and spit to the side. He was a rank little man, but his voice carried as if on board.

"Yeh'll be wondering why we got all this bad luck, now, won't yeh? Well, I can answer that for yeh! 'Tis the witch we have among us. Th' red-haired maker of evil spells stands right here amongst us; can't yeh see it? We should stone her and then yeh'd see our luck turn, right enough. No more evil here!" He picked up a large stone from the beach and threw it with deadly accuracy at Ardath, catching her on the side of the head so that she went down with a thud.

Immediately several men fell upon her, throwing out their arms. I could not tell whether they meant to beat her further or to shelter her from his missiles. Most people were shouting and jumping away from Ardath. I wrestled my way through them, toward her. I was almost there when the sudden report of a firearm sounded.

"Arrest him!" Major James said to two men beside him. They fell upon the sailor, Mr. Scroggs, who was bending to get more rocks. They yanked him down. "Attention! There will be no more of this hysteria on my watch!" James said, pistol in hand. "Does anyone offer to defy me?"

Of course, no one did. I dropped to Ardath's side and found her bleeding

49

from her temple, pale and unresponsive. Major James picked her up like as if she were a bouquet of roses and took her to the pallet where Ibrahim examined patients. He was magnificent in his rescue of my sister. And to my surprise, James looked genuinely alarmed for her.

Ardath would not believe that, I thought. Then, I was struck by the fact that I might never get to tell her that, might never talk with her again. I found myself unable to stand, except that the strong hands of Mrs. Perry held me up.

Ibrahim called for Isa to bring cold cloths and began a gentle examination of Ardath's injury. I knew from working with him that a blow to the temple could be fatal. Hopelessly, I began to pray.

CHAPTER 11

May 1751
Ardath

I AM FLOATING. PEARLY white mists swirl around me. I am in white also, long dress flowing out. My hair flies behind me, bright color in the air. I am warm, at peace. I feel no fear, only wonder. Everything is perfect, and so the next step must also be perfect. When will he come? Though I am complete, still I long for him.

And there he is, tall, strong, moving on his cat-feet, a wash of browns and blues. Brown of hair, blue of eye, sweet light-brown skin. He smells of wind and sea. He takes me in his arms as if I am indeed a floating feather. But he is solid, sure, safe. He takes me down to the brown earth, and the sky is blue above.

I want to ask if it will hurt, but I do not speak. His lips cover my mouth, soft but insistent. Salty, warm, bringing me to him. He turns us and lies beneath, I above. My body presses into his, feeling his hardness, yet he is gentle.

"Ardath," he whispers.

Both of us longing. We are skin to skin, like some boneless sea creatures set to mate in the waves. His hands, O marvelous instruments, roam across me. Every touch shines with light, transforms me again and again. Tingling, moving against him, I say it, "Booth."

His hands cup me. I pull him in. He pulls and pushes until I am screaming with it. Then, sweet God! I am full and exploding. Arching, arching, arching against him, crying out, free.

Suddenly, I am on the ship. Wind and rough seas threaten me. I grab for a rail. Alex is across from me, struggling to hold the wheel. The ocean gray and deep seems to reach up, wanting to take him. His face is gray as well, his eyes black. The wind throws him to the end of the rope. It frays and separates before our eyes. He looks into mine and cries out, "Ardath!" He is hurled away, arms and legs reaching back toward me in supplication. I cannot save him, for all his longing. Yet, still I hear his voice, calling for me.

Then it is Mother, calling me with great tenderness, but she needs me too. And Gwyn, wringing her hands and trying to be brave, tries to reach me. Ibrahim wants my help with someone ill. It is crushing, like my head is crushing my brain. The pain is like fire, the weight too heavy to lift. I could not, for my life, lift that head.

They cannot call me anymore, yet they do. I must rest. Don't they know that? I cannot hold up the world now, or even myself. Leave me alone; let me be. I go deeper where they cannot find me.

CHAPTER 12

May 1751
Gwyn

As Ibrahim and I bent over Ardath, she began to moan, mutter, and arch her back. "Ibrahim, is she convulsing?"

He looked carefully. "No, I think not," he said.

From the gathering of our remaining shipmates, who were a few feet away, I heard a sarcastic laugh. "Consorting with the devil himself! See her swive him! She can't hide it now. We all see it. There will be hell to pay." It was the ship's carpenter, Muckle, his scarred face a mix of glee and fear.

Oh, no, in my concern for Ardath, I had forgotten her enemies among us. Scroggs was confined, but there was Muckle still accusing her of witchcraft. I looked around for Major James, but he had disappeared after laying Ardath down on the pallet.

"That's enough, Muckle," said a male passenger. "You'll scare the womenfolk."

"We should all be scared, for true! That knock to the head only sent her running for her Friend, and now Old Harry shall be close among us. We're doomed now, if we weren't before. We won't be safe till that witch is dead. See her twitch? That is the devil himself coming in!"

"For heaven's sake!" exclaimed Mrs. Perry, newly come on the scene. "She's had a bad head injury; that is all. Everyone go find something useful to do. Gather more wood for the fire, if nothing else!"

Some muttered as they drew away, but they went, somewhat hangdog, as if scolded by their mother. Even Muckle shuddered and went away toward the beach. I fervently hoped we had heard the last from him. I would ask Ibrahim to talk to James about it.

Ardath lay quietly now. I tried to stop the shaking that had overtaken me. "What can we do?" I asked Ibrahim.

"I would like for her to wake. You could try calling her. She may respond to your voice." His lips were pressed in a straight line, as if he doubted that it would help.

"Ardath, please wake up. Come back to us, Ardath," I said, clasping her cold hand between mine and chafing it.

"Ardath!" Ibrahim called also. She did not stir.

"We can keep her warm and hope for the best," Ibrahim said then. "I will watch over her. Please see if you can bring James here. We need to learn what his plans are."

I approached the major with some trepidation. He was standing on the beach, conferring with Muckle about the ship's possible repair. The wind blew his hair across his eyes, but he tossed it aside in time to see me coming. "Miss Rhys, how is your sister?"

"Still unconscious, I'm afraid. Ibrahim asked you to please come to him as soon as you can."

"Certainly. Are we finished for now, Muckle?"

"Yes, sir. As I say, sir, I do not believe she can be repaired." Muckle seemed almost pleased to be able to pronounce his message of doom. Perhaps he relished his role as expert.

"Thank you for your assessment, Mr. Muckle," James said, as he turned away. "That idiot," he muttered under his breath. His brow was furrowed above his deep-set eyes.

He strode across the beach and into the defile, glaring at the ground, so that his forehead creased even more. I hurried after him, taking many steps to each of his long strides.

He entered the defile and immediately began to address Ibrahim. "I understand that there was more of the witch-talk from Muckle. I'd have him in irons if we were not so in need of his skills."

Ibrahim stood up. Though he was a tall, lanky person, he only reached up to the major's shoulder. "What does he say about the repairs?" he asked in his soft voice.

"That they can't be done, an unacceptable answer if ever I heard one!" As Major James said this, he paced about in the small area of the sickbed like a tiger in a cage.

"Perhaps we need to consider another opinion," said Ibrahim.

"Well, anyone can have an opinion, but I need someone who has the skills!" said James.

"It happens that we have such a person among us, sir," said Ibrahim. "The African Omar was a carpenter in his country. While he was not a carpenter on vessels, as far as I know, he has many skills with wood. His son, Ahmed, is a blacksmith of great skill also, from what they have told me."

Major James's mouth pulled down at the corners. "Damnation! I don't suppose they speak any English?" he said.

"Very little as yet, but I can interpret for you," said Ibrahim.

Major James sat down on a rock, hands clasped between his spread knees. He stared intently at those hands, as if they could impart some wisdom to him. Then he lifted bright-blue eyes to Ibrahim. "This is madness, but let us call them over and see what they have to say."

Ibrahim went to fetch Omar and Ahmed, leaving me alone with the major. I was speechless, as I usually was when around him. I'd never been around a man of such authority before, except my cousin Rice. James didn't remember that I was there, but ran his hands through his brown curls and sighed. Then he peered at Ardath, who lay as still and white as a marble statue. He sighed again. How I wanted to know what he was thinking!

Just then, Ibrahim returned with the Africans and Walt. The Africans stood quietly, with hands held loosely at their sides, but their eyes seemed alert as they watched Ibrahim speak.

"Omar says that he has been studying the hole in the hull. The problem he sees is the need to bend the timbers to conform to the hull's shape and make a tight-enough seal. This requires steaming the wood. We have plenty of water for this, but whether we have enough firewood to make steam, we do not know."

James looked thoughtful.

Walt said, "Sir, we have the timbers to make the repair in the bottom hold, though they are not as long as the hole. We have an extra mast also. It is not as large as the one that broke, but we could probably make do with it. The shattered mast could serve the fire."

"Yes, but if we cannot make the ship seaworthy, we will need all the firewood to keep us comfortable here," said the major.

"Either way is a risk," Ibrahim pointed out, "but this seems an isolated place and inhospitable as well. I doubt that we can look for a rescue from here. Our stores will eventually run out."

"Hmmm. I'd sooner take the risk that calls for action," said James. Ibrahim translated, and all the men, African and English, nodded. "I'll not enjoy wresting his tools from Muckle's grasp, or"—he smiled—"perhaps I'll enjoy it very much!" His relief and rare smile were contagious; the men trooped off in an apparently better humor.

Ibrahim turned to me as they left. "Can you watch Ardath while I get them started?"

"Of course. I'll be here," I said.

"I could send Mrs. Perry also," said Ibrahim.

"No, I am fine. She is needed at the fire," I said. In truth, I wanted to talk to Ardath in private.

When they were gone, I again held her hand in mine. Her skin was like porcelain. A blue bruise stood out against the creamy complexion. I brushed her fiery hair away from her face with my other hand.

"Just rest now, Ardath. Heaven knows no one deserves a rest more. Thank you for looking after me. Now it is my turn to tell you that everything will be well. Remember that so many do love you, Mother and Alex among them, wherever they are."

As I sat there in quiet, breathing deeply and intensely wishing my sister well, a clear impression came to me. I knew with a pure conviction that Mother and Alex were alive. Where, or how, I had not an inkling.

CHAPTER 13

May 1751
Ardath

I WANDER THROUGH DARK tunnels alone. Water drips around me. When I touch the walls, they are smooth, cold, and wet. At times I am in caves with strange markings on the walls, animals of lyric beauty and grace, or fantastic, birdlike, almost-human figures of tremendous power. In such a place, my Celtic forebears must have made their sacrifices and called upon an earth mother to help them work their spells. In such places they might have reenacted the birth of living people from the sacred caves underground, out into the world of light and forest, of sky and stream, of sun and moon.

I have my wish. No one calls me now. I am as alone as ever a person can be.

Perhaps I will wander this dark world forever. Or perhaps I will be drawn to some light, some world that I cannot now see. And as I think this, there is, after all, a light, dim and far from me, but growing brighter. I find that I am ready now to follow it to the upper world, if that is where it leads, or to some land beyond death.

It shall be as it shall be.

CHAPTER 14

May 1751
Gwyn

IT SEEMED ONLY A moment ago that we conspirators rather cheerily planned an escape from the "island," as we supposed this desolate place to be. Now Ardath lay unresponsive in the defile, and men argued outside in several languages about patching up the ship. The number of men left was a mere twelve, not counting the seaman, Scroggs. Of the women and children, we had about the same number, a sad decimation of the original group.

Walt came over to the rock on which Ardath lay. I had sat by her side for so many hours that my seat was numb and it was beyond my ability to feel anything other than the cold desolation of my heart.

Walt stood awkwardly next to me. He seemed not to know what to say, just gazed at Ardath with dismay. I wanted him to comfort me, but that was beyond his means. Of course, he was just a child, after all.

"She's about the same," I said, trying to keep my voice level.

"She will surely be better soon. They could really make use of her out there. They just argue and get nothing done. She is smarter than them all!" he said, as if just discovering that for himself.

"I know. What are they saying?" I asked.

"The carpenter, Mr. Muckle, says that it can't be done, which makes Major James angry. His face started turning purple. Then Ibrahim says that Omar the African can do it. That really set off the passengers—the men, I mean, because the women were sent away before the talk started. I would think they'd have some say, too, but the major is not allowing for that. But no one wants to believe a slave could do something a free man couldn't. I think that is the main argument. They have been at it for hours." Walt scuffed his feet in the pebbles and sat down heavily beside me on "my" rock, brushing his hands through his red hair. "They won't even let him try. And they will need help from all the men to attempt the repair, so they *have* to agree to it."

I sighed. "Well, there's not much we can do about that. Can you tell me how far Ardath got in explaining to you how the quadrant and the charting work?"

He looked at his feet. "Uh, I can't tell you much about that. She gave me the maps and the quadrant but didn't have time to explain it. She said that the quadrant must be used at noon on a sunny day and that we were driven far north by the storm. That is all I know, but I have everything safe, if she…"

We had an awkward moment of silence then.

The only thing I could think to do was a pale imitation of what Ardath would do. I turned my face from the haunting question of whether a pale imitation of my sister was all I ever was to be. Well, at least I could do something practical.

"Walt, maybe you could ask Mrs. Perry to organize the women to get things off the ship. If there are any reluctant to work, she could shame them into it. We could use more cloaks and blankets, at least. It sounds as if we may be here for a good while," I said.

He looked grateful to have something he could accomplish. "Well, one thing the men have settled, that's to use the high tide to get the ship onto dry shore, so that they can more easily get the supplies off her. High tide should be tomorrow morning. I'll get Mrs. Perry ready." He hurried off to find her, his feet scrunching in the beach pebbles.

I thought that probably everyone had had these ideas already, but I had done what I could do.

I looked out to the men. Their arguing seemed as silly as hens squabbling over a bug! The hole in the ship *was* of a frightening size, being about five feet wide and four high. What choice did we have but to attempt repairs? Who cared whether our best hope was a man of "unacceptable" color? I turned away in disgust.

I looked back to Ardath. Her face was lovely in repose, but repose was not a natural state for her. I wondered what world she wandered now.

CHAPTER 15

May 1751
Ardath

THE LIGHT GROWS SO bright it hurts my eyes, even my head, but there is nothing to do but to follow. I stumble, somewhat blinded, forward. So it is to be the same world I left; I can tell that by the pain. Beyond that, a terrible thirst, but also Gwyn, my beloved Gwyn.

"Gwyn," I said as loud as I could. My tongue was swollen, my mouth wretched.

"Ardath!" she cried. I could hear the love and joy in it. "Oh, thank God!"

"Water," I croaked. And there it was, gently dripped into my mouth with loving, careful hands. "How long?" I asked.

"Two days," she said.

Suddenly, I remembered it all, even the pain of the blow. "What is happening now?" I asked.

That was when Gwyn told me the events following the attack on me. Some progress had been made, with the main concentration being on the possibility of getting the ship repaired. Apparently, the arguing continued as I lay there.

I wanted to get up and put things to rights. That was not to be. My head presented a major obstacle, weighing a ton as it did. Gwyn went to fetch Ibrahim. I hated being unable, but in truth, from what Gwyn was telling me, it would not be wise to approach the gathering, which consisted of men only. Major James had been adamant about not allowing the women to be present. I recalled the conversation I had overheard between the two gentlemen on the ship's deck when the pox was raging, about the iron rule of his mother over her sons. But there was some advantage with the men hot in argument.

Perhaps I could talk with Ibrahim and Walt and never be noticed. As it happened, Ibrahim and Walt came back with Gwyn.

"Ardath, I am so grateful to see you awake!" said Ibrahim, taking my hand between his long-fingered ones. His hands were cool, his smile warm. "How is your head?"

"Ibrahim, you know I'd be up if it were not so bad," I said. "It is very heavy, but I seem to be able to think and remember clearly."

"That is good," he said.

Walt stood back shyly but looked as if he would like to hug me then and there. He twisted a lock of his straggling red hair.

"Miss Ardath, I have taken care of our secrets very well." He looked around carefully, but no one was close. He grinned. "I can learn more at any time," he said proudly.

"Then sit down and we will work," I replied.

Gwyn protested. "But you should rest! Shouldn't she rest, Ibrahim?"

"I have rested quite enough, I think," I said briskly.

Ibrahim only nodded and steered Gwyn away. "Gwyn, I would like to see *you* rest now," he said to her as they moved away. "Besides, it will take her mind off her head. I should return to the meeting."

"Now then," I said to Walt, "what do you remember about the quadrant?"

Walt was an eager pupil, if not an especially quick one. Once he mastered an idea, though, it seemed to stay with him, so I tried to be patient about the number of repetitions he needed. We even had time to bring out the quadrant and look it over before anyone noticed that I was awake. Then Walt quickly stuffed it back into the bag and hid it in a corner. Even then, it was just Mrs. Perry, come to check on us.

"Ardath, I rejoice to see you! Now! I know how important it is, the work you two are doing, but we must try to see if you can take some food," she said. "One of the women found some cress and wild onions. Nothing is better for you than a soup of those, if I do say so."

This broke up the lesson for us, but I really felt more tired than I should have anyway.

"Walt, go over these things in your head until they stick with you," I said.

"I will!" he said, and went away muttering to himself.

Taking the soup was an ordeal. My neck refused to move smoothly, sending shocks of pain through me. I dribbled on my chin. No dignity! But the soup was soothing, and I found that I could rest better after I ate.

A few minutes later, Ibrahim came to see me. To my surprise, James had followed him up from the beach. He ignored me and spoke directly to Ibrahim.

"I've had my fill of those idiots!" James said. "I'd court-martial them all, if they were in my army. Damn it! I'm going to get your Africans started early tomorrow morning. Perhaps their work will shame the dissenters into helping out, eventually." He paused and glanced my way. "Oh, Miss Rhys, forgive my rude language," he said. "How are you feeling?"

"I'm much better, thank you. Not really able to help out much yet, though."

"Oh, no, no need. We have several women to tend to the fire and cook already," he said.

Immediately my gorge rose, but I gave him a simpering smile and said nothing. I was very happy to see him go then. Ibrahim gave me a very specific lesson in the Africans' language so that I could help him with them as they worked with wood and iron. Ibrahim looked as tired as ever I had seen him, even in the throes of the epidemic.

*****

The next morning dawned bright. Nothing could keep me on my pallet, although I thought I might carry my head in a basket, if such were possible. Gwyn helped me wash. Though the air was cold, at least we had fresh water. Mrs. Perry had warmed a pot of it for me. It was like going to heaven to get most of me clean. When we were finished, we watched the scene on the beach.

The high tide had come in early, as Walt had predicted. The Africans

Omar and Ahmed were already unloading materials from the ship. The slanting sun glinted off their well-muscled arms, wet with sweat. They were making quick work of moving planks of wood and some long iron bars from the ship onto the beach. Nearby, Mrs. Perry had women, including the African Isa, building a pile of driftwood into a pyre. Willing male passengers, directed by Major James, brought down pieces of the shattered old mast to pile beside the fire for later fuel. From a distance they looked like a well-ordered nest of ants working at their tasks.

The carpenter, who had reviled me as a witch, Muckle, jumped up and down in fury as Major James brought his tools from the ship and set them next to the Africans. I could see that Ibrahim kept a careful eye on the proceedings.

"Gwyn, everyone is too busy now to notice me talking to Walt. See if he can come over and resume our lessons," I said.

"Gladly," she replied, and set off at a jaunty pace to find him.

When Walt appeared, we began our lessons again. He really seemed to be understanding more this time, which gave me hope. We made plans to take the quadrant up to the hilltop the next day.

At midday, I went to the beach to give Ibrahim a rest from translating. The atmosphere of the crowd around the Africans felt heavy and hostile. Muckle had been restrained and was thankfully out of the scene, but others of the men and women were plainly unhappy with Major James's decision to put the Africans in charge of the repairs.

Fortunately, James had a corps of willing helpers who had ignored the muttered comments and hauled netting to the edge of the ocean. Into the netting, they and the Africans loaded the planks and secured the whole to some of the larger boulders with thick lines. Major James stood by with his pistol clearly visible in his hand.

"Ibrahim, would you like to rest? I can probably direct the men in what needs doing," I said to him. I was not aware that James had crossed to our area of the beach just then.

"Miss Rhys, you will be doing no such thing!" he exclaimed from close behind me. "You will immediately take yourself completely out of this area. I will not tolerate seeing you here again!"

I confess that I jumped at that order, as unexpected as it was. I turned to face him. I'm sure my face burned red in that moment, which I hated! "You will not address me in this way! Your mother would be mortified to see you act like this!" Well, I had said exactly the wrong thing, of course. His face went from as red as mine to some shade of purple. I thought he might suffer a stroke, which I secretly hoped for. He was insufferable!

Ibrahim gently took my arm and proceeded to walk me away. If I had not had so much respect for him, I might have struggled to turn and say everything I was feeling at that moment. There would have been no charity in it.

"Ardath, this will not help. I know that you want this process to go well. Sometimes we must swallow our pride and our needs for the common good," Ibrahim said, very sympathetically.

I knew that Ibrahim had learned this from the many trials he had endured in all his years as an outsider, so it did not feel like a sermon to me.

"Thank you. I would have not helped the cause," I said. I tried to present a calm exterior, but inside I was seething, boiling, burning with desire for revenge. I delighted in picturing all that I wanted to happen to that self-satisfied martinet!

I went back to my pallet, hoping that I could be calm, but I tossed and turned as my mind threw up pictures of the men I had known in my life. First was my father, that disgusting crow who had deserted my beautiful mother and left us penniless, all for the "glory" of his religion. Then the men who had leered at me or called me "witch" (or both). Those scoundrels who had attacked me on the ship. The slave trader who had made my Africans into rats in a hole. The dandy on the ship who cared more for his clothes than people. Now this "leader of men," raised a gentleman, who was nothing of the sort. He was an arrogant coward who could hear nothing from a woman, who disregarded half of the human race. For the first time, I hoped there was a hell, so they all could burn in it!

CHAPTER 16

May 1751
Gwyn

SOMETHING TERRIBLE HAD HAPPENED between Ardath and Major James. She didn't help on the beach, where she might have interpreted for the Africans. I saw her looking at him with squinted eyes, as if she might shoot sparks at him. If she was giving him the "evil eye," I couldn't very well ask her what had happened, because the "evil eye" might turn on me. Anyway, she had been in a fury all afternoon.

Whatever it was, it must have happened when I was gathering driftwood for the bonfire. It was no mean task to gather the driftwood that was left. It was almost like tree trunks compared to the small pieces that we had gathered at first. To drag these heavy logs warmed me up but left me tired and breathless too. However, feeding the fire was the most important thing that we could do now.

Omar and Ahmed needed heat to bend the iron and timbers into shape for the ship's side. Omar, being the carpenter, was directing work with the wood. Ahmed had brought down an anvil-shaped cleat and a sledgehammer from the ship. He intended to beat the iron into shape on the cleat and use it to help brace the timbers, Ibrahim said. Major James stood by with his pistol at the ready in case anyone made a move to interrupt the progress. All other weapons had long since been taken and locked up in a chest.

Despite everything Ardath felt about him, I couldn't help but think that the major cut a handsome figure. I wondered how it would feel to have those arms catch me, if I were to stumble under my load of wood. But I didn't stumble; I let my load slip off my back near the stack. The fire was giving a mighty roar as we fed it, like the scary, hissing, popping beast that it was.

The men used long poles to push the logs toward the center, concentrating the heat in a smaller and smaller place. They planned to let it burn down to coals so that it would be at its hottest by morning. I put in a little prayer that it wouldn't rain that night and ruin our chances. The sky looked very clear, though.

It was getting too dark to see very far from the fire, so gathering had to stop for the day. I didn't regret this in the least. Mrs. Perry had a soup on the cooking fire. I didn't think I'd ever been so hungry! Some of the men had been throwing nets out from the rocks and actually catching a few small fish. There were some mussels attached to the underside of the largest rocks that I got whenever the tide was down. People were very leery of getting out into the surf, because it was freezing, but also because nobody could swim.

Once again, I was grateful to our mother, who told us it was foolish not to know how. She taught us in the pond near our woods. I never got very good at it, but Ardath took to it like a mermaid. She even did it for fun and became quite strong, frolicking about and staying underwater until I feared she wouldn't come up. Well, I could at least venture to collect food from the slimy green rocks. No one helped, but no one hesitated to eat it! The fish and mussels made the soups less watery, more meaty.

I brought a bowl to Ardath. "Please eat if you can. You need your strength," I said to her.

"Thank you, sister, although I seem to be rather useless here," she said. "I still would like to feel stronger."

I didn't know what to say to that. It must have been a great frustration to Ardath, who had always been active and essential (never useless!), to be feeling this way. This journey was showing us a wider view than we had known in our little house near our little village, where we had lived more in a women's world.

In our current world, she was not valued as she had been there, where my mother and she were known and respected as midwives and herb women.

True, we didn't have the status that our Celtic women ancestors had. Mother had educated us about that. (She included me as a woman, though I was too young really to claim it; I had not yet had my courses.) She told us that the idea of women as equals to the men had been swept away by the English centuries ago, when Wales was finally conquered. I did hold out hope that the New World might be different. Surely, anyone with talent would be needed to tame the wilderness. I thought of Father and his plans. He might have given us the best opportunity we ever could have had to make a new life. I thought for the first time (not without a little guilt) that we might be freer to have this life without him there.

We had finished our soup in silence. Ardath looked at me.

"I gathered the mussels," I said, with some pride.

"You are a good sister," she said. This was high praise from Ardath, who almost never said anything about how she felt. I was overcome with love for her and gratitude that at least we were in this predicament together.

"I suppose everyone who is able will be working hard tomorrow," she said.

"Mostly, I think it will be the men, who need to put the soaked timbers over the rocks to bend them into shape." (For the rocks had been rolled into place before we started the fire, to be the points over which the wood would curve.) "I don't know what Major James will do if some of them won't help."

"Major James will stride about and flourish his pistol. I wouldn't worry about him for even a moment," she said with gritted teeth. "Perhaps we useless ones can find something else to do. I can take Walt up to the headland to work on the quadrant while they are distracted. Please ask him to come up in a minute."

*****

Walt came back with me. "Miss Ardath, I will not be needed early tomorrow. Gwyn told me of your plan to go to the headland with the quadrant. I think I understand what you have been telling me about it, and we can try to make it work."

"It really needs to be used at noon, but I think a trial with it would help anyway," Ardath said.

"But are you able to make the climb up there?" he asked.

"I will help her get there," I said.

"Walt, can you please bring up the quadrant, in case anyone catches us?" asked Ardath. "That way, we can keep to the story that you are the one who knows about it."

"Of course," Walt said. "I have kept it safe in the bag."

*****

There was no rain in the night, and the next morning, the men were busy on the beach. Ardath had had a restless night. I had noticed, since I slept in the pebbles near her. But she still appeared ready to go to the headland. Walt shouldered the bag, and we commenced to climb up the hill through the boulders. I had to give Ardath a good amount of support. Despite my complaints to myself about the driftwood, I found that I had developed some strength carrying it and was well able to help her. She leaned heavily upon me as we wended our way up on a path of sand and shale-like rock. The wind hit us full on when we arrived at the top, but we had become used to the cold and I, at least, didn't mind it.

"Ah, Walt, it is a clear day," Ardath said, after she caught her breath. "This will be good for our lesson, for we can see to the horizon."

"Yes, ma'am," he replied and began to empty the bag. The quadrant was a strange-looking object with projecting arms and odd knobs. With this, Ardath was able to tell us where we were and somewhat where we should be, which seemed like a miracle to me.

"I believe that this is the way to hold it," Walt said.

"A little more level and steady, though," said Ardath, as she showed him. "Now, if the sun were at its zenith, as it will be at noon, you would be able to make an accurate reading on this dial here."

"Yes, ma'am and tell me again, please, what the numbers mean."

"Well, the numbers tell us what latitude we are on. That is, where we are north of the equator," Ardath replied. "Liverpool is at 53.40 degrees latitude, for example. Captain Whitsun told me that we were to land in the New World at 39.95 degrees latitude. If the number for our latitude here is higher, as I suspect, then we are north of our planned course and must make our way south as well as west. I remember from the charts that there is land to the north of the course we were to take. If possible, we can go along a coastline in hopes of not being blown too far from some kind of land, in case the ship repair is not completely sound."

"That would actually make me feel better," I said. "I no longer feel very safe on the sea after seeing her power at work." They turned to look at me, and I felt myself blushing.

But Walt smiled at me. "I know what you mean, but *never* tell anyone that!" he exclaimed.

It was a moment of lightness in our sea of worry.

Then Walt asked, "Miss Ardath, what is an equator?"

"Well, that's not too easy to answer. Let's see, you know that the earth is shaped like a ball," Ardath replied.

"Yes, ma'am."

"If you went halfway down the ball to the middle and drew an imaginary line all around the ball, that would be where the equator is on the earth."

"Imaginary like fairy folk or like imagining we are somewhere on a chart?"

"The latter. Of course, there isn't a line, but it is a measure we can use, drawing more circle 'lines' up from that to the top of the earth. Those are the latitudes."

"How far north we are?"

"Yes."

"But how do we know how far we have gone to the west?" Walt asked.

"I don't think there is any one instrument that can tell us that. At least Captain Whitsun didn't show me one, so we won't know that until we can spot some marker, like a point of land. Then if the charts are right, we may know something."

So I thought, if we had the sun, we could see which way was west and how far north we were, with the quadrant, but that was really all. Even I could see that we were going to be sailing "in the dark" for a while. I wished we had someone who could sail us by the stars, as the ancients were said to do.

CHAPTER 17

May 1751
Ardath

ON THE MORNING THAT the men strained on the beach to bend the sodden timbers over the hot coals, even the dandy, Mr. Towler, was pressed to work. He still wore his blue silk suit, which was showing signs of hard wear, having been drowned in seawater and filth during the storm, rubbed and bleached to tattered threads and grayish color by rock and sand afterward. Apparently, he had brought nothing but the finest attire for impressing the citizens of the New World and hoped to make it there with the rest of his wardrobe intact in its trunk. He wore his (formerly) white wig, now slipping sideways on his head and looking like a wet chicken in a windstorm, feathers awry. But James was not letting anyone lay out on this occasion. The men grunted and pulled the ropes that held the ends of the timbers, shouting curses and encouragement to one another. Ibrahim would be busy tending to blistered, cut, and burned hands later on. Foremost among the hard workers were the Africans, who had barely any rest for days but worked on harder than ever. My admiration for their tremendous strength and endurance deepened.

After Gwyn, Walt, and I had gone to the headlands, I had come back to rest, with the plan to return when the sun was overhead, for a real quadrant reading and a serious look at the charts. Then Walt could go to Major James to let him know where we were, without involving me. Ah, it was a well-laid plan!

I was eager to go, but Gwyn insisted that I eat. We had some hard bread and water before the men were to take a brief break. Then we slipped away up the same path we had trod earlier. In truth, my legs noticed that I had exercised them! Even more, I had to lean against Gwyn. Walt was there as planned.

"There is bright sun and a clear horizon," I exulted. "We can get a good reading!"

"I think this is how you sight it," Walt said.

"Exactly right," I said. "So now we can turn this and take our reading."

"Yes, ma'am," he said with excitement in his voice. His red head and mine came together. We almost had it! Gwyn crowded close to us. At that moment, there was a growling sound. I was surprised but held on to the quadrant with both hands.

We turned to see a red-faced Major James staring at us in apparent disbelief. "What do you think you are doing? That is valuable ship's property you are playing with! Put it down immediately!"

"Sir, if you would allow us to explain," said Walt.

"Explain? Explain why two women and a boy have sneaked up here without permission with stolen property?" Major James said.

"Well, first, we were not playing!" I said. "We are taking a reading to—"

"Miss Rhys, you have caused quite enough trouble! Do I need to place you in restraints?"

"You, sir, have lost your reason! Pigheadedness will not get us out of our predicament. Even if the ship can sail, we need to know where we are and what course to take to our destination," I said.

His voice became low and menacing. "Miss Rhys, give me the instrument immediately."

With my teeth gritted, I said, "And what will you do if I refuse? Wrestle me to the ground and take it by force?" At that moment, I was ready to fight him.

"Ardath," Gwyn said, putting her hand on my arm, "please give the quadrant to Major James. No good can come of this!"

I shrugged off her touch but took a deep breath to calm myself. "Someday, Major, you will understand that everyone is needed if we are to make our way forward. Your arrogance does you no credit."

I handed over the quadrant carefully. From the corner of my eye, I saw that the martinet then grabbed the oilskin bag full of the charts and books as well and was slinging it over his shoulder.

I turned on my heel and started for the beach, picturing him burning in the red flames of hell. In my mind, his mouth stretched wide in agony, his flesh melted before my eyes. Devils prodded his naked body with sharp spears. He danced on a huge bed of coals, his feet red and steaming. Envisioning this, I hardly saw the path before me.

After a while, I became conscious that I was on the beach. Walt and Gwyn had silently followed me down. We had never finished the reading or looked at the charts. Now they were in the hands of a man who didn't know how to use them. A man whose damnable stupidity made him blind to his own prejudices!

CHAPTER 18

May 1751
Gwyn

I BLAMED MYSELF. IF I'd been doing the job I had promised to do, I would have sensed, or seen, or heard Major James coming up the path. But the wind was in our ears, and I was watching for the moment of revelation to know where we were. Now it was ruined! Two of the hardest heads in our little world were the major and (as much as I loved her) my sister. I couldn't see a reconciliation between the two. Walt was beside me as we stepped back on the beach.

"Gwyn, come, don't feel so bad," he said.

"I should have watched," I said.

"We all should have watched. Come. I'll show you the tide pool I found with its strange creatures around the next point." Walt peered at my averted face and pointed around to the left of us. Normally, I would have jumped at the chance, as I loved to look at strange animals and plants, but today I had not the heart.

"I'm sorry. I can't right now," I said. Walt moved away with his own head down, kicking at pebbles and rattling his way along the shore. At least the scene there was diverting to me. Men of all sizes, shapes, and descriptions sweated in the noonday sun, pulling on ropes, slipping in the pebbles, or gripping as tight as possible the heavy timbers they sought to bend. Some were formed and had already been carried the short distance to the boat. Larger men were hoisting one up to the broken side. The hole had been neatly trimmed. Ahmed had fashioned two bars of iron, top to bottom, down the center of the opening. I could see that it had holes in it, as did the plank they lifted up. The men above had the full weight of a soaked plank to lift. To my surprise, Major James was among them. If possible, these men sweated even more than those bending timbers at the fire, their muscles standing out with the strain of the dead weight, their faces in grimaces of pain. Ahmed was among them, and I wondered to see black and white arms work so close together. As I approached, I heard a great shout of encouragement from the major, and the plank slid into place.

"Watch out!" one of the men cried. Before my horrified eyes, the rope broke. The plank fell on a man standing too close. His arm was pinned beneath him at an unnatural angle. I ran for Ibrahim and Ardath. The men at the fire ran for the one pinned down.

I found Ardath quickly packing medical supplies at the rear of the defile. "Where is Ibrahim?" I asked.

"I don't know. Gone to pray, I think. Gather those splints for me, and the opium."

I did this quickly. "Go help. I'll be right there," Ardath said.

I ran back to the beach. The injured man was screaming as the others lifted the plank off him. It was none other than the dandy, Mr. Towler. His face was white from the shock of the blow.

"Don't move him," I said. The men stood back. That was a badly broken bone. I could see its jagged whiteness jutting out from the tired silk of his suit arm.

Just then, Ardath arrived. She spoke calmly to Mr. Towler, urging him to lie still. She administered the opium, murmuring to him all the while and testing the sharp edge of her knife blade. With care, she split the coat arm away from the bone. I looked up to see Major James there beside us.

"Where is the physician?" he asked in a quiet voice.

I stood to answer him. "We do not know. Ardath said he went away to pray. Ardath has done this many times. You can trust her," I said.

He opened his mouth as if to protest, then shut it firmly. He watched for a moment while Ardath efficiently set about feeling the wound and gently moving the arm into place, then said, "Stand back, men, let her work."

She looked up at the sound of his voice. "Major, I need your help with

76

this arm," she said. The major's face reddened, but he knelt down at Towler's side.

"Hold his arm straight at the count of three. You will have to pull strongly, but steadily. Are you ready?"

"Yes," he replied.

"One, two, three!" The major pulled steadily while, on the other side of Towler, Ardath pressed downward on the bone. The bone fell into place. Towler tossed, but the major held him down. Ardath applied a healing herb powder and stitched the wound. She placed the splints on each side of the arm and wrapped it all tightly with cloth strips. It was a neat job and well done! I was once again so proud to see Ardath at work.

The major stood up. "Make a travois from two poles and some canvas," he said to Mr. Smythe, who was standing close by. Smythe hurried to do this. Major James looked down at Ardath, who was checking Towler's eyes.

"As well done as on a battlefield, Miss Rhys," he said, and he seemed to mean it sincerely.

"Thank you, Major," she replied, as if she had not been ready to kill him mere moments ago. She did not look up at him, however. Was this civility an act, I wondered, or had they declared a momentary truce?

By the time that Mr. Smythe had a travois ready, Ibrahim had appeared and nodded approval at Mr. Towler's repair and condition. The major and another man placed Towler on the travois and carried him to the sickroom.

Ardath was tired. She slumped down into the pebbles. "How can I help you?" I asked. "Can I get you some soup?"

Her green eyes looked up at me. "That would be a wonderful thing!" she said.

I went off to the cook fire. Bless Mrs. Perry! It never went out night or day now while she fed the workers. While I got some soup. Major James had gone back down to Ardath. I could not hear their conversation, but he was soon helping her up off the ground. He led her away toward the defile where she had been sleeping, supporting her there with one arm around her waist. When I took the soup, I really did not mean to spy on them.

"That was bravely done. I have seen many a break ill-treated during battle, yet you seemed to know precisely what to do," he was saying.

"I have not been in battle, but there were many occasions in our village for injury from physical work. My mother taught me well."

"It seems among the womanly skills to give succor at such times."

Oh, dear, the conversation was about to take a bad turn, I thought. Rather too loudly, I said, "Ardath, here is your soup."

"Oh, yes, thank you, sister. If you will excuse me, Major…"

"Certainly," he said, giving a nod to Ardath.

As soon as he left, she was muttering into her soup. So much for the "truce," then!

"Ardath, he was really admiring you," I ventured.

"Sister, please leave me now," she said.

I didn't want an argument; she was so set against him, and I didn't want to listen to Towler moaning on his pallet. I moved away toward the beach. Major James had called a halt for rest, which was wise. These were not hardened men he commanded, and I think they were somewhat unnerved by the accident. Mr. Smythe, who had become the major's second-in-command, spoke with him near the ship. Their backs were to me, but I heard him say, "Booth, that was an admirable job she did with Towler."

"Yes, it was," the major replied. "I tried to tell her that, but I confess that I fail with her. She seems to hate me on sight. In all my life, I do not believe I will ever understand women."

"Perhaps none of us will!" Smythe said. "She is quite the handsome woman too. Tall and statuesque, like a Greek Goddess, perhaps Diana."

"Why, Smythe, are you sweet on her?"

"For myself, no, but I think you are attracted to her, Booth, if you would but admit it."

"It could go nowhere, *if* I were as you say. She is of a common class. It's impossible," the major said. (I was taken aback by that, but yes, this was the upper-class view of us.)

"Well, you may not find many of our station in the New World, and it's

78

not as if you would be presenting your wife at court," Smythe said.

"Smythe, you are rubbing salt into the wound here. It is true that I did not part on the very warmest of terms with my parents, but we are civil. And as to the title and inheritance, my brother will succeed, and there is no need for me in England, all true, but there are standards to maintain nonetheless."

"If this is the way you speak to Miss Rhys, I can see why you fail with her. As for me, I plan to be free of some of these strictures once we are in the New World. I shall marry whom I love, be she a mere guttersnipe."

"Very romantic. But, what will people say?" asked the major.

"I plan not to care what 'people' say. I'll make my fortune and my own way."

"Well, you are planning to stay, to make it your home, but after I finish with the Indian problem, I may return to England. And it may be the New World, but it is still an English one!"

"Oh, Blimey!"

"Smythe!"

"I'm practicing, you hard arse! I'm practicing to be a new man in a New World. Perhaps I will take another look at Miss Rhys myself, she of the pale, creamy skin, the violent red hair, the flashing eyes, the strong face, the admirable skills! And most of all, the passion." Smythe chuckled as the major's face reddened.

At this point, they had shifted somewhat in the pebbles so that I feared they might see me. I turned away and busied myself taking fresh water to the men. They had dropped onto the beach where they had labored. Their faces were sooty, and their hands raw. They took the water with gratitude and sometimes sloshed it out of the cup as they drank, their hands being numb with the cold and hard usage.

As I did this, my mind was on the conversation. The major's attitude seemed immutable. I liked Smythe for his humor and forthrightness, and again, my hopes sprang up for the New World. Perhaps there would be a better, less-strictured life for us there, too, if such attitudes as Smythe's prevailed over those of the major. Of course, it depended on us getting there! Everything depended on that.

CHAPTER 19

Late May 1751
Ardath

I WAS BORED. I had cut all the bandages we could need for an army of men. I had at ready the medicines to use for injuries. I could do nothing more for Towler, who would have to sleep off the pain. Keeping busy could not keep me from my anger, but I was bored with that as well. James wasn't going to change. Eventually, I would find a way around him to do what must be done, but I missed the books and charts that he had taken. I might have learned more, if only I could have looked at them. I reviewed in my mind everything I knew about the sails, how to present them to the wind, and other things like measuring speed with the log on a knotted rope. It wasn't much, when I considered the ship on an open ocean. I knew that it took men many years to learn the craft of skillful sailing, and that was with thorough tutoring by experienced sailors. Well, we could only do the best we could with what we knew, supposing that the martinet let us.

At least the plan was working with the repair. I walked down to the ship, where Gwyn helped with the water bucket. A breeze, which would have been pleasant in warmer air, rustled around us.

Gwyn looked up from her work and rested the bucket on the beach pebbles. "Work resumed soon after Towler's injury," she said. "The timbers are almost all in place. It is so exciting! They seem to fit well. The men are fastening the timbers with iron nails that Ahmed made for the holes."

"I can see. The hole in the side has practically disappeared!"

"Walt found the oakum they will need to caulk it. They have to wait until the timbers dry some, though, because the boards will shrink. The one sailor left, Mr. Scroggs, says that the sails can be repaired or replaced."

Indeed, some men were throwing canvas overboard, mostly onto the beach. I turned to see Mrs. Perry leading the women down to pull it up further. I went to help, as best I could.

"Ardath, don't do this hard pulling. You are not recovered yet," Mrs. Perry told me. Normally, I might have bristled at that, but it was true. "You can help by laying out our needles and cord on this board." She handed me a bag of sewing equipment quite unlike any I had seen before. I laid out heavy needles made to poke through the tough canvas. And "thread" that looked more like thick twine.

I threaded these while the women looked at the tear that ran as jagged as a lightning bolt through the cloth. The men wouldn't be the only ones needing salve on their hands tonight! But hands used to silken threads had been roughened by carrying driftwood the many days we had been marooned here. I was proud to see the women leap into the work as if at their knitting circle. Away they went with their repair.

Mr. Smythe approached to see how we did.

"This will not take long for you ladies, at the great rate you are going," he said. "I believe we have good cause for hope when I see you at work!"

I smiled at him. I liked Smythe, who seemed a good-humored man.

He tipped a hand at his forehead, as if tugging a forelock in salute. His hair had turned blonder in the sun, though, like all of us, no less greasy, and he had lost the pasty-pale English look. With his too-lean face and beaked nose, he was not a handsome man, but amiable.

"Might I have a word with you, Miss Rhys, if you can be spared?" he asked.

"Of course," I replied, getting up from the beach.

He gave me a hand. We walked out of the hearing of either the men or the women. I leaned back against a boulder. I was still more tired than I wanted to be.

"I have been wanting to speak to you about my friend James," he said.

I inclined my head toward the ground, so that he could not see my expression.

"I know that the two of you don't always agree," he said.

I said nothing, waiting. Maybe this was an opening to get what we needed from James through an intermediary, but could I trust a friend of James?

"So I came to ask if you would meet with him, to discuss what you know about the ship and its running."

Ha ha, I thought, *too cowardly to approach me himself.*

"Did Major James send you?" I asked.

"Well, no," he admitted. "I happened to notice that you made yourself familiar with certain aspects of the ship when Mr. Whitsun was still with us. I feel that we can use your knowledge in our hopes to complete this journey."

"Umm," I said. "You may also have noticed that Major James and I are not on the best of terms."

"That seems a shame, as I can tell you are both strong leaders," he said.

"That is kind of you, but I am a woman and should know my place," I said, mocking James's words.

He stooped and turned his head sideways to see my face. "Is this what he said to you?"

I had to laugh; he looked so comical upside down, like a bird with a cocked head.

"Well, that is very close to many things he has said."

"I regret that, and I'm sure he must also." He straightened up again, and I found myself looking at him face-to-face. His wore a slight smile, but not a mocking one.

Here was an unusual man, one who addressed me as a person of intelligence. I valued this considerably more than good looks, which, I was learning, did not show the true nature of a person.

It was such a relief that I found myself comfortable with him and ventured to confide, "I did come to know how to use the quadrant and a little about our course and about reading charts, but as I was working with these, the major came and took them away." I didn't mention Walt or Gwyn's part in this, in case this confidence landed me in trouble.

"Ah, umm," said Smythe.

"Do you think you could have some influence with him, to let me look at those again?"

"Well, it is patently absurd not to use what you know, but the major has strong views. I don't know how to persuade him, *yet*, but as I am bound to be a solicitor in Philadelphia, if we make it there, then I must learn to make a good argument."

I was surprised. He was obviously a gentleman, but he actually intended to work for his living. I had thought most gentlemen, even if in financial straits, preferred to marry well rather than work.

"At the least I could teach you what I know and the major would not have to endure the shame of being taught by a woman."

"It wouldn't hurt him to learn some humility," he said, to my surprise.

Unexpectedly, fate seemed to have handed me an ally. I hope my mouth did not drop open too far at the very thought.

CHAPTER 20

Late May 1751
Gwyn

ARDATH DID NOT TELL me much of her conversation with Smythe, either that day or the next. It seemed to have gone well, but the excitement on the beach was all about the completion of the ship repair. Of course, there was much more work to do, but it looked as if we might be afloat within a few days.

That night, the fire was a gathering place full of celebration. The major even broke out some of the rum supply. Mr. Scroggs, the sailor, had reformed his ways after the major had put him in irons for stoning Ardath. He worked and celebrated with as good a spirit as anyone nowadays. He called for the Irish passenger to find his fiddle. The fiddler played dance tunes that made our feet twitch. After some rum, we all danced, just by ourselves, with other women, men, or whoever was near. Mr. Scroggs capered about like a happy monkey.

They called for me to sing. A jolly song like "The Devil and the Farmer's Wife" seemed the best. I was roundly applauded, which didn't even make me blush.

The next day, we felt the effects and were long in rising from our pallets. Then it was back to work. The men carried hogsheads to the stream. Through the bunghole, we women ran hoses and filled them up. Omar devised a sort of wheelbarrow, which helped the men get the huge barrels back down to the beach. It was slow work, getting them down and back onto the ship. One full hogshead broke loose and careened down the hillside to smash itself on the rocks below with a great gush of water.

Pulleys, again devised according to the Africans' plan, helped load them on the ship.

"Ardath, what would we have done without the Africans' help?" I asked.

"It would have been impossible. We never would have made it off this godforsaken place! Now we will, and try to go west, I guess."

"Did Smythe offer you any hope of the major relenting about the quadrant?" I asked.

"Ah, sister, you are a smart girl! He actually thought he could find a way to talk to James, but he promised nothing. He knows James well."

Over the following days, the men, directed by Mr. Scroggs, caulked the ship thoroughly, new and old parts as well, inside and out. The sea had flushed out much of the old caulking in the storm. The men were a nasty, splotchy brown from the oakum, but no one cared. We had several more happy campfires before we were ready to float.

Major James addressed the men at the last fire. "Tomorrow we will attempt to float her. Tonight, all those who do so should pray for our success." It was a good moment for us all, and I assuredly prayed with all my heart that night.

CHAPTER 21

May 1751
Ardath

THE NIGHT BEFORE THE launching, I waited until everyone was asleep, then crept from my pallet. Instead of taking off my shoes at bedtime, I had wrapped them in a thick wad of cloth to muffle my movements, so they made little sound in those blasted pebbles. I had a candle handy, but the nearly full moon gave enough light without it. The night was very beautiful, cold, clear, with stars filling the soft sky as they did no other place I had ever seen. No wind stirred the air. I stood for a while at the edge of the defile to make sure I was not noticed. There was no sound beyond the quiet snorts and farts of the sleeping company and the surprisingly calm swish of the surf. I crept on, flinching at every small sound my feet made, following the little path that I had scouted during the day. The scene was otherworldly. I felt like a dim ghost moving over the beach to the ship.

The ladder the men had been using was still hung over the side, so I climbed it slowly. My feet made muffled thumps hitting the side as I pulled on the ladder. It took strength to pull myself up, strength I didn't have yet. My arms and legs burned with the effort. My lungs hurt from the cold air. Regardless of my condition, I was not going to miss the experience and watch passively from the beach with the other women. I found a place amidships to hide, under a tarp folded there. I inhaled a deep breath of the salt-sweet air before ducking into the stale space beneath, which smelled of a mélange of rotted fish, men's sweat, and moldy cloth.

It was none too soon. I heard the crunch of heavy steps in the pebbles beside the ship. I picked up a small edge of the tarp. It was Major James, pacing on the beach with his hands clasped behind him. The moonlight glinted in his hair. In a moment, he stopped and stared at the ship as if it could give him answers to his deepest questions. I ducked further down. The piles of rough, spiny rope stored in my space pricked at me and crowded me. Although it was most uncomfortable, I didn't move. The last thing I wanted was for the martinet to know I was aboard. Eventually, he moved away. I had hoped to look for the charts and books on the ship before the night was over, but he might be back. I ventured another peek, then settled the ropes in a more comfortable arrangement. I was tired enough to sleep there with my wrapped shoes as a pillow.

*****

The next I knew, the ship's bell was ringing for the men to board her. They clambered up, chattering with excitement, and spread to their stations across the ship. No one was really near me. The early light was still dim. So I rubbed the grit from my eyes and climbed from my "bed." I stayed close to the mast.

They would not attempt to sail today. This was a test to see if the boat would float. High tide had surged in during the last part of the night. The rollers Omar had made were placed under her. The men on the beach pushed her out with long poles. Yelling a great "Hurrah!" they watched her float on her own. To everyone's surprise, she kept rolling out at a fast clip. The prow turned sideways and then out to sea, jerked by a strong crosscurrent near shore. The ship shuddered but kept moving.

I saw Major James realize the danger. He rushed to the anchor, yelling for help to throw it out. In their hurry, two men immediately threw the anchor. James was standing over the rope. A loop of it caught his right leg and pulled him overboard with it.

The men stood in horror and confusion. They tried to pull back on the rope, but it only burned their hands and slipped through them. They couldn't swim; they looked over the edge helplessly. He would drown if I didn't get him. Stupid men!

I ran, stripping my skirts off, leaving nothing but my vest and shift. I dived over the side. The shock of the cold almost made me draw a breath of water. The plunge took me down some ways, but the salt buoyed me up so that I had to fight to force myself down. Below me in the crystal water, James twisted and flailed, still firmly pinned at the bottom by the rope and anchor.

I used the rope to pull myself headfirst down to him. His flailing threatened to swamp me as well. I floated out from him to avoid his kick, then swam close again. I put both hands beside his face. His blue eyes were frozen wide in panic. I made him look at me and shook my head, gesturing for him to stop struggling. For a moment, he stilled. I dived farther down. Clasping the rope, I pulled it down. I wound it back from his foot. He was free, but no longer conscious. I thanked the sea for her buoyancy.

My chest was bursting for want of air. I pushed and pushed, until he finally began to rise in the water. I followed, pushing him up ahead of me. When I thought I could stand no more, we broke through the surface. I inhaled a great breath of air, so sweet!

Smythe had seen what happened. He already had a plank lowered to the sea next to the anchor rope. I saw him peer down at us as I hauled James partway onto the plank.

"Take him up," I gasped. They pulled his limp body up the side, using the ladder to get down to him, boosting him up. I bobbed in the water until the plank came down for me shortly thereafter. I hardly had the strength to pull myself onto it. But I had to.

Ibrahim was on the shore. No one was going to know how to revive James. I took a bruising ride bumping to the top, shivering. I became aware that I had lost my vest and was clothed only in my drenched white shift, showing my nipples and red bush through it for all to see. Well, so be it! The man at the top averted his head from my nakedness and covered me with a blanket.

On deck, Smythe had a blanket covering James and was chafing his blue hands in his own. I grasped my blanket, stumbling the few steps to him. Shoving Smythe aside. I dropped painfully onto my shaking knees. Pushing on

James's chest, I caused some water to bubble from his mouth, but he was not breathing. I put my mouth to his and gave him my breath. Alternately, I pushed his chest again. I never looked up. I breathed and pushed again and again, until I saw stars. Finally, he coughed some water. I turned him on his side. Water and vomit poured from his mouth. He took a gasping breath. I was kneeling next to him. He looked at me with bleary eyes.

"You," he said. I couldn't tell if he was glad I had saved him, or ready to curse me for my unladylike behavior.

In either case, Smythe now had me in his arms and held me to warm me up. He took me below out of the cold breeze, rubbed my arms and legs briskly. Without a blink, he had me out of my frozen shift, for it literally had frozen in the air on deck, and into clothes from a handy sea chest. It happened to be Mrs. Perry's, so the clothes in no way fit me, but I was glad for every layer. There was even a cloth to dry my hair; he toweled it briskly.

He had arranged for the stove to be started in the galley. In time, we drank a cup of tea together. Nothing had ever been more welcome.

Smythe smiled at me. He had good teeth, though quite crooked. "Well, she floats," he said. "Perhaps too well for our skills in handling her!"

"That she does! We must have Mr. Scroggs, the sailor, and Walt continue to train the men. They mostly have no idea what to do on the sea. And we must know more about where we are and how to return to our route. Have you had any luck in making a case with James about the quadrant and charts?" I asked. It had not occurred to me until that moment that I was speaking so openly with a man I hardly knew. I stopped abruptly.

"I have broached that with him, but I think you made quite the case your-self today, for the usefulness of a unique woman in unusual circumstances," said Smythe.

"Well...thank you, I guess. But I do thank you most sincerely for the care you showed for me and, of course, for the major. I might have frozen along with my clothes. Uh, to speak of clothes and my lack thereof...'"

"No, we shall not speak of it. I will swear on any number of Bibles that you dived into the water fully dressed and reappeared at the top of it in the same state, only wetter."

"But others saw me too," I protested.

"I have spoken to them. They saw nothing out of the ordinary except extraordinary courage."

"You seem rather more calm about this than some men might be," I said.

"Ah, comes from having three sisters, very proper ones, of course, but the female figure does not hold much mystery or terror for me."

I smiled. How could anyone not smile at this unusual man?

"I will return your clothes when they have warmed some more in the galley. We must spend some hours here, waiting for the tide to turn. I suggest you rest in this bed."

"How will we get back to shore, even with the tide coming in? We won't be close enough."

"Happily, Omar is on board with us. He is making a raft from spare planks and an oar and pole to get some of us closer. We will take hawsers with us to help pull her in."

"Oh, good." I relaxed.

"In the meantime, I am bringing James down here for a fuller rest. I'm afraid the poor man is quite tuckered out."

"No, I don't wa—"

But he was out the door before I could finish.

He brought the major back with him and put him across from me in the tiny cabin's other bed. I gave Smythe a red look, but he exited right away, leaving the major and me in uncomfortable silence. Unfortunately, even in his almost-drowned state, he was a handsome and well-formed man, in some ways very admirable.

"I hope you are feeling better," I managed to say.

"Mmph," he said. So he was angry, or embarrassed, perhaps. I didn't try again. I was frankly too weary to care what he thought or said. I drifted toward sleep.

His flat voice came at me. "I must thank you for my life," he said.

"Of course," I said. That seemed ambiguous enough.

"Ahem…is there some way I can return a favor to you? I have little money, but my family does, and I have some influence in society in the colonies."

I spoke too quickly. "There is something. If you could let me teach you or one of the men, discreetly, of course, to read the quadrant and the charts, we would have a better chance of getting to the New World."

"You are the most…," he started, then curbed himself. He drew a long breath. "I owe you my life. Though you are unnatural in your wishes and behavior, I will honor your request."

"Thank you for being so gracious about it," I murmured. What could he do with that reply? He fell silent. It was almost too easy a victory. My eyes were closing as I spoke. "We should get some rest," I said.

CHAPTER 22

May 1751
Gwyn

THE MAJOR WAS QUITE fevered. Ibrahim and I worked on him, Ibrahim bent, listening to his chest, and I arranging his covers. He was wrapped in a blanket and had no other clothes, not even a breechclout. It was not as if I'd never seen a man like that before, of course, from helping my mother and Ibrahim, but I felt my eyes wanting to linger on him. So many times I had thought of my hands on him, stroking his hard muscles, feeling his warmth. And here was need for me to do it as a helper. It made me feel timid to think of it.

"Gwyn, you must bathe his face and chest with cool water to get the fever down. I have given him willow bark. His chest sounds well at this time, but we must take no chances. I need for you to watch him carefully. I'll fetch water for you to bathe him with, but then I must see to Mrs. Herman. Can you stay?" asked Ibrahim.

"Of course," I said to him. *Oh, dear,* I said to myself. But there was nothing for it. I stilled the trembling in my hands and began work. I willed myself not to think as I had in my fantasies, of him reacting to my touch, turning to me and saying, "Gwyn, how could I have thought of you as a child? I see now that you are my beloved. I will always love and protect you." Of him kissing me with soft yet insistent lips. Oh, dear, I was thinking of these things and furthermore imagining that he glowed hot with love for me, not fever. Oh, foolish girl that I was! How grateful I was that no one could know my thoughts or feel what I felt just then.

The major did not stir as I bathed him; his skin did seem to cool somewhat. The willow bark must be working. And he must not be very sick, or Ibrahim would never have left him. I took some moments to smooth back his hair. He had a noble forehead under those brown curly locks, and his lashes lay long on his cheeks. Normally smoothly shaven, he was starting to get a stubble on his chin. It had a shade of red in it, unlike his hair, more like the hairs around his cock, which was nestled innocent and soft in his crotch. Oh, no, not again. I had to blush this time. Why did I have to have such thoughts when it seemed that I would never be a woman, never be able to do something other than moon about in a lovesick way? I wriggled on my seat and focused on ways to help him.

Just then, any struggle with myself came to an end, because he began to speak. With a fevered tossing of his head, he moaned, "Ardath, don't hate me so! I am not a bad man! You must come to know me. You must come to love me." He broke off into unintelligible mumbles.

That burst the spell. I continued to bathe him, perhaps not as gently as before. I watched my silly dreams fall like dead sparrows at my feet. So he wanted Ardath. How could he not? She was a full-blown woman, beautiful and resourceful. I wanted to retreat into my heart and curl up there like a snail in its shell.

Ardath strode up the beach toward us. "Oh, Ardath, he wants you!" I exclaimed, without thinking.

"What? What do you mean, sister?" she asked.

"Uhh, he's feverish and talking of you. He wants you to give him a chance…"

"What? Hah, if that is truly how he feels, he's not likely to win me. He must be raving." She looked at me more closely. "You admire him, don't you? After all he has done, you think him a worthy man. Or…" She looked at me again. "Oh, Gwyn, you haven't become enamored of him, have you?"

Now I really was blushing. "I just think you don't give him any quarter. It is true that he doesn't seem to think that a woman could be his equal, but you seem determined to prove that you are *more* than his equal."

"No, that isn't necessary. I certainly know that I am more than his equal."

93

"Ardath! You will never be happy with a man if you always see yourself as superior."

"I can't help the truth. I'll feel that way until I meet a man who shows me otherwise."

That seemed quite arrogant to me, but I would not say that, as it would only lead to an argument. Once Ardath was set on something, it was of no use to debate it.

She bent to examine Major James. "He will be recovering soon. I have to say that he will probably walk with a limp from the wrenching the rope gave him as it dragged him to the water."

I swear that she said that last as if it gave her satisfaction. I was beginning to see a certain hard-heartedness in Ardath that chilled me. I had always adored her, unquestioning. She had been everything to me since we lost our mother. Now I felt alone, as I never had before.

Smythe approached, greeting us with the question, "How is he?" He seemed to be asking me as well as Ardath. I waited for her to answer, and when she didn't, he looked to me.

"I think that his fever is coming down. Ibrahim says that his chest is clear, which is a good sign."

"Ah, good. Has he said anything?"

"Oh, no, not really, just mutterings," I said.

"How about Towler? Will he be ready to move soon?"

"Yes, I think so. The arm is very sore, of course."

"Well, it can be sore on board as well as here. Ardath, now that you have shown me the use of the quadrant and maps, we have an idea of where we are. I think we should get on with our journey as soon as possible. What do you think?"

"Yes, Mr. Smythe," she said.

"Please call me Gregory," he replied. "If we are to be in this venture together, we can be less formal when in private. How about you, Miss Gwyn, are you ready to go?"

"At a moment's notice," I said. Weren't we all eager to leave this godforsaken place?

While they discussed the tides and timing of a departure, the major awoke.

"Where are we?" he asked.

"Ah, Booth," said Smythe. "So glad to see that you are awake. We are still on the shore, but planning our grand departure. Scroggs has been drilling the men, and they are as seaworthy as we can hope for, I believe."

"How long have I been unconscious?"

"Much of the last two days. How do you feel?" said Smythe.

"Foolish, I vow!"

"Nothing foolish about letting your body rest," said Smythe. He pushed a lock of blond hair from his eyes and looked at Ardath. "We have been discussing leaving at next tide out. Do you feel ready to be moved to the ship soon, James?"

"Certainly, I will not need to 'be moved.' I am quite able to move on my own." With this, the major swung his legs over the side of the pallet and tried to stand up. Smythe jumped to help him. The major's right leg buckled under him. He leaned heavily on Smythe, his lips pursed and white. "Perhaps I will require a cane," he admitted as he sank down again.

"No shame in it, no shame," said Smythe. He caught Ardath's eye, signaling with his head that she should leave. No one noticed me, so I stayed.

"Smythe, how go the plans?"

"Well, I think. The quadrant and charts tell us that we seem to be near Greenland. We hope to follow the coastlines until we can reach Philadelphia. A rather-slow trip, most likely, but a chance for us to find a landing."

"We?"

"Well, of course, Miss Rhys has done as you suggested and taught me to read the instruments."

"And you consult her at every turn, I suppose." The major's mouth turned down at the corners.

"Booth, you must drop this enmity toward her. We need everyone to help in this effort. She needs to teach you these instruments as well. Furthermore, I suspect that your animosity toward her springs from a frustration in your hopes to court her."

Before the major could reply, Smythe looked up and noticed me. "Miss Rhys," he said, chagrin written on his face. "So sorry for our bad manners."

"Of course," I said. I blushed because I had hoped to escape notice and because the major had shown himself so petulant. He had the grace to look down but did not apologize for himself.

"Well," said Smythe, when he saw that the major would not speak, "let us make for the beach straightaway."

CHAPTER 23

June 1751
Ardath

WHAT A RELIEF! AFTER weeks on this island, we were finally setting out. The morning's tide was good. The air was fresh; I couldn't remember what a city smelled like now. The men were alert, especially so, it seemed, after James's accident, and trying to do careful jobs at their stations. James was ensconced in a chair on deck and looked recovered, when he was still. Smythe was everywhere, as was Scroggs, making sure the launching went smoothly.

Smythe had learned everything he could from me, which we had done privately. Then I worked with James. In teaching him the instruments, I had had to get quite close to him, wrapping my arms around his to show how to hold the quadrant. I was conscious of his breathing, his smell, his heart pumping, the strength of his arms. Those lessons had made my head spin, I confess.

Walt ran the rigging as always, now with another boy that he had been training. They looked like the monkeys I saw with sailors in Liverpool, scrambling about above us, bare feet hugging the ropes like extra hands. Mrs. Perry had taken charge of the galley, with Gwyn assisting her. Ibrahim had few patients and spent time in prayer or gazing in contemplation at the water.

We eased out of our rocky bay. Immediately, the waves were rougher, the wind was up, but so it must be to get us there!

And I did have hope that we would get there. It made me look to our money belts and think about the New World as a real place that we must conquer. Gwyn seemed remote from me, spent more time with Mrs. Perry now. I supposed it was about James's mutterings. I wish that she would not suffer over him. James was a dead end for either of us, though he was very civil to me since I pulled him from the water and was quite subdued, perhaps by his lameness. We would need a man to help manage our affairs in Philadelphia; it wouldn't be James, who would be intent on army matters. From his apparent trustworthiness and what he told me about his business plans, Smythe would be a good choice. I didn't plan to trust our uncle.

*****

After we rounded the headland, we began to see ghostly blue-white shapes in the dark-blue sea. Icebergs!

"Keep far away, steer to port," Scroggs called to Smythe at the wheel. "They be bigger than they look."

We dodged that monster and several others in the days to come. In eluding them, we lost sight of land and traveled blind, in cold white mists, going southwestward by the sea compass. Many of the women knelt on deck, or down below, to pray aloud for our safety. Who could say if it helped? But several days later, the weather cleared. We saw before us a long coastline, rocky and barren in appearance. It had to be the main coast of Greenland!

"What do you think, Scroggs?" Smythe asked the sailor. "Should we try to go ashore?"

"Too dangerous, I'd say, sir. I'm not well-knowing of these waters, and we could run aground," said Scroggs.

"Mrs. Perry says the onboard water is still in good supply and fresh enough," I said. "I think we should push on."

"I agree," said James, giving me a nod of acknowledgment.

"'Tis rumored among the old whalers that a current here will take ya right around the place, if it be Greenland," said Scroggs.

That settled it. We sailed on. It was smooth traveling the current, if that was indeed what propelled us, around the south of Greenland and then swinging up north to sail around its western side. The men got a break from the constant vigilance they had maintained on the other side of the coast. We stayed well out from shore, but it was still good to see land on our starboard.

One day, Scroggs, Smythe, James, and I stood on deck. According to the quadrant and maps, we were swinging too far north and needed to take the leap across open ocean, southwest to Labrador. By going southwest at this point, we were bound to hit some kind of landmass.

"If yer thinkin' it will be an easy trip, yer wrong now!" said Scroggs. "This next part, say my whaler friends, is where the icebergs float extra thick-like this time o' year."

It was late spring or early summer by now. I hated to think how overdue we were in Philadelphia.

"Well, we can't wait for a better time to go," said Smythe.

"Yes, that is plainly true," said James, looking off toward the west, with one hand shading his eyes. "We will just have to put on constant watches, as we did before we saw Greenland."

"Aye, ye will that!" said Scroggs, who wrinkled up his pug nose, making his face even uglier than before, if that were possible.

"We are very short of men for the watches," said James. He was gradually resuming his leadership among the men, as he recovered further. Indeed, they called him Captain.

"Perhaps I and some other women can help this time," I ventured.

James looked at me steadily. "That may be wise," he said with some warmth.

I kept my face still so that he could not see my surprise. "I can ask among the women for volunteers, those with the best eyes," I said.

"Please do. We cannot afford to be caught midocean by those mammoths," said James.

I organized the women's watches. Mrs. Perry was excused since she was needed in the galley to keep heartening soups and stews and hot drinks at the ready. I was surprised that most women wanted to help. They squared their chins and assumed their duties with stoic bravery.

Our breaths showed a misty white as we stood on opposite sides of the ship and worked in pairs so as to keep ourselves awake, especially in the night watches. Some of the younger women could be seen to shiver at the horror of our situation. We were mostly alert through sheer terror. One glancing blow of an iceberg would be our end, after all we had endured to get this far!

Either Smythe or James was always at the wheel, with Scroggs catching rest on a nearby pallet when he could. At night, we cast out a sea anchor so that we did not propel the ship into the ice, but still the icebergs, breathing out their devious mists, floated toward us out of the blinding muck. The passage was as bad as it could be. The worst nights had little moon to guide us and reflect off the ice, but both day and night, we were eternally in thick fog and threading our way through looming frozen mountains.

There were twelve of us women who could see well enough to keep watch. We placed ourselves on the fore and aft of the ship and on both the port and starboard sides. At first, four women watched for eight hours, but the constant strain on hearts and eyes was too much, so we divided the watches into four hours each.

On the night when Gwyn and I took the first fore shift, we gripped the rail under a new moon. It shone weak strands onto the black water, yet at least the sky was not cloudy. The always-lurking, frigid fog soon closed in all around us, blurring the moon into insignificance and making us strain our eyes into its murk, hoping to *not* see a monstrous white shape moving toward the ship. I was on the starboard side because I thought the ice mountains were more likely to come from the north. I hoped to spare my sister the sight of one bearing down on us.

I glanced at Gwyn, who shivered in our "watch cloak," the heaviest covering we women had against the cold. She was moving her bluish lips in what might be a silent prayer or a song. We didn't speak, because in the fog, the noises of the ice might give us a warning. So far, nothing!

The hours plodded by, and I struggled to keep my mind alert, though I hadn't slept well since we entered the ice field several days before. As I concentrated on the night sounds of the waves slapping against the ship, the groans of the boards, and the slight whine of the rigging, I heard a different kind of groan across the water, then a creak of massive proportions and a rush of something heavy falling into the water.

"Calving ahead, starboard side!" I shouted to Scroggs at the wheel.

"Aye, aye!" he yelled, turning the wheel away from the threat.

Still the massive wave flew over us. Chilled to the bone, we hung to the ship with all our might. I saw Gwyn crouched by the rail, submerged in its flow. The wave jerked me off my feet. Any sounds that came to me then were muffled in the eerie underwater pressure against my ears.

The railings and uprights on the port side stopped my tumbling course. I opened my eyes in the swirling water to look for Gwyn. Thank the Goddess, I had landed very close to her. I crawled behind her, still gripping the uprights, to protect her from the blasting water. Now the wave pulled off us, but behind it came the second wave, and worse, the screaming of ice against wood. Something had hit the ship and seared along its side for what seemed an eternity. The ship bobbed to port on the sea anchor. Gradually, the ice let us go and the ship wallowed in its wake. The women at the rear were hanging on to the uprights as well and appeared unhurt.

"She's afloat, Captain!" yelled Scroggs to a drenched and staggering James, who clung to the mast, looking around him with eyes narrowed against the stinging spray.

"Misses Rhys, are you all right?" he asked of Gwyn and me.

We both coughed and nodded, too tired to do more. He checked the women on the aft end as well.

Omar came on deck to report. "Captain, the ice hit us, but we can repair as we sail."

"Aye, Captain, we was lucky where it hit, near the decking, where we'll do all right if we don't have high seas," said Scroggs.

Everyone was on deck by now, looking shaken but relieved. We were still afloat. "Man your stations now," I called to the first four women who appeared. "We four need a rest," I said, pulling Gwyn to my side to help her belowdecks.

When I had a moment, I longed for green fields and a warmer season we hoped to come to. It was hard to believe we would ever see anything but winter and hardship.

Eventually, the fog lifted, Walt cried "Land ho!" and we saw Labrador. It was early morning, but everyone ran to the deck. Some broke into impromptu jigs. Smythe ran up and twirled me around by my hands.

Then James limped forward from the wheel and took my arm gently. "None of us would be here without all that you did," he said. I didn't even question how he had come from dislike to a seeming admiration for me. We had worked well together and grown in respect for each other.

Now we were near land, and British land at that!

"Well, now, I must say I didn't think we'd make it," said Scroggs.

He was roundly booed.

CHAPTER 24

June 1751
Gwyn

"LAND HO!" WERE THE best words I had ever heard. Surely, the worst was behind us. We were at Labrador and could now sail along a British-held coast all the way to Philadelphia. The rocky headland before us showed a muted green, barren of trees or habitation, but *land!* Even the ocean seemed to be moving our way, sweeping us past the shore.

Major James was in charge again. I had finally gotten over my disappointment from hearing him talk about Ardath. They had developed a relationship that seemed to work for them, perhaps one of some warmth. She laughed with Mr. Smythe, but she and James were like close business partners, heads together, intent on getting the ship onward.

It had been soothing to work with Mrs. Perry in the galley. The routine of physical work left me busy enough not to be constantly agitated in my mind. Mrs. Perry, of all the people on the boat, had the most cause to worry about her circumstances when we reached Philadelphia. She and her husband had spent their last penny to pay passage on this voyage. He had planned to work there, and now she had no means of support. Yet she was among the most cheerful and practical of us all during all these trying weeks at sea. I fingered the heavy money belt under my skirt and determined that we must find a way to look after her needs when we arrived.

Thus I was musing when it happened. They say the watched pot never boils, and so it was with me. While I waited and lamented that I would never be a woman, my courses never came. Yet when I forgot totally and lost myself in helping Mrs. Perry, suddenly one day, I felt the warm stickiness on my thighs. Mrs. Perry found me cloths; the other women were kind and showed me how to tend to myself on the ship. It seemed a rather-messy beginning for the august state of womanhood, but I was happy nonetheless. That is, until I thought of how my mother would never know that, or anything else about me. Then I found myself tearful, which the women also seemed to understand, though I had not told them why I cried.

After I washed and changed my clothing, I went on deck. There I found Ardath in conference with the major and Mr. Smythe. Major James sounded quite cheerful as he said, "It is likely that we will see a ship of the king's royal navy soon. They must be patrolling these coastal waters." He gestured widely all around him, then addressed Ardath. "Miss Rhys, are you sure that we present no danger of infection to other ships?"

"Yes, we are as clean as any ship could be after an epidemic. All boards have been scrubbed with oil of tar, and of course, all clothing and bedding used by the infected were boiled or thrown overboard long ago," said Ardath.

"Good."

Then, as if the major were prophetic, we heard Walt call from the crow's nest, "British ship ahead!" In all the excitement, I forgot to tell Ardath my news.

We soon caught up with the ship in question as we raced down the coast, and she turned to meet us, signaling us to stop and be boarded. When they pulled alongside, the naval ship dwarfed ours. It looked shipshape, as Walt would say, burnished and bright in the sunlight. I thought it very exciting to see a captain of the navy in full regalia.

"Who commands this vessel?" shouted the naval captain from his deck way above ours.

"I do, sir, Major Booth James of His Majesty's army at your service."

"Booth James, you scoundrel! I've hardly seen you since Oxford. How did you go from major to captain? I'm not surprised they had to find another place for you. Disgraced the army, did you?"

"I admit that going from army to navy would be a disgrace," responded the major, laughing. "How are you, Wiley?"

"Most happy to see you. We thought your vessel lost. Permission to come aboard."

"Permission granted."

So with some adjustments to the ships, we were tied together securely, and Wiley, or Captain Wiley, as the rest of us called him, came aboard. He shook hands with Smythe and James and bowed over Ardath's hand as if she were a lady of great standing. He turned to me with a quick bow; I saw a merry look in his eye. He seemed a man who loved his position in life.

James took him below to the captain's cabin for a private meeting. No one noticed that I slipped away to spy on them. I hoped to find out even more about James when he spoke with his friend. The oaken door was massive, but a knothole in a nearby wall afforded me a good listening post. I curled up in a rough storage space against the wall and put my ear to the hole. Captain Wiley was speaking. "Booth, what happened here?" The major told of our epidemic and our shipwreck. He gave full credit to Ibrahim, to the Africans, and to Ardath for their parts in saving us.

"That is a remarkable story! Also, a remarkable woman you have in Miss Rhys," Wiley said. "And you somehow managed to float this wounded vessel with two sailors and a few civilians here from somewhere near Greenland? This is a story worth telling, I'll vow!"

"As you know, the need for survival can bring a motley crew together, to do things we all wouldn't have been able to do separately," said James.

I peeked through my hole, one eye against the prickly raw wood. The men stood together in the middle of the cabin, James taller by some inches than Captain Wiley.

"Well, you're in my waters now. I can provide you with some sailors to get you to port more easily. You also will have an escort, as we are headed for New York." Captain Wiley stood next to the wooden table and rapped his knuckles on it. "We are close to New France, and as you know, they have been raising the Indians against us. But that is more inland. The coastline is mostly secure, but there are always threats from privateers. We may not officially be at war now, but they claim their rights to maraud anyway. For now, we will take you with us. Are your supplies adequate? Did your cargo survive?"

"We need fresh water. There was very little cargo. Mostly, it was passengers, and we lost many of those to storm and illness."

"A brutal crossing! We will send over water with our sailors. My first officer can command your ship, with your permission, of course."

"Of course. I give up this command eagerly. I am no sailor."

"What about your plans? Still headed for Philadelphia?"

"Yes, I am to report to the colonel there for orders. Have you any news of my family?"

"Ah, so sorry, of course. I've had letters. It seems that your sister has been under the weather but is expected to recover completely. Your mother is with her at Glenmorgan House. Your father is in London still with business matters. Your brothers are there also, in good health. Of course, they asked if I had heard from you, which is why I knew of this ship. I can send them a message from you via a naval vessel, which will be quicker."

"Yes, thank you. Hmm, sometimes it is a small world, for all its vastness," said James.

"Aye to that! And thank God, a British world more and more!"

"God save!"

"God save!"

At this, I sensed that the conversation was coming to an end. I squeezed myself into my rathole further. The two men came out the door within inches of my hiding place. When they were well gone, I breathed deeply, my nose assaulted with the rank smell that never left the area belowdecks, no matter how much it might be scrubbed.

I unfolded myself from my cramped position. To my chagrin, I felt the bloody stickiness on my legs. The rag had slipped out of place when I hid. My skirt was wet with a huge red stain, which I should have to get into cold water as soon as possible.

Being a woman spy was different from being a child spy. It made me think that many other things in my life would be different too. I would have been grateful to go above into the sweet-salt air of summer, but first I crept away, hoping to encounter no one, to the women's cabin to clean up.

CHAPTER 25

June 1751
Ardath

WHAT A TURN OF events! We could even leave our ragged vessel at times, rowed in a long boat to the naval ship. We now ate almost nightly at the captain's table on board the HMS *Charlotte*. It was a formal affair, with several courses each time. Gwyn and I had no proper clothes, of course, though the women passengers gathered together the best they had and insisted that we use them. Mrs. Perry turned out to be a good seamstress and cut down the smallest woman's gown to fit Gwyn. It was blue, which made her eyes stand out even more than usual. Her cheeks were filling in from the good food. In the swinging, warm lantern light, she was suddenly beautiful.

All the men were courtly with us, complimenting us, pulling out our chairs, etc. Mr. Smythe, Gregory, had taught us how to handle the many pieces of flatware and glasses that we were not used to seeing on a table. How he got them off the naval ship, I do not know. With his easy ways, though, he made friends instantly.

Secreted in a cabin on our ship, he had laid them all out on a table. With mock seriousness, he bowed and said, "Pay attention, ladies, and I will give you the secrets of elegant dining, in a nutshell. These frightening forks are used in order from the outside in." We giggled like silly girls. The whole thing seemed absurd, but I knew that everything we learned about society could prove useful to us in Philadelphia. After all, Gwyn was becoming a young woman; I had to think of her possibilities of marriage. We had a little money for independence, but we didn't want to look so lower class that we could not join in the social events there. Philadelphia was becoming a more sophisticated city in the last few years, according to Gregory.

At dinner, we did well enough with our implements, and the conversation proved very interesting, as the captain knew Philadelphia well. One night, Smythe raised the subject of prominent citizens of Philadelphia. "I hear that a Mr. Rhys is promoted to assistant rector at Christ Church this year," he said to the captain. "Do you know him?"

"I do, and a good man he is, by reputation. He's overseeing the raising of the high spire on the tower at the church. Philadelphia now aspires—oh my, bad joke—to be a high-class city. They even have some paved streets now, and of course, Mr. Franklin has his hand in every good deed that goes on there," replied the captain.

"So you know Benjamin Franklin?" Smythe asked.

"Well, yes, he's in politics and rising quickly. I think everyone knows him. It would be a good idea for you to meet with him concerning the city. He knows all that goes on there and could probably be a help to you in your business."

"Thank you. I don't have a letter of introduction to him, though."

"Oh, he doesn't stand on ceremony, never fear, but I can send a note with you." There was a lull in the conversation.

I asked the captain, "Could you please tell us more about the Reverend Rhys? He is the uncle that we had hoped to meet when we began this journey. Unfortunately, our father died before he had time to tell us much about his brother."

"My sympathies for your loss," replied the captain.

"Yes, it was a terrible shame," I said, with no trace of sarcasm in my voice. I glanced at Gwyn across the table. She looked down steadily.

"Ah, let's see," said Captain Wiley. "Mr. Rhys is about forty-five years of age, married, of course, to a very religious lady, Mrs. Priscilla Rhys, a stalwart of the Church of England. They have a son in the Carolinas who is building a plantation there, not far from the Great Wagon Road. Many sons of prominent Philadelphians have migrated there. David is reputedly very industrious, sure to make a good go of it. He must be in his early twenties now."

"Interesting. When we reach Philadelphia," I said, "I suppose that we will go first to the Reverend Rhys and let him know of his brother's death."

"And then where do you propose to go? He will surely take in his brother's orphans!" said the captain, raising his eyebrows.

I glanced again at Gwyn. She looked stricken. Perhaps she had not thought of us as "orphans" until that moment and that someone who did not know us (perhaps did not even know *of* us) would have to take us in. She missed our mother, Carys, all the time, as did I, though I never spoke of it. My mother had always instilled in me that I must take care of my sister. All the hardships Gwyn had faced, so young! Well, she'd never know more hardship if I could prevent it!

I paid little attention to the rest of the conversation that evening, absorbed as I was in thoughts of how to make Gwyn's situation the best possible. It wasn't just Gwyn that concerned me. I had the three Africans to consider, and Gwyn had pleaded with me to help Mrs. Perry also.

Later that night, James rowed us back to our ship. After the others went belowdecks, we stood together, looking at a half-moon that shone on the water. "It has been a remarkable journey, but we should soon be there," he said.

"Ummm," I said, still trapped in overwhelming thoughts of my responsibilities.

"I know that we started on the wrong foot, or rather, I started on the wrong foot, but I feel we have grown closer in running the ship together. I wonder if I could call on you in the city," he said, moving nearer to me. "I have come to recognize your amazing strength, your intelligence, your beauty!"

The moon shone silver on his hair. I couldn't see his face, but I could feel his warmth next to me. Warmth, safety, shelter, protection. I wanted to melt into it.

"Oh, that is very good of you, but I am not of a suitable class for you!" I exclaimed. What in the world was he thinking?

"Well, you know, the more I hear about the relative freedom from tradition in parts of the new country, the more it appeals to me. I have no future in England. I want to make my own way, without regard to my family's position. The army affords me a chance to do that, as I train the militia and lead maneuvers on the frontier. I now think more of a person's character than of their station."

"I see. You sound like Mr. Smythe," I said.

"Well, yes, he has influenced me with his good sense. The truth is also that I don't like my family very much. I find them cruel, small, and unjustly prejudiced. I learned on this voyage that I would much rather be useful than rely on my family's name. And as much as I may, I would like to be useful to you and, uh, of course, your sister."

"So you wish to be of service to us poor girls," I said, laughing.

"Well, not just that," he said.

I could hear the small smile in his usually serious voice. He moved his hands to my shoulders and turned me toward him. I leaned in; I rested my head on his chest, where his heart beat fast. I wondered if I would come to regret this literal leaning on such a man. Just in a moment of weakness? Then, he was kissing me, and I stopped wondering about anything but how his lips could fit mine so perfectly.

CHAPTER 26

March 1, 1751
Carys

THE BABY HAD BEEN safely and happily delivered after a long labor. The mother would survive, but it had been a near thing for both of them, with her severe bleeding, the initial weakness of the infant, and his breech presentation. He was now nursing well and making up for lost energy.

I said a prayer of thanks to Brigid, the ancient Irish Goddess of midwives, mothers, and healing. I felt sure that the Christian male triad could not be as present with women.

The grateful parents had asked me to stay the night, but, though exhausted, I was eager to get home to my girls. I hated leaving them for days, as I had to in this case.

The moon was already gone from a very dark sky as I walked on, picturing Ardath or Gwyn at the fireside with a cup of steaming tea, and even better, my bed! Going down Bridge Street, I looked ahead to the walk under twisted oaks and ash up the Estate Road to our stone house in the Castle Woods. I'd soon be past the chapel and graveyard, with its stone gates leading onto the Rice Estate, then up the hill, past the sleeping sheep, to our oak copse above the Tywi River.

I had passed the thatched row houses of the Dinefwr Estate workers and was approaching the bridge, but I was not watching every bush as I should have.

They came from nowhere, rough, filthy hands across my mouth, hard nails digging into my arms. My struggles were in vain. One had my head and arms, the other my legs, all tight as a vise. Directly, I was dumped into a splintered wagon bed, still tightly gripped and unable to move or cry out. A stinking rag was forced into my mouth so that I could hardly breathe. My heart raced. My lungs ached for air. I tried to slow my breathing and conserve what little energy I had. The light under the trees where the wagon sat was not bright enough to see their faces, but they soon bound my eyes as well as my hands and feet. I could hear in their speech that these were hard and ignorant men.

The one with a deeper voice said, "Be ye sure that this's the right 'un?"

The other replied in a nasal whine, "Oh, yea, it be her, no doubt. I followed her from that cottage. She's the birthing woman, no doubt."

After they muttered together a few more moments, I felt the jerking of the wagon as they mounted into the seat. I had succeeded in slowing my breath and heartbeat, but I was very sore already from the hard boards beneath me and could not brace myself or get into any reasonable position, trussed as I was. Worse, I pictured what my daughters would be going through when they found me missing.

We crossed the creaking wood bridge over the Twyi, then jolted along for many hours sometimes uphill, sometimes down, in the cold night air; that was all that I could tell. I was fast pierced by splinters and felt bruises swelling. I prayed to Brigid, for her intervention and healing. Although Wales had been Christian for over a thousand years, and even the Irish now called her Saint Brigid, I held on to the knowledge of her Goddess aspect. That information had been passed down by women in our family through the ages, following the past intermarriage of Irish and Welsh nobility. No one but my daughters knew of my belief, but I felt it was a special connection for midwives and healers. And I could see I was going to need divine help to find a way out of this trouble.

I could no longer hear anything but the rattles and thumps of the wagon over the rough ground. It began to rain in torrents, needling my face and drenching my clothes, adding to my chill misery. We had been going forever when we stopped with a jerk. Rough hands again dragged me around. They pulled me up and set me on sodden earth. The mud sucked at my shoes as I made my legs carry me forward.

"They'll be at the Manor House, I warrant," the deep voice said.

"Aye, they will that," said the whiner.

The Manor House? I thought. Where was there a manor other than New Town anywhere near our village? Or perhaps I had been unconscious and we had gone farther than I believed? I could see no light with my eyes bound so tightly. It could be past daylight for all I knew. After we'd taken a long stumbling walk, the men opened a creaking door and pushed me into a room, where I fell hard to the floor. It was cold, wet stone, but I could feel warmth from a crackling fire nearby.

A cultured Englishwoman's voice said, "Pick her up, take off her blindfold, and wait outside."

Rough, cold hands pulled me up by my shoulders. My head snapped around as they jerked off the binding blindfold and grabbed the stinking gag from my mouth.

"Water," I pleaded. I couldn't see anything but the blur of the fire. The woman sat me on a chair and put a cup of water to my mouth. I was still trussed like a chicken set for roasting. I was at least near the fire. Steam rose from my clothes as they began to dry. I had no idea where I was or why I was there.

"I regret the circumstances that you find yourself in," said the lady.

I doubted that very much but said nothing. As my eyes cleared, I saw that she wore a whitish opaque veil over her face, in fact over her whole head and neck. She was dressed in dark clothes that gave little hint of her figure, but she sounded mature.

"I must ask your help with a poor village girl under my care who has compromised her future with an unwanted child. She is about to deliver her babe. You are a midwife, I believe?"

"Yes, but why have you brought me here like this? It hardly makes me want to help you!"

"Well, then, the poor girl will die from our lack of courtesy, I suppose," she said, in a voice muted by her veil. "And of course the innocent child."

She knew how to reach me, a smart woman, whatever else she was.

"No, I will help. I will help," I said. "But I need hot water and clean cloths. Did your men bring my supplies with them?"

"Yes, and I will get the girl," she said and left me there, still tied. This whole business was strange, to say the least, but if I could aid a woman in distress, I must surely do it. I shook my head, trying to throw my red hair out of my face, and my eyes cleared some more. I could then see that there was a narrow bed next to the wall. The room was round and entirely made of stones, ancient stones with very old mortar, no windows in sight. I knew it was on a level with the ground; otherwise, I would have said it was a dungeon. The bed seemed not a bad one. It had adequate supports and would do as a birthing spot. There were even pillows, quite nice ones, with white lace that did not match the room. They would probably be ruined in the process, but it was good to see that the "mistress" cared that much about the girl.

Soon the men returned with my bag of herbs and instruments. One locked the door with a large key and stood guard, while the other untied me. I stood, rubbing my wrists and ankles, which were worse for the wear.

The "mistress" returned with the girl in tow. The older woman ordered the men outside. The other woman seemed young and was bent with labor pains. She had on a veil also. It stuck to her face with every indrawn breath.

"You must let her take the veil off. She needs to be able to breathe freely. I would never reveal her identity, if that is what concerns you!" I said.

The "mistress" hesitated for a long moment but took off the girl's veil. She was young, her face beet red from breathing hard, but her features were refined, and her hands delicate and soft, not the hands of a typical villager. Her brown curls stuck to her face, and her blue eyes were wide with fear and pain. She was advanced in her labor, but when I examined her, I found that the opening to her womb was not expanding as it should have. I began to massage it open with warm cloths, telling the girl not to push at this point. She nodded, biting her lip, brave even in the pain. After I had encouraged it, her womb began to open on its own, giving me hope for the baby and for her.

"What is your name?" I asked.

Simultaneously, the mistress said "No" and the girl said "Elizabeth."

I ignored the woman. "Elizabeth, you should push out when I tell you. The baby should be coming soon."

But it didn't. Something was wrong with the baby's position. I leaned way over her, both of us sweating with effort. The child was a big one, stuck sideways, which at least was not breech. The butt was to the left and head to the right.

"I will have to turn the baby so that it will be able to come out," I told her, looking deeply into her blue eyes. She nodded and braced herself as best she could in the bed, white hands gripping the bedposts above her head. I leaned my weight into her and shoved the baby steadily clockwise. The first effort only shifted it a little. She lay gasping and weeping when I stopped. "We must do it again," I told her. "I'm sorry."

"Do it," she said with determination. I was beginning to have more and more respect for her bravery. We took a breath and tried again. This time the baby slipped readily around into a head-down position, but the face was point-ing upward. I was not able to turn it now. The baby was coming too fast. After a great burst of blood and pain, the poor girl was finally delivered from her labor.

It was an exhausting birth for all involved, but in the end we had a squall-ing, healthy boy. I cleaned him, wrapped his squirming body in clean cloths, and handed him to his mother. She reached for him, her eyes glowing with love.

Immediately, the "mistress" took him away, to his mother's weak pro-tests. She gave the girl a draft to "help her sleep." I attended the girl as she drifted off to sleep, then turned to the baby again. To my amazement, the "mis-tress" had opened the door and handed the baby to one of the rough men who had brought me here. He obviously did not even know how to hold him.

"What?" I began.

"And now for your pay," said the "mistress" to me.

"I do not require any payment, only ask that I be given a swift ride to my home. My daughters will be worried about me," I said.

"My men will be away with you soon, then," she said. "I regret that they must blindfold you again, but we must protect this poor girl's identity from her family's wrath."

Sure enough, they blindfolded me again and the whiner led me, more carefully this time, away toward the wagon.

Before we had gone very far, I heard the "mistress" say to Deep Voice, "Get rid of her and the child!"

If I was chilled before, it was nothing to what I felt now. I twisted away from the whiner and, dragging off my blindfold, bolted into the field beside me. The day had turned to dusk. I might make it to the line of trees ahead and hide there successfully. I ran like the devil pursued me, stumbling over clods of dirt, and made for the trees. My breath was rasping in my throat. I could still see enough to dodge the trees as I ran, desperate with fear, hearing the shouts behind me. Brambles dragged at my skirts and ripped into my legs, but I hardly felt them.

I had run for what seemed to be a half-hour. Suddenly the shouts stopped. I stopped, too, gasping as quietly as I could. Without the shouts, I had no marker for where the men were. The woods were now in full dark. I crept on all fours amongst the bare bushes, straining my ears for sounds. I could smell the wet duff of the wintery forest under my nose. I edged into a muddy hollow and piled oak leaves over myself. I had to rest.

My hope was that they might miss me in the wide woods and give up the search. I was chilled beyond chill, but my limbs would no longer carry me. I was not a young girl any more, who could go many days working hard, with no sleep. Now that I was not pursued, at least for the moment, the fear began to sap me as well. It was like a child's worst nightmare, where you try to run but cannot get away.

Then I thought of the baby that I might have lost this day yet finally saved during his birth, a beautiful boy who was going to die, so like the boy I had lost at birth twenty years before, my first baby with Jacob. Which made me think of my girls again and how I might survive to get back to them.

These thoughts fled quickly when I saw lights bobbing through the woods on my left-hand side. So they had not given up the search, only stopped long enough to light torches. My heart sank. I nestled further into the clammy leaves and breathed prayers to the Goddess of women to hide and protect me.

The Goddess had other plans.

In their blunders about the woods, one man's large legs came closer and closer. I could hear the thump of boots near me, even see them walking a few feet away. While I prayed fervently, he stepped on my head, rolled, and pitched forward in the ditch, stripping leaves off me as he fell. My head was a fiery ball of agony. I let out a groan.

"Fucking bitch!" he yelled, which brought over the other man. Their torches shone directly into my staring eyes. They dragged me back to the track, tied me, threw me in the wagon, and off we rumbled.

I was too tired and pained to care whether I lived or died, but then I heard the baby crying. I knew I had to live.

CHAPTER 27

June 1751
Gwyn

As we went in safety down the seaboard, I don't know what caused it—maybe that comment by Captain Wiley about us as "orphans"—but I dreamed every night of our mother. Perhaps it was just the hope that we would be safe from here on out, or at least as safe as one could be in a barely settled country. In my dreams, she was very much alive and going about the business of helping people as she did in her life in Wales. She didn't seem to be in Wales, though. I recognized no landmarks from there. Anyway, I loved being in her presence once again, if only in imagination. It made me feel safe, inside my soul. Yet at the end of each dream, I felt she was trying to tell me something that I couldn't quite hear. I hated to wake each morning without her.

Ardath seemed to be drawing closer to the major. I saw them together more and more, talking almost in whispers with each other. It still made my stomach knot up, but in general, things were better on board. It was nice that we were clean now. My poor hair got a reprieve from its former lank and greasy state. The men complimented me at dinner. Gregory was especially attentive.

During the days, now that we had real sailors tending to the ship, we had leisure time. I found myself with Gregory more and more. He had a good voice, which blended well with mine. We sang together, teaching each other songs we knew. Gregory was also teaching me how to do a dance step that he said was popular in Philadelphia. I never could figure out how he learned these things. Sometimes he invited Omar, Isa, and Ahmed to join us, and we danced in a circle on the deck. Ibrahim liked to watch, but Walt would never come, nor Mrs. Perry, who claimed that she was "too old for such!"

We made up our own song to dance to, and it was a silly one that got us laughing too hard to move sometimes. One day, we gave up dancing entirely. Gregory pulled me off to the side, and we flopped down, out of anyone's view, on some piles of rope there, laughing and sweating, for it was getting warmer each day as we went south.

He brushed my hair back from my forehead gently and said, "You shall have to be an Indian princess soon and pull this lovely hair back in a braid." He was close, looking at me rather intently. Suddenly, he was kissing me! I was very surprised and hardly noticed how it felt, my first kiss. I did feel a quickening in my body and wanted him to keep on, but he pulled away.

"Oh, dear, I shouldn't have done that," he said.

"Why not?" I asked, then regretted asking, because he was sure to say, "You're too young."

"Because I want to do it more and I have not asked anyone's permission to do so at all, especially yours," he said.

"I give my permission," I said solemnly. I stared at him to see what he would do.

He looked back at me with softened green eyes. He turned his head to the side and smiled a crooked smile. "I'm not a handsome man. You could do so much better!"

I took his face in my hands. His face was flushed, warm, my hands, cool. "No, that is where you are wrong. There is no one better than you!" I said. "You are the best friend we could ever have."

"Friend?" he said, pulling a long face.

"Give me a moment to think of you as something else," I said. "Another kiss would help."

"Oh my," he said. This time, I was ready for it. My breath grew raw. My hands were all over him. I never wanted it to stop. So this was why men and women wanted to be together. It was like a magical ride to another realm.

Finally, he stopped me. "You will rob me of all breath and I shall die right here on this miserable ship!" he said. "You are a tigress! That is a high compliment, nothing else. But we should get out of here before we melt together and can never be separated."

And that was how it began, totally unexpected and unasked for on my part, the last thing I could have imagined actually happening, a romance with a grown man. He never asked for my hand. I asked him not to tell anyone. We found our moments together, whether in the stinking hold, behind an oak door, under a pile of canvas on the deck, at night far from the watch. My body began to feel like a woman's. I do believe that my tiny breasts grew a little each time he kissed me. Anyway, nothing seemed to matter to us, least of all the age difference, which should have been the worst obstacle, he being almost ten years older. But he seemed a child at heart, so maybe it was not so odd. I would look at him over the captain's table; we would smile secret smiles. The clatter of silver and the tinkle of glasses, all the conversation would fade away while I drank him in.

When we were discovered in one of our moments together, it was by Walt. "What ho?" he said as he swung above us in the rigging. His slight body was outlined dark against a creamy blue sky. "I'll have to tell," he teased.

"If you tell, she might kiss *you*," said Smythe.

"What a terrible threat! She'd never catch me!" Walt laughed and scooted back up a rope, swinging across to another spar.

"Seriously, we have to tell someone, before we are pointed out," I said.

"Who should it be?" he asked. He had stopped joking now and looked me full in the eye. It made me melt at once. I couldn't think; I was overwhelmed with love for him.

"Ardath, I suppose," I said with regret. If Ardath knew, it was no longer a game. She would have to have answers and *plans*. I was not ready for that. "I don't want to."

"Maybe it is too soon," he said thoughtfully. "We should cool down now before we reach Philadelphia, then start seeing each other in the open. We have your reputation to think about."

"Oh, don't be so honorable!" I said, but I knew he was right.

"Why, I think honor is my best feature, don't you?" he said. He grinned at me with such a merry eye and straightened my dress carefully, brushing his long fingers across my breasts as he did so. I practically screamed with frustration.

So our longing had to be confined to looks across the supper table, singing, and fast dances on the deck. In truth, I didn't know that anyone, certainly, that Ardath, would have noticed hidden kisses, she being so involved with the major at this point. Gregory and I did talk more, though. No one could skewer us for that.

I confessed my hope that my mother might be alive, as we sat on the deck in bright sunshine. "I don't know, of course, I suppose it isn't likely, but they never found a body. There are many woods, caves, and fields where a body could be..." I choked up at this.

"Well, I understand that you would hope for her to be alive," Gregory said in a gentle voice. "I don't think that is unreasonable at all. What was done to search for her?"

"Our villagers loved her, no one could not, so they searched hard all around our area, even the hunters and woodsmen. The sheriff questioned the family where she had delivered the baby. She had left at night, and no one had seen her after that. There was no sign of violence, no blood found anywhere, though it had rained later that night, so it would have been hard to see."

"What has made you feel lately that she might be alive?" he asked.

"You will think me foolish..."

"I could never think that of you."

"Well, dreams and mostly"—I paused—"a feeling."

"Umm, what do you want to do now?"

"There's nothing I can think of to do. I guess, look to the future as much as possible. The rector in our village church promised to contact us through our uncle if anything was discovered about her disappearance. That does comfort me somewhat. I will write to him when we reach the city, in case he thinks that our ship was lost."

"That's good. I will ask among my contacts in Philadelphia if any rumors have come their way. They also have friends in ports all along the American seaboard who will have heard any British gossip."

"Who are your contacts?"

"Mostly traders and merchants," Gregory said. "They are among the men I believe will be my law clients."

"Oh, Gregory, thank you! At least we will be doing what we can."

"Family is important, although I must say that mine has both disappointed and disinherited me," he said.

"Whatever for?" I was incredulous.

"Father doesn't like the idea of one of his sons, even the runt of the litter, not pursuing the life of a gentleman. Because I want to work, well, perhaps he fears I will become a Puritan, you know, assume a dour expression and wear black and seek out witches to persecute."

"No, you silly, that is far from you," I said. "But don't you miss your family? Do they refuse to speak to you?"

"My favorite sister is on my side and sends me newsy letters. I believe that, in the end, I shall spite them by living a happy life. That is what I had intended on doing, anyway."

"But how will you get on with your business without money?"

"My aunt had already provided funds for me to use in the business. Of course, I shall pay her back. But happiness is more important than money to me. With you on my arm, I can hardly be unhappy, can I? But I told you, I am not handsome, and now you see, also not rich. You could do better."

"Stop that!" I ordered, batting at his arm.

CHAPTER 28

June 1751
Ardath

JAMES WAS AN ARDENT lover, kissing me with an abandon that was very unlike his calm exterior. We lay on canvas in a dark corner of our ship's deck after supper the night after our first kiss. He bent forward and hurried to take off his coat and shirt. I explored his chest with open palms, running over his hard muscles with delight. I stroked and marveled at the broad shoulders that had strained his uniform to the bursting point. He nuzzled my neck, taking little nips that sent chills through me. I ran both hands through his soft curls while the moonlight, released from clouds, flowed over us. His hair smelled of the sea. I inhaled him. Slight beads of sweat formed on his forehead and clean-shaven upper lip. I licked them off while he groaned. His cock, hard and huge, soon strained against the bindings of his breeches. I could feel it through our clothes, which somehow made it even more exciting.

"We must stop before I lose control," he panted.

I did not want to, but agreed.

"I must lie here a while before I can walk," he said. "Would you sing to me?"

"I would, and gladly, but I have an execrable voice," I said.

"No, I don't believe it. You are a Goddess, Ardath, in form, in intellect, an intensely sensual creature. You could never be truly bad at anything."

"You must believe me…"

"No, I don't."

I launched into an execrable version of "God Save the King" to prove my point. He tried to be polite, but soon we were both groaning again. It had a different tone this time. This performance served to check any passion we might still be feeling. Sometimes it was worth it, being truly bad at something.

We had to be careful after that not to spend too much time alone. The excitement was in knowing what lay open to us when we could find it. But neither one of us was sure that we could stop, and who knew what the future might bring? Certainly, an unwanted child could blight it all. I didn't even know if I ever wanted to have a child. It seemed enough that I had so many responsibilities already. I dreamed someday of flying free from it all, into the unknown, some life in which I left behind all hindrances and lived only for the excitement of the moment. Was it foolish to think that this dream might be real in the New World?

The New World! My thoughts turned more and more to it as we approached Philadelphia. *The HMS Charlotte* had left us in New York, with enough sailors on our decks to make an easy journey. We settled into our own ship's routine, as if coming back down to earth.

In the morning of a fine day, I found Gregory in the prow of the ship, alone. He was not often alone, being one of those people who thrived on the company of others. "Oh, Gregory," I called.

He turned, as if pulled from a dream. "Ardath, how are you? It seems as if we hardly see each other lately."

"True, but I think of you," I said.

He seemed to flinch slightly at that; for what reason, I did not know. "Oh?" he asked.

"Yes, I am wondering if you can help me and my sister manage our affairs in Philadelphia when we arrive."

"Oh, indeed," he said quickly. "I would be most happy to do so. But I must say, I will not know the town well until I have had some time there and set up an office. I have contacts with a reputable banking house already, however. But will you not use your uncle to help with your affairs?"

"I don't know my uncle, but I wouldn't think a clergyman would have the best business knowledge," I said.

"Hmmm, well, in any case, I am happy to help," he said.

"I will need it to be confidential," I said.

"Of course, that goes without saying. Is there something I can help you with now?"

"We have some money in the form of English pounds and Spanish gold."

"That is rare and must be well protected! Where are these coins now?"

"My sister and I have been wearing them around our waists in money belts. I have the Spanish coin, which is probably the more valuable." I turned away from him. Ensuring that there were no observers, I sank to the deck and slipped the money belt down my legs. It was, of course, the money that Alex had given me from the slave trader when he died of the pox. Handing Gregory the warm belt, I felt no embarrassment. He had seen me in worse conditions than these when he helped me recover from James's rescue.

He carefully opened the belt. It was so full that the coins fairly spilled out on their own. Gregory paled before the sight. His hands shook a little as he poured the rest into a golden pyramid. They shone in the sun, warm with their own light, and shiny as if newly minted. We both drew a sharp breath. They appeared to be stamped with some royal insignia; they were truly beautiful. I had never counted them, but there were many.

"My dear Ardath, you are a rich woman!" he exclaimed. "In the first place, the treasuries of Spain have trouble even producing such coins at present, so they are becoming rare. In the second, the only people who have these now are pirates and slave traders who have become, by far, more wealthy than the landed classes. I do not ask you how you came to have these, and you should tell no one, not even me. I think we should put these in a secure bank. I can work as your agent so that no one will know your identity. By law, I cannot be forced to disclose my clients. It frightens me to know that you have these on your person, and Gwyn, too?"

"She has pounds sterling in her belt, the money that our father had saved to make our start in America. It is more money than I have ever seen, but no fortune."

"Still," said Gregory, "some of that should be put away also. For one thing, it will make interest for you and increase in size. Do you have plans for this money otherwise?"

I hesitated. "Gregory, please tell no one this," I said.

"Of course," he said.

"I might like to start a business of some kind in Philadelphia, or perhaps on the frontier."

His eyebrows flashed up, but he said, "Well, you certainly have the money to do so!" He was looking like an earnest bird. I smiled and began to pack up the coins. Sure enough, he cocked his head and looked at me with bright eyes. "And your sister, what does she want?"

"Honestly, that is a good question. I suppose to marry and have children. I don't know. I need to talk to her. Mainly, I need to know that I can provide for her until our future becomes more clear. I haven't talked to her about your managing the money. Give me this afternoon to do that, please, and then you may speak to her about it, always in confidence, of course."

"Agreed. This is a wise plan, indeed," said Gregory. "Well, if you want to entrust the management of this money to me, I will put heart and soul into making it productive for you and your sister so that you may live the lives you choose."

"I know you will. I trust you for this. It relieves me greatly," I said. "These coins are all the surety we have in a world that we don't know and where we have no friends."

"Well, I hope that you will consider me a friend, and there are others on board who feel much the same," he said.

"Oh, of course, I'm sorry. It is just, with no parents and no clear purpose here, there is that melancholy." He said nothing, just covered my hand with his in sympathy.

We gathered the gold pile quickly and stuffed the coins back into the belt. He left me to don the belt again. It seemed heavier now.

*****

Buoyed by Gregory's promises, I sought out Ibrahim. We had not had much sickness to deal with and had talked little during the past weeks. He was sitting in the shade of some canvas, teaching Omar, Isa, and Ahmed more English words. They sat around him in a semicircle, all with legs folded, as if children on the ground. It amazed me how effortlessly they all unfolded and rose to their feet. The Africans were, of course, dressed as whites would be and, having benefitted from decent food, now had the sturdy bodies of strong workmen. They all inclined their heads at me. I had forbidden them to make more obeisance than that. I had given up my studies of their language, but they were speaking English quite well. They were quick learners, which I always respected as a sign of intelligence.

"Oh, I did not wish to interrupt your lesson," I said.

"We are finished for today," said Ibrahim. "May I help with something?"

"Yes, thank you," I said to them all, for the Africans began to leave immediately. "Ibrahim, may I talk with you about our futures?"

"Of course," he said, brown eyes exploring mine as if seeking to see and cure my troubles.

"What do you plan to do when the ship lands? Will you ship out again on another vessel?"

He smiled, creasing his brown face with deep lines. "No, I think not, after this journey. I had hoped to settle somewhere soon anyway, somewhere I could use my skills at healing on dry land. I plan to explore whether I am needed in Philadelphia."

"Ibrahim, you are a great healer. You would be needed! Would you have a practice of medicine there?"

"No, I would most likely not be accepted in that community. I don't have the degrees from a medical institution that others would recognize, and I have strange ways." He touched his turban with another smile. "Not to speak of my skin, always a little too dark."

"Fools! Leeches!" I said, bitter for him. I thought about it for a moment. Something was stirring in me, an excitement, an idea that might help us all. "What about an apothecary shop? Then you could help people without upsetting the leeches. Apothecaries can give advice. Since yours would always be good, you would attract a clientele. You would have to have someone at the door, turning the excess customers away."

"Thank you for your trust in me. I have never sought to be a wealthy man, only to use my skills for helping. As a result of that, though, I have no money to set up a shop."

"But I do," I said. As he started to shake his head, I added, "Wait, this would help me. I want a place to work, and I have money that my father saved for us to start in the New World."

I didn't mention that it was to be money for his new church originally. I felt it was our right to use the money as we wished, given all those years he had not provided for us as children.

"I want to learn more of the herbal remedies you know and more skills you have not yet had time to teach. I could be an 'herb woman' already, but I'm not satisfied with what I know. There will be new plants to explore in America, which we could learn about together. I believe a shop could help us both."

"Hmmm," he said.

"Please think about it. As a woman, I might be laughed at, trying to start out on my own. You could do it, though."

"Ah, Ardath, you are always so far ahead of the rest of us. I will think about it." He paused, searching my face again. "Is there something else?"

"No," I said. "Well, I would like to review what each of us knows about preventing conception, for the other women who ask me, of course."

"Of course," Ibrahim said.

CHAPTER 29

March 1751
Carys

THERE WAS NOTHING FOR it. I was in their hands again, in a makeshift camp they had set for the night. The child, poor little thing, was there too. While they chased me, he had been left to cry in the wagon. Now he was worn-out, had stopped squalling, and just whimpered into his fist, a pitiful sound. I was tied to a tree near a fire, so at least I wasn't freezing in my mud-caked dress, and they had let me hold the baby to keep him quiet. My head still pounded from the rough boot that had tromped on it in the ditch. My scalp was torn and still bleeding in a trickle that I tried to blink from my eyes.

During the trip back to the wagon, they had called each other by name, Deep Voice being John and Thin Voice, Joe. Now John said, "We should just kill them now and hide them in these woods."

"Naw, the lady wouldn't want it done so close, where it might be found out. I say take them to the shore and drown them," said Joe.

"Speaking of found out, them drownded bodies always wash up somewheres! We could just slice open the boy and hide him easy enough, or maybe cut him up and give him to the hogs. They'd eat bones and all, they're so hungry this time of year," said John.

"Hallo, there!" I yelled, as if I were too far-off to hear them.

"What, Miss Biddy?" asked Joe.

"You don't have to kill us. I won't say a word. I have no idea where we are, or who gave birth, or who the lady is. I can go far away and take the baby too. No one will ever know, and you won't be in danger of being caught by the sheriff!"

"Oh, I don't think we can trust in that, do you, John?" said Joe.

"No…but it gives me an idee. If we was to cut out her tongue, she couldn't say nothing to nobody, ever, and we could make use of her some other way, maybe sell her to a whorehouse up in Liverpool."

"No, that won't suit the lady, and she has a long reach all over England and Wales. She'd hear about it and come after us," said Joe.

"Well, we gotta make them disappear, or the lady will make us disappear, but seems like we could make a profit on it somehow or other. How about we take her, at least, to the port? I know a captain there what takes prisoners and indentured servants to the New World and asks no questions where they came from," said John. "But the tongue has to come out, and the baby, well…"

"Listen, if you cut out my tongue, I will die from the loss of blood. I know this. I've seen it happen," I lied. "Then there'd be no profit. I have no story to tell here. I can pretend to be mute, and you can sell me to that captain."

"Hmm, she has some points there," said Joe. "As long as they disappear, the lady won't know. Maybe just cut off the tip of her tongue. She still couldn't talk plain. How much do you figure we could get for her at the port?"

"A pretty penny, with that red hair. The captain might take her for his own whore. She's still in good shape and got her teeth and all," said John.

I said, "What do you think, that he will like his whore to be disfigured? And I could die from cutting off the tip, even. There are many blood vessels—"

"Shut up, whore!" said Joe.

"Well, by then, she'll be too scared to talk, I'm thinkin', and the captain won't be listenin' to her anyway," said John.

I carefully stayed quiet for several minutes to let them think. They were still planning to kill the baby. Finally, I spoke. "If I take the baby on board, you can probably get more for the two of us. There are people in the New World who would pay for a white baby. You could get the captain to sell him there," I said.

Joe turned to John. "How much?" he said. I couldn't hear the rest of what they were saying. My hands were free to hold the baby. I stretched out over him. My fingertips could almost reach my bag. I had in it some sugar candy that I used in long birthings. I could make him a sugar teat to keep him alive and quiet for now. There were still some clean rags in the bag also.

"What you doin' there?" Joe asked.

I explained about the sugar teat and how it would keep the baby quiet until we reached the shore. "I'll need some hot water too, please."

"I'll say! You are a ladylike bitch! Who said we were going to take you an' him there?" said John.

I stayed very still then.

"Haw, look at her face, Joe. She thinks we will still kill her, oh, and we could, easiest thing ever! But I've had a good idee, so we shall take them on, first light, and see what silver we get out of this," said John.

So we passed another miserable night. The baby slept from exhaustion and the lethargy that comes from lack of nourishment. I could not sleep. My thoughts kept returning to Ardath and Gwyn, picturing their distress and worry when I had not come home. Who would help them? I had no idea where their father was. The vicar in the village had found him once. He reported that Jacob had joined a radical sect and was preaching on street corners, going from town to town in England, seeking converts. The vicar would try to help my girls, but he was desperately poor, as were almost all the people of our village. Lord Harleigh at the Manor House had been kind to us in the past, even letting me use his library. (I had secretly used his books to teach the girls, always keeping the books very clean and returning them carefully.) He was gone back to London and in poor health, the house closed up in his absence. Well, we were accepted in the village. I finally calmed myself by hoping that the vicar would find some kind of help for the girls if I could not return soon, or they could go to the Rices up at the New Town Manor House.

*****

It turned out that we were not that far from the coast of Wales, thank God. The babe and I survived the wagon trip and arrived in the dead of night at the sea.

I could hear its restless waves and smell the dank salt air. My captors took us bumping down a steep cart track to a small cove where a ship stood offshore. It was lit from behind by the bleary gray light of dawn. It flew no flag and looked like an unclean vessel even at a distance. The shrouds were flapping, and men leaned over the sides, vomiting—drunk, I presumed. My heart sank at the sight of it. My hands were free, so I was able to bind my red curls under a rag headcloth. I spread gritty dirt on the cloth and on my face from the wagon bed. My dress was still mud-stained and splattered with blood from George's birth. I hoped to look as unattractive as possible, preparing to go aboard a ship where discipline plainly did not reign!

"Wot you doin'?" asked John. "Stop swirmin'."

I sat still at that. They had me well bound by ropes, and worse, I was bound by my desire to protect George. I might have tried to escape again if not for him. As it was, I determined to make the best of my fate for now.

"Ho, bitch, I see ye besmirch yerself," said Joe. "That'll not do for getting us a good price!" He jumped off the wagon seat, grabbed a dirty rag that they used to wipe down the horse, and proceeded to spit on it. With the gob of spit still running down the cloth, he swabbed my face roughly. I had to cry out when he ground his hand into the spot where the massive bruise spread across my face and scalp.

"Oh, ho, Joe, better you'd left it filthy than show that messed-up face!" said John. "Well, it matches the rest of her, and Captain Smog ain't too particular anyhow."

Then it was a forced haphazard slide down the shale of the beach to where a rowboat waited. I held George near my heart and stumbled into the boat, as my feet were still tied. They rowed out into deep water. John slit my bonds with his long knife.

"Look pretty for the captain, now," he said, holding my face by the chin. I could see that he thought himself quite the wit. Well, I felt relieved that I would be rid of my captors. Surely to God, the next situation could not be worse!

CHAPTER 30

June 1751
Gwyn

As I STOOD AT the rail, staring out, hoping to catch a glimpse of our destination, Ardath drew next to me. The setting sun made her hair glow golden, like a nimbus around her face. Sometimes her beauty surprised me anew. She spoke and surprised me again.

"Gwyn, how do you want to live once we reach Philadelphia? What do you want in your life, I mean?"

It was not a question I was accustomed to considering, or to answering. "I…I don't know. I suppose we will have to live at our uncle's house and be ladylike."

Ardath snorted like a horse at that. Her nose even looked a little long and horsey for a moment.

"We have money, so we don't have to be charity cases. Gregory will manage it for us, so we will have it in privacy. Two sisters can live together independently, I believe, without too much scandal. And," she said, smiling now, "I thought we could ask Mrs. Perry to join us."

I was overcome with gratitude at this. "May I be the one to tell Mrs. Perry?" I asked.

"Of course, please do," said Ardath. "And think what else you want."

Suddenly, I felt a shiver of fear. With this many choices, the future seemed wild and formless to me.

"Perhaps you can't answer me now, but you must think about it, you must *know* what you want!" she said, with some impatience.

"I want to find our mother," I blurted out. I touched my face, which was hot with passion and embarrassment.

"Oh, Gwyn," she said, almost patiently. "You surely know that that is unlikely."

"I won't give up. I feel her!" I declared, close to tears.

She drew back and twisted her neck to stare at me. She began to speak, then checked herself. After a moment, she shifted on her feet, gripped the rail, and resumed in a strong voice, "Well, whatever we decide to do, you should know that we have the means to do it. You should tell no one of our money. Most men will think it should be in their hands, not ours, and they may attempt to make that so, if word leaks out."

"No, of course, I won't say a word. I am glad that Gregory will help us, though."

"Yes, he is an unusual man."

I was tempted at that moment to tell her about Gregory and me, but I held my tongue for now. As it transpired, that was a good decision.

Then I had the pleasure of telling Mrs. Perry our plans. Though she had never uttered a word of worry to us, I knew she had wondered about her future.

I went to her cabin, where, by candlelight, she was slowly packing what remained of her worldly goods in two sea-stained leather satchels. She didn't see me at first, and I caught the sad look on her shadowed face. I knocked on her open door.

She immediately turned with her round face wreathed in a sweet smile. "Oh, Gwyn, are you excited about our next adventure?" she said. "Come and give me a hug. Whatever awaits, you are ready for it!" Dear Mrs. Perry, always more interested in encouraging another rather than dwelling on her own troubles.

"Mrs. Perry, we shall *all* be ready for it. I have the best news for all of us! At least I hope that you will think so. Ardath wants to lease a house. We hope you will come to help us with it, as I very much doubt we could handle it all on our own. Please say you'll come!"

"Oh, dear," she said, and almost broke down. Her voice cracked "I wondered where I would go. Are you sure? I have no money…"

"That isn't important. Our father had a little money saved for the New World so that we could get established there, but we need your help." I thought she might refuse the offer as charity if I didn't stress how she would be helping us.

"Oh, dear girl, of course, I would help, with anything you wish. I really can cook if given some fair ingredients, and you could use a new dress, and oh my, this is an answer to my prayers!" In the flickering light, she, who had declared herself "too old for such," danced around the room, her spirits were so brightened. The joy she felt couldn't have been any greater than my joy to see her so happy!

*****

The next day our journey finally came to a close. In the pearly gray dawn of a beautiful day, we saw that we were now upriver. On the shore we saw giants of chestnut, ash, plane trees, and some others that I didn't even recognize, towering above the shore in their summer glory. We soon entered the harbor of Philadelphia. As the sun hit the city, I suppose I expected a cluster of alabaster buildings set on streets of gold, but the humble dirt streets and modest warehouses were still exciting to see. We all were gathered on the prow. I had to look at Gregory. He smiled, and my happiness was complete!

It seemed as if it took forever to leave the ship, with all the business that must be done with the harbormaster, agents, and customs officials. Thankfully, we had a note from Captain Wiley as to our cleanliness and did not have to stand quarantine. His letter probably smoothed our way considerably through the (still) tedious process. The ship's agents had heard our story, by another letter sent ahead. They had to board before we could dock. They were now ensconced in the ship's best chairs at a low table on deck.

Major James stood by them, as the interim captain for the last leg of the journey, giving a full accounting of what had happened on board.

"Major, we understand that there are slaves aboard, which are abandoned property. We will want to take possession of these straight away," said the portly Mr. Allen, already wiping the summer sweat from his massive throat.

"No, sir. These are not abandoned. They are the property of Miss Rhys."

"Well, where is her husband? We would have an accounting," said the slimmer agent, a Mr. Swampter.

At this, Gregory came closer. "She is not married. I am her solicitor and can speak as her agent."

"And this is the Miss Rhys of whom you speak?" Allen said, gesturing at me. "She does not appear to be of legal age. I will speak to her father."

"That is also Miss Rhys, but the lady's sister." He nodded for Ardath to step forward. She came with head held high, and she looked imposing, not at all humble. I feared she would speak her mind; it was easy to guess what she would say! However, she had agreed to let Gregory do the talking, and to my relief, she stuck to it, her lips tightly pressed together.

"This one does not seem of legal age either, and she is not married? How do you expect me to deal with a girl? This property cannot belong to her," said Allen.

"As you can see, she is in possession of these slaves." He pointed to the Africans, who had approached Ardath and now stood behind her. "Furthermore, she is a 'feme sole,' being of age and unmarried, with equal property rights to those of a man."

"This is ridiculous! We claim possession immediately!" Two burly men who had stood silent behind their chairs now came forward and laid hands on the Africans, bringing with them hand and leg chains.

James strode forward. "Desist!" he shouted. The men stood back, uncertain.

Gregory cleared his throat. "Ahem, gentlemen. We also have a proof of sale signed by the previous owner and witnessed by your Captain Whitsun."

"Humph," said Allen and Swampter together.

"Forged, no doubt!" said Allen.

"I believe that you will find Mr. Whitsun's signature matches what you have on file with his employment agreement. You have not a leg to stand on if taken to court," said Gregory.

"Beware! We have no chancery or equity courts here! Women have no standing without a husband or father's protection."

"That is of no consequence. Even common law must recognize a 'feme sole', rare though that status may be. You do not want to face me in court with this argument."

"Then where is the purchase price? We certainly claim that."

"I'm afraid that many of our possessions were swept overboard in the storm. We are fortunate to have even our few souls surviving," Gregory said, with a sad glance at the deck. Whether the last was for the sake of effect or real sorrow, even I could not tell. He was wonderful!

James faced the agents. "My friends, we are all gentlemen here. It is a gentleman's duty to admit defeat graciously. These slaves belong to Miss Rhys, and there can be no doubt of it. Let us turn to other matters."

James was magnificent. They had to agree and did, grumbling only for a moment. Some of my tension drained away, but I noticed that Gregory and Ardath had not completely relaxed and were quietly urging the Africans out of sight down the deck. The interrogation of other crew members concerning the events of the voyage continued, but of course, everyone's story was the same, being the truth.

After awhile, I saw Walt waiting in line to talk with them. I waited with him.

"What will you do now?" I asked him. "Will you stay in Philadelphia or go back to England?" Walt and I, for all our closeness during the epidemic and shipwreck, had grown apart since we were picked up by the HMS *Charlotte*. He had spent all his time with his new friend, mostly running the rigging, but I still appreciated what he had done for us before that. Of course, I had been involved with my change in status at the same time, and then involved (I blushed a little to think of it) with Gregory.

"Well, Miss High and Mighty, now you speak to me?" he replied. "All grown up and such?" His freckled nose looked white and pinched. Was he angry?

"Oh, Walt, I'm so sorry! Have I neglected you so much, as things changed on the ship?"

"Aw, Miss Gwyn, I can't keep angry with you," he said, looking abashed. "Really, my plans changed too, and now I'm looking to sign up on a new voyage. The sea's my life. Even with all the bad things that happened, I'm meant to be out on the waves and up in the rigging."

"When will you leave again?" I asked

"Well, I've heard there's a ship sailing tomorrow for the Indies. After nearly freezing to death, I think I'd like to try the tropics!" he said, with his old good humor returning. "These agents may have a place for me." He'd grown taller, I suddenly realized as we stood there talking. That made me think of the clothes he had loaned me.

"Would you like to have your clothes back? It was most kind of you to loan them to me."

"Naw, you keep them, Miss Gwyn. Who knows when you might need 'em again?"

"Oh, Walt, thank you so much for being such a good friend! Please come to see us when you get back to Philadelphia." I had to give him a hug, from which he turned a bright red. At that moment, the petitioner ahead of Walt stepped aside, and it was his turn to present his request to the agents. I moved away, glad that we had been able to say goodbye for now, sorry that I had left him flustered.

I gazed across the water to the dock, where a tall man in black clothes with a white clerical collar stood, with his hand shielding his face from the morning sun. Surely, this was our Uncle Thomas. Beside him, in an equally dark set of clothing, stood a woman with a deep scowl on her face, surely our Aunt Priscilla. I hoped that the scowl was brought on by the glare of the sun, but I suspected that it might be the thought of her new kinfolk that caused it. I feared that she might be hard to please.

Gregory came up, with his wide-brimmed hat in hand, mopping the sweat from his face.

"My, you look lovely today, so happy," he said. "It went well, I thought.

Your sister was most restrained and demure. And she and Ibrahim are most wisely keeping the Africans out of sight."

"Good. I can't wait to get onshore. Walt told me sometime back that I would walk like a duck when I was first on land. I hope you won't be embarrassed for me."

"Never! I will be at your side so we may waddle forth together, perhaps with a nice 'quack' or two just for good measure. Actually, the plan is for us to go as a flock, so that James and I can prevent any incident regarding the Africans. Ibrahim has instructed them to keep their heads down and act servile. James and I will find housing that can accommodate them. You and Ardath will go with your aunt and uncle, of course. I will go to a rooming house for now, and James is expected at the colonel's."

"Thank you. That is a lot to arrange," I said. "I will speak to Ardath about us, if you are ready, so that you may call on us without need for secrecy."

"Yes, I would like that very much. In the meantime, I can call on you both as your agent, if nothing else."

"Well, duck or not, I'll be glad to be on ground," I said.

I went alone, then, to look for a last time around our cabin, not that I would be sad to leave the ship, of course, but it had been our home through many changes, losses, and gains. Of the losses, the first was our mother, back in March in Wales, when she disappeared. My sorrow would never cease over that. I somehow felt that I could never be whole until I at least knew what had happened, even if it were the worst, as everyone seemed to think it was. I sighed from the soles of my feet.

Then, so soon after we had begun to know him, we lost our father. He was the first of the many people, the good and the bad, like the slave trader, who had all died horrible deaths from the small pox. Then the captain, who had died in the mutiny. Then those lost in the storm, like Alex, who had loved Ardath so much and been so kind to us. It seemed the losses were overwhelming.

Still, the things I had gained were very important. Growing closer to Ardath. My friendships with Walt, Mrs. Perry, Ibrahim, and others aboard, my experience of lives so different from our own, like the sailors and the Africans.

My new womanhood and, of course, Gregory! The promise of a new life made me hopeful. I fancied that I had attained a new strength through all the losses and the gains. I imagined that I was a woman of the world. Only good and exciting things could come to me now. That was how little I knew of what was to come!

CHAPTER 31

June 1751
Ardath

THE TIRESOME BUSINESS ON the ship was finally done. In late afternoon, we docked and were permitted to leave. I saw that my aunt and uncle waited for us on the dock. At least I assumed it was them, since he was dressed as a cleric. His wife had the sharp face of a battle-ax, but why should we expect anything different from the religious?

As we had planned, James led the way off the ship. He inspired confidence with his authoritative stance and his full army uniform flashing in the western sun. The people waiting below parted for him and the rest of his entourage, which included his supposed slaves, that is, Ibrahim and the Africans, and the "women of his household," Mrs. Perry, Gwyn, and me. Gregory brought up the rear in his role as the apparent manservant.

James strode over to the cleric. "Have I the honor of addressing the Reverend Thomas Rhys?" James asked him.

"You are correct, Sir," answered our uncle. "And you must be Major James."

"I am Booth James, at your service." He gave a half-bow. "May I present your nieces, Miss Ardath Rhys and Miss Gwyn Rhys?"

To my surprise, my uncle held out his hands to us, then enveloped each of us in his arms. His black clothes were warm from the June heat, and he smelled of fresh ironing. "My dear nieces! I am very grateful that you have come through the terrors of this trip alive!"

"Thank you, Uncle," I said, moved in spite of myself by his kind welcome.

Gwyn actually shed tears in his arms. "I am glad to know you, Uncle, and so sorry that we do not have our father with us," she said.

"A great loss for all of us, my dear. And so soon after losing your dear mother. My sympathies to you. God works in mysterious ways," he said, casting his eyes down at the wood of the dock for a moment. He blinked and looked up again.

"My wife, Priscilla." He gestured toward our aunt, who contrived to plaster a look of sympathy and welcome on her face. After that fleeting look, though, her face settled into what I took to be her normal expression and such a sour countenance I had seldom seen. Why did it seem, as our mother had noted, that kind men often married women who were not?

At any rate, after introductions all around, our uncle settled us into a waiting rented wagon, first inquiring of the others if they had lodging available. James wrote the address of the colonel's house for me. My uncle gave Gregory the address of an inn within walking distance. Gregory took Ibrahim and the Africans with him, probably to sleep in the inn's stable.

"Uncle, Mrs. Perry is with us. Have you room for her also, or should she go to a rooming house?" I asked.

"Of course, she must come with us. There is an extra bed in the maid's quarters," he said, and all was arranged for now.

As we squeezed into the wagon, my aunt looked as if she smelled something foul, and indeed she might have. We had washed as well as possible on the ship, but it had been a long, hot day of business and waiting. She seemed particularly disgruntled when Mrs. Perry climbed up. The wagon did sag dramatically as Mrs. Perry put her weight on its boards, but perhaps it was the idea of riding with a servant that upset Priscilla.

When the horses strained to pull us up the slight hill, Uncle hopped out like a man half his age. Mrs. Perry followed with a mutter that she could do with her own two feet, thank you.

We looked around at our new "home city." I must say that after the docks were passed, it looked cleaner and smelled better than Liverpool, though that was not saying much. The houses here were of wood or brick, mostly small but nicely tended, with little gardens in front or with boxes of flowers on the windows. The road was dusty. Puffs rose from the horses' hooves.

We very soon arrived at the parsonage and gratefully debarked. All I wanted was to be still for a moment. The street seemed to sway beneath my feet. Uncle Thomas was quickly at my elbow and ushered me into their brick cottage. After the front parlor, a narrow hall led to small rooms at the back of the house. Gwyn and I were to share one, while Mrs. Perry and their maid, Nancy, were to rest across the hall. I was so tired that I fell in bed as I was. Gwyn also fell into her bed immediately. While the room swirled around me, I slept like the dead.

I awoke to muttered conversation in the hall. "Look at those slovenly girls, would you?" I heard my aunt say. "Lying all over my clean covers in their dirty dresses."

"Now, Priscilla, they are exhausted from their journey. Can you not have some charity toward our nieces? I ask you for my sake and for the love of Jesus, who hears your every word."

They moved away, still talking, but I could no longer understand them. Priscilla, the old biddy! It took no second sight to foresee trouble for us in this house; I wondered how soon we could find other quarters. Gwyn lay face-down on rumpled bedding. Creases from the pillow made lines on her smooth skin. She was so childlike at that moment, her face pink and innocent in sleep. It reminded me of my promise to protect her. We would need to meet with Gregory as soon as possible.

The maid, Nancy, came to our room to announce supper. She was small, malnourished, pale, and mousy in appearance. Probably one of the indentured servants that James had said were prevalent here. I had been struggling with my money belt, which in the close quarters of the house felt heavier and more oppressive than it had on the ship. I straightened up quickly when Nancy entered.

"Thank you, Nancy. We will be out shortly."

"Come soon, please, or the mistress will swat me right hard," she said.

So we hurried to the dining area, which was a small nook off the hall.

The kitchen appeared to be a separate building outside the house, at the end of a brick walkway. Uncle arose quickly from his seat at the head of the table and pulled out our chairs for us. Priscilla appeared in the doorway. "Do not spoil them, Mr. Rhys," she said. "They will think they are to be ladies of leisure here in this house, where there is plenty of work to do." She gave us a brief forced smile.

"Mrs. Rhys, they are our guests," he said, but made no further argument.

I turned to him quickly to ask him about our father, but he had bowed his head in prayer.

"Dear Heavenly Father, bless us this day, especially our nieces. Bless this food so that we may have the strength to do thy will here on earth. Amen."

"Amen," Gwyn and I repeated. In the short silence that followed, Mrs. Perry and Nancy placed simple fare before us. I was very happy to see some greens, as we had had so few on shipboard.

"Do you raise these greens yourself?" I asked Aunt, in an attempt at polite conversation.

"Yes, we must. The farmers hereabout are unreliable, uncouth, and lazy. Don't you go getting yourself involved with any of those!" she said.

"Well, I shall take that under advisement," I said. She peered at me closely to see if I mocked her.

"You must, however, get engaged soon. No niece of mine will be a spinster. Why, you must be eighteen by now."

"Yes, just," I said.

"There are several men at the church that might take an interest in you. There is a shortage of marriageable women here. But you must keep that hair under your cap at all times if you expect to attract a suitable man."

I swallowed a smile. "I am in no hurry, and I believe Major James might ask to call on me."

"Hmmm," she said, and turned to Gwyn. "You, young lady, are entirely too young, so don't think about seeing anyone for a few years yet," she said. Gwyn turned a scarlet red and stared at her plate.

Our uncle rescued us. "Mrs. Rhys, the greens are divine. Could you ask

Nancy to serve more, please?" While our aunt was out of the room, our uncle turned to us, his thin face sober and lined. He looked somewhat like our father, except kindly and concerned where Father, with much the same features, had always looked harsh and unforgiving. "We will need to speak at more length, of course, but I will assume guardianship of you, Gwyn. I know that you may have worried about your future, but with no need. Ardath will stay here until she is married, but you must consider yourself our child from this day forward."

Gwyn's eyes were enormous and deep blue. She stared as if hit by a rock, stunned.

I rushed to explain our situation. "Uncle, I appreciate your kind offer, but I believe that I may be able to assume Gwyn's guardianship as soon as my solicitor can look into it. We have just been through circumstances that have tested us, and we feel more adult than we might otherwise. We wish to establish our own household here in Philadelphia with Mrs. Perry's help."

Uncle's eyebrows flew up. He gave a slight shake of his head, which, had I been more observant, would have stopped me, but oh no! On I prattled. I didn't see that Aunt had crept up behind us like a spider. "But you see, Father left us some silver, and we will be able to—"

"What are you saying, foolish girl?" Aunt said from behind my chair. I admit that I jumped a little in surprise. "Do you wish to go about humiliating this family as soon as you have arrived by shunning our hospitality? If you have any money, it belongs to your uncle. He will see to it that you are provided for. A woman, indeed a mere girl, cannot be trusted with such."

I struggled with my temper. I wanted to blast the woman to hell! "I'm sorry, Aunt. I believe I need a walk to clear my head," I said.

"You girls were clearly raised in a cattle shed. You cannot go about the streets by yourself. It is not at all seemly."

"Please excuse me," I said, and walked to our room as calmly as possible, trying and failing to take deep breaths.

Mrs. Perry, bless her, came down the hall soon thereafter. She stopped in and quietly closed the door behind her. "My dear, I heard. She shall prove a hearty nuisance to us, I fear," she whispered.

"Mrs. Perry, I need to see Mr. Smythe as soon as can be arranged. I shall be raving mad if I stay here," I said. Indeed, I felt like tearing the hair from my head still.

"If he is not here in the morning, I'll find him for you," she said. "In the meantime, I could bring you some tea."

"Yes, please!" I said, and she went away. We had been introduced to China tea as a regular drink in Liverpool. It was not readily available in our Welsh village. On the *HMS Charlotte*, the captain was most generous with it. I had grown very fond of it. James had talked Wiley into giving us some before he left, which was now long gone, of course. Perhaps it would clear my head. Certainly thinking of being a prisoner in this house would *not*.

Instead of sparking my brain, the tea soothed me. Again, I fell into a deep slumber. When I awoke, morning sun was creeping down the hallway from the rear of the house. Gwyn was already up, apparently working in the garden. "Pull those weeds with some vigor, if you want to see more greens," I heard my aunt say.

"Yes, ma'am," said Gwyn meekly. Aunt was already turning her into a servant!

I arranged my clothing as best I could. When I entered the hall, Uncle was standing outside the dining area. "Good morning, Ardath. I trust that you slept well!"

"Yes, thank you, Uncle."

"I hope you will take a walk with me before breakfast," he said.

"Yes, that would be good," I said. Finally, a chance to have a reasonable conversation!

Without a by-your-leave from Aunt, we were soon out the door into the new day. It was glorious, sunny, still cool, blue sky. The green leaves made patterns in the shade. I walked better than the night before.

"Ardath, you are not accustomed to living in a town, I know, and some of our ways are different from those in your village or even in England." He tipped his hat to a lady walking by, her servant woman trailing behind. "On the ship you had, by necessity, to do whatever it took to survive. Here we must go by the local customs, especially those of us who are a Church of England family. My wife sounds harsh, I know, and I regret that. But she makes points with which I must agree. Gwyn must become my ward, and you must not seek to live on your own away from us, until you are married. I shall do my best to be a father to you in place of your own."

My heart had sunk when I realized that what he intended for us was not to be discussed further. The thought of living under the same roof as Aunt made me want to run, screaming, down to the river and jump in. His last sentiment was my opportunity to change the subject, at least.

"Can you please tell me more of our father? You may know that he left when we were young and we hardly knew him."

Uncle sighed. "Yes, I know. Jacob was a good man. He truly loved your mother and married her against the advice of the family, but then he heard the call to ministry, which can be a powerful voice. Even then, he was fervent in his beliefs, but when the Anabaptists got ahold of him, he became more radical than the worst of them, seemingly putting himself on the streets to be stoned, never willing to bend an iota! The sect may have sent him here as their most tenacious believer, fearless enough to set up a church, or perhaps he was too much even for them! We will never fully know now what he intended. I believe this, that he never intended to hurt his family. He was very caring, very spirited, in all senses of the word, even as a boy. I have long grieved for that little boy."

So my father had been loved, if only by this brother. Could Mother have loved him, too, at some point? If so, it still seemed unthinkable.

"Uncle, do we have other relatives? I know of none still living on our mother's side."

"No, I am the last, except for our son, David, and his children. This is a dangerous world we live in. We must thank God for our lives every day." He stopped to adjust his collar.

"But what about your son, David?"

"He is the only child we have. I believe my wife's spirit died when he moved to North Carolina. He spells his name R–e–e–s–e, to be understood more clearly on the frontier. Now I have more children of my blood." He smiled. "I have you and Gwyn," he said.

I could see that it was going to be hard to disappoint this kind man, but of course, I had not given up my plans. I must simply think harder about how to manage them. At the moment, I was hit by inspiration on one point.

"Uncle, Gwyn is in no immediate danger now. Would you humor me by waiting a while to make her your ward? It is very kind of you, but our heads are still whirling from all the changes we have been through. We need time to adjust to them."

"Of course. You don't know me yet either. There need not be a hurry with it. The main thing is that she be protected from unscrupulous men, but of course, she is too young to have dealings with them yet."

"I can assure you that there is no one on her horizon in that regard," I said. As we returned to the house, I believed that we were both in better humor. I hoped we would find Gregory waiting there. After that, I must see James as soon as possible. I longed for his arms around me, his kiss on my lips, physical release. Keeping myself under control was wearing on my body and my spirit.

CHAPTER 32

March 1751
Carys

As WE APPROACHED THE dark ship, I realized that I was truly leaving my country and my daughters behind. I had chosen my life and George's over their security and peace of mind, for which I felt awfully miserable. There was nothing for it now but to go forward and make the best of whatever awaited us.

John took out his very sharp knife and sawed through the bonds that held my upper arms to my sides. Awkwardly, I wrapped George tighter into the sling across my chest as our boat banged against the side of the ship. The boat swung and bucked with alarming force as he did so. Joe pushed me so that I had to grasp the swinging rope ladder that hung over the side. As I struggled up, the ladder threatened to throw us off into freezing waters at any moment. John impatiently pushed at my backside to make me go faster.

Above our heads, an otherworldly keening pierced the air. I crawled faster, pulled myself high over the top of the rail to prevent harm to George, and heaved myself sideways, half-falling onto the filthy deck, John close behind me.

The rising sun outlined a terrible sight. A scruffy sailor held the bluish inert body of a newborn over the side with one arm, while with the other, he pushed away the wailing mother, who clung to his legs, reaching with imploring hands for her baby.

With a harsh laugh, he dangled the little body to torment the poor woman. I wrested myself from John's grasp and went to her, squeezing her shoulder gently, murmuring that she was not alone. I peered up to confirm that the baby was dead. He was, by several days; such a sad thing never failed to overwhelm me.

I joined the woman, kneeling on the deck with her, holding her as she allowed it. "So sorry," I whispered. Eventually, the wails became sobs, great tearing things that rose from the very roots of womankind. Then came the tears, and after, she collapsed into my arms. The sailor had long ago given up on further fun. We had not even heard the splash of the baby hitting the water.

The woman's clothing was tight across her chest, with her milk letting down in streams from her breasts. That and the jostling had awoken George, who sent up a weak wail of his own at the smell of the milk. "You have a baby too?" asked the woman.

"Yes, but he is in need of milk, which I don't have for him," I said.

"Oh," she said. "I could maybe help your baby, since I canna help mine." She again sobbed for a moment. "I'm Kate."

"Kate, that would be the greatest gift. You would save my baby, if you are willing," I said.

Her red face brightened some as I unwrapped George. He rooted toward her breast and gnawed his little fist with frustration.

"Oooh, come dear, be ye hungry, then?" said Kate, peeling aside her shirt straight away. With a sigh of relief, George latched onto her breast and sucked greedily. "Oooh, he's a strong one, aye?" Kate asked. She actually smiled a little.

"He will be now," I said. Of a sudden, I realized that we had been wrapped in the world of women, with no attention to the world around us. In that space of time, a rugged older man had appeared. I rose from the deck, facing him. He was large, with rheumy brown eyes and a bulbous, veined nose that spoke of too much drink.

"So," the man said, turning to John and Joe, "this is the woman you have brought me? A midwife and a comforter of women. I grant you, I could use her on *this* boat! Hmmm, yes, yes, I could."

They moved aside to negotiate a deal, I assumed, because in a few minutes, John and Joe left down the ladder. I could hear a small clink of silver in their leather bag. The large man turned to me again.

"I am Captain Smog," he said. His thick lips slurred even those few words. "What's your name?"

"Carys Rhys," I said. We took each other's measure. He looked as thoughtful as a drunk man could. I must have looked as dirty, cold, and disheveled as I felt. However, I kept my chin high.

"Well, Mrs. Rhys, I am taking a group of disorderly women on this ship, those who have been sentenced to 'Transportation.' Everyone wants rid of them. They don't notice a few who leave early." He stopped to belch mightily from his paunch. "I have customers in the West Indies who will pay good prices for the healthy ones. You, my dear, will keep them healthy." He wove sideways but managed to stay upright. "Go clean yourself and report to my cabin."

I had no time, now that George seemed safe, to consider throwing myself overboard. The very sailor who had tortured Kate grabbed my arm with hard hands. I snatched it back.

"Now, miss, don't take it wrong. I'm to show you to some warm water. Not so bad, eh?" He lurched at me. He now had me in a viselike grip. I cast a hurried look back at Kate and George, but they seemed engrossed in the feeding.

In any case, I had no choice. Down the hatch we went. The smell of rot, vomit, and excrement gagged me as I fumbled down the ladder. We slid across the slimy floor, to a large cabin, maybe the captain's. The sailor closed the door and latched it. Water sloshed in a wooden tub, and clean towels were laid on a chest nearby. They could not have been expecting me. Apparently, I was to have the bath that had been prepared for the captain. In any case, I was very grateful to see soap.

"Take off yer clothes," said the sailor.

"You must leave me in privacy for my bath," I said.

"Oh, no. Must stay right with you, says Captain Smog, he does," he said. I could hear the salacious grin in his voice. "I've seen it all before, running these 'lady ships,' ya know."

"Well, at least have the decency to turn around," I said. I hoped he hadn't seen me glance at the porthole on the opposite side of the room.

"Nope, gonna watch every minute," the sailor said. "I hear you can be a slippery sort."

Damnation! I sighed and turned my back to him. I pulled off my crusty clothes, hardly recognizable as garments anymore, and let them slide to the floor. I grasped the sides of the tub and lowered myself into tepid, but at least fresh, water. I made quick work of washing every inch, including the sores and scabs and bruises from my rough treatment. I even washed my hair, though the water was cold by then. I did not know when I'd have a chance to clean myself again. Of course, my wet red hair stuck out wildly in all directions. The sailor leered but made no comments and handed me a towel at the end. He unlatched the door.

At that point, the captain jerked open the door and lumbered in. He was carrying a dress, which he thrust at me. "Dress quickly," he said. "We are soon underway." He watched while I turned away and dressed. Such was my exhaustion that I no longer resisted. The dress was made for a smaller person; on me it came well up my leg. The bodice, cut in a V shape, showed large portions of my breasts. He looked amused.

"Didn't know we'd have an Amazon aboard. Scully, get her a shawl," he ordered the sailor. "Now, then, let's parley, shall we?" he said, as Scully went out.

We were standing face-to-face. His breath was horrible, but I didn't flinch. I took a breath through my mouth and pleaded with him. "Captain, there has been a mistake. I am not a convict, nor have I done anything wrong. John and Joe captured me as I was walking home from a birthing and have brought me here against my will," I said.

"Ah, madam, I am shocked. I have never heard of such a thing. Please sit down," he said, gesturing to a straight chair. I sat with some relief. "We must get you back home immediately. Your family is perhaps worried for you." He leaned closer; his face showed no hint of irony. I almost let myself believe him. The next moment, a great guffaw broke forth from the bottom of his huge belly. It smelled of drink and sickness. He yanked me off the chair.

"You, my dear, obviously do not understand your position. You are mine, bought and paid for. You are no less my slave than if you had black skin and a nose ring!" he said with a triumphant grin. He wagged his head as if greatly impressed with his joke. I loathed him.

He took me to a much-smaller cabin and threw me into the room. I heard the bolt thunk into place. The cabin was barely large enough to turn around in, but it had a bunk, into which I sank as if it were a field of clover. Scully came in a few moments later and threw a shawl, a water bag, and some weevily hard bread in with me. I was alone at least. I trusted Kate to tend to George; perhaps I could now think clearly. But the exhaustion of my trials in the last days had left me numb. I drew the shawl around me and slept.

When I woke, the ship was moving. I had to find George. I tried to open the door, but it was still barred on the outside. I wanted to scream my frustration. I was considering how the bar might be lifted from the inside when I heard it being raised. A grizzled sailor appeared in the doorway.

"Missus, I'm Pete," he said. "I'm to show you to the captain."

Pete, although dressed in shabby clothes, appeared to be clean. He was about my height and did not smell of drink or vomit. Neither did he grab my arm nor, indeed, touch me in any way. I pulled my shawl around me. We retraced my steps from the night before, back to the captain's cabin. When we entered, the captain actually stood up to greet me. "Mrs. Rhys, I hope you will forgive our treatment of the past night. I'm afraid that we were in rough shape to greet a lady."

I was astonished, to say the least, and vowed to keep quiet and learn why he had changed his demeanor. "I feel better for some sleep," I said.

"John has told me that you have many skills, among them healing abilities."

Now I was shocked again to see that the captain had my satchel in hand. "I wish to return this to you so that you can help on the ship," he said.

"Thank you, Captain," I said quite sincerely. I opened the bag and found my herbs and tools in good shape. "Of course, I shall be very glad to help as I can, but I need some assistance from you also."

His eyebrows pulled down in a grimace, but I continued as if I had not noticed. "I came aboard with my child, George, and shall need to see him and have access to him at all times, or I may not be able to work well for the worry I would bear."

"Hmmm, I see. Well, you can't stay in the room that locks. I shall need that for some of the hardened prisoners we will pick up in several days at St. Mary's. You must give me your word that you will not try to escape. We shall arrange the other cabin for you."

"That would do very nicely, I'm sure," I said, going along in this conversation as if we were gentlefolk in someone's drawing room. I did not give my word, though.

Pete took me back along the corridor at the base of the hatch, only a few steps in these cramped quarters. Another room opened off it, one I had not noticed the night before. It was tiny, too, but actually had a porthole, not big enough to get through. The room shared a wall with the captain's cabin and had a table bolted to the middle of the floor. The bunk was on the left-hand wall, leaving some space on the right, where a person might stand. It was dusty, as if unused in some time.

"I mought clean it for ya, miss," said Pete quietly.

"Yes, that would be good."

"And I mought say that you will sleep better in the rough seas to come if I rigged a hammock for you, uh, if you wish," he added.

"Thank you, Pete. That is very kind. Could you also find my baby for me? Kate was tending to him."

"Yessum," he said, as he backed out of the room. I rushed to the porthole and tugged on the corroded latch. It wouldn't open, but I wiped the grimy glass with a corner of my skirt. All I could see was rolling sea, no coast. I had no idea where we were.

CHAPTER 33

Early July 1751
Gwyn

UNFORTUNATELY, MY WORRIES ABOUT our aunt were proved true. No matter how much I worked or how little I said, I could not please her. Uncle wanted to claim me as his child; I no longer thought of myself as one. Ardath had told me of their conversation. She hadn't revealed my relationship with Gregory to Uncle, since I had never told her; that was both a blessing and a curse. At least my aunt had one less thing to abuse me about, but I had little way to be with Gregory, and certainly not alone. Ardath assured me that she would find a way to move us to our own place, but after all the promise Philadelphia had seemed to offer, I felt let down, almost melancholy.

Seeing Gregory on the second day after our arrival helped some. He came as our agent, and he had some good news. Aunt allowed the three of us to meet privately in the parlor.

"Major James sends regards and regrets he could not be here," he said. Ardath nodded. "So sorry it took me some time to find out what might be available to you," he continued. "The best news is that an apothecary shop has recently become available for rent or purchase. It is in a respectable part of town and has ample living room on the second floor for Ibrahim and the Africans."

"That *is* good news," said Ardath.

I was busy looking at Gregory's face; he was smiling as he told us. Then, his expression sobered. "I have not had any luck with finding suitable housing for you sisters and Mrs. Perry. There is nothing to buy or rent and no rumors of any coming available soon. There are only plots of land, which can be purchased and built upon. I am sorry."

"Oh, dear," I said without thinking. Gregory's gaze shifted to my face.

Ardath looked grim. "I'm afraid this is not a good living situation for us here. What do you and James plan to do?"

"I have office space in a solicitor's house, a closet really, but it will do. James and I will live at the rooming house for now. He doesn't know if he will be assigned here or on the frontier. He is busy with the colonel every day."

"Well, at least we can get the others settled. How soon can we see the apothecary shop?" asked Ardath.

"Why, today, I should think," Gregory replied. "I can inquire and come back."

"Yes, please," Ardath replied. I longed to get nearer to Gregory before he should go, but I shook my head at him when he came closer to me. I saw comprehension in his eyes. He nodded to me and showed himself out the door.

We checked the hall, but Aunt was not to be seen. "Ardath, I must speak to you, now," I said in a low voice. She appeared to be distracted by the news Gregory had brought but responded civilly enough, turning to me and gesturing to reenter the parlor.

"What is it, Gwyn?" she asked when we had the door quietly but firmly closed.

"I, uh, haven't found the right time to tell you this. I fell in love with Gregory when we were still at sea, and he loves me also." I paused to draw a shaky breath.

"Goddess Brigid preserve us! Are you with child?" she said, drawing back and looking at my waist.

"Oh, no, nothing like that. I just want to see him, and now Aunt says no, and I can't stand it," I said.

She looked very relieved. Relief quickly turned to anger. "Oh, don't whine, then! We will figure something out," she said. "It is sure that we can have no freedom here. I will speak to Uncle about meeting with our agent in his office near the assembly. Meanwhile, I must see James. But you remember how babies are made. Don't do that, no matter what!"

It was my turn to be relieved. Ardath could have been so much harsher with me. I was vulnerable to hurt where Gregory was concerned.

We turned to our chores again to make time pass, but Gregory was back very quickly. He explained to Aunt that he had some business to conduct with the two of us and did not let her object. We left the house that imprisoned us, almost at a run. After we turned the corner, I held his arm for a moment. "I have told Ardath," I whispered. His face lightened, but I explained that Aunt and Uncle thought I was too young to walk out with him.

"Oh, the freedom of the New World!" he exclaimed. "Don't worry, Gwyn, we shall work it all out." Suddenly, I noticed the sun was shining and birds were singing over the clatter of the city.

*****

We were not prepared for the filth and disarray we found at the shop. It looked as if it had been deserted for years, with cobwebs dangling from the ceiling, dirt coating the one window, and leaves scattered across the floor. The room was furnished only with pieces of two old chairs. It was so dark inside that it looked even filthier than it was. We lit a lantern that hung from a hook by the front door in order to see the place clearly. It would take some hard work to make this a presentable place for business. The stairs leading up from the main room to the residential floor looked solid, but we didn't venture up them.

"I know it looks derelict, but Omar has examined the structure and found it sound," said Gregory. "Of course, it needs much work, especially a thorough cleaning."

Ardath and I had never been shy of work, and we had the Africans to help us, so that was not a problem.

"I believe that we can get the price lower because of the appearance, if you want me to argue for it," said Gregory.

"Yes, we must jump at the chance, I think," said Ardath, and I agreed. "I think it would be prudent to purchase it," she said.

"I agree," said Gregory. "Until we get better-known here, I suggest that we use the silver rather than the gold. Even silver is not common, since most people here use Pennsylvania's printed currency, but silver will raise less suspicion, especially since you just brought it from England." We nodded together, remembering that gold was often seen as the currency of pirates and slavers.

We went to see Gregory's office near the great assembly building. This was a new construction of which the city fathers must be very proud, a long building of fine brick with many windows.

His office in the solicitor's house nearby *was* like a closet. He ushered me into the windowless room but stayed in the hall while I extricated the money belt I wore. When he and Ardath came in, we all checked leather belt, which was the worse for wear, a tired brown, mottled and tattered, like an old snakeskin. It had been through a lot, like the rest of us, but still held together. We spread the coins out on the table that served as Gregory's desk.

While he and Ardath counted, I leaned against the wall and studied his slight figure, his elegant, long-fingered hands. They would have looked right on a musician or a poet, I thought, as would his glossy blond hair, with its wayward forelock that kept slipping over his face. I was very glad that he did not wear a wig for business, tailing or queuing his hair instead.

"All right, we are set on the offer, then?" Gregory asked.

"Yes," said Ardath.

"I will see the current owner today. Am I authorized to go a small amount higher? I don't think that I shall need to, but…," Gregory said.

"Yes, that is still a fair deal, I think," said Ardath. "I shall wait in the hall while you have some time together." She nodded to me and left.

"Oh, Gregory, it has been hard!" I burst out, but his lips were already on mine, gentle yet insistent. He pulled my body closer so that I felt his warmth and his fast heartbeat. I explored his smooth head, his face, with trembling hands. We entered a place of timeless comfort, where everything else melted away. I don't know how long we stood together, but I awoke as from a dream to a knock on the door. I hastily rearranged my clothes and hair. Gregory stood back from me with a silly expression of pure delight on his face. It was Ardath,

luckily, who stuck her head around the corner of the door and smiled know-
ingly at us.

"I must get a lock for this door," said Gregory.

"Yes, you must," I answered promptly.

The rest of the day was a whirl of happiness. Gregory walked us back to
the parsonage. Nothing my aunt said could rile me. He arrived later with the
good news that we now possessed a shop, which he had been able to purchase
for less than we had dared hope.

"Please just keep the key, but have another made," said Ardath. "Ask
Ibrahim to start getting the materials together for the cleaning and repair. Omar
is going to need the tools of his trade, anyway, so ask him to get good ones.
You can use the extra money for it and to pay yourself for acting as our agent."

"Oh, no, I ask no fee for helping friends," said Gregory.

"No, we are adamant on this, aren't we, Sister?" said Ardath, as she
turned to me.

"Yes, indeed! Remember that we are your first clients," I replied, grinning widely.

"My ladies!" Gregory replied with a very low bow. "I would be greatly
blessed if I always had such clients. I will be about your business, then, and I
expect the Africans and Ibrahim to make short work of this."

"I miss them," I said.

"I shall return when that work commences, and we will go to see it in
progress," he said.

I hated to see him go, but we now had our own tasks to do. I found Mrs.
Perry at work in the kitchen, pushing the hair from her red face. She had happily settled down to work at our uncle's house. She liked having a job to do,
she said. No one else was about, so I told her our news, reminding her again
that we must keep it secret.

"Bless me! You will soon be businesswomen of the town. You *must* have
new clothes," she said.

"I don't know how much we will get out to see other people," I sighed.

"What? You don't mean that you want to get out of *this* house," she said in a conspiratorial whisper. "Perhaps to see a certain person," she said, looking over her shoulder. I loved Mrs. Perry. Somehow she had known about Gregory and me and never opened her mouth.

"Well, I have to do some shopping in town later, maybe look for some cloth. Would you like to go? We could be two servants together. Auntie could not object, surely," she said.

Aunt had gone to a church meeting, so Mrs. Perry and I sneaked off to the market. On the corner of Market and Third Street, just off the cobblestones, were a cluster of stalls selling everything from hog jowls to scents and fabric. Both women and men chatted and sauntered through the area, laughing and bargaining with the sellers under the bright July sun.

We found some lovely linen in a periwinkle blue for me and a warm green for Ardath. I had along some of the smaller silver coins from my money belt, which was only a little bit lighter now. I was unaccustomed to using money, but Mrs. Perry bustled around as if she had been doing it forever. She also bought the necessary items Aunt needed with the coin she had from her.

"Mrs. Perry, I would like to buy something for you. You are working so hard for no pay."

"Oh, bosh! I have room and board and my girls. I am happy."

I said, "Yes, but—"

"Well, I do spy some hard soap that comes from France there." She pointed to a stall that housed imports brought by recent ships. It was a real bar of soap with the lavender of the old world in it. It smelled heavenly and it was my joy to buy it for her. We returned home like the happy conspirators that we were.

CHAPTER 34

July 1751
Ardath

JAMES WAS GONE FROM me already, I felt. So busy was he that I never saw him for the first weeks we lived in Philadelphia. I tried to bury myself in my plans for the shop, which was so important to complete as soon as we could. The Africans had had worse accommodations on the ship than the straw beds they slept in at the stable, but I wanted to get them established in the community so that I could liberate them into some kind of productive life. Gregory was working on the papers needed. Also, I was concerned about Ibrahim. It was warm now, but the stable was no place for an older man when autumn came around. I needed him to be hale and hearty for our business.

We had found that Aunt would let us out of the house if Mrs. Perry, whom she instructed to keep an eagle eye on us, was along, so Gwyn and I went with her daily to the market, if needed, and to the site of the apothecary. I longed to roll up my sleeves and pitch into the scrubbing and rearranging of the shop, but by-passers were watching with great curiosity, so we often stood by as if mere onlookers ourselves.

If necessary, Mrs. Perry would stay with Gwyn in front of the shop while I consulted with Ibrahim in the back as to supplies needed, because it would take some time to acquire everything. There was a stillroom in the rear, which was the first finished, its weathered boards whitewashed into fresh glory. There I filled the shelves gradually as old world products became available in the market. Some we could not get or were too expensive. After cataloging each item, Ibrahim and I would slip out into the woods behind the shop to gather herbs that we recognized, to be dried for later use. This proved to be a treasure trove beyond what we had first imagined. In fact, the great diversity of familiar herbs in the woods astonished us.

There were probably also some plants of use that we did not recognize. I wished I could find a local herb healer to consult, but apparently, there was no one since the old apothecary had died. That at least could bode well for our business, but we both wanted to learn more about the abundance of plants in this new land.

*****

In the third week after our arrival, Major James came to the door, asking for the Reverend Rhys. Luckily, Uncle was at home. "Major James, how are you? We have awaited your visit, one of us in particular!" Uncle said. I could hear the smile in his voice as I listened outside the parlor door. My fate was being decided; I would have continued to listen shamelessly had not "the spider" found me. She gave me a shove down the hall and a disapproving click of the tongue. Nevertheless, I was happy and trusted James to handle the situation well. I went into the garden, where the flowers were abundant and the bees buzzed in ecstasy. The purple, pinks, and yellows, the ripe pollen scents, made me almost dizzy.

Then, there he was, looking dashing in his uniform, immaculately kept, I imagined, for his audiences with the colonel. He ran a hand through his brown curls and smiled at me. Did I detect a slight hint of mischief in that smile?

"Ardath," he said, "it has been too long. I am so sorry."

"I'm just glad that you are here," I said, stepping close to him.

"Oh, not here," he said, looking around for Aunt. "I have permission for us to walk out, and I have just the place in mind."

We walked up the street arm in arm. It was exciting to be so close to him, to smell his spicy scent, but I kept my head bent, trying to look demure. We went across town, past the apothecary, which he knew about from Gregory, and into a little lane that very shortly veered into the woods. Our conversation had been general, if important, but now we didn't talk for long! He pulled me closer under the trees. My arms went around him.

"Oh, Ardath, how I have missed you, like a part of my body was gone, like an ache that ate at my insides!"

"I have too," I said, gasping for breath through his kiss. Yes, we'd kissed before, but nothing like this, not the longing, the desperate passion for each other! He even kissed my breasts, as much as my kerchief would allow, making me go wet below. Finally, we paused, panting, for a moment. His back was against a smooth tree. I had seen men's whole bodies when helping my mother as a healer and, of course, during the small pox epidemics. I had also seen men in pain. James's face, as he leaned his head back, showed the furrowed brow, the tight lips, the fiercely shut eyes, that said he was suffering.

When I looked down, I could see why. His cock was straining so hard against his breeches that the buttons must be digging into flesh. I knew what to do, because I had seen the shepherd boy at home relieve this condition when he thought he was alone. I slipped down and hastened to unfasten the buttons and free him. With much striving and twisting, my fingers finally got one of the rows of buttons loose while he groaned above me.

I almost jumped back when his immense cock leapt free and throbbed, engorged and purple, at my head. Something like *that* I had *never* seen. He drew me upright, kissing me again, hard. Then he thrust me back as he came, discharging a creamy fluid from that fevered organ. Some splashed onto my skirt.

"I'm so sorry. Please forgive me," he said, his face red with embarrassment. "I lost control. This was bad judgment to bring you here." He tucked his cock into his pants, shook out his handkerchief, and began to clean my skirt.

"I wanted to be with you, too," I said. Indeed, these sensations had whetted my appetite for more, though the size of his cock had made me hesitate. "But how could *that*, as it was"—I pointed to his now-shrunken organ—"get inside me without a great deal of pain on both our parts?"

"I can assure you that rather than pain, it brings a sublime pleasure," he said, smiling.

I raised my eyebrows as if in disbelief. We were struck with the absurdity of it all and bent over laughing. That was fortunate, for it broke the spell and reminded us of the danger. He quickly buttoned his pants.

"I know how to prevent a child, but you cannot have me just any day. I am not always prepared," I said. "We must be careful."

He gazed steadily at me. "I would never endanger you."

"I would like to give you pleasure," I said.

Now he looked me in the eye with an expression of surprise on his face. "You are the most extraordinary woman I have ever met. How have I had the great good fortune of knowing you?"

"Well, not exactly 'knowing' me," I said. "And in case you are wondering, I am a virgin."

Now he went beet red and turned to adjusting his uniform, with his back turned toward me. I stuffed my hopelessly unruly hair into its cap and tucked in my bodice scarf, in truth still feeling a little wobbly with desire. Deep breaths, I counseled myself.

*****

"I must tell you," he said, as we walked slowly back to town, "I do not know where my future lies, whether here, the frontier, or the Canadian provinces. It seems that we are set upon with threats from many directions. There are few regular soldiers here, and the king seems unlikely to send more. Probably, I will serve as a spy to begin with, to find out the strengths of the French along their river lands to the west. I would need an Indian guide, of a tribe that is loyal to us. It will take time to find that person, I believe."

He stopped and turned me toward him, holding my elbows. "It may be prudent to marry soon, before I am sent away," he said. "Then I can get you safely established here."

I tried not to look as surprised as I felt at his urgency. I swallowed against the dryness in my throat. "James, you know that I love you, but I have no thought of marriage now!" I looked into his blue eyes earnestly, hoping against hope that he would understand.

"How can you say that, after what we just did in the woods? I thought you a respectable person. I know our classes are unequal. I am willing to overlook that, but I still must be sure of decorum in a wife. As an officer..." He stared at me as if I were insane. "How can you even say it?" His brows pulled down, his nose sharpened into a beak. Here it was, the return of the James I had known when we first met.

So, his transformation had only gone so far. When one of his precious principles was disturbed, he returned to his old ways. Better to find this out now, I thought. But I was infuriated, at him and at myself, for believing this could work. I shook my hair out of its confining cap and strode off down the street.

He hurried to catch up, his longer strides accomplishing that quickly. "Put your hair under your cap and slow down," he snapped. "You are *not* going home on your own and looking like a harlot!" He glanced around quickly to see if we were being observed, but the few people on the street were hurrying about their own business, largely ignoring us.

Just to get it over with, I stuffed my hair back in and assumed a quick but measured pace back to the rectory door. "Thank you for seeing me to the door," I said with exaggerated politeness.

He had himself under control also. "Certainly, Miss Rhys." He turned and walked away with a stiff back. I thought that this was the last I would ever see of him, that English prig!

CHAPTER 35

March 1751
Carys

WHILE PETE LOOKED FOR George, I did the best I could to make myself presentable, although it was doubtful who might care. I combed my tangled red hair with my fingers and tried to smooth it down into order. I was always throwing off my cap at home, but I wished for it now, if only for its slight warmth. I rubbed the crusty sleep from my eyes, dragging my cold hands over my face as if washing. I flapped my arms, all to feel that I was truly awake and not in the bad dream I might have been living for days. How many I really didn't know; I vowed to keep count. I had been taken on the third of March. It must be March seventh, at least, by now.

I heard a rap on the door. When the bar lifted, I flung it open, hoping to see Kate and George. It was Pete with an apologetic look in his green eyes and a furrow in his brow. "Uh, missus, I think you'd better come with me," he said.

My heart sank. "Is it George? Is he all right?" I asked in a shrill voice.

"Yessum, I believe so, but Miz Kate won't give him to me. I don't know…" His voice trailed off.

"Well, let's go. Take me to them!" I pushed past Pete and pushed the door open further. The hinges squealed, but we were away, I almost running, Pete behind.

"No, ma'am, this way," he said and pointed to the stairs descending to the next level. I scrambled down into an even worse smell than filled the first deck. Choking with it, I felt my way through the semidark.

"Over here," said Pete, pointing with two fingers. Next to the wall, I made out the bundle that was Kate and the baby, wrapped together in a large plaid cloak. I heard a whoosh as Pete lit the lantern he had with him.

"Kate," I said, approaching slowly so as not to startle her. "There you are. How are you feeling today?"

"Get away, you'll not take my we'en! I know you for a faerie. You want to take my son from me and trap him in your world, but you won't get him. I'd see him dead first." I could see her crouching and turning away from us with George held possessively against the wall under her cloak. The lantern showed her eyes glinting madly at us. Sweat and tears ran down her face. My heart hammered in my chest, but I kept my voice low and calm.

"No, Kate, I am no faerie. I have only come to see your bonny boy. What is his name, then?" I asked.

"It's my Dougie. You know that. Don't be trying to trick me!"

"It's all right. I don't have to see him now. How is your Dougie today? Is he feeding well?" All this time George had been quiet, but whether he knew my voice or became uncomfortable, I didn't know; he began to cry.

"See, evil woman, you have waked him!" she said.

"Perhaps he is hungry," I said. I hoped that if she fed him, she would be calmer.

"Well, he's a real strong boy, is my Dougie. Must be fed all the time, it seems. He's been like this since the first. A healthy babe, for sure." She pulled down her shirt and began to nurse him.

"And when was Dougie born?" I asked.

"Oh, aye the time flies when you've a little one. Must be four days old now. My man, Donald, will be so proud when he sees him. Such a broad chest and a strong cry. Dougie'll be a true man of the Scots someday."

"Where has your man been?" I asked.

"Och, he had to go to the hills when old King George's army came 'round, but he'll be back soon." She stared down at the baby. I looked at Pete, who shook his head.

"Well, Kate, I am happy for you that you have such a bonny boy. Can we get you something to eat and drink? It takes a lot from a body to feed a braw boy like him."

"Well, I haven't et in days, I reckon," said Kate. "But I'll take no faerie food!"

"Well, no one will take your baby. Let Pete get you something from the ship's stores." I rose slowly and began to back away.

When Pete and I had left the lower deck, I stared at him in the lantern light. "What has happened to her, Pete?"

"I happened to know her husband, who was killed at Culloden. She was taken by the British army from near there." Pete wiped his nose on his sleeve, waving the lantern as he did so. "I guess they got tired of using her when she was with child, and threw her on the streets. She stole some bread. That got her in Newgate, then to a prison hulk, where we picked her up. Then, of course, her baby was born on this ship and died almost right away. Reckon she's gone bad in the head. Seemed a nice one before that, once was pretty too. I knew her Donald before he were killt."

"That's a sad tale, Pete."

"Yessum." He paused. "I can take her some hard bread," he offered.

"Yes, I think that would be good, and how about ale? Surely she would see it is not faerie food. I can make her some tea with calming herbs also. I had better stay away for now. It might help if you told her you knew Donald."

"Yessum, and we can boil water in the galley for the tea," he said.

Pete showed me to the galley, an even tinier room than I had seen before. It was as filthy as the rest of the ship.

"Not much here, of course, since the cook jumped ship," said Pete, but he fumbled around at the spigot of a large keg. He drew some water into a tin cup. It smelled reasonably fresh.

"There's no fire here to boil water," I said.

"Yessum, I reckon I could start you a fire," said Pete. "Then I'll take her some water and bread. Got no ale till we stop again." With some fumbling and muttering, he got a good fire started. He took the cup and bread out the doorway. I put on the kettle.

He was soon back to report. "I had to leave it on the floor near her, but I think she'll take it. She must be famished by now."

"Good, the tea has to steep for a while," I said. He stood there with his head hanging.

"What is it, Pete?"

"Well, you are in the doctor's old cabin, and you seem to know how to physic, and well, I've got a problem, you see…"

"Oh, maybe I can help. Can you show me the problem, or tell me more about it?"

"Reckon I should show you, but not here, ma'am." A deep pink blush was creeping up his neck.

"Well, in the doctor's quarters, then?" I asked.

"Yes, ma'am," he said and led the way out the door and took the few steps into my room, closing the door behind us. He was struggling to stay calm; I saw him breathe deeply. He didn't seem to know what to do with his eyes or his mouth, working the latter back and forth as he looked anywhere but at me.

"It's all right, Pete. I've seen everything, you know. Just as a doctor does."

He turned his back and yanked down his breeches. Even though I'd seen lots of things, the boils on his bottom and legs took the prize. I didn't know how the poor man was walking, standing, or sleeping with such painful sores on him. They were plump, ringed with dark-red steaks, and oozing yellow pus. If not treated, the skin would die soon and poison his body.

"Pete," I said very calmly, "I'm glad you showed me. We must lance those boils and clean them up. It will hurt you some, but it will be very serious if we don't. I must go back to the galley for some water. Could you lie down on the bunk there for me? Oh, and do you have a sharp knife?" He dug in his pocket and produced a little knife with a sharp point that would do nicely.

"Don't tell the captain," he said.

Whether he meant his sores or the knife, I didn't know, but no matter. "Of course not. Doctors do not talk about their patients," I said. I grabbed my bag and ran back to the galley, where I set willow bark tea steeping for Pete and the calming herb tea steeping for Kate.

I soaked cloths and the knife in the remaining boiling water. With another pot, I set some more to boil for the comfrey I would use in the compresses. I hurried back, afraid that Pete might change his mind. He lay obediently on the bunk and muttered away, perhaps praying.

"First, I'll cover these sores with the hot cloths. It may burn a little."

He lifted his head to nod. "I've been many years on the sea. I've seen some pain. I can bear it."

"Of course you can. I just want you to know what I am doing." I proceeded to soak, then lance, then wipe the boils down as they collapsed. Blood and pus poured out, a blackish red and yellow, down his butt and legs. Pete tensed at times but said not a word. I went back for the teas and made the comfrey compresses. I fastened the compresses on with clean rags as best I could. He leaned on his arm to struggle up and drink the willow bark tea. "You should lie here on your chest to let your back heal," I said.

"Well, ma'am, that is kind of you, but I'll be missed, you know."

"But you must keep this area clean or the boils will come back. And you must come here for me to check these tomorrow, or at latest, the day after. Stay here as long as you can. I'll take the tea to Kate now."

I climbed down the ladder one-handed, careful not to spill the tea. When I reached Kate, I bent to leave it on the floor in front of her. She still turned George away from me, but I could hear him burbling away contently, so I was satisfied for now.

I heard her say "Faerie…" under her breath, but she didn't threaten him or me.

"Do you need some cloths for him?" I asked. I hoped that she had been changing his diapers.

"Oooh, yes. As fast as he eats, then he's dirty again," she said and actually looked at me without much spite.

"Is there anything else that would make you feel more comfortable or help you and Geor—uh, Dougie? Perhaps a blanket, if I could find one?"

"Aye, if you please, for the we'en," said Kate.

It would be a process, but I had hopes that I might soothe her with kindness. Right now, I was her enemy because my presence threatened her with the truth she could not bear. Thank the Goddess that I had a good supply of herbs, especially valerian root, that would soothe her, perhaps let her sleep.

With my "patients" cared for, for now, I went away to scout the rest of the ship. It occurred to me that I had not been seeing many of the men aboard. I had certainly heard them shouting. I guessed they were mostly on deck, as we seemed to be moving at a surprising speed. I climbed the ladder to the main deck. It was a scene of rapid movement, with men running the rigging, working the sails, and crossing the deck with quick steps. The source of this commotion seemed to be that the ship was approaching an island. It was quite a beautiful place, with long white-sand beaches and wild cliffs above them.

Immediately, the captain spotted me. "Scully, take her below and confine her," he ordered.

This Scully did, with apparent relish, his blackened teeth grinning at me. "So now it is 'milady' again, is it?" I was back and locked in the room before I could think about it. They would take no chances of me getting away near land. Damnation! But then, I couldn't leave George with poor, mad Kate either, so I planned no escape for now.

CHAPTER 36

July 1751
Ardath

IT WAS ONE OF the few times in past months that I had no idea what to do. Of course, I should have known that James would permit some "liberties" only if we were engaged. I was angry with myself for not thinking this through.

Gregory had warned me that once I married, everything I owned would belong to my husband. If Uncle then adopted Gwyn, he would own everything of hers. The money that I had thought secure melted away before these thoughts. And I had no idea how I felt about marriage, other than it seemed a sure way to become dependent and lose any chance at directing my own life. That was intolerable to me.

Suddenly, I wanted someone to give me advice that I could count on. I trusted Gregory with his legal advice, but I could not ask him about personal things. No one came to mind except our mother; I missed her terribly right then.

To my surprise, Colonel Ellis's servant came to the parsonage that very day, with an invitation for me to join the colonel at his table for dinner the following night. Of course, James would be there. I hesitated to say yes, but then, why not? I needed a wider society, and this would be one way to reach it. We would manage the awkwardness somehow.

I was very happy that my green linen dress was ready. It was beautifully crafted, with a boatneck lined with whitest lace, a bodice that made a V down to accentuate my waist, and tight three-quarter-length sleeves, also trimmed with lace. The gathered skirt blossomed out from my hips. My money belt made up some of the stuffing, with soft cotton for the rest. Mrs. Perry had made a light-green hat adorned with two long feathers to wear with it. I had always looked good in hats, so on it went, to tame my springy red curls at least somewhat. James would be glad to see that I looked a proper lady, though most of the ladies would doubtless be wearing silks.

The colonel sent a carriage for me, which was quite elegant, with satin seats in a caramel color and a driver who assisted me into it. The colonel's house, borrowed from the governor for this occasion, was well lit with thousands of candles. It was the single biggest house I had seen in Philadelphia and made of brick with white trim. It seemed more than a small dinner had been planned, as many people were already streaming up the steps toward the house.

A black servant in purple livery escorted me to the door. I met the colonel and his wife in the foyer. He was a tall man with a white wig. He seemed to look down his long nose at his guests. His mouth was drawn into a thin line, but he greeted me cordially. His wife was pretty, plump, with very dark hair and a porcelain skin. Her hazel eyes sparkled at me warmly. Although other women were cordially conversing in small groups around the main hall, she insisted on taking me over to James straight away. He was chatting with other men, all shorter and somewhat stooped compared to his military bearing.

"Ah, Miss Rhys, let me introduce you to these gentlemen," said James, taking me by the elbow, but not actually looking at me. I met all the men, who bowed to me gallantly. I wasn't paying much attention to them until he introduced Mr. Benjamin Franklin. He was not on the short side, and at least I wasn't looking down at him. He was not handsome, just a little plump and starting to bald. All this mattered not a whit. He had the most kind and intelligent eyes I had ever seen, and they were definitely twinkling at me. He charmed me before I could think about it.

"Miss Rhys, I have been hearing about you from the major and the colonel. Your adventures have been most remarkable, and now I see that your beauty excels even those wonderful stories. Gentlemen, you will excuse us if we talk privately together. I want to find out what I have missed by not knowing her before."

I thought this quite wonderful but wondered what the other gentlemen, chiefly James, would think of our abrupt departure. He escorted me to a curtained window seat away from most of the crowd.

"My dear, you are going to be quite bored in this company, for the most part, but hopefully not with me," said Franklin.

I laughed. "I have heard of you also, you know!"

"Oh, dear," he said with mock horror, lifting his eyebrows.

"You are not the only one wanting information. I hear that you know everything that goes on in this town and direct a lot of it yourself."

"Modesty forbids," he said solemnly, pushing out his lips. "But first, I must hear of the daring rescue of the major from the icy waters."

I described the sequence of events that led to James's rescue. He made me feel very special; I got lost in the telling of the crystal waters and the struggle to release James from the rope, as Franklin seemed lost in the tale himself. He never took his eyes from me.

"This was very unusual, you know. The courage it took to risk your life that way, and even the rarity of a woman who can swim. Most men I know, including the young and fit, do not swim and would have stood by helplessly or killed themselves trying to rescue him. I have loved swimming since a young boy in Boston and endeavored to teach and encourage other men to do it in the river here, upstream of the tannery, of course, but hardly anyone takes me up on it. It is a fine exercise and obviously a skill needed on a ship, but even the sailors don't learn it."

"Yes, you are right. Perhaps they think, if lost overboard, that there is no hope for them, but it does seem strange," I said. "Do you still swim?"

"Oh, yes, when I have time. I once thought that I would go to sea. I am fascinated with it. But then several friends and I tried to sail from NY to Philadelphia in a small boat. We ran aground so many times that we all were disgusted by it. Not exactly the high seas, though." He laughed. "My wife, Deborah, hates the water and would never sail with me, even to England."

"Where is she tonight?"

"She hates parties almost as much as the sea. Tell me how you managed to get the ship here after the wreck."

"Well, we had a quadrant that I had learned to use from the captain before he was swept off in the storm, and charts that helped us somewhat. During part of the trip, the ocean itself seemed to help us along."

"Admirable! And it is fascinating how much you have observed. I hope to prove someday that there are stable currents that run through the ocean, like currents in a river. Perhaps that was at work for you during those parts of the journey," he said.

"Ah, not the breaths of the gods on the 'wine-dark seas,' then?" I laughed.

He paused, those eyes inspecting me again. "How is it that you are able to read charts and quote Homer?"

"My mother thought it was important for us to read and had a way to get books loaned to us. The ship's charts called for a great deal of guesses, though."

"Amazing once again! Why, when we started the Library Company here, a lending library, there were barely fifty good readers who could join. There are more now, but all men, of course."

"Are there no women who can read?" I asked.

"There surely are, but women usually don't tell people, lest they be thought presumptuous."

"So I can't join the lending library, then?"

"Hmm. There are ways around such mores. You could get a man to sign up in his name for you." He saw me begin to grow red with anger. He sighed in a philosophical manner. "There are many inequities in regard to the sexes. For example, most women would not consider knowing figures, yet my wife has been much better at that than I ever could be. Indeed, my business could not have prospered as it did without her help. I have not such an orderly mind as she does."

I half-rose and spoke, making emphatic gestures with my arms. "It just seems so unfair! Do you know that if I marry, everything I own, down to my hair ribbons, then belongs to my husband?"

"Yes, I know." He discreetly pulled more of the curtains across the window seat, blocking us from view and muffling our voices further.

"And now, now, Major James has asked me to marry him. I would have no say in my life if I marry."

"Do you want to marry him?"

"I don't know. No, I think I could not tolerate losing my independence!"

"And have you told him this?"

"No, not exactly. I told him I didn't know if I wanted to marry. He was furious. I don't know what to do."

"Hmm. Well, without knowing more, I can't give you good advice, if that is really what you want. You are a most forthright young lady. I like that. In some situations, that will cost you more than it is worth. I would only say 'More flies with honey than vinegar' is a good thought to keep in mind." His eyes smiled at me again. Here was a man very comfortable with himself and others.

At that moment, the curtain moved aside and James stood before us. I hoped the red was gone from my face and that I looked more composed than I felt.

"Franklin, you must not monopolize the young women so," joked James, "even if she is the most beautiful one in the room." He extended his arm to me. "Dinner is served," he said. He walked me into the dining room, it seemed, without the least embarrassment.

As it turned out, I was seated next to Franklin at the table, so we were able to continue our talk. We had so much to say that we quite ignored the people to either side of us. We spoke in murmurs, with heads close together, so as to keep some privacy to our words.

"My dear, you are about to witness a spectacle, the likes of which you have probably never seen," said Franklin, gesturing to the head of the table, where the colonel stood over a steaming china cauldron of some kind of soup. He dished this soup out, handing it to the people around him. Manservants in full dining dress then took bowls of the soup down the table to the rest of us, maybe thirty people in all. Mrs. Ellis took her place at the end of the long table, with special friends seated around her.

Manservants began to place the first course in front of us. This was to be a sumptuous affair, as we saw when the crawfish soup was served. Pieces of white meat swam in a sherry-laced broth. Steam from the soup clouded Franklin's eyeglasses, and the rich smell tempted our appetites. The rest of the table was soon covered by the remaining victuals.

"Venison pasties, mutton cutlets, boiled goose and stewed red cabbage, boiled trout, tongue and turnips." Franklin discreetly pointed out each dish in the morass before us. "Hard to tell at first. Best to eat the soup while it's hot. Then eat one or two of the others."

"Oh my!" I said. "I'm a good eater, but this is a difficult task."

"The key is to slow your pace and just take small bites."

Men stood and lifted their wineglasses to toast one another. Conversation never lagged around us. Crystal and silver made tinkling sounds whenever there was a break in the conversation, which was rarely.

Franklin wanted me to tell about the small pox epidemic on the ship. I explained that my sister and I had been variolated in Liverpool and were spared from the disease, so we acted as nurses to the ship's doctor, Ibrahim. I told him about our mother, about her midwifery and herbal healing skills.

"You lost your father in that epidemic, I heard. So sorry," he said.

"Yes, we did. Thank you for your sympathy."

"I lost my Franky at just four years old, some years back. I loved that boy so much, but he had the flux and I dared not vaccinate him. It was a terrible thing." He hung his head. I put my hand on his arm in sympathy. "Some thought I had opposed the vaccination, but it was not that. Some opposed it because people could contract the disease from it. It was a large debate."

"It is true that some get the disease from the variolation, but it is usually a light case and can be cured. Ibrahim has methods that reduce the risks greatly. Perhaps people will trust it better if he has better results."

"It seems that you are close to Ibrahim. Many of the finest doctors were Moslems in Spain several centuries ago, so he might have been well trained."

"He is. He didn't sign up for another ship, but is renovating a building here. He will be an apothecary there, on Arch Street."

"That is good news, indeed," said Franklin. "And how are you involved?" He smiled, spooning up some more crawfish.

I sat in confusion. "Why would you think I would be involved?"

"Forgive me! After hearing your story, I can't believe much happens around you without your involvement."

I was struck dumb in confusion for a moment, before letting my enthusiasm take me over.

I waited while servants whisked away our plates and bowls and placed moist slices of dark roast duck in the center of the table. Around this were side dishes of cherry tart, jellies, blancmange, and roast pigeons, supposedly the lighter fare of the "second course!" I was already feeling full from the rich soup, strapped in as I was by my stays. Franklin had no difficulty enjoying his duck, cherry tart, and a roast pigeon, though!

I sighed and continued with my account of the apothecary. "Well, Ibrahim and I have searched the woods hereabout for herbs that we know. There are some that we recognize, but many more we don't know, which may have healing properties, but we have no one to ask," I said.

"Ah, I must introduce Ibrahim to John Bartram," said Franklin "He has a garden of native plants that he is studying. He is a great botanist. His son William draws plants well and may follow in his steps. John is a member of our American Philosophical Society. He knows more about the plants than anyone. We try to have a scientist from every area of inquiry in the Society."

"How many women?" I asked, to tease him.

"I suspect that you can answer that one." He smiled. "I, for one, am relishing my retirement from the printing business or at least from the day-to-day work of it. I am doing experiments in electricity now and corresponding with the Royal Scientific Society of London."

"What do you know so far?"

"Not much, but I theorize that lightning is a form of electricity. It is a dangerous thing to work with, but my son William helps. We attempt not to get struck by it."

This time the servants brought out a "third course," three small tarts of puff paste filled with cherry, apricot, or damsons, fricassee of rabbits, forced cucumbers, and Jerusalem artichokes. I took small bites of puff paste; I had to stop eating or my seams would burst. Once again, Franklin merely sat a little straighter and ate all three puffs, dabbing at the crumbs that collected on his lips.

It was an unusually bold move, but perhaps James had been watching Franklin and me in our intense conversation. Across the table, the major leaned slightly forward, over the dishes. "Excuse me, Franklin," he said, "what do you think of our military resources?"

"I have been telling the powers that be for some time that we need a regular militia to protect the city, but they have not agreed as yet," said Franklin. "It seems that there must be an imminent threat to organize one and then it is too late."

"We must talk more about this," said James, then leaned back to address the lady next to him, who was asking about his role in the protection of the colonies.

So the evening flew by. I hoped there would be an opportunity to talk with Franklin again after tonight, especially since he knew so much about things that interested me. He could be a great resource for us.

After supper, the chairs were pulled back in the reception area and dancing began. The ladies were all dressed sumptuously, most with their hair piled high. The prosperous Quaker ladies wore shades of gray in beautiful materials, watered silks graced by pearls, smoothest satin with contrasting patterned ribbons, lace overlays of light gray over darker. The other ladies wore colors that ranged from my light green to a pearlescent peacock blue, punctuated by a few reds, and pinks for the younger ladies. Amber, amethyst, and pearls, set in gold and silver, adorned their necks, glowing in the candlelight. The dancers whirled around me with flowing colors, gay smiles, and voluminous skirts.

James came to me, bowed, and put out his hand for the dance. Seeing me observe the women around me, he said, "Don't worry, you are the most beautiful woman in this or any other room." He carefully tucked a red coil of my hair behind my ear and swung me pleasantly through the crowd.

I must say that the men shone in their equally elegant outfits. I was reminded of Towler and his pride in his clothing, as I looked at shining white neck stocks and lace cuffs, coats of deep green, cobalt blue, burnt ochre, gold, and grays, all distinguished by the richness of their fabrics and the brocade and embroidery that adorned them. And of course, most wore those silly white wigs in the late July heat. Ah, England!

When the guests began to leave, James guided me down the steps to the carriage silently. We had not spoken a word during the whole evening about our argument.

CHAPTER 37

August 1751
Gwyn

ARDATH WAS HAPPY: THE work on the apothecary shop was almost completed. She had been out in society several times, going to various suppers, thanks to the influence of the colonel and his wife. But I was far from happy. I had seen Gregory a few times in his office, with a lock on the door now. Being away from him so much, and becoming increasingly miserable at my aunt's house during the day, I began to have miserable dreams at night as well. They were always about my mother, who was seemingly under stress, cold, hungry, and alone. That had the strange effect of making her feel even more alive to me, as this life is surely full of danger and dismay.

We had not heard any word from England or Wales about her. Though we had been several weeks in Philadelphia, it seemed that the days passed at a snail's pace so that each day was a week long.

Finally, I was so filled with unease that I welcomed any hard work Mrs. Perry or Aunt could find for me, since at least I was distracted by it. Working in the garden became my favorite pastime. The smells of earth and flowers, the buzz of bees, the cool of the shade, and the heat from the sun all soothed me. I never thought better than when my hands were in the dirt or were busy snapping beans from their stems.

However, thoughts of our mother went round and round their old beaten paths, like a mule around a grinding wheel. I usually tried to steer off these, as they only frustrated me. I tried to make plans for our future but was not able to imagine what we might do if not trapped here. Would we have a house where

Gregory could come to see me without causing caustic comment? Would we be free to walk out in the woods? To sing something other than hymns, and dreary ones at that? Right now, it was even hard to find privacy to talk with Ardath.

One day, Aunt had gone to yet another church meeting. I was in the garden, working in the cool of the morning. Ardath appeared in the doorway, dressed in old clothes suitable for work. I leaped up to cling to her, which she didn't like, but I couldn't help myself.

When I held on to her, she said, "Don't worry, sister, I'm here to talk with you. We must make plans. We have things to do!"

"Oh, thank you. I am so unhappy here, and you haven't been here much and…" I trailed off.

"I know. The Africans and Ibrahim are moving into the apothecary shop today, and I think we both should be there. I will take the blame if Aunt is displeased," she said.

"But we are both in our work clothes! We can't go out," I said.

"Of course, we can! We must hurry! Take off that apron," she said.

I rushed to do so, and off we went. I felt freer than I had for weeks. It was lovely.

I hurried to keep up as she strode on her long legs up the street. "Ardath, we have to get out of Aunt's house!"

"I know. Have patience!" she said.

*****

The scene at the apothecary shop bustled with people, black and white, moving things with much loud, cheery talk. Omar wiped his brow with a white handkerchief and looked our way. Before he could say a word or finish his bow, I was on him. I completely forgot decorum and hugged him there in the dusty street.

"Whoa, little miss," he said, in deep but lilting English. A grin as big as the ocean split his face. His even teeth then parted to accommodate a belly laugh such as I had never heard from him before. At that moment, Gregory came around the house.

"Gregory, would you like to do the honors?" asked Ardath.

"Omar, please bring Isa and Ahmed too," said Gregory. Very shortly, all three Africans stood in a line before us. Then I noticed that Mrs. Perry and Major James had come as well. Ibrahim was there too, so that our old shipmates were all gathered together for the first time since we had reached the city. What was happening? I felt an anticipation arise from the group like a surge of light.

"It is my distinct honor and pleasure to announce that Omar, Isa, and Ahmed enter this house today as free men and woman. I present you with the papers of manumission. Henceforth, you are never to be slaves to anyone again as long as you live, nor will your children and grandchildren suffer that awful state. Be sure to keep the papers with you at all times! This is due to the kindness of Misses Ardath and Gwyn Rhys. May your lives be full of peace and contentment," Gregory finished up, handing a document to each of the newly freed Africans.

I was in tears from the joy of this. Everyone rushed to shake the Africans' hands. Whoops and huzzahs followed. I grabbed Gregory and commenced to dance one of our silly shipboard dances. We sang our own made-up words about the freedom that we had foreseen for ourselves in America. Soon, the others caught the spirit and danced right there in the street while passersby sent us looks of either censure or understanding, depending on their own philosophy. "In our New World," we sang. "Only here can we meet headlong our dreams!"

Then we went inside, a crowd for that small space, which had become a clean and well-ordered business since I had seen it last. Two wood chairs sat on either side of the doorway. A long counter with a built-in gateway crossed the room. Behind that was a gray floor-to-ceiling curtain, which divided the front area from the back stillroom and storage.

I gave a mock bow to Ibrahim for his accomplishments. He was always a quiet, usually solemn, man, but he radiated happiness now. His face looked ten years younger; this was truly a new start for him. I turned to Isa, who was beaming and gesturing toward the stairs. I followed her up to the second level, which I found adorned by colorful materials, with curtains framing the windows, and bedcovers in bright blues, yellows, and reds. It was another celebration of their new life.

There were three small rooms, one for Ibrahim, one for Isa and Omar, and a separate smaller one for Ahmed. I tried to ignore the jab of envy I felt that they had a home of their own. They deserved this!

Ibrahim served apple cider to us all. I went to Gregory while everyone was talking and drinking. He quietly pulled me through the stillroom and out the back door. Then we were kissing and laughing at the same time. "I'm so happy for them," I said.

"Yes, greatly happy!" said Gregory. "But I wish that you and I had a little house of our own to go to now."

"Gregory, I would love that. Or even a house where we could meet in some privacy. I can't stand it where we are. Ardath keeps saying I should be patient, but she is allowed out more than I."

"Hmmm, well, I am trying to ask you to marry me," he said. He looked utterly serious.

"I...I, uh, you *are*?"

He got down on his knees on the path before me. He took my hands in his. "Miss Gwyn Rhys, you have my heart in your hand. Will you be my wife?"

I suppose my amazement showed clearly on my face. "Oh, Gregory, how kind of you!"

"Kind? I would call it utter self-interest on my part. I have loved you since I saw you, full of compassion for the sick on the ship, a loyal sister even under duress, a hard worker and deep thinker, funny and silly when allowed, the lovely woman who grew before my eyes."

"Oh, dear. That is so beautiful! But...and I hesitate ever to say this, I agree with Aunt and Uncle on this one thing. I don't feel old enough to be a wife. I know some girls are married at my age, but I don't feel settled in heart and mind."

He had come to his feet now, still holding my hands. His eyes were full of longing, but also of sympathy. "It is true. Neither one of us is ready yet. I must make a successful business that will support you and the children. You have your own desires to establish yourself in this new land and, I believe, to pursue the whereabouts of your mother. I just want you to know my intentions toward you. If ever your family consents to let you out of the house, I know that you will be besieged by suitors. I hope you will let me be the first to court you!"

"Gregory, you know that I love you. Even should the prince himself pursue me, he is not you, and it is you that I want."

"That makes me very joyful!" He paused, looking at the ground thoughtfully. "In the meantime, we must do something about the housing situation for you."

"I could not agree more with that," I said.

Ardath entered the garden just then. Of course, she was there on business and ignored how close Gregory stood to me. Nevertheless, we stepped apart.

"Gregory, we have accomplished much here today," she said. "I thought we were here to work, but everything seems to be done."

"Yes. It has been a great pleasure to see this house and the manumission finished. Has Omar spoken to either of you about taking the Rhys name as their surname?"

"No!" Ardath and I said together. I had never thought about them needing a surname.

"Legally, it is a simple matter, but they asked permission."

"Of course," I said, and Ardath nodded.

"Good. Ahmed has already begun working for the livery behind the guesthouse. I assume that you would like for him to claim his earnings there." We nodded together. "Omar can now look for work as a carpenter. I believe you wish him to keep the tools he has used on this house." We nodded again. "The Reverend Rhys has recommended that he seek work at the site of Christ Church, where the tower is to be erected. Mr. Rhys will speak for him and feels sure he will be well-employed."

Once again, we had reason to be grateful for our uncle's kindness and help. Ardath and I looked at each other. Her image blurred as, again, I found myself with tears of joy and gratitude, on this day that had started with such gloom. "This is wonderful," I said.

"Isa will keep house for the men here and help Ibrahim with the shop until it is going well. Then she may hire herself out as a housemaid, or take in washing, or be a seamstress."

"Whatever she wishes, in short," said Ardath, bitterness creeping into her tone. Gregory and I both turned to her. "Well, they have been freed from slavery and we have *not*!" she said. I realized that she still struggled with our position here in Philadelphia, and probably with what to do about Major James.

"What can I do to help?" asked Gregory. I loved him even more, if that was possible.

"Get us out of that house!" Ardath said.

"Yes. Please!" I said.

CHAPTER 38

April 1751
Carys

THE SHIP WAS AT St. Mary's Island in Wales, to pick up a large load of passengers from the prison, Pete had told me. Apparently, the wardens here were more lax or greedy or both, as this was where they commonly got most of their women for transport (or as I called it, slavery). I heard a huge splash from the heavy anchor and the rasping of the long boats going down the sides, from my "prison" cabin. The boats were gone most of the day, as far as I could tell by the movement of the sun.

Near evening, they returned. I could hear footsteps and shouting once again and whistles from the men as they greeted the new inmates above me. Then the higher voices of the women sounded over them. They didn't seem afraid but rather seemed resigned to their fate. Who knew what horrors they had become accustomed to? They were then handed down into the lowest hold. I heard the rattle of their chains as they went past my door and down the next ladder. As soon as that noise stopped, the ship moved out toward the open sea and we were off at speed again. Like me, the women were given no opportunity to attempt escape.

At last, I heard a key turn in my door lock and realized that I had dozed off, probably from pure hunger and upset, not having been able to see George, or Dougie, for more than a day.

Captain Smog stood in the doorway and eyed me, seemingly in a jolly mood. "Mrs. Rhys, will you join me for dinner? We have much to discuss, you know."

I had no idea of his plan but hoped for something more to eat than weevily bread and water. I straightened my clothes and brushed my hair back with my hands. "Of course, Captain," I said, with as much dignity as I could muster.

The captain showed the way with his arm extended. We entered his cabin to delightful smells. Fresh food from the island and well-cooked, roasted game hen, apples, cheese, and fresh bread. A large jug of wine. He must have noticed my surprise, as he laughed. "Yes, the best food. We obtained not only that but also a reasonable cook from among the darlings we rescued. And I have a bottle of heavy Madeira, fortified with brandy. Please, sit."

I sat at his table, set for two, and wondered what other surprises were to come.

"You see, my dear, we can treat a lady as she should be treated here, provided the lady treats us well in return."

I didn't like the way he spoke or looked at me. It made my skin crawl. I made a noncommittal sound and sat in the proffered chair. My hope was that he would overindulge in the wine and pass out before he could bed me. In any case, I was hungry enough to want the meal. If I played along, I might see an opportunity to make my escape. I pretended to drink lots of the very strong wine and made sure that his glass was steadily full while we ate the sumptuous meal. He had years of drinking experience, though, and could hold his drink longer than the usual man. In the end, he kept his faculties about him.

"So, Captain," I said, "you wish me to get the women through the journey in good health."

"Well, yes," he said, drawing out the last word, "as long as it does not cost me any coin to do so."

"It seems likely to be worth some small expenditures to get as many women saleable as possible," I said.

"Come, my dear, we can talk of this at another time," he said with an unctuous smile. He leaned over the table, pressing his face next to mine. I swallowed. I was determined not to lose my supper over this.

"Captain, surely you cannot mean that a gentleman like you would take advantage of a lady?" I asked in a rising voice.

"My dear, just why do you think I have allowed you on the ship? Of course, I would like our women to be healthy, but more than that, you have caught my eye. It will be a long voyage, better spent in some pleasure that benefits us both, don't you think?"

"But, I have my courses."

"Oh, I am not so nice that a little blood puts me off. Sit here on my lap, and you will see."

He pulled me down on his lap. I searched my mind for something that might repel him or lead to my rescue. No one on the crew was going to risk a captain's wrath at sea, so no help there. I would have liked to shit on him, or vomit, but my body did not cooperate. Unfortunately for the situation, I had a sound digestion.

He licked my neck with a greasy tongue and munched on my cheek as if it were a pear ripe for the taking. It was disgusting, but I reminded myself that I had been through worse. If I relaxed, it probably would not be too painful. It didn't matter if he thought I was agreeing to this treatment, because I would ensure that it did not happen again. I set my mind on that plan and tried to ignore what he was doing to my body.

He pulled my dress off my shoulders and bared my breasts. He slurped away on one breast, and then the other, like a slobbery, grizzled baby. My nipples stood up in the cold air, which encouraged him to slurp some more, meanwhile wriggling and grinding his pants against my bottom.

Finally, he sprang up, as if stung by a bee, ripping off my dress entirely and, with trembling hands, pulling his pants free from a massive erection. I cried out then in surprise, which I was sure he took for delight.

Throwing me on his bunk, he climbed on top of me and commenced his business, which fortunately for me was soon done, as he rubbed me raw. He was a right aqueous man, proceeding to slobber and sweat upon me until I felt I had fallen into a greasy sewer. He then held himself on stiff arms above me in the bunk to look at me in triumph.

"Hah! Loved it, didn't you, milady? Not too many women lucky enough to be bedded by the likes of Captain Smog! I can see we'll have a fine voyage together!"

I said nothing as he collapsed onto me, completely senseless. Thank God!

I felt that the Goddess was not here, or this would not have come about at all, so I didn't thank her then. I'd ask her later to help me with the best plan to prevent this in the future. I crawled out from under, shoving his limp body away toward the wall, where it made a satisfying thump. He slept on. I rubbed down my body and then mopped my crotch gently with his shirt, which was reasonably clean. How I longed for a full bath, but that was not to be! I dressed myself in my clothes again. I ran my fingers through my hair as best I could.

It was my chance to rummage through his things, where I found a chain of keys to my locked cabin, of which I took one, and a purse. I helped myself to a little of his coin, but not enough so that he might miss it. I also took some apples and cheese to hide in my cabin, against the day when fresh fruit was gone or I was shut up again. Finally, I stole one of his nutmegs from a small drawer where several rolled around. I had to keep preparing for an escape of any kind I could manage for George and me. I would go to see him as soon as I flushed my body of Smog's cursed seed.

The plan formed as I cleansed my vagina with vinegar and worked on the herb tea that discouraged conception. Given that he had enjoyed drinking before bedding me, I planned to mix into the muddy-colored wine a concentrated brew of valerian root, disguising its slightly fetid odor with some nutmeg. After all, I had heard it was the fashion among gentlemen to add nutmeg to wine. Nutmeg, when used judiciously, could also create a warm feeling of languor that led to sleep. I planned for the captain to bed no one but himself!

*****

I was weary when I finally got to the middle deck. I could tell by the added scent of many unwashed bodies that this was where most of the sailors now slept, leaving the worst deck below for the women. I lit my lantern and saw the swinging, bulging hammocks. Kate still maintained her spot with George, or Dougie, as she called him.

I approached her as quietly as possible, but she lurched around toward me as if I had startled her with loud shouting. "What be you wanting?" she hissed at me.

"I brought a blanket for you and Dougie," I whispered.

"Aye, I can use it," she said.

"Are they feeding you well?" I asked, knowing that this had been a long day for both of us.

"If ye call extra weevils in the bread and rank water, then, aye, I am well-fed," she said.

"I brought you some cheese and a piece of apple," I said, laying them out where she could see them in the lantern light.

"Oh, aye, that will help with milk for Dougie."

"And how is Dougie tonight?"

"Well enough. I don't think he likes all the stinking men here, though. He'll be ready to go home soon."

"Well, that would be best, wouldn't it? Home has a good sound," I said. It did, but neither of us was likely to see home again. It wouldn't help anyone to see the tears come to my eyes, so I hastily bade her good night. "I'll try to bring you some better food each night, if I can," I told her.

"Right kind you are," she said, looking at the floor. I knew that Kate was a good woman at heart, and felt for the misery she had been through. George would not have lived without her milk. I needed to be patient, though I longed to grab the baby and take him with me to my dreary cabin. I imagined his warm body against mine, the cozy feeling of a baby asleep. I pulled myself to my feet and returned to the "doctor's" cabin, where I gratefully lay down in the hammock Pete had put there for me. It swung me to sleep.

CHAPTER 39

September 1751
Ardath

WE HAD A HAPPY day with the opening of the apothecary shop, but I could see that even the saintly Gwyn was reaching the end of her tether with staying at Aunt's house. I had thought that I would be needed more at the shop, but Isa was proving to be an exceptional businesswoman and assistant to Ibrahim. She was particularly good at figures, which took that aspect off Ibrahim's shoulders. Most importantly, she excelled at finding herbs and learning their uses. In fact, she began to teach me about plants that she and Ibrahim were finding. She had known the African healing herbs well and looked for similar uses in American plants. Through Mr. Franklin, Ibrahim had received an invitation to Mr. Bartram's garden to learn more.

Franklin had proved to be an excellent ally for us. I was able to talk with him at several parties given by the colonel and others in his circle. Finally, I asked for a private meeting. It was an unheard of thing to do and had to be done with an eye to my reputation. So on a pleasant September day in Philadelphia, we met at Chelsea's, a ladies' tearoom. Elderly ladies from throughout the city met there for conversation and Chelsea's excellent, buttery shortbread.

"Oh, Mr. Franklin," several ladies called out as he entered the shop. He stopped at every table to greet them by name. They all flushed with delight. As much as Franklin liked to speak with young ladies, it seemed that the mature ones really had his heart. But it put everyone in a positive mood, which we hoped would forestall gossip. He gestured to a table in the corner where we could speak quietly.

After we were seated, he said to me, "How are you, my dear?" He watched me carefully, his eyes large behind his eyeglasses.

"Some things are going well."

"Ah, the apothecary shop is doing good business, I hear," he said, smiling and taking a sip of his tea.

"Yes, thank you. It seems to be filling a need. I have a suspicion that you have sent business our way."

"It is my pleasure to support a business that does not compete with mine," he said, laughing. "If I may ask, how is the housing situation that you spoke of before?"

"Unhappy! But we are stuck. No place to rent or buy," I said.

"Hmmm. I have a tenant leaving a shop on Market Street. The place is really not suitable for a residence, but if you are desperate, it could provide temporary shelter. The problem I see with it is that it may anger your aunt and uncle for you to leave them so soon. We are the biggest city in the colonies, but still a very small town, in many ways. They will worry about the propriety of it also." He paused. "Ah, I see that you are exasperated."

I felt the heat in my face; I must be flaming red. "More than that! I am afraid of what I might say or do to break out of that prison. Gwyn would endure it forever, but I cannot!" I took a large breath. "We have Mrs. Perry to move with us, so it would not just be two young women alone."

"That would be helpful. Is Mrs. Perry perhaps thinking about a business for herself? If so, it could be seen as primarily her shop, with you there to help her. That might enable the situation to pass muster. However, it puts you in a different social category. That is not quite so important here as in England, but still…"

"What, no more parties at the colonel's house? No dashing young aristocrats to meet there?" My laugh was sardonic. "Gwyn has already chosen her suitor, and I have one, at least on the face of things, and I am not looking in any case."

"This is a short-term rental that we are looking at, but the future springs from the choices we make now. You may find that you regret jumping out of the frying pan and into the fire."

"Oh, as you did when you left your brother's apprenticeship in Boston?" I asked.

"Oh my! I have indeed regretted leaving my brother in the lurch and have tried to make amends for it, but overall, you are correct. It was necessary for me to leave. My life here was possible because of that move. But—and I hesitate to say this—"

"But you are a man! That's what you want to say, isn't it?" My blood boiled. I scraped back my chair, ready to leave.

He put a quiet hand on my arm. "Don't shoot the messenger, please! You know that it is true, and you know my opinion of the inequity, especially in the case of someone as talented and intelligent as you."

I sat down and raised my eyes to his. He was right. I tried to calm myself. I needed to think. Perhaps the shop would work for us. "Mr. Franklin, you are a patient and wise man. I beg your pardon," I said. "Let me talk with my sister and Mrs. Perry. Does the shop have sleeping quarters above it?" He nodded. "Do you have an agent I can contact about renting?" He took some paper from his pocket and wrote a name and address for me with a curious stick of wood called a pencil. He showed how it contained a writing lead within it.

"By the way, should I ask, or not ask, about the major?" he said.

"Of course, it is fine to ask. I have explained that I am not needed to actually work at the shop. It seems to help him reconcile my business venture, if I am only to be an owner, not a shopkeeper. As to our future, little has been resolved there. I remain confused."

"Well, I believe that all shall become clear in time. I must get to an appointment now, but let me walk you at least partway to Ibrahim's shop."

"That would be very nice. Thank you. You have again given me much to think about." My heart lifted as we left the tea shop. We might have a path to follow now to get our own lodging.

When I got to the apothecary, Ibrahim was just coming in from visiting Mr. Bartram's garden. He held his head high and had a soft smile on his face.

"Tell me!" I demanded.

"A very interesting trip. Mr. Bartram's farm has a large plot devoted to American plants. Most of what we need to know is to be found there. Mr. Bartram has given me permission to revisit his garden and study it at leisure."

"What did you find today?" I asked.

"I admit to part ignorance on this point, but he showed me ginseng, a root prized by the Chinese and, he says, used by the Indians. I knew that it was prized as an herb to strengthen endurance in all parts of the body, but I didn't know that it grows in the woods here and especially down the chain of the southern mountains. If I can now identify and procure this for us, it promises to be a truly helpful product. It would be something unusual to offer that might help your business. Although, he did say the woods here had been somewhat picked over by Indians and others…"

"Ibrahim! You must be truly excited. I have never heard such a long speech from you!" I said, smiling at him. "But you must say 'our business,' you know."

"Oh, ummm, yes, I guess so." He looked at the floor, but still was clearly pleased with his news.

"I wonder if my cousin David in North Carolina has seen this plant. Can you draw it for me?"

Ibrahim could indeed draw it, and very beautifully. As he drew and described it, I could picture the dark-green leaves, spread in a fan shape, three larger, two smaller, like spread-out fingers, the small white blooms on a single stalk, the berries that would soon be turning bright red. Most importantly, of course, was the gnarled brown root that, when chewed, could deliver energy to flagging muscles. I felt that this plant would be important for our future. I shook my head firmly. Gwyn was the one with "the sight." But I could not wait to get back into the woods to look for it.

CHAPTER 40

September 1751
Gwyn

ARDATH HAD BEEN MORE absent and more secretive of late. She didn't tell me where she went, most days. She had developed a certain countenance when facing our aunt, such that even that dragon stood back. This was better than the explosion I was afraid Ardath would erupt with someday. She now went freely about the city, unchaperoned. I could see in Uncle's eyes that he feared for her and was ashamed for her. The air was thick with disapproval, even when she was not here. I did not think it was possible to feel worse staying here, but it *was* worse now. Aunt had only me to correct and control. My attempts to comply with her every wish led to no relief. Now I just felt angry and lonely.

"Ardath," I said, as she prepared to leave yesterday, "at least tell me where you are going all the time."

"You shall know soon. I promise it is in a good cause, the cause of getting us out of here."

"That is not enough. You must tell me or I'll go mad."

"I don't know enough yet. I must go." Out she went with her head high, into the street, where I could not readily follow.

I ran to the kitchen, where Mrs. Perry was preparing luncheon.

As soon as she saw me, Mrs. Perry turned from the fire and wiped her hands on her apron. "Oh, my dear, I can see you're in a tussle. What is happening?"

My breath was ragged. I was beyond all sense or reason. "You must get me out of here, Mrs. Perry," I begged.

"Hush now, Mrs. Rhys is right outside in the garden. Let me stir the stew one time. I will make my excuses to her and we shall go to the market for a missing ingredient," she said. She moved quickly, though not quickly enough for me, tidying the kitchen and pulling the stew pot off the fire.

When we went out, she said, "Mrs. Rhys, Gwyn and I must hurry to the market. I like a touch of allspice in the stew. It is edible without it, if Mr. Rhys is home before we return. The pot is resting on the hearth."

"I don't know why you two must be flitting around when you could be here working! Get Nancy out here to carry on, then, if you *must* go," Aunt said.

Nancy dragged herself into the kitchen at Mrs. Perry's request. She stared openly at my face, which must show my distress. I wiped my cheeks and stood straighter before leaving the kitchen. Aunt's gimlet eyes seemed to bore into me as we passed.

As soon as we got to the street, Mrs. Perry took me by the arm and steered us into a nearby alley. "What is it, Gwyn?" she whispered. I wanted to sob in her arms, but I held myself tight.

"I want to go to Mr. Smythe's office right now," I said.

"Well, we can do that, of course, but is it really going to do you any good?" she asked. When I didn't answer, she started back for the street in the direction of the assembly hall, looking around to make sure there were no onlookers. We walked at a good pace, which helped calm me some. I really had no idea how it would help to see him, just knew I must. The streets passed in a blur. I could see nothing but some gray miasma of my misery.

By good fortune, he was in his office and not engaged with a client. I rushed to him, enveloping him in a desperate embrace. I felt him nod to Mrs. Perry, who shut the door behind her as she returned to the hall. "Gwyn, Gwyn, what has happened? I am here. It is all right now."

"Please marry me, right now, today! I can't stand it! I can't go back there!" I cried out. Then the sobs came, wild, out of my control. My body shook his body—so great was the force of them. He held me with such love and tenderness that I let myself melt into him. When the sobs finally lessened, I said, "I'm not a bad person. I don't want to cause any harm to anyone! But here I feel I am being punished. I'd rather be on the ship and in grave danger than safely imprisoned on land!"

"I understand," he said gravely. "We had freedom on the ship that we don't have here. The dictates of society can be very limiting. If I had more physical courage, I'd say, let's set out for the frontier. But I am not built for that, and my profession needs people and a city."

I drew a long breath. "No, I'm not proposing that we venture into the wilderness, although my aunt seems to think we were raised in a cowshed." We had to smile at that.

Gregory raised his eyebrows, pursed his lips, and let out a long, low "Moooo." He took my hand and sat me down in a chair. He pulled up the other chair.

"Seriously, we must do something for you. I can't stand your being so unhappy," he said.

"But you won't marry me…," I said, pulling my mouth down in a mock pout.

"You know we can't do it today. The banns must be posted for three weeks before, at least. But I have no place to take you, living at the inn as I do. I also am trying to ascertain whether we might sign an agreement concerning your fortune, to allow you to hold it regardless of marriage. That is possible in some other colonies, but the Quakers here influence the laws toward the idea of unity, that is that the man and wife become one in the eyes of God and should also in the laws of man. As you know, I have little savings and no property. I would not like it said, in coming years, that I married you for your money."

"But I know that you would not!" I said.

"Yes, but I am finding that people in the City of Brotherly Love are like people anywhere. They love to gossip. The truth is nothing next to a good story!" He smiled that sideways smile of his that was so endearing to me. "I confess that I am breaking a confidence in telling you this, but Ardath and I have been talking to Franklin about getting you a place to stay. Ardath had hoped to keep it a secret, but I think your peace of mind is more important. It is not a wonderful solution to your problems, but there is a shop in the market area which could be fixed into a residence, though it is barely more than a room upstairs. There is a space for a garden in the rear, I believe."

"Oh, I don't care. It need not be fancy at all, just ours." I faced him directly. "Gregory, what about us?"

"Can you wait?" he asked.

"What choice do we have? But I can't go back there today!"

"Hmmm. What about sleeping at Ibrahim's tonight? We could say that you have a fever and he is tending to you at the shop. You could sleep with Isa, perhaps."

"I would sleep in a stable if necessary!" I said.

"Ah," he said, "my beautiful dear. It is very hard to wait." He put his palm on the side of my head.

"I don't want to put you in a bad position between Ardath and me, Gregory, but I don't want to rely on her all the time. She has her own ideas about what she wants, and I feel like I am just hanging onto her coattails. Hanging on for dear life, most of the time. I can't get settled in my mind. I can't be as strong as she is."

"I understand your position very well. At the same time, I don't believe that she means to be so overbearing. We must think about how you can feel more secure. Your life will not always be so tied to hers, surely. But I know that you are a very loyal person..."

"When we were in Wales, we had only our family. Now I have only her."

"You are very different from her, but her strength does not mean that you are weak. There are different kinds of strength, you know," he said.

"You are so wise. Are you older than you look?" I asked.

"Please address me as Grandfather, or perhaps Cradle-Robber, as people would call me if we married now."

"Umm, and that is all that concerns you? My vastly younger age?" I said, batting my eyelashes at him.

"That and the fact that if you stand here much longer, I will ravish your body here and now."

We laughed. I felt much better, but still not ready to return to Aunt's house. We found dear Mrs. Perry waiting outside in the hall for us and told her of our plan.

"Let's say that you have a headache, the kind that only Ibrahim knows how to cure, and must stay there with them until you recover," said Mrs. Perry.

"That sounds good," I said.

She left us to go tell our story to Aunt, while we walked to the shop together. I loved walking under the shade trees that William Penn had so thoughtfully planted when he started the colony some seventy years before. On this early September day in 1751, they were mature and stately.

I commented on them to Gregory. As usual for him, he knew more about everything. He had a lively mind for history.

"William Penn was an avid Quaker and risked life and fortune to make this colony a refuge, not just for Quakers, but for other religious groups that were persecuted in Europe as well. The Quakers still have a strong voice here, for many of them are talented merchants who increasingly improve trade and prosperity. The current proprietor is Penn's son Thomas, who appointed James Hamilton as governor. I am hoping to get business with them, which would give me an inside view of how things are run."

"Hmmm. How is your business going?" I asked.

"Philadelphia is growing rapidly. I will soon have no lack of business. Ah, here we are."

I stood before our little shop, feeling proud of Ibrahim and the Africans. A line of customers had gathered outside the door. They had no lack of business either! I heard one woman with a basket under her arm say, "Mary told me that he cured her skin problems in just one visit, can you imagine? She suffered for years with that!"

We went through the narrow side yard to the back of the shop, where we found Isa tending to herbs in the garden. She straightened up with a joy in her round face that made me feel very welcome. "Miss Gwyn, I never see you, so happy to!" she said.

"Oh, Isa, I need your help," I blurted out. Gregory put a steadying hand on my arm. "I need a place to stay tonight. Can I stay with you?"

"Oh, yes, yes, please!" She beamed at me.

"Gwyn, it looks as if you are situated nicely, then," Gregory said. "Forgive me, but I must return to work if I mean to make a living. Isa, can you walk her home tomorrow?"

"Oh, yes, yes, please," Isa said.

"Thank you for your help," I said to Gregory, hating to see him go. He smiled at me. My heart melted as it always did.

As soon as he left, Isa brushed the dirt from her fingers and handed me her apron. I put it on while she fetched another. We happily weeded the herbs together. Enjoying the heady scent of rosemary, savory, and sorrel, I was soon at peace again.

I slept that night in Ahmed's bed, while he had a pallet on his parents' floor. I had not slept so well in a long while. Isa returned me to Aunt's house in the morning. It was still cool, and the birds sang cheerfully. I turned the doorknob and waved goodbye to Isa, already starting off to her home.

Aunt was waiting immediately inside. "Hah!" she said, startling me. "So the little whore returns! You conniving minx. All the while, I thought you were chaste in my household, when you were out with that weaselly solicitor, having your licentious fun. Not to speak of your wanton sister flitting about wherever she wants with a gentleman! Well, you will pay! Shaming your good uncle and aunt!"

She slapped me so hard that my ears rang as I fell to the floor. I shook my head to clear it, but Aunt kicked me savagely in the stomach and even harder twice in my ribs. While I gasped for air, she seemed to rise straight above me like an avenging angel ready to deliver the death blow. Then, rising even further, suspended above the floor, she showed a look of surprise. I looked behind her through the spots that floated before my eyes. I realized that Ardath had Aunt grasped by her upper arms. White anger blazed on Ardath's face. Her eyes were narrow slits, her mouth a hard line.

"Ardath, no!" I shouted, with my first breath.

Ardath let go, and Aunt slumped away from her, real fear written on her face. She fumbled for a chair and crawled into it, her eyes never leaving Ardath.

"You will never touch my sister again! You will never have power over any of us again!" Ardath shouted. She turned to Mrs. Perry, who had arrived in the hallway. "Get our things together. We are leaving this house this minute!"

My ears still rang, yet these words got through. We were leaving! I got myself up, with the help of Ardath's strong arm. Brushing past Aunt, I stumbled to "our" room and hastily stuffed my clothes and a few other possessions into a large bag, while Mrs. Perry got Ardath's. She then reappeared from her room across the hall with her own things.

A pale and frightened Nancy peered at us from the rear door. "You can't leave me here!" she pleaded.

"I'm sorry, Nancy. We will try to help you in time. Right now we have no lodging ourselves," Ardath said to her. Nancy stared at us blankly, then ran for the back garden.

We left that miserable place. There was nowhere to go but Ibrahim's shop, so that was where we went. I was not able to straighten my body and had to go slowly, bent over and leaning on Ardath.

CHAPTER 41

April 1751
Carys

Captain Smog was in my cabin the next day while I still rubbed the sleep from my eyes. I hastily rolled out of my hammock and faced him.

"Ah, my dear, how delightful to see you this morning," he said.

My lip began to curl down of its own volition, but I changed it to a smile. "Captain, I trust you slept well," I said, pulling the shawl over my chest.

"The best for a long, long time. You have proved a fine tonic for me. We shall enjoy our pleasures again this evening." He swept his arms into a mock bow. "But meanwhile, you have a boatload of slatternly women to examine. They must be cleaned, scrubbed really, so that their stench may become bearable. I have simple dresses to clothe them in, as their rags must go overboard. I'll not put my men to the task, as some of them are no more than animals. I will not have the women ruined." He smiled, as if expecting praise for his gentlemanly sensibility.

I smiled tightly. "Where is the clothing?"

"I'll have Pete bring it to you. Be careful. I have myself inspected them for weapons." A lascivious look spread over his face. "But you never know with these wenches…"

*****

I faced my new job with a great deal of curiosity, as I climbed down the stairs to the third deck, where the women were held. I went softly and heard moans and crying. Suddenly, an authoritative voice spoke, "Hssst!" and silence fell.

I proceeded more openly, holding my lantern higher when I reached the bottom of the ladder. Though it was broad daylight outside, we were below water level here and no light reached the room. I took a deep breath through my mouth, which helped somewhat with the smell. In the semicircle of light cast by the lantern, I saw women pressing forward. Their eyes glinted in the lamplight. They seemed neither suspicious nor slatternly but were pitifully thin and dirty.

In the front stood a woman of some height, with a demeanor of leadership about her. She had her dark hair done up in a bun and wore a dress that once might have been rather grand, a low-necked gown of faded maroon damask, splotched with spots of dirt and water stains. Her face was streaked with smut, yet she had her dignity intact.

To this woman I said, "My name is Carys. I am the healer on this ship and have come to help you all in whatever ways I can. Like you, I'm a prisoner here, but am allowed on higher decks in order to do my work."

"Welcome, Carys," said the woman in a deep voice as smooth as cream. "I am Margaret. My girls will need your help most assuredly. We need water and food soon, as we have not even had a crust since we entered this ship."

"No one has fed you?" I asked, incredulous. "Then that is the first order of business. I know a crewman named Pete who is trustworthy. I can ask him to bring you some supplies. We will have some water for washing yourselves as well and clean clothes for you."

"We have some who are sick from the rough seas. They are in the 'seasick corner.'" She pointed to a side of the ship beyond the range of light. "There are others who concealed their illnesses or pregnancies in order to get off the prison hulk who will need your help as well."

"I will bring another lantern when I return and some peppermint that may help with the seasickness. Pete should be here soon with food and water. You can trust him."

I hurried from that deck with a great feeling of purpose. If I could stay in the captain's good graces, I might be able to do some good here. That and ensuring Dougie's safety might be enough to keep me going, even in the face of my captivity and my sorrow over leaving Ardath and Gwyn.

I spent the rest of that day with the (mostly) young women. Many of them had stories similar to Kate's. They had fallen on hard times, been forced to steal food, and imprisoned for that or other minor thefts, or had turned to prostitution to keep themselves alive and were imprisoned for that way of life. A woman on the streets was in constant danger. It was no wonder that most women married at their earliest opportunity with little regard for what that life might be like.

I was very grateful that I had my skills to keep me and the girls going after Jacob left. Ardath had been almost fully trained when I was taken and, beyond that, was smart and inventive. I trusted in her to keep the girls together and safe.

It was a slow and arduous business to feed and clean the many women. At one point, I left them with Margaret in charge and dragged myself up to the next deck, where Kate had been keeping Dougie.

I found that Kate had relaxed in my presence and no longer accused me of being a faerie. Her story explaining Dougie stayed the same. She showed no awareness of who I was to him but did accept my help. I had arranged for a pallet to be made of blankets and straw for her and Dougie. They also had some separation from the main room by a blanket hanging from ropes over the timbers in their corner. The men who now strung their hammocks on the same deck left her alone. It was clearly known that she was mad; apparently, they hoped not to catch the same disease!

Today, Kate let me hold Dougie while she used the chamber pot in their corner. He was growing to be a fine and healthy boy. He had a solemn manner about him and stared at me intently, as if memorizing my eyes. He seemed like a little wise man. I shuddered to think that he, and I, might easily have been dead for several days. It appeared that his eyes would remain blue, and he was growing a thicker head of curly brown hair. Well, his mother had been a beauty, so he had a good chance. Kate kept him clean; he had a sweet baby smell. He was warm and well-fed. He drifted off to sleep in my arms, growing heavier as each moment passed.

It took me back to the days when I had had young babies, the boy who died and the girls who lived. The sweetness of that heavy weight! It was a magic bond like no other. But soon Kate was back and I had to give him up again.

In sitting still, I had found that I was bone-tired. I had to find Pete again to check his backside before I could rest. As I climbed up to my cabin, he had begun coming down the ladder but clambered up again when he heard me. "Mistress, how do you be?" he asked.

"Oh, Pete, we must take a look at your sores. Can you come to my cabin now?"

"Yessum, I'm ready," he said, sounding proud. Sure enough, when I examined him, his sores were healing nicely.

"Good job," I said. He actually blushed.

"Could be that most of us rascals could have cleaner habits. I even washed those clothes and rinsed them in fresh water, though the men laughed at me. I told them that they could use some of the same, and they laughed harder."

"Oh, well, Rome wasn't built in a day! I'm so glad that you are better."

"Yessum, best get some rest. A hard day you've had!"

"Both of us. Thanks for your help today."

"Yessum, rest well."

As Pete left, I sighed, wishing to slump down into my hammock and seek blessed sleep. It wasn't to be, of course. Captain Smog had had a much easier day, I imagined, and would be upon me at any time now. I struggled to keep alert, to prepare my valerian root mixture and remember all I must ask him for. Not too many things at once, I cautioned myself.

Sure enough, a light scratching on my door soon followed. I put on my best smile. I opened the door, and there he stood. He had put on his wig and looked even more ridiculous than usual.

"Why, Captain, how good to see you!" I said with false cheer.

"My dear, and you also." He pursed his lips. "I hope that you can join me for dinner." He cocked one eyebrow to show that he meant more than dinner.

What a surprise, but I kept up my act with him.

"Let me freshen up a little and I shall be right there," I said, as I still needed to put the root mixture in a less-conspicuous bottle. I found one, made for infusions, that was small enough to fit in the palm of my hand. I filled this quickly after he left. Then I splashed some water on my face to keep myself alert.

The meal tonight was again almost worth the struggle of dealing with the captain. Fresh fish and some pears from our last port, even somewhat-fresh bread. I fell upon it in a most unladylike manner. The captain, of course, was steadily drinking. As soon as he turned his back for a moment, I slipped the root mixture into his jug of Madeira. I moved the decanter to my side of the table so that I could steadily refill his glass.

When he turned back to the table, I smiled sweetly. "Captain, I have heard it is all the rage for gentlemen to grate some nutmeg into their Madeira. It is said to have a beneficial effect on, ahem, certain organs."

"Oh, my yes, I've heard that! Not that any of my organs is in need of help." Here he winked mightily. "But let us try it. Will you join me?"

"Of course," I said. He rummaged in the nutmeg drawer, triumphantly raised a nutmeg in the air, and grated it into both glasses.

"I have seen it done thusly," I said and grated even more into our glasses.

"Here's to it, then!" he said in a jovial voice and downed his wine. "Why, quite tasty! You never fail to amuse me, Carys."

I concentrated on eating and pleaded for more provisions for the women below. "We have cleaned them and clothed them in the dresses provided, but many are seasick and underfed. They need more fresh water and food, especially greens, to keep them well."

"Well, my dear, we don't want to coddle them."

"I hardly think clean water and decent food is coddling," I said, smiling sweetly and pretending to be shy about it.

"You show your ignorance of sea voyages. Conditions will be rough. A lady such as you are"—here he looked at me smugly—"would not understand, naturally."

To this I merely raised my glass, hoping he would keep drinking as before. In this I was not disappointed. Although I took the barest sips from mine, he downed his glass and reached for the jug again. I leaned across the table toward him, distracting him with my low neckline while I poured more treated wine into his glass, reminding him, "Don't forget the nutmeg, my dear."

Eventually, the captain became more and more sleepy, and I was able to steer him to bed, pretending to be amorous and climbing in with him, undressing him while he still was able to help do this. I tousled his hair, pulled off his shoes and stockings, all the while telling him how magnificent he was. He fell asleep when enough of his clothes were off to look convincing. The process had rumpled his bed also. At last, with a truly exhausted sigh, I rolled off the bed to the tune of his sonorous snores.

I returned to the table, wrapping the extra fish, pears, and bread in a cloth I had brought with me. I hadn't succeeded in getting any promises from him to help the women that night, but I did get to eat and then steal enough food for Kate and myself. A good night, then!

I don't remember hiding the food or getting into the hammock, fully clothed, to have a fine rest.

CHAPTER 42

September 1751
Ardath

WE HAD GONE SEVERAL blocks up the street when the red rage began to fade from my eyes. We had instinctively followed the substantial form of Mrs. Perry, who was making speed away from Aunt's house regardless of the bundles she carried. I had my right arm around Gwyn, who still seemed stunned by the blows Aunt had delivered, her delicate complexion marred by the imprint of a hand. The skin had split open where that hand with its rings had hit her cheekbone. Blood dripped from it.

My gentle sister, who would never hurt anyone, slapped and kicked by our demon aunt! And for nothing! I almost retched from the fury of it but held on to my gorge and forged ahead, murmuring to Gwyn, "It will be all right. We will take care of you. We will be at Ibrahim's soon." Some of this was to comfort myself, as now the guilt swept in. The one thing my mother had asked of me was to protect my sister. I had failed. All my petty concerns paled before this fact.

It felt like a long, miserable trip to the apothecary. Entering the front of the shop, Mrs. Perry and I gratefully put down our bundles. Ibrahim looked up as we went back through the curtain, into the cool of the stillroom. His face fell when he saw Gwyn.

"What has happened? Sit here, Gwyn. Let me look at this."

"I am fine," she said, before bursting into tears, covering her face with her thin white fingers. Ibrahim waited quietly, then gestured to us to leave them alone. Mrs. Perry and I walked through to the garden, where we found Isa, as usual, kneeling in the dirt.

She hastily rose to her feet, looking at our expressions. "Mistress Ardath and Mrs. Perry, something goes wrong. I get Mr. Smythe!" Before we could say a word, she slung off her apron, shook off the bottom of her skirts, and ran out through the side yard.

"I'll make us some nice tea," said Mrs. Perry, patting me on the shoulder as she returned to the house. This left me with nothing but my own thoughts for company. These thoughts held no solutions, only whirled around like the winds that were blowing up the river under a darkening sky. I heard the cracks of lightning, soon followed by the rumble of thunder. As the wind slapped my hair in my face, one thought settled in my mind. I wondered if Mr. Franklin were running out to test his lightning theories. That led me to my disappointment that Franklin's tenant had decided to stay on Market Street after all, so even that possibility of lodging had vanished.

I longed for the simplicity of our life in Wales, where we had not much, but enough. To have even a cabin to ourselves would seem like the height of luxury to me now. The fat drops of rain bounced on the stone path and splattered, cool, on my head.

I went inside to the small kitchen. Mrs. Perry had the door open to the storm. Fragrant tea steeped in a white porcelain pot entwined with painted roses. I sat on a stool and leaned my elbows on the counter, staring out. She poured tea into a tin cup (we must get some better crockery here). I drank gratefully and sat in silent misery for some time.

Mrs. Perry put her arm on my shoulder. "This isn't your fault, you know," she said, as if reading my guilty thoughts. "That woman will someday get her due. The good Lord will see to that." I didn't have time to answer her, which was good, given what I was likely to say.

Omar stood in the inner doorway; the storm water ran from his body in sheets. "Oh, I will mess floor too bad," he said, looking down, and moved with animal grace to the outer door. Puddles formed at his feet, but he was at least under the eaves there. Mrs. Perry handed him a towel, which he used on his upper body before wrapping it around his waist.

"Were you on the church tower when the storm hit?" I asked.

"Yes, m'am. We saw it come. Dey told us 'Get down,' and we did." Here he grinned, his wide mouth showing the square front teeth. He looked at me more carefully then. "Mistress Ardath, something wrong here?"

Mrs. Perry jumped in. "I'll say there is. That witch aunt of theirs struck Miss Gwyn hard and, when she fell, kicked her even harder. I was there. I saw it! Suffice it to say we won't stay there anymore!"

Omar's usually sunny face darkened. "Hit Miss Gwyn like a slave? No, dat is so bad. A bad woman. Christians say dey are taking care of others, loving others. What do you say when dey do not?"

"Hypocrite!" I said. I could not find a close word in his language, other than one that meant a sham, which I tried to say for him. He seemed to understand. He stood stock-still, hands hanging at his sides, while the storm raged behind him.

Finally, he said, "Not right. We have our house and you have none. We move out. You have dis house."

"Thank you, Omar, but maybe there is another way," I said. At this point, Isa returned, puffing from her run and fully as wet as Omar. She moved under the eaves as well, gently pushing him aside. He put his arm around her, bent down to her ear, and quietly told her what had happened. A look of horror spread across her round face.

"You stay here. No go back to bad woman," she said. "Mr. Smythe, he come soon."

"Thank you, Isa. We will need shelter at least tonight," I said, not knowing what our real solution could be. Thank God we did have this place!

With the help of towels, Omar and Isa were finally dry enough to come into the kitchen. The little space was becoming crowded, but we were not through having company. Gregory appeared a little later, with his heavy cloak held above him for shelter. He came straight in, after shaking his cloak under the eaves. He hung it on an outside hook and turned to us.

"Where is she?" were his first words. I pointed the way to Ibrahim's stillroom. He barely nodded at us as he hurried the few steps through the room.

I could hear him greet Ibrahim and whisper to Gwyn. I imagined him holding her in his arms, surely the tonic she needed now. What tonic did I need? It occurred to me that this was it. My circle of friends around me, all feeling the same anger and need to protect as I did. I let my tight body relax in my seat. I was not alone in this.

The next time I looked up from my cool tea, James was in the doorway, his head ducked low to enter. He wore not his usual red uniform, but a suit of dark mismatched clothes, the shirt being a brown buckskin with only one sleeve, showing the white shirt beneath. He stared at me, his brow furrowed. His deep-blue eyes carried anger, hurt, and determination in equal parts. Trickles of rain ran down from his curly hair.

"Ardath, are you well?" he asked, rushing to me. I was taken aback by the concern he showed. There he was, strong, able, and in love with me. He embodied protection; I wanted it so much right then. He took me in his arms, disregarding all the observers standing around. I slid off the stool and leaned into him. He smelled of new leather, rain, and his own spicy scent. His muscles were hard beneath the soft buckskin. I laid my head against his chest, where his heart raced as if he had run the whole way. He led me away beyond the curtain and into the waiting area. He closed the shop door and put out the CLOSED sign. When he crossed to me again, he addressed me earnestly.

"Ardath, please marry me. I want to protect you, to give you a home, and be helpmates together with you for as long as we shall live. What can befall us that we cannot overcome together, two such as we?"

I understood what he meant, but my mind cried out, *Why, life, life can undo us, and death as well,* but I did not say anything to him, merely leaned in harder, hoping he would know how much I did love him, somewhat to my own surprise!

He continued to hold me, as if savoring the moment. He spoke again, with great regret in his voice. "It seems that a guide has been found and I will be leaving in the next few days for the frontier." He shrugged the shoulder with the missing sleeve. "I just came from the tailor, who is helping to give me the backwoods look. The colonel is eager for us to get as much information on the enemy as we can before the weather turns for winter. I hope to get back before the worst of the snows fall, but I can't be sure what lies ahead. If you marry me now, you could live at the colonel's house, both you and your sister, of course, while I am gone."

"But how could we marry now, if you are leaving so soon? The banns…"

"It can be done under the colonel's authority. Since I am a soldier under his command, he can make arrangements for us to marry quickly in the name of a hardship calling, which he considers the frontier to be."

"I see. But we have talked before about my need to conduct my business independently, which is not something that ladies of your class would do, and to keep control of my own coin as if a single woman."

"Yes, I have worked on that with Smythe. He has drawn up an agreement in which those conditions are spelled out. Honestly, whether it would hold up in Pennsylvania courts, Smythe is not sure, but if it won't, we will move to a colony where it will. You can trust me that I do not wish to take from you some of the things that make you so appealing, your strength and independence, for example."

This was the first time I had heard him so clearly declare the extent to which he would defy convention for me. Arriving at these conclusions must have cost him much thought and self-examination. It spoke highly of his regard for me as I really was, and that turned the tide for me. "Then yes, I would marry you," I said. "But I don't think we could do it in a church."

"You make me a happy man!" he cried. "No, under these circumstances, we must do it before the army chaplain, and I suggest it be a simple affair, as we have time for nothing else." He trailed a dripping hand through his hair, wetting himself and me further with falling drops.

I preferred simplicity myself, but something held me back still. "I don't know, James. I prefer not to have a rushed marriage. It doesn't seem right somehow…"

His face fell. He stood back from me. "You still don't trust me," he said slowly.

"It's not that, really, I just don't feel ready. I must take care of Gwyn. I have failed her so badly. I don't want to jump into a marriage when I need to focus on her. My mind is not settled. We still need to make every effort to find our mother…would you wait until your return, perhaps? We could be engaged while you are gone, if you wish."

He turned away slowly, speaking as if to the floor. "All that you must do, I could help you with. Do you not understand that you don't have to do everything alone?"

Thus he echoed my thoughts of the day, and still I held back. "I'm sorry," I said, "I must see how Gwyn is doing."

James followed me through the curtain but moved on to the kitchen, which apparently Gregory had done also. I entered the stillroom and sought Ibrahim's eyes, to read there the serious nature of Gwyn's condition. He had her lying down, cushioned with pillows to each side and under her knees. I stepped close to her. Her face was still pale; the catgut stitches made ugly tracks on her cheek. Her eye was swelling, a livid purple color, though Ibrahim had put a cool rag on it. Most of all, she seemed hardly to breathe. I looked again at Ibrahim.

His quiet voice was soothing, as always. "The blows have broken some of Gwyn's ribs. I have bound them, but they will be painful. She should not be moved any more than necessary. Luckily, I had the softer pad on the table when we placed her here. The lungs seem to be functioning well now. We don't want that to change." He didn't say that broken ribs could puncture her lungs, causing much worse problems. He knew that Gwyn was listening care-fully to all we said.

"I see. How can she sleep on such a narrow bed, this far-off the floor?"

"I will ask Omar to build sides to the table to make her secure," he said. He nodded and left the room to us.

I turned to Gwyn again. "I am so sorry. I should have gotten you out of that house. I was working on getting a place, but I didn't want to tell you and then have it fall through."

"Oh, Ardath, it's all right. Please don't blame yourself! I will be all right, I promise, and we can work on it together. I'm not a child anymore, you know!"

I smiled at her, my lip trembling only a little. At the moment, I was the child, wanting to burst into tears, but of course, I did not. "Well, at least we are out of that house," I joked weakly.

"We are indeed. We will come up with a plan soon," Gwyn said.

"Now you should rest." I went back to the kitchen, where the others were gathered. Mrs. Perry quickly left to stay with Gwyn. Ibrahim was explaining to Omar what was needed for Gwyn's bed. Isa had provided tea and ale and was busy over the hearth with what smelled like a stew in the making. Gregory looked at me with misery in his eyes. He, like me, must wish he had been able to protect Gwyn. I put my hand on his arm. James just looked at me, said nothing. Nevertheless, we had a room quite crowded with people who cared about Gwyn, and that lifted my spirits. Outside, the storm had passed, though rain still dripped from the leaves.

Ibrahim and Omar stood up. Before Omar left, he said to me, very simply, "I will not work for the Christians anymore. I will make a house for you." I nodded my thanks.

Gregory, who was leaning against the doorjamb, unfolded his arms, and said, "He could do that, you know. You could buy an empty lot. Quickly done, it would not be a fancy house, of course, but it would be secure. Three good lots have been offered for sale as one piece, just today, very near here. They would be more expensive than others, but they would provide you plenty of privacy. I believe it would be good for you to be close to your friends here at the shop. Other lots for sale are farther out on the edge of town and not very safe. I have been looking hard for some solution…"

"Gregory, thank you for always watching out for us. I wonder if we could be in a house before winter. What do you think, James?"

"Would you not consider staying with the colonel this winter?" he asked.

"It is a most gracious offer, but we hardly know them. For now, Gwyn needs to stay here until she heals. And we do not want to be at the mercy of others, no matter how kind they might be," I said, knowing that I disappointed him.

"It would help your reputations, certainly, if you lived at the colonel's," said James in a tight voice. His face was tight also, but I could read it. He was afraid that I didn't care about reputation. Truly, I didn't. I expected that Aunt would gossip about us, if only to make herself look good. She would ruin our reputations anyway. We would become, in the public's eyes, whatever she made us out to be. It was galling, but true.

To James I said, "Don't you see? Our aunt will ruin us. She has hated us from the start. Now she will spread whatever lies she wants about us. The colonel and his wife might regret taking us in, in the end. Those who do care about reputation should stay away," I said. And I meant it as a warning to him also. In the end, he might not want me for a wife.

I turned then to Gregory. "Buy the lots if you can, now, today."

"But don't you want to see them?" he asked.

"No. I will stay here with Gwyn. Ask Omar to go with you to see how buildable it is. Negotiate if you can, but spend what you must," I said. I was relieved; action always made me feel better.

"James, do you know the tentmaker for the army in town? We will need two tents here to house everyone," I said.

"Yes, I'm talking with Courtland about a tent for my expedition. I can ask him for you also. He makes them rainproof, or nearly so." He pulled himself off the stool he was occupying. "First, I must return to the tailor. I think I scared the poor man, running out so fast." He was actually smiling; James liked action too. I hoped we could come to some sort of agreement before he had to leave for the frontier.

"Thank you for your offers to help," I said, making it deliberately vague and praying that he would understand all that I meant.

I walked him out into the wet street. "Would you consider us engaged until you return?" I asked.

"Yes, perhaps that is for the best, not to rush it, but I hold you to your word," he said, gently tucking a piece of my hair back under my hat. His fingers brushed my ear and made it tingle.

"Yes," I replied. "You may trust in that."

I wasn't to see him again before he left. He sent word the next morning that he and the scout were already setting out and that our tents were in the making.

CHAPTER 43

September 1751
Gwyn

FOR SEVERAL WEEKS, I was confined to the narrow bed. Isa had to hold a shallow basin under me for my bodily wastes. She did it, as with most things, with unremitting good cheer. She used the opportunity to learn English words as well; I would have tried to learn more of her language too, but unlike Ardath, I am miserable at languages and had given up long ago.

Being more out in the world, Isa's husband and son were ahead of her with English conversation. We did have some amusement over her attempts, though I tried not to laugh, as it hurt very badly. She and Mrs. Perry kept me fed and as comfortable as I could be. After the first week, I could sit up a little and enjoyed some books that Ardath got for me. Defoe's amazing *Robinson Crusoe* was a favorite of mine, although I did think we had had almost as many adventures ourselves while at sea.

I overheard Ardath one day telling Mrs. Perry about our aunt's slanders against us. "Mrs. Perry, it's as I feared. Rumors about us are flying around the town. They are preposterous, of course, but people believe them. I'm afraid that it will hurt our business here, though it seems that it hasn't yet."

"Well, perhaps your aunt's ways are better-known than you think. People might consider the source. However, it is best that you do not go about freely until this dies down."

"I agree. I have plenty to do with the house building on our new lots anyway. True to his word, Omar has been working all hours to get the house ready. It is simple, but he will make it solid. People are making do with much less on the frontier."

"It will be good to have our own place, although they have made us very welcome here," said Mrs. Perry.

"True, with all the Africans staying in tents at the new house site, we have fared well enough here," said Ardath. "But of course, we will all be better off soon."

"You heard nothing today about Major James?" asked Mrs. Perry.

"No." There was a pause while she apparently pushed down her worries about him. I heard the tension in her voice as she said, "We should have heard something by now, Mrs. Perry. I'm going in to see Gwyn."

Ardath parted the curtains that shielded "my room" from the rest of the shop. "Gwyn, how are you?"

"Bored and feeling better. When do you think I can get up and come to help you with the house?"

"Ibrahim will have to say. I should think that you'll be up and walking soon. Then soon after that, you can come to see it. No hard work for you, though."

I had not seen Ardath so relaxed in a while. The hard physical work she was doing seemed to agree with her and actually to cheer her up. She left early every morning and returned only as light faded. She wore a broad-brimmed hat to shade her from the sun. She took this off now and wiped her brow. "We have finished clearing, and the foundation was started today. As the house is set, there will be plenty of privacy from neighbors. We are building more toward the middle of the lots rather than putting the house close to the street," she said.

"We can pretend that we are back home in Wales," I said.

She smiled. "Yes, we can. The woods will wrap us 'round like a comforter. Omar says that the work should go more quickly now. Since it is nearing the end of September, we will need to work fast to get it weather-proofed before snows start. He already has a mason to do the chimneys. Ahmed is helping with the carpentry at every chance he has. He wants to make us iron railings for the steps and porch. He has also found a freedman in need of work to help Omar."

"That sounds wonderful!" I had to ask her how she was feeling about a subject few dared to mention. "How are you faring with James gone?"

"I must be patient, about so many things, but especially about him. I can't think about him without worrying, so I concentrate on the work of the house. Most likely, he will not be back before it is finished. Gwyn"—here she took my hand—"I don't know how I feel still. Will it ever be clear to me? Beyond the house and the business, the future is a blank."

I turned her hand over in mine; it was rough and red despite the gloves she wore for work. The nails were irregular, with some broken. I pretended to read her palm. "Let's see. A long life line, but only if you behave. Many loves in your future—ooops, James would not like to hear that! Prosperity and hard work. Beautiful children, hmmm, six, I believe…"

By this time, we both were giggling, which caused me to gasp and remember my ribs. "Really, Ardath, have you forgotten that you are in charge of your future? My turn to ask you what *you* want."

"All right, that is fair. Here's what I want: to make a successful business, to make our lives secure, to find our mother, if that is possible, to explore this new land more fully, to be free of society's restraints and go about as I please."

"Well…" I smiled. "I don't hear anything about marriage or children, Ardath."

She stared at me as if I had said something shattering. "Then what am I doing, promising to marry James? Despite the error of his ways, I do not want to tease him, when his feelings for me seem sincere."

"I'm sure they are sincere. Do you still not see how you affect men? Half the town is probably in love with you," I said. "You need to face up to that or you will miss the truth of things."

Ardath was speechless at this. In her headlong pursuits of results, she was never really aware of how attractive she was.

"But looks are not important. Looks do not get things done."

"Looks *are* important. Perhaps too important, but you have more than looks. You have vitality, power," I said.

"Am I then to choose a life without a companion, without children?" she asked this more of herself, perhaps, than of me. "That sounds rather dreary too. How can I make decisions now, for the rest of my life?"

"Just because Aunt says that you are a spinster at eighteen years old, you do not have to believe that. Ardath, I have had much time to think, having to lie still here. It seems that you can do what you want, as long as we have the funds. Even a true spinster, of any age, could be interesting to men if she has her financial independence. And since looks are important, you should think of our mother. You resemble her very closely. I believe you will keep your looks and vitality as she has. There's not a gray strand in her red hair, and her skin is almost as creamy and smooth as yours."

I stopped then, realizing that I spoke of our mother as if she were alive, which she was, to me. I drifted into thoughts of her.

"If I could know that our mother is alive, where and how she is, I would happily stay here in Philadelphia, in a modest house, and marry Gregory and have his children. That would be all I could wish for."

"Oh, Gwyn, I understand. We must find a better way to search for her. Uncle has had no word from the vicar in our village, which must mean that she is not in Wales. I will ask Franklin if he knows of agents in port cities here who might get rumors of her, since Gregory has heard nothing from his contacts. The colonel also has inquired of his contacts in England and in colonial areas with no success. It isn't as if we haven't tried. Word travels slowly over these long distances, so even now we may hear something before spring. But I will ask Franklin, if he is still speaking to me."

"Why would he not speak with you? Because of Aunt's rumors? I can't believe that of Franklin. If not, perhaps Gregory could ask him," I said. "I do hope Gregory's reputation has not been sullied because of us."

I was suddenly worried. It was true that Gregory often came to see me since I was confined to my bed, but it had always been at night. I had thought him merely busy, but maybe he didn't want to be seen coming here. My heart sank into a deep well. I felt the cold water rush over my head. I couldn't speak.

"I don't think he has been badly hurt because of us, although apparently Aunt has accused him of seducing you, a young and naive girl, and courting you for your connection to her and Uncle, to advance his standing in the community."

I resurfaced to cry, "But that is ridiculous!"

"Of course, it is. This will surely die down and fall of its own weight eventually. I'm sorry if I upset you."

"No, it is better to know, but how awful! Oh, dear! I must think about this. I don't know," I sputtered. "Do you think James has been affected by this also?"

"Since he's not here to hear the rumors, I assume that he is blissfully unaware. His standing is less likely to be affected than Gregory's. The army is not likely to care like the ladies of the city or Gregory's customers might."

"If everyone is believing these rumors, then Uncle must also. We haven't heard from him at all since we left. I want to see Uncle. I know he has cared about us. He *must* know the truth about what happened."

"I understand. I have considered meeting him at his office, but perhaps it would be better to ask him to come here. Do you want to speak to him alone? Considering what a whore I am...," she said with a smirk.

"Oh, Ardath, don't even joke about that. Yes. I need to do this by myself. I need to know if he can believe me. Perhaps Mrs. Perry could go to ask him?"

*****

I really didn't want to talk to Uncle. I was afraid that I would break down and become incoherent, but we *had* to make him understand. The day after Ardath and I talked, Mrs. Perry set out early to his office. When she returned, her mouth was set in a grim line. "He is coming," she said. "Do you want me to stay?"

"No, thank you, Mrs. Perry. I must manage this on my own. Please just tidy the room and put on some tea." I dared not ask her why she looked so severe, but it could not be good news for me.

When Uncle arrived, she ushered him in, offered him a chair and some tea, and left immediately. I looked at his eyes and steeled myself. I had never seen the poor man look so confused and outraged.

"I am sorry that I was not able to come to you these last weeks. I'm sure you would like an explanation of what happened at your house," I said.

"Your aunt has explained it to me," he said. "I have asked the good Lord to forgive you. I continue to pray for your soul, and your sister's as well." He slumped into the chair, frowning.

"Thank you, Uncle. You are a very kind man." Then I felt a rush of anger that took me by surprise. "Do you also pray for Aunt's soul?"

He must have heard the edge in my voice but continued in a calm, sad way, looking at the hat he turned in his hand. "Your aunt is always in my prayers. But she is not in the wrong here. She told me how you and Ardath conspired against her, pushed her, and threw her aside as she tried to help you turn from your wanton ways."

I sat back in disbelief. So everything that Ardath and Mrs. Perry were hearing in the streets and market was true! "Uncle, I know that you must trust your wife, but she is not telling the truth. Just the opposite happened. Aunt struck me, bruised my eye, and tore my face." Here I turned to show him the cheek with the stitches in it. "When I fell, she kicked me so hard that my lower ribs were broken. I have been lying abed these last weeks so that they may heal and not puncture my lungs. She might have continued to attack me had Ardath not restrained her. I am not wanton, and neither is Ardath. The night before this happened, I became ill and had to spend the night here under Ibrahim's care. I sent word to her, but she did not believe me, would not let me explain."

Here I stopped and studied him earnestly. His face was a stone mask. Haunted eyes gazed out at me.

"I understand that you must justify your actions against my wife. When you are ready to tell me the truth, please send for me again. I do not wish to hold ill will toward my own kin. I will continue to pray for you and for your reformation." With this, he stood and replaced his hat. "May God forgive you!" he said, stepping away from my bed.

"Uncle," I called after him, "hear me, please. We are blood. You are like a father to me."

He hesitated, his hand gripping the curtain, as if he might turn around to me. Then his shoulders slumped. He shook his head violently, as if to shake out my words, and pulled the curtain aside. "I can't...I can't," he said.

The other side of the curtain jerked away, showing Mrs. Perry's face, swollen with anger at Uncle. "I was there. I saw her beat and kick Gwyn. You can't listen to it, you coward! You can't face that your wife is a demon." I heard her follow him to the door, saying more in angry, low tones. I fell back against the bed, aching, undone.

CHAPTER 44

April to Early June 1751
Carys

IN SOME WAYS, MY plan succeeded. As the weeks passed, I was able, while pretending to have an amorous relationship with the captain, to win some privileges for the women in the hold. They were allowed to go on deck once a day when we were out to sea. They stood straighter in the fresh air and talked to one another in a livelier way. They had to be kept away from the men during these short visits on top, of course. I joined them as a sort of guard. In time, we slowly lengthened our visits to the deck, without the captain objecting.

Although the air invigorated us all, it made our quarters even less bearable, especially as the air was warming on our southward journey. As time passed, the women grew less seasick and more nourished. Some were able to work. Together we scrubbed down their deck, carrying bucket after bucket of filthy water and rags topside to wash in seawater. The smell diminished somewhat, though the bilge stank to high heaven always. I ran out of peppermint oil for our noses. We had only rosemary to stick behind our ears; its pungent smell helped some.

Kate did not come on deck, or let anyone but me touch Dougie, who was growing apace. Kate was benefiting from the captain's leftovers, and so was Dougie. It was the delight of my days to snatch some moments with him. His fresh baby smell, soft skin, and gurgling laugh pierced me with joy.

One morning I went again to see Kate before the women climbed out for the trip to the deck. I sank to my knees on the rough wood beside her. "Kate, good morning. Have you passed a good night?"

"Yes, Dougie slept well, and so did I. I have just fed the wee hulker."

I smiled at her. "You are taking good care of him. The other women on the ship are going up to the deck. Would you join us in the clean air? I think it would do you and Dougie good."

"Oooh, no. I won't be doing that. These women would envy my Dougie and might try to steal him." Her eyes were full of real fear.

"What if I got permission to take you up when the women are below?"

Her eyes widened. "But then the men would see me and, worse, see Dougie. You know the sailors are a rough lot, except for Pete, who shows me kindness. He knows my Donald from Culloden. But the sailors, they might throw my boy over the side, just to see me cry. I'll not let nothin' happen to my Dougie."

"I understand your worry, but I would be there to protect you." She smiled a little at that but shook and shook her head. "Well, if you change your mind, just tell me," I said, suppressing a groan as I forced my knees to straighten. Neither my days nor my nights were restful. As I moved away, I also worried about ever being able to claim Dougie from Kate. I quenched the thought. One day at a time, I reminded myself.

We stopped for an unusually long time in a harbor at the Canaries. I didn't see Smog on the ship for about ten days and was relieved of my nightly game with him. I asked Pete why we delayed here so long.

"Oh, the captain, he has a ship wife here. Likes to spend time with her, drinking mostly, I think. But he's due back tonight, so ready yourself for his bad temper, from the leaving of her."

Indeed, that same evening, I prepared to play my usual farce with Smog. Pete was outside his door, awaiting orders, I presumed. Pete shook his head in warning. As I entered Smog's cabin, he slouched over the table.

He smirked. "Mrs. Rhys, I see you have donned new clothes to please me," he said with irony.

I mock bowed. "Indeed, if I had new clothes, I would gladly wear them," I said. The same old dress I had worn since the first night on the ship stank almost as badly as the bilge, having much of the same substances—offal, vomit, dead skin, and pure filth—on it.

"Perhaps I shall tire of you if you remain so besmirched," he said. I didn't like the angry tone barely hidden by his hard grin.

He had drunk his decanter almost dry, though it was before dinner. "Let me refresh your wine for you," I said and started for the table. He gripped my wrist. "Sir, that is painful," I said, trying to twist away.

"I think you are getting pretty cocky, for a *slave*. I don't want a slave to touch my drink or food. You are filthy. I have befriended you out of the kindness of my heart, and now I know that you are a mere slut. Been seen spending time with Pete, I hear."

"Sir, I only speak to Pete to get help with caring for the ladies of the ship. Whatever would make you think it was more than that? Provide me with clean water and clothes and I shall improve my appearance for you, but don't desert me. You are my strong protector!"

I was frightened not only for myself, but for the other women on the ship and what his anger at me might mean for them. And he knew I cared about Dougie, of course. A chill flashed through my heart.

At my pleading, he let go of my wrist, which I rubbed ruefully. Perhaps he would let me talk him out of this mood. He'd been staring at me with his bloodshot eyes, as if to plan his next move.

"You know, I never remember our swiving." He paused; then a thought seemed to dawn on him. "I think I need to *see* what it looks like. You will be my predining entertainment tonight," he said. Stumbling to the door, he called out to Pete. "Come here, wretched man."

My weary legs gave way. I slid into a chair. I could tell by the look on Pete's face that he knew the worst was coming.

"Now, see here, Pete, I know you are a special *friend*, shall we say, of this whore who claims to be a lady. I want to see how you love her. Show me. Kiss the wench!"

"But, sir, I do not want her," Pete stammered.

"Oh, she is good enough for me but not you!" roared the captain.

"No sir, I only meant…"

"Stop whimpering and take down your pants," said Smog to him. I rarely cried but felt my lips start to tremble at his cruelty. Pete slowly took off his pants and held them before his private parts, with his head hanging. Smog grabbed a whip out of the cabin corner. With his left hand, he jerked the pants out of Pete's hands. "Now take her, you fool!"

Smog pushed Pete at me. I clung to him; we held each other up. "Pete, it is all right if you must do this," I whispered to him.

"Hah! See, I knew you were *friends*," Smog crowed.

"Oh, no, missus, I can't," Pete began, but his words ended in a sharp scream. Smog's whip had lashed the back of his legs.

I couldn't stand for this. Smog had the right to whip his crewmen to death if he wished. I kissed Pete on his grizzled cheek. "Let us pretend to be amorous," I whispered, running my hands over the poor man's back.

"I can't, ma'am, 'tisn't right!" he sobbed, as the lash fell again.

"He can hardly be in the mood if you whip him," I said to Smog, my voice shaking.

"So right," Smog said.

Then he lashed me. Liquid fire ran over my back. I cried out and fell, almost passing out at Pete's feet. He reached to help me, then screamed and fell over me, jerking as Smog lashed him again and again. I felt each lash as though it had hit my own body.

Finally, Smog said, "I won't ruin a crewman, worthless as you may be," snatching Pete up to standing. "Go get me Scully!" Pete limped from the room, red blood streaking down his bare legs.

I huddled on the floor, lying very still, trying to breathe through the burning pain. Smog paced the room, muttering curses, as foul a language as ever I had heard, the very devil's language.

In a short time, Scully pounded on the door. Smog let him in, cackling a devil laugh. "I believe we have a solution here. Scully, I find myself in need of watching tonight. Take her and take her rough, as the slut deserves."

I lay as if insensible on the floor, but neither man was fooled. They circled me like wolves might circle prey. "Have at it, man," said Smog.

Scully rolled me onto my burning back and wiped the drool from his mouth with the back of his hairy hand. His eyes glinted in the lantern light; he seemed to be savoring the pain he could cause.

He chuckled and nodded at me. "Well, high time I had you in this position!" he said. He dropped on me then, wrestling my skirts aside as I fought, pausing only to shove his breeches down while his hard arm on my breasts held me pinned to the floor. He rooted around in my private parts, spitting on his fingers when he found no moisture there, jabbing spit into me. Then his gross member stabbed me, repeatedly. I could do nothing. Nothing but hate, and that I did. It warmed me. It kept me alive.

When Scully was done with me, Smog shouted, "Get you to the lowest hold with the other whores!"

Scully wiped his hands on my dress, then dragged me down the ladders like a sack of flour and dumped me on the hold floor, slamming the door behind him.

"Carys, is that you?" a welcome voice asked. Margaret!

"Margaret, I must ask your help," I said, trying not to whimper.

"Oh, what have they done to you?" she asked, lighting the precious lantern I had stolen for her, which only came out for emergencies. I didn't answer, only tried to sit up, which showed her my back.

"Oh, Mary, get the bandages and the salve," said Margaret. "There you see, you have taken care of us, Carys, and now we will take care of you."

This she did, and a good job of it too, though each of her tender touches caused me fiery agony. Finally, I felt able to say, "I'm afraid this will go badly for you. The captain has become disenchanted with me."

"Don't worry. Sleep. We have all endured the worst of what men can do to us. We will endure Smog's wrath as well. We are stronger because of you, and we will stay strong together."

I heard no more as blessed blackness took me away.

CHAPTER 45

October 1751
Ardath

As I WALKED FROM Ibrahim's shop to the new house site, I could feel the change in the weakening sun. The days were growing shorter. The trees were almost finished shedding their glorious reds, bronzes, and yellows. Thankfully, the house was coming along well. Everyone working on it was determined to get it sealed against the elements. Omar and his crew, which included Isa, Ahmed, John, a journeyman carpenter, and myself, were putting up the roof this week. We had hoped for clear skies; so far, October shone with them, cloudless and blue, day after day.

I had arrived at the site and stood a moment to watch the progress. The house was not a conventional one, of brick or board. Rather, we had decided to raise the quickest style we could, a log cabin such as might be found on the frontier. The dense vegetation around us would shield us from sight summer and winter, so our neighbors could not complain about it being unsuitable. The walls were nearing completion, though due for another round of caulking later in the week. The sturdy logs had been cut from the timber cleared for the house and garden sites, so there was no waste of material. I was proud of what we had done in just a few weeks. It was a building that suited its wooded surroundings well.

Behind me, I heard Gwyn call "Hallo." She had been Ibrahim's assistant at the shop ever since she had been able to move around. This enabled Isa, who was quite strong and most dedicated to us, to help with work on the house. Today, however, Gwyn had come to see the building I had been so excited to tell her about.

I hugged her, feeling both happy and grateful. "Gwyn, I'm so glad you came today. I'm sorry you have had to miss so much of this happy process!"

"It's not important. I was glad to help in the way I could, at the shop," she said. "But now, I want to know everything!" Her smile brought out her dimples. Her face revealed no trace of pain, another reason to rejoice.

"For example, how did Omar get the logs flat on the side so that they would fit together so neatly?"

"When we were clearing, we had a sawyer come to cut the downed trees flat on two of their sides. His mule hauled out the saw from his shop and powered it. The flat logs could be laid level on top of one another to raise the walls. But Omar insisted on making the notches by hand so that he could be sure that the logs locked together perfectly at each joint. Of course, the wood is green. Even though they fit so well now, we will have to keep caulking this winter to keep out the chill."

"What will the inside walls be like when it is finished?" Gwyn asked.

"Let's go in and I'll show you." I said. "One of my jobs was to clear the bark off the inside of the logs with an adze and plane, so bark won't drop onto our floor. It's fine for it to drop off the outside over time. But they will be much like what you see now." I led her into the house.

Gwyn said, "The walls are very smooth. Let me see your muscles!"

I rolled up my sleeves to show how unladylike those muscles looked. "Whew!" she said, with mock wonder. "But, Ardath, I had hoped we would have windows, and I don't see any openings. I know they are costly, but…"

"You shall have your windows! We were merely waiting to see where you want them," I said. "The house is about twenty-two by twenty feet. To start with, we will have heavy curtains on a rod, about one-third of the way down the length, dividing the space in two, with the hearth and table in the larger back room. Above that area is where we will put the sleeping loft. It is good to have that above the fireplace, of course, to keep us warm. The front room, we can use for a parlor and working space, a sitting area for reading and so many other things."

"Then, can we have windows in each room, and on each side of the house?"

"Yes! That's a good idea. And we'll have real glass, not isinglass, for our windows."

Gwyn grinned happily at that.

"We'll have heavy shutters to keep out winter storms. Since the logs are thick, we'll put shutters on both the inside and the out."

"But what about the floor?" she asked, looking down at the hard black dirt we stood on.

"Normally, wood floors would be done in the early stages, but we didn't have time. It can be a winter project for Omar if we can find enough dried boards to buy."

"Hmm," she said. I could see she didn't like the idea of a dirt floor.

"I promise that we'll do everything we can to get the wood floor down," I said, squeezing her arm gently. "Also, I need your help finding or designing furniture for the whole house. Oh, and since you love animals so much, we should pick out our livestock together."

"I will love to do that! Chickens? A cow? Perhaps a dog...?" She raised her eyebrows and almost pranced in her happiness. "Well, it is marvelous what you all have done in a short time! What are you working on today?"

"Come out and you will see!" I said, showing her out the back door.

During the short time we had been in the house, John, Omar, and Ahmed had carried a truss for the roof to the back yard and stood briefly to wipe sweat from their eyes. Gwyn greeted them with a large smile and wave, which they returned.

"This truss will serve as a model for the rest of us to copy," I told Gwyn. "After we have made seven of these, they will fit over the roof beams to support the boards on which our roof shakes will lie."

Omar said to Gwyn, "Your sister is good with a hammer! I think we will let her build the rest of the house."

"Yes, just let me carry these trusses around for you, too!" I replied. Omar chuckled at this, white teeth gleaming.

The work had pulled us all closer together. Omar's skills and good nature helped us work in harmony. Unlike his father and me, Ahmed could not work with us every day. His smithing was in high demand in the city. I could foresee a day when he would need his own blacksmith shop and an apprentice besides. Despite his main job, he worked very hard with us and never seemed to tire. I looked over the yard to the camp Omar, Isa, and Ahmed had set up. Their tents had served well. Isa had made a fire ring and cooked us delicious meals on it, primitive though it was. When the rare rains came, we huddled on stumps under an oiled tarpaulin spread over four posts and told stories.

"A penny for your thoughts," said Gwyn. I realized that I must have been staring out over the yard while she sat quietly on a stump.

"Oh, yes, sorry. Let me show you the new path to the stream," I said. "Isa and I decided that the old path would be too slippery for wet weather. We will need to haul water until spring, when we will have time and warmer ground to dig a well."

She readily straightened up, wincing only briefly, as if her ribs hurt. We followed a path through the clearing that would one day be a garden for our herbs and vegetables. The earth was rich and dark there. The stream was quite close to our new house. We had smoothed the bank and built in three-level stone steps down to a deep pool. A bucket hung by a rope from a handy branch. "Another bucket hook will be outside the back door," I told Gwyn.

Tears rolled slowly down her cheeks, one smooth as an apricot, the other with the small track marks of stitches.

"Oh, Gwyn, what is it? What have I said?" I asked.

"Oh, no, it's not that," she said, and smiled through the tears. "It reminds me of home, the cozy cabin, space for a garden, a stream flowing through. I can be very happy here. We will labor together to make it our new home. It's just…"

"It doesn't have our mother," I said slowly.

She nodded, fresh tears flowing. "I'm sorry. You have worked so hard here. I don't want you to think I don't appreciate that."

"No, of course, I don't think that," I said.

"But, Ardath," she said, raising her eyes to look into mine, "you are engaged to marry James. What will I do then?"

"Well, we will all live together, then." In truth, I preferred not to think about James, since those thoughts reminded me of danger he was in. There was nothing I could do about that, so I had determined to put the worried thoughts out of my mind.

"But he may have other ideas, want only to be alone with you. This house does not plan for that; forgive me for saying it…," she said.

"Why, if he wants that, we can build another room on the back. After living in the wilderness, this should seem a mansion!" I said. I hope I didn't reveal the discomfort this thought gave me. It rushed in on me like an unexpected wave; I truly had not consulted him, nor had I thought of making room for him, during the planning of this house. Of course, he had not been here, but still, this did not portend well for our future.

Once again, I questioned my decisions about James. In truth, Gwyn thought about his opinion more than I did. The "we" in my life consisted of myself, Gwyn, and Mrs. Perry, if I faced up to it.

Gwyn tugged at my sleeve. "Ardath, you seem stricken."

"It is the same problem as before. I keep believing I have solved it, but I really am only diverting myself," I said. "I don't think of myself as engaged. I don't think of myself as someone's wife. Perhaps every woman goes through something like this?"

Gwyn, honest Gwyn, looked doubtful. "I don't know about that, Ardath. It seems that he should be the main thing on your mind."

We were distracted by a call from the yard and walked quickly back down the path.

"Miss Rhys," said a jovial voice. It was Franklin. "I've come to see your new home. Ah, both the lovely ladies are here. How fortunate I am!"

"Mr. Franklin, how are you?" said Gwyn, dropping a small curtsy. I smiled and bowed for him.

"I hope you don't mind my nosiness in dropping by to see your progress," he said.

"Oh, not at all," I said. "Please be welcome. Draw up a stump."

He grinned at that. "I can't stay. I came to let you know that I have not heard anything from my personal contacts or from my articles in the *Gazette* concerning your mother. Please do not be disheartened, however, as communication moves very slowly. I still hope to hear something."

"We understand. Thank you for looking," I said, sighing. He sighed in sympathy.

"Also, my bitch has whelped. The puppies are quite adorable, if you would like to see them," he said, swiveling his gaze toward Gwyn, who smiled in delight. "Just go by anytime and Mrs. Franklin will show them to you," he added.

"Well, we were just exploring our creek. Would you like to see it?" I asked.

"Yes, indeed," he said. Off we went, retracing our steps. Franklin was very polite about the bucket system we had planned but had another idea. He pointed toward the pool.

"If you submerged a pump here, you could perhaps pump water into a pipe that would bring it to the house, where it could be stored in a barrel outside your door for easy use. Then you would not have to make a trip with a bucket each time. I have such a pump that you could try," he said. Once again, I admired his endless clever ideas.

"Thank you. That's a splendid idea! It would save us much unnecessary work in the coming winter," I said. "How I admire your agile mind!"

"I'll bring the pump by when I next have an opportunity," he said. "Meanwhile, if you will excuse us, Miss Gwyn, I would like to speak alone with your sister for a moment."

"Of course," said Gwyn. She went to speak with Omar.

He watched her go, then turned to me. "I am so sorry about the injuries your sister sustained at the hand of your aunt."

"Then you don't believe it was our fault."

"No, but I want to warn you, others do believe it still, those who think a Christian woman would never lie. Myself, I see that people are the same, regardless of religion, some good and some bad, who nevertheless profess to be good."

"I have been worried that this scandal would redound badly upon Major James, as I am promised to him."

"Yes, I heard that you are." He studied my face, but I looked down to hide my confusion. "I hear many things but repeat few," he said slowly. "You could tell me what is going on, if you wish, and it would not reach another ear."

"Thank you. You can probably see that I am still confused. There seems no easy answer to this. I just do not see myself as a wife."

"What do you plan?" he asked.

"Most likely, I shall simply explode," I said, smiling at myself. After all, this was not a world-shattering situation. "I shall marry him, or if I am very honest, I shall call it off. Of course, that is easier to say than to do when he is near."

"You will regret not being honest, I think, because you are an honest person."

"Either way, I may break his heart. I don't think I could stand that. He doesn't deserve that."

"You *could* tell him everything and let him decide what he wants to do under the circumstances. You are not the only one who needs to make a decision; he does too," he pointed out.

"Mr. Franklin, has anyone told you how very wise you are?" I asked.

"Modesty prohibits me from saying," he replied with a slow smile. If he were younger and unattached, in that moment, I'd have had no problem marrying Franklin!

CHAPTER 46

October to November 1751
Gwyn

THE SNOWS CAME EARLY and steadily that year. Their white blossoms fell silently over woods and houses, muffling the sound of hammers at our house site, for, of course, the house was not done yet. We had a roof, thank goodness, and sturdy walls, doors in place, and window holes with shutters attached and firmly closed. Omar and John still worked on the floors. Ardath had agreed that we needed them for the winter, even if we had to delay our move.

The Africans slept in the house now. The chimney provided warmth, especially in the loft. They were on-site to start work each morning.

I helped Ibrahim in the apothecary. It was interesting work and very busy, as the weather became colder, with agues and lung fevers starting to abound. I learned much from watching Ibrahim and often fetching the ingredients needed for his patients or assisting him as another pair of hands. Many of Philadelphia's society came to him and seemed quite content to, despite his skin color and religion. It was a simple fact: his cures worked better than the bloodletting that many doctors preferred. He even began to be called to houses for those unable to come to the shop. Most patients could pay, usually in Spanish silver dollars or paper money, and our business was therefore financially successful, which pleased Ardath and Gregory.

When it came to getting help for their illnesses, folk didn't let rumors about Ardath and me get in the way. The subject never came up at the shop. I also received a note one day from my uncle, delivered to the apothecary. In it, he apologized for his rudeness at our last contact and hoped to renew our relationship at some future time. I was glad that he would not shun me completely and wondered if he had been swayed by my words or Mrs. Perry's. I remained cautious, however, having no wish to be hurt by him again. I sent Uncle a return note but decided to let time pass before seeing him.

Although I was out and about, I never saw Gregory. I didn't quite know what was happening to us. He only came to see me at night, and not often.

"How are you feeling?" he asked as we sat by the apothecary fire on one of his rare visits.

I looked at the sewing in my lap. I always sat on his left, trying to keep the injured side of my face away from him. "I feel well, thank you," I said. "And you?"

"Well, but tired. If I am not working, I am meeting potential clients in taverns or homes. It can be tedious, but I must do it to increase my business," he said.

"I hope Franklin has been helpful with introductions," I said.

"Oh, yes, he has. It is right to be busy at this for now," he said.

"Umm," I replied, picking at my sewing, holding the cloth as if examining it.

"I understand that you are being a great help to Ibrahim here," he said.

"I hope so. I learn so much in the process. He is a kindly instructor, as you can imagine," I said. I sneaked a look at him sideways. He sat on his chair in a stiff posture, his normally mobile face a passive shield. On the ship, had we exchanged this amount of conversation, we would have been laughing, singing, even kissing, if we could. Despite the warm fire, the room felt cold.

"It is fortunate that the weather remained mostly clear for your house building," he said.

"Oh, yes," I said. So now we had only the weather to discuss. Appropriate for the strangers we had become. I missed the warmth of his body against mine, his sweet kisses, the shoulder I used to rest upon safely, not to mention his humor and, especially, that look in his eyes that had made me so sure of his regard for me. I hoped it was because he was so intent upon building his business, not because he had tired of me or found me less attractive with a scar on my face.

"Well, we are both tired. I'm afraid I must retire now," I said.

"Of course, so sorry if I kept you up," he said. Hat in hand, he hardly looked at me as he rose and made a swift exit.

I was horribly upset when I thought about Gregory, so I tried to concentrate on work as Ardath would do. I was certainly weary enough at the end of a busy day to sleep well, which was a blessing. I was also becoming aware that I could learn quickly and be useful, which made me feel more sure of myself. It helped that Ardath was absorbed by the house building and was gone to the site early every day. I was not constantly reminded of her natural superiority in almost every aspect of our life.

Mrs. Perry kept house at the shop for Ibrahim, Ardath, and me. She and I sewed by the shop fire and by candlelight after supper each night. Even when the glass and shutters were in place, we would need the curtains to shut out the cold and wind and to add some spice to the caramel color of the log walls.

"I'm really glad that we found some heavy cotton fabric in this rich red color, Mrs. P," I said one night.

"I love it myself," she said. "You are showing yourself quite skillful in sewing, by the way. I had no idea you had such talent."

"Oh, Mrs. P, you are so kind to me, always," I said, "but you are the skillful one. Do you ever think of being a seamstress? Philadelphia will become a fashionable city soon. Already, Franklin presses the proprietors for paved streets. Who knows what civilization might follow!"

Mrs. Perry chuckled as she pulled the bright thread through the cloth. "In fact, I do think of it. I dream of my own shop where the ladies may come to get their frocks rather than wait for gowns from France or England. But we have been too busy so far to really act on it. When we move and get ourselves settled, I can imagine myself sewing in our front room by the fire to keep my hands warm. I have some designs in mind. I have seen drawings for sale in the marketplace…" She shifted on the hard stool we used by the apothecary fire. She wiped pearls of sweat from her ruddy forehead with the back of her wrist.

"You have been a constant blessing to us! Please let us help you get a shop," I said. "I just know that you would be a great success!"

"Perhaps we could talk about it in the spring. This fall and winter, we will have plenty to do at home," she said.

We resumed our sewing in companionable silence. After a pause, I asked her what she thought might have happened to Major James. "We should have heard something by now, don't you think? I daren't bring it up with Ardath, as it is a sore subject. He's on a very dangerous mission, after all."

Her bright eyes fixed on mine. "Do you still fancy him?" she asked. She asked it gently, but still!

"Oh, no, no, not like that. He's to be my brother is all." I could feel the heat rising up my neck and across my face. I seemed to worry about him more than Ardath did, that was true, but it was just my nature to worry, wasn't it? I bent my head to my work again, but I was filled with consternation. I thought I had thrown off all desire for James long ago. I had to admit that I did think of him out in the forest. He would be as stealthy as a panther, prepared for any danger, melting between the trees like a forest fay. I groaned. My thoughts were like some piece of pathetic poetry.

"I wonder," said Mrs. Perry, changing the subject gracefully, "if it is too late in the season to engage a long-hunter to get venison for us? It makes the most tasty stew, in my mind."

"I don't think it would be too late to get fresh meat. I certainly never want to eat salt pork again. In the spring, we could buy animals of our own. Chickens!" I exclaimed. "And their manure will be excellent for the garden." Suddenly, I was struck by it. We were to have our own house and garden. We truly were rich! Mother would be proud to know how we prospered here in the New World. The thought of her drove off my enthusiasm. I sat in silence, my red cloth lying forgotten in my lap.

*****

Our moving day had finally arrived. Ardath had told us at a certain point that we must wait until all was finished to her satisfaction at the house before she would reveal it to us. This only increased the excitement we felt. It was an important day for us, the one that most signified our independence. Even the weather cooperated with us that day, as we moved our few personal possessions by pull cart up streets empty of snow, under blue skies. Though it was now November, we were having a brief break from the storms that had beset us all the past month.

Nevertheless, we were very happy that our housewarming gift from Omar was a pair of snowshoes for each of us, even Mrs. Perry. We grasped them gleefully. He presented us with these before we started down the narrow path to the house. We needed them to get through the snow that had not melted, because close-hugging bushes shadowed the path. When we came to it, the house looked settled in its spot, enclosed by the dark-green rhododendron, bright hollies, and feathery firs. Smoke curled from its chimneys. We did an impromptu dance on our long front porch, waving the snowshoes around like batons and stamping on the wooden floors to make a great pounding sound as we cleaned our boots.

Ardath led the way inside. The floors gleamed with polish, which left a lemony smell in the air. She had hung our red curtains over the real glass windows, letting in a lovely pinkish light. Our small table with its oil lamp, three big cushioned chairs, and a chest inlaid with mother-of-pearl completed the furnishings. Though the furniture was sparse, it was of good quality. I had helped choose these, but they looked even better in place than at the cabinet-maker's shop. A cozy fire burned in the front fireplace.

Ardath pulled away the heavy off-white curtain that divided the room. At the far end, the hearth fire, snapping and crackling, beckoned us. The table stood proudly two yards in front of the hearth, with six high-backed wood chairs around it and a bowl of dark-red apples in its center. Rocking chairs with red cushions sat on each side of the fire. Bright blue and white crockery was stacked on the shelves to the left of the huge gray stone fireplace. Cast-iron pots and a frying pan hung in reach on the right wall, along with all the hearth implements we could need. Then came the door to the rear area, and through it, the stairs to the sleeping rooms. A beautiful walnut hutch stood in the corner to the right of the door; it included a pie safe with tin doors. I was proud of helping Ardath find it and collecting the kitchen implements. Seeing it all in order was enough to make me hold my breath! It was almost enough to make me want to cook.

Then I chanced to look up, for the biggest surprise of all. The sleeping loft was enclosed, a real room instead of an open loft, made with boards similar to those of the floor. I ran to the stairs. At the top floor landing, another surprise awaited, for the "loft" had two rooms, each opening onto the chimney's heat from both sides of it, but with doors that could be closed off for privacy. One room had a large bed, ample enough for two people; that would be for Ardath and James. The other, for Mrs. Perry and me, had two smaller beds.

"Oh, Ardath," I said to her. She had come right behind me to witness my surprise. "What else do you have to surprise me with? No wonder you made me stay away so long!"

"Hmm, well, I wanted you to know that I can plan ahead in my life, after all, and make room for James," she said, smiling. I laughed at her. "Come back down now. I'll show you the rest," she said.

We clattered down the stairs. I stopped to notice that the door off the hearth area did not open onto a mere hallway but onto a large storage space, with shelves for jars of food or whatever we might wish to keep there. Furthermore, there was an enclosed passage that led from that room out toward the yard. Ardath had had the carpenters build a passage to the stone necessary. No tromping through the snow in frigid winter nights for us! That wasn't the end either. On the other side of the stairs, I noticed yet another door. This connected to a room about the size of the storeroom, which was empty and had a dirt floor.

I looked at Ardath, who had been beaming at my surprised delight. "This can be for animals in the winters until we build a barn, or if we decide to have only a few of them."

"I am overcome," I said, throwing myself at her with abandon for a big hug, which she returned. She was warm and sturdy, her arms and back hard-muscled from all her physical work. She smelled of soap and eagerness.

She took both my hands in her rougher ones and continued. "The animal room can be for the dog at night, unless you want to have him in your bed."

Now I was more than overwhelmed with her generosity. "We can have a dog, truly?"

She grinned at me. "You know that Franklin's dog had puppies several months ago," she said. "Although we haven't seen them, he says we are sure to admire them. Of course, you would have to pick one. You *know* we need a watchdog." She pursed her lips to keep the smile in, but I wasn't fooled. She had wanted all this for me even more than she wanted it for herself.

CHAPTER 47

Early June 1751
Carys

I AWOKE IN PITCH-DARK. Like a wounded animal, I dared not move or cry out in my pain, lest the predator be near and find me. My mind whirled to place myself. I was bruised and torn but could feel nothing broken. A rough wood floor, but not bumping, so not back in the wagon. Movement and stink all around—ah, the ship, then. But where?

A gentle voice spoke. "Miss Margaret, I believe she is awake," she said.

"Right, then, let me see," said Margaret. The spark from flint and steel, and then the lantern glowed above me. "Mrs. Rhys, can you hear me?" Margaret asked.

I blinked in the sudden light. "What am I doing here?" I asked.

"You are safe. Scully brought you here last night. We have tended to your wounds as best we can, with the herbs you left with us. Tell us what else to do and we will. Do you remember?"

"My mind is muddled. Is it day?" I asked. "Where is Pete?"

"Yes, it is morning. They will be down with food soon, I hope. Are you hungry?"

"I…I don't know. So tired…" I felt myself falling back into sleep, the blessed escape of the sick at heart.

As I slumped back to the pallet they had laid me on, I heard Margaret say, "Rest is best. We must find ways to fend for ourselves now, my girls. We must care for her as one of us."

*****

I awoke with a start. The women of the hold were busy around me, going about their morning routines as Margaret and I had taught them to do. They awoke at about seven each morning and immediately attached their hammock rings to a single hook, so there was room to walk. They straightened their shifts and took it in turns to use the four buckets we had for their necessary business. Then, in turns, they swept with the little piece of broom Pete had found for us. I had a brush in my bag, which I had used in Wales for women who had given birth. It was a precious article for the women, who brushed one another's hair daily. It was not for them to feel like the helpless slaves they really were.

And I, well, this time I raised my head. I ached all over, but I must not give in to despair. I had to rise, though unsteady, to visit the necessary buckets in the far corner. Hands reached out to pat me as I walked. Most women murmured in sympathy. I was one of them now. As I hunched over the pot, my urine burned sharply. With a shudder I remembered Scully's dirty hands in me last night. I would get an infection, most likely.

Pete! Oh, no, Pete was hurt, and how could I help him, and where was my bag?

I must take one thing at a time. I wiped myself with a nearby rag. Someone had put me into one of her unbleached shifts. It was loose and clean at least. I felt some relief to be out of the ridiculous costume that Smog had made me wear. Perhaps my best bet was to be as anonymous as possible. Or perhaps Smog would decide he had been too harsh with me, if he even remembered the night before. My stomach turned to think he might favor me again.

A mate named Mick brought us food. At first, I stayed in the darkest corner but then felt encouraged. Mick was one of Pete's friends. Someone was remembering us. I rejoiced at that. I wove my way through the women reaching for food.

"Mick," I whispered. "Is Pete all right? Is someone seeing to his wounds?"

Mick leaned across the women. "Yes, ma'am, we are giving Pete the usual help with the stripes. Believe me, we have all dealt with it before. He'll be better in a day or two. All are staying out of Captain's way right now." He turned his attention back to the food distribution.

"Can you get me my bag, please?" I realized my hands were together in an attitude of prayer.

"Sorry, ma'am, not now. We'll check the captain's weather tomorrow. He's dark today, and we dare not cross him."

"I understand. Thank you," I croaked, my throat suddenly dry. Of course, I wanted to visit Dougie very badly too, but I had to wait to see whether we were to be allowed above decks after last night's incident.

"Are we...?" I began to ask, but Mick had already turned to hurry away. He probably didn't want to take the chance that someone would report him for being too long with the women, especially with me.

"Come sit down," said Ann, a young and gentle girl who had helped me tend to the others in the hold before. Ann was thin and small, with straight blond hair pulled back from a pale face.

She could have been mistaken for a nun. She was sweet-tempered and modest in her manner. Like the others, she had a hard story, thrown into the vilest prison for stealing an apple from a street vendor. She had never again seen her younger sister, for whom she had stolen food, and was worried the sister might be imprisoned also.

"She'll never make it in prison. She's so thin already," Ann had lamented to me in an earlier visit I'd had to the hold. She had been raped by a prison guard and was about six months pregnant. I was very fond of her. Her sweetness reminded me of my younger daughter, Gwyn. I sent a prayer to the Goddess that Gwyn was safe with *her* older sister.

Now Ann carefully helped me back to my pallet. As I lay down, I felt the bruises and exhaustion again. She offered me some water, which I took, turning away the bread. I was too tired to eat.

*****

After the next rest, I began to feel more myself again. Margaret brought me a sharp knife and a mobcap. "I think you should cut your hair off sufficient to hide it under this cap," she said. "Might be better if you blended in more for a while."

"I must agree with you," I said. "It would be a relief not to try keeping it neat also."

So the two of us proceeded to saw away, which took us a good while, as my hair grows thick and curly. I felt lighter when it was done, my red curls bouncing around freely. I felt I could hold my head higher, a good feeling. I would put on the cap to hide my hair color.

No one else came that day to the hold. This made me suspicious that we were no longer going to be allowed on deck. If so, I'd have no chance to slip into Kate's area to see Dougie.

When I shared my worries with Margaret, her brow wrinkled. "Perhaps you're right," she said, "but they must feed us if we are to be any value to them in the long run. It may be that we will get more information from the mate that feeds us.

"From what I have heard the sailors say on deck, we are headed down the coast of Africa to pick up slaves before we sail west to the West Indies. They will have to let us out at times, I believe. If it seems hot now, it's going to be worse soon. Worst of all, there is no place for the slaves to stay but in this very hold. I don't know his plan, but I don't think Smog will risk us getting sick down here."

I was grateful that I had another experienced woman to talk with. And I did talk with Margaret quite a bit. Indeed, most of the women proved good company. Their spirits were generally good; whenever possible, they made light of our situation.

The next morning, Ann approached as I readied myself for the day. "Miz Rhys," said Ann, a girl of about thirteen, "I expect you'll make a mother of me soon now. I'm hoping for a boy, so's he may make me worth somethin' in this world, be a field hand or somethin'." This didn't sound like the best life to me, but she grinned broadly when she said it. I smiled too, not knowing whether she joked.

Nearby we heard another call, from Mary, Ann's pregnant friend. "Miz Rhys, I'm needing you now. I had a gush of water all on me legs, an' I don't know what to do!"

Mary hobbled over and stood with legs spread apart, a look of terror on her face, clutching her stomach through her shift.

"Come, Mary, we have a place prepared for you. Don't fear. We will take care of you," I assured her. I led her carefully with my arm around her shoulder, to my pallet, which was the one we had prepared for childbirth a few weeks ago. I turned my head toward Ann, who was following close behind.

"Ann, get the lantern, a clean shift, and rags, soap, and the best water you can find." She hurried away while I slipped a clean cloth over the pallet for Mary to lie on.

Mary's face was ghostly pale in the midst of the dark. She was all of twelve years old. She had been chosen for the ship because, at about seven months, her stomach barely showed evidence of a baby within. Now that we had been two months on the ship, she was close to having what I could only pray was a reasonably healthy child. And I did pray now, silently and with solemn fervor. "Goddess, help us!" Without my supplies and with the conditions in the hold, it had to go smoothly if mother and child were to live.

Ann hurried to us with the lantern. The candle was already burned almost to the nub. We must make use of the light while it still sputtered away. The other women, feeling the tension, muttering to each other, brought any cloths they could find, mostly empty sacks they had smuggled into their hold.

"Let's stuff one of the sacks with rags to serve Mary as a pillow," I said. This was quickly done, while I asked Mary to bend her knees and part her legs. I washed my hands and forearms as best I could in the water and soap Ann had brought. I lifted the light to examine Mary. "I'm going to put my hand inside now, Mary, to see how you are coming along." She tensed. "It's all right; you can relax now," I told her. The cervix was beginning to thin, as it should. I breathed a quiet sigh of relief.

Turning to the cluster of women around us, I asked, "Has anyone had experience assisting with childbirth?" Margaret came forward, as I should have expected. She probably had helped with many deliveries in her life as a madam.

"Oh, good, thank you," I said to her. "You can all go about your business. We will call on those we need later. Now, Mary needs some air. Ann, please be ready to help with the food when it comes, and please ask again for my bag. Thank you all!" I said.

The baby lay in a good position, head downward in the womb, so there was little to do for a while. Mary was dropping off to sleep. I nodded at Margaret. We extinguished the lantern to save the candle. Sitting in the dark, I became aware of the temperature in the hold.

"It is so hot today," I said, wiping my brow with a rag.

"We must be close to the hottest part of Africa now," Margaret said. "Apparently, we are behind in schedule to pick up the slaves. Smog has enjoyed his drink and shore time too much to keep a trim ship. He will be in trouble from those who fund his voyages if he doesn't move on quickly. That may explain his treatment of you, to some degree."

"May his neck be on the chopping block!" I said. "Well, except that he might treat everyone else as if they are the troublemakers, not him."

"Most true!" Margaret replied. "Typical of a tyrant!" She shook her head in disgust.

Mick came with the food soon after. He proudly handed Ann my bag of herbs and instruments, with a wink at her.

"I believe Miz Rhys could use this," he said. To Margaret he said, "Ya must prepare the ladies for a move. Today we will bring down the slaves we are picking up in port. Ya will be moving to the mid deck before the night is out."

"Might you spare us a candle, kind sir?" said Margaret. "We have a girl in childbirth."

"I must go now but will try later," said Mick.

After he left, a buzz went through the room. "Moving up, are we?" asked Mary, awakened by the sounds around her. "So we count for more than slaves, then?"

"I suppose so. Here is my bag, Mary. I can't make a tea as I would like but will spread some honey on the willow bark so that it will not be as bitter.

It will give you some help with the pains. You can chew on it now," I said, popping it into her open mouth. She chewed with lips pursed. I pushed the dangling curls from my face and, reaching beyond Mary, grabbed the cap to keep my hair back.

How we could move a woman in labor, I didn't know, but again, I told myself, one thing at a time.

Margaret reappeared. "Might as well be the original Mother Mary in the stable, eh?" she said as we propped up our Mary.

"After all, I have been through worse, such as the time a man tried to beat his wife while she was lying in labor," I said.

"Umm, what did you do?" asked Margaret.

"I had to take the blows to shield her, until I got in a good blow of my own, with a backward kick of my foot to his balls."

"Mrs. Rhys, I know that good trick, as well you can imagine," she said. We both chuckled. For a moment, I contemplated how my cultured, noble mother would view my situation, laughing with a prostitutes' madam in the hold of this wicked ship. She said nothing good would come of my marrying Jacob Rhys, so maybe she wouldn't be surprised, but she was wrong. My girls had come from that union, and they were pearls.

CHAPTER 48

November 1751
Ardath

LATE NOVEMBER WAS A busy time for us, and thank the Goddess for that; I needed the distractions. We settled down in our new home, and none too soon. After a few milder days in which we had moved, the raging storms of snow and its nasty cousins, sleet and ice, came back upon us immediately. I was beyond worried about James in such terrible weather. He should have been here by now; even the colonel was worried and had come by to report he'd had no word of James or Manja.

We seldom tried to go out. The house worked well, with the covered hall to the necessary protecting us from venturing out into the elements, both chimneys providing crucial warmth, the windows supplying as much light as winter made possible. Still, it was a challenge just to get through the winter day's labors. Ahmed and Omar helped us get in the vast amount of wood eaten by the constant fires and brought us water, chipping through the thick ice on the stream and barrel to get to it. A long hunter brought us meat, venison and rabbit, which I had to butcher, but at least it was no problem to keep it fresh, as it froze within a short time in the outside shed. All this I had to direct and coordinate to keep the household running efficiently.

Everyone else was busy with his or her own work. Through contacts of Franklin's and the colonel's wife, Mrs. P had orders coming in for holiday dresses faster than she could sew them. Gwyn had become her constant sewing assistant. They were set up in the big chairs near the sitting room fire, fabric draped over the laps and the arms of the chairs. Going to Ibrahim's daily in this weather was out of the question for Gwyn, anyway. When we heard from Isa and Ibrahim, they were overcome with work also. Many people had broken bones from trying to move about on the icy ground, and there were more than the usual winter agues in the freezing conditions. Omar helped them get to the injured if necessary, pulling them on a sled. Omar and John had found some inside carpentry work, at least part-time, as well.

Ahmed was still very busy as a blacksmith. My goals for spring included setting him up in his own shop. Gwyn had spoken to me about Mrs. P's desire for a seamstress shop. At the rate she was going, she would need that by spring also.

These needs had me spending many hours with the monetary books Gregory had helped me set up. Gwyn and I had a share in all the business the others carried out. Everyone contributed to the common coffers but had separate accounts also. I meant not to profit from their work, but to help them manage the money and the businesses to their best advantage. It was a pleasure to see our common fortunes grow, even though we had spent so much for the apothecary and to build the house, not to speak of the tools for carpentry and smithing. I was pleased that the men wanted me to manage their money. It showed respect for my skills; I felt useful when busy.

Still, as day followed day, we heard nothing from James. The colonel had promised I should know immediately if he had word of him. Every storm that we endured in town would be vastly worse in the wilderness. In the times when I sat idle in our sheltered house, disquiet for him haunted me.

One night, I heard a noise over the howling wind. I wrapped my shawl around me, took up the pistol that James had left with me, grabbed a lamp, and opened the front door. Cloudy breath was raked out of my body in an instant by the swirling frigid gusts. Light from my lamp spilled a golden color out onto the porch.

A man leaned sideways, hunched against the railing, as if barely able to stand. He was dressed in woodsman's clothing with a battered wide-brimmed hat pulled low. Dark blood splattered his clothing.

"Rrrrrr," he stammered, raising his head briefly.

Both Mrs. P and Gwyn stood behind me with lamps raised high. Gwyn recognized him first. "Ardath, it's James!" she shouted into the wind.

With a shock, I realized she was right, threw down the gun, and began supporting him, an icy block against me, while the wind tore through my clothing and his. The three of us wrapped arms around him, dragging him into the house. Mrs. Perry struggled to bolt the door, closing it against the whistle of the wind with a heavy thump. We helped him, stumbling, to the fire. We lowered him carefully to the hearth.

"I'll get blankets," said Gwyn, running away.

James was wet from the snow; his clothes were frozen to him. He shook in my arms in great spasms.

"I'll get tea on," said Mrs. Perry, brushing snow off her sleeves.

"Get the brandy as well!" I yelled as she hurried away. She was back quickly with the glass of brandy, the jug gripped in her other hand. I lifted some to his blue lips. I could see him concentrate, trying to still his head in order to take it in. "Yes!" I whispered to him as he succeeded. Immediately he began to shake again, but in time I was able to get most of the liquor down him.

We leaned him forward and wrapped two blankets around him as best we could.

Mrs. Perry was then able to help him sip her tea. Gwyn had scurried to build up the fire, which now roared before us, snapping and crackling, shooting out sparks.

I checked his hands, as we warmed him up, for the telltale signs of frostbite. I admit that mine shook almost as much as his, from relief that he was here. The white, red, and yellow colors had indeed already shown up in his fingers; I was sure I would find these in his toes as well. "Get basins for his hands and feet," I said to Gwyn. "Heat water, but not over-hot," I said to Mrs. Perry.

We made an efficient team. I was briefly proud of that. Then I looked into his eyes; they were rolling back in his head. "James," I said firmly, "you must stay with me. Don't you dare pass out!"

"Wouldn't dare," he slurred, blinking and trying to focus on me. I could see that he was trying to smile, but his face was too stiff. I touched it carefully.

The tip of his nose was very white, not a good sign. *Oh, James, don't lose your fine nose,* I said to myself. The silly things we care about; he was alive, after all. Nevertheless, I put warm compresses on his nose for hours, as we soaked his feet and hands in basins, changing out the water each time it chilled. Of course, he was clumsy and water slopped over repeatedly; we wielded the mop continuously. Towels and blankets piled up several feet high on the floor, but Mrs. Perry soon took them to dry by the hearth fire.

Mrs. Perry made him a padded pallet on the floor in front of the fire, where he lay. After some time spent getting him warm, we ventured to peel off his wet clothes, now steaming from the heat of the fire. We placed a towel as a cloth diaper around his private parts, which did not appear to be frostbitten, thank the Goddess! We turned him like a chicken on a spit, back and forth, in front of the fire, until his skin began to be more flexible and felt a good temperature. With luck he could recover without losing any extremities. All the terror that I had held at bay for months threatened to overwhelm me. I could no longer pretend that I was indifferent to his fate. The force of my love for him shook me to the bone.

He stayed somewhat awake, as ordered, during most of this, until I was satisfied that we had done all we could to protect his body. Then we placed him facing toward the fire and I, having stripped off my outer clothes, curled up behind him on a quilt, putting my body as close to his as possible to warm him in sleep. I gave in to exhaustion as Mrs. Perry and Gwyn trudged off to their beds.

*****

In the morning, I woke wondering where I was. I wasn't in my bed in our new house; the light was all wrong, the bed too stiff. Something hard was sticking into my leg. I groaned. I felt as if I had been lifting logs all night, just as I had in my dreams. I opened my eyes to stare into dark-blue ones. James! The night before came rushing back to me. He was smiling at me; I was suddenly aware of my state of undress and just what part of him was sticking into my leg.

"James, how are you?" I asked, scooting away from him just a little.

But strong arms were pulling me to him. "I feel good!" he said, his smile changing from merely happy to quite lascivious.

"We can't right now. It is full daylight. Gwyn will be here any minute," I said, gathering one of the blankets firmly around me.

"Oh, dear, how quickly they forget! Have you become a lady of the manor in my absence?" He smiled a devilish, crooked smile, which almost melted me.

At that moment, Gwyn came in, looking worried, until she saw that we were propped on our elbows and talking. "Oh, you are all right, then. I'll let Mrs. Perry know to start breakfast." She hurried back out, drawing the curtain behind her.

We shared a wicked laugh but covered our mouths with the rough blankets to muffle it.

"I have to dress," I said, standing up in my blanket, "but it appears that you will have to wear your blanket to breakfast. Your clothes are rags and still soaked, I imagine. You gave us a bad scare last night."

"I was barely aware where I was last night. Seeing such angels, I thought I had frozen and landed in heaven, which seemed unlikely, but then I couldn't be sure of anything."

"Show me your hands," I said. They weren't perfect, still off-colored, but much better. His nose had resumed a pinkish tone. "Those hands will probably blister in the next few days," I said.

"Don't sugarcoat it for me, please. I can take it," he said, grinning.

"Wrap up in that blanket now. We'll come to get you when breakfast is ready." I went upstairs to put on fresh clothes. I brushed my hair out and splashed freezing water in my face. It was not an angelic visage reflected in the mirror, but nobody was going to look her best this morning.

Breakfast was a celebration of sorts. We were all cheered by James's presence and apparent recovery. He could walk to the back of the house with very little help. We sat him on the side of the table next to the hearth. He ate like the starving man he had been, still shaking, even with arms braced on the table. I watched him over the board. He was thin, bearded, and brown-skinned. Almost giddy with the relief of being alive, I guessed, when he finally had put away his food and began to tell his story.

"I had been out on the trail for four weeks, speaking through my guide, Manja, who knew many of the Indian dialects we encountered. We found, as we had expected, that beyond the civilized portions of Pennsylvania, most Indian tribes had allied with the French, especially those Iroquoian tribes from farther north and those in the river valleys of the Ohio. Most of their contacts with white people had been through French traders. They value the iron tools and weapons that the French exchange for animal pelts. They are convinced that the British are white devils who will take over their land and massacre them," he said.

"But if you were one of the 'white devils,'" said Gwyn, "how did they trust you?"

He smiled at her, his teeth showing even whiter against his tanned skin. "I am fluent in French and pretended to be a new trader trying to learn the ropes. And I had been well supplied with tools and trinkets for trade, even tomahawks. We stopped short of selling them muskets, with which they could shoot British settlers."

"But obviously something went wrong, since it took you so long to return," I said.

"Well, yes. It went terribly wrong. In the last tribe we visited, there was a suspicious warrior who questioned us sternly before the whole gathering in the chief's longhouse. I thought Manja had answered him well about our origins, but later we discovered that he had shadowed our every move and probably overheard us speaking in English when we thought we were alone. After we departed the village to return here, a band of warriors followed us and attacked our camp at night."

Here James paused and pressed his lips together in a tight line. "Manja put his body before mine to shield me. They killed him with their knives." He stopped abruptly, looking down at the table.

"James, you don't have to tell us everything now. Come and rest by the front fire. I need to look at your hands," I said. He blinked and followed me, wobbling slightly, to the sitting room, as we now called our front room. His shoulders slumped. Losing his guide had obviously hurt him badly. I steered him into the softest padded chair and looked in his eyes. Unshed tears had welled up. I sank beside him and held his face to my bosom while he shook and wept. He had been through a great ordeal; I wanted to protect him. I murmured sweet things in his ear as if he were a child. Very shortly, he fell asleep. I rose, wrapping a second blanket around him. I stirred up the fire, putting on several logs, though it was quite warm already.

Mrs. Perry offered to get help at Ibrahim's, and I accepted gladly. She put on her snowshoes, into which Omar had driven short nails for traction, and grabbed a walking stick from beside the door. The storm had moved on, leaving a crystal clear day with sun so bright it hurt our eyes. The surface, covered as it was in a layer of ice, would make walking treacherous, but she gave me a reassuring pat on the arm and tramped off with a smile.

Gwyn was at the hearth, cleaning up. "I put your porridge back on the fire to keep warm. You should eat some more and go to bed," she said. "I will attend to James until the men come." She set about warming bricks for my bed.

"I truly am beyond tired," I said. I ate the porridge to keep up my strength, though it tasted like ashes to me. "I'll go to bed to warm it for James. Omar and Ahmed must bring him up there, where he can spread out. He's going to need complete rest for at least a few days."

I wrapped the warm bricks in towels and went to my bed. They seemed too heavy to lift; the stairs were a mountain before me. But it didn't matter; James was here. Whatever doubts I had about marrying him had disappeared when I realized that I might easily have lost him forever. I called myself petty for my concerns about marriage. We belonged together.

CHAPTER 49

Late November 1751
Gwyn

OUR HOUSE WAS A different place with a man in it. The formerly serene space seemed to contract with James there. I felt him everywhere I went, certainly. The house's activity sped up, and I felt a heightened energy all around us.

In addition, there were soon many other men. Ibrahim arrived with Ahmed and Omar shortly after Ardath had gone to her bed. We had helped James back to the front fire after breakfast. Ibrahim stepped to the fire to check James right away, examining his hands and feet in detail.

Ibrahim nodded to me. "You have done all the right things with him," he said. Our plan had been to take James upstairs to recuperate, but Ibrahim continued. "It would be best to keep him here by the fire if you can. Frostbite is a serious malady for an active young man. He needs to keep all his appendages. Can you manage him here?" he asked, looking up at me.

I was flattered by Ibrahim asking *me* this question rather than Mrs. Perry, but then I had been at his side for many patient calls by this time. "Of course, we will do anything to help him."

"I'm right here, you know," James said in a strong but rather-croaky voice. He raised himself up from his pallet on one elbow, but spoiled the effect by collapsing back to the pallet immediately.

"Yes, but you are the patient," I said. "That means you have to be patient."

He had the strength to grin at me at least. "Hmmmm" was all he said to that. "I must report to the colonel right away, though."

I looked at Ibrahim. He shook his head slightly. "We think it best if you do not go out into the chill again," I said. "Perhaps Ahmed could ask the colonel to come here?"

"Oh, please, I'm fine," James said.

"Major James, I must insist that you not stir from this spot except as absolutely necessary for the next week at least," Ibrahim said. "You won't be a difficult patient for the ladies, will you?" he asked James.

"Oh, no, sir," James said with a smirk. What in the world was wrong with him? His responses were strange, almost giddy. The morning was just breaking as we talked together. We had opened the shutters to let in light, which slanted across us as the sun rose. The brightness reflected off the snow made the cabin look white. James squinted as if in a snowstorm. Something had happened to him other than walking and starving in the wilderness. I could feel it, the wrongness in him.

"You must rest now and take light nourishment, drink the good water from the stream and some ale for strength," Ibrahim said.

"But I must report," James said, becoming agitated. His brow creased, his thin face emphasizing the hawk-like nose. He was a bird of prey again, as I had seen him on the ship.

"Then I will send Ahmed to fetch the colonel. You must rest and take your condition seriously," said Ibrahim.

"As you wish," James said, more calmly this time.

Ahmed went for the colonel after the wintery sun was fully up.

Mrs. Perry prepared a broth for anyone who wished it and insisted that James take some. "Mrs. Perry," he said, after taking a spoonful with clumsy hands, "I have never tasted anything so delicious!"

"Well," I said, "perhaps you should let me help, so that you may actually get some in you, instead of on." He seemed unperturbed by the spill but allowed me to feed him. His full lips closed around the spoon. No sooner was the bowl empty than his eyes closed and he went to sleep again.

I settled to sew in the largest chair, which was turned away from the door and toward the fire. I tucked my legs up under me. I suppose I got some sewing done, but really my mind was spinning out possible scenes of the coming months. Where would James go next? He couldn't return to the wilderness in his condition, with the winter so hard. It made sense for him to stay here, but even I thought he should not do that without marrying Ardath first. I didn't know if I was prepared for that. I set about making myself ready for whatever might come. I pictured James with us all winter, as my brother. It felt more like an invasion than an addition.

Here we were, just now settled and content in our home. I stopped myself, amazed at my own selfishness. Surely, my feelings should not matter as much as the happiness of two people important to me. But I wondered, frankly, whether Ardath would be happier. It seemed unfair for her to get the love I craved when she didn't seem to care about it. I examined myself: Did I really love Gregory, or was he just a substitute for one I could never have? This thought led into another: Did Gregory love me, or had that vanished too? Had he sensed that I had feelings for James? I found myself in a muddle of confusion. I gave up trying to sort it out. I had to let it be.

While I stewed in turmoil, Ahmed had brought back the colonel. Not realizing that I was tucked into the chair, the officer came to James's side. With his hand on our patient, he spoke quietly. "James, how do you fare?"

James awoke then. "Colonel, how glad I am to see you! I regret it has taken so long to report."

"Don't concern yourself with that. It is very fortunate that you survived."

"Manja did not," James said.

"Yes, I know. He was a good man."

"He died saving me. He provoked the Indians so that they would take him first. He died most horribly. They tortured him before my eyes, cutting off small pieces of his body while he screamed. They laughed, scalping him alive, leaving his face to collapse, leaving him to die slowly of his wounds. All the while, I wrestled with my bonds. When the Indians became too drunk to observe me, busy with their fighting and carousing, I got free and slashed his throat to end his agony. I backed away until I was no longer within the circle of firelight and fled with only my clothes and the bloody knife. I left him there." James put his head in his hands.

The colonel bent closer to him. "James, there is no shame here. This is war, and we must do as we must in war. It was a great accomplishment to make it back here, in brutal weather and without aid or provisions. Do not be distraught over Manja, though I know he had become a friend. The horror of war is in losing our friends for the greater cause, but he was a soldier too, and soldiers know they face death."

"But such a death…," James said.

"Yes. It was hard. Rest now. You can finish your report later," the colonel said.

James fell back onto his pallet with a groan. The colonel went off toward the hearth at the rear of the house. Neither man knew I had overheard them. It made sense now, the wrongness I had felt from James. The horror of his capture, the giddiness of his survival, the guilt over his friend's death, all mixed together in a jumble.

I slipped out of the chair and knelt beside him. James had his eyes closed; I assumed he was asleep. I tenderly brushed the hair out of his face, touching his forehead to check for fever. Suddenly, I was looking into blue eyes. "Sister, you were here? You heard?" he asked.

"Yes. I didn't mean to…"

"You should not have to know these things. I am sorry you heard. These are a man's province."

"Women are not so fragile. We saw countless horrors while treating the small pox, I assure you," I said. "I would do what I could to comfort you."

He held me in his gaze, eyes clear. "Amazing" was all that he said, but I could see that he admired me.

I stepped back from him. "Ardath has gone to rest. What can we do for you?" I asked.

"Some water, please," he said. I put the cup to his mouth. He drank a goodly portion and eased himself down again. "Can you send Ahmed to take me to the necessary?" he asked.

"Of course," I said. I tried to move away in a stately motion, not to trip on my own skirts. I was suddenly in deep waters, for which I was not prepared.

The shock of it hit me. I was in *no* way prepared for a grown man to admire me, much less prepared to know myself whom I truly loved, or to marry. Yes, at fifteen years of age, many girls were married, and maybe some were really ready for it. I was still a young girl, not sure of who I was and what I wanted, still looking for my mother.

I stumbled away to fetch Ahmed, but these thoughts occupied me in misery throughout the day and for many thereafter. I tried to concentrate on my sewing, for we could not get behind on that regardless of circumstance. Mrs. Perry was pleased that the work went along well. I didn't tell her what was on my mind as I sewed.

Finally, I realized that I could suffer this way or I could have other thoughts that reflected the reality of my situation better. I didn't need to get married anytime soon, so it was all right if I didn't know myself well yet. Major James was to be in the house with us. Again, I could suffer every time I was close to him or I could focus on having a brother, regardless of my attraction to him. Of course, I would never be stupid enough to make things worse by acting in such a way that invited everyone's censure of me, including my own. If I wanted to know what it was like to be admired but not loved in a married way, then this was an opportunity.

Furthermore, wanting to find my mother did not make me a baby, though sometimes I thought Ardath believed it did. Again, if I allowed Ardath to tell me what I was, I would never have the courage to find out for myself. Well, it was all very well to think this, but time would tell just how much courage I had. Nevertheless, I felt better having made this step toward independency.

CHAPTER 50

June 1751
Carys

TOWARD EVENING, MARY WAS delivered of a sweet girl. The babe seemed healthy, but I worried that she was so small. Mary took to her right away, and the babe took the teat avidly. All this was good, because we heard the "Land ahoy" and, shortly after, the anchor splashing into the water. We were at the port to pick up slaves, and we had to move. Mick brought us candles. The women had already packed what little they had.

Now we climbed up the stairs, I balancing the pallet for birthings over my back and clutching my bag in one hand. It was an awkward trip, but I rejoiced, because we would have portholes and, I hoped, hammocks. If they hadn't moved Kate, I'd see Dougie again.

One of the first into this upper hold, I was able to set my goods down next to Kate's canvas shelter. As I peeked around the hanging, she looked up from feeding the baby. All still seemed well there. "Hello, Carys, did you bring food?" she asked.

"I'm so sorry. I have nothing for you today," I said. "Captain Smog no longer favors me, so I am moving here to be close to you."

"Ah, too bad." She looked down at the babe. "Dougie does well," she said, as he pulled off her breast with a smack to look at me, leaving rich milk dripping from the teat. He smiled at me, the first smile I had had from him. Milk bubbled from the corners of his lopsided mouth. I loved him more passionately than ever, if such were possible.

"Oh, Kate, he is a darling!" I exclaimed. My heart yearned to take him from her that instant; I loved him so.

"That he is, miss!" she said proudly. I had to keep reminding myself that Kate thought he was hers. In an important way, he was. But to me, he was my lost David, sent to make up for all those years spent mourning him. My mind flashed to the oak tree under which we had buried his tiny body and where I had visited him every day until I was taken.

"The women from the lower deck are moving up here. They will not steal or harm Dougie, I promise," I said. "It would be good for you to make some friends, since we are all here together." Kate merely looked at me with suspicion in her eyes. I let it pass for now.

"Kate, since Dougie is a hearty eater, let's try him on some pap soon. Would that be all right?" She nodded.

"Carys," Margaret said quietly from behind me. I had told her of Kate and Dougie's story. "May I meet your friend Kate?"

"Is it all right, Kate? Miss Margaret is a kind woman who is very good with babies," I said. She shook her head desperately, so I shook mine at Margaret. "Well, perhaps another day, then."

"We are indeed blessed to have the hammocks here," said Margaret as I stepped out of Kate's tent. "This space still stinks of men, though. I would like to see it cleaned out."

"Yes, hopefully, once we are at sea, we will be allowed on deck to get seawater," I said, wondering how I'd ever face the cruel captain or Scully again. I was sure to see them if I went on deck.

At this moment, we heard a commotion above us. The slaves were being brought on board. Their chains jangled as they were dragged across the upper deck. I had seen drawings of these poor people in the chains, which were very heavy and allowed little movement. My friend Lord Harleigh was a humanitarian, influenced by Oglethorpe in Parliament. We had discussed his writings against slavery at length. I had seen the broadsides depicting their conditions, which were appalling. A beast should not have to endure the treatment they regularly faced. Unfortunately, too many in Parliament benefitted from the practice of slavery, if not the trade itself, and my friend's words fell on deaf ears.

Now I was to witness this barbarity firsthand. My heart sank for the captives. As wretched as we women were at times, we at least were not chained. Further, I was running out of helpful herbs and wouldn't be able to do much for them, *if* I could even get to them. The weight of this dreadful world threatened to press me to the floor.

I turned to work instead, helping the younger women with their unloading, making sure that Mary and her baby, whom she had named Becky, were secure on the pallet close by my hammock, where I could keep an eye on them. I tried to ignore the groans and clanking as the slaves dragged themselves down the stairs, the curses of their drivers, the increasing stench that we could smell even through the stout door.

As soon as the slaves were settled, the ship took off with much creaking and moaning of timbers. We could hear shouts of the sailors putting on all the canvas, running the rigging, and thumping on the deck. Apparently, Margaret had been right; the ship needed to make all speed toward the West Indies. By the next day, Pete returned to bring our food. At least it included some fruit, which I urged the doubtful women to eat.

"Pete, how are you?" I whispered as soon as the food was given out.

"I be good, thankee, Miz Rhys," he said. "Captain had to treat me right because I'm the one what bargains for the slaves, so he been treating me well. How be you?"

"I'm all right, Pete. You are the one who buys the slaves?"

"Yessum, I know how to speak that trade speech. He keeps me on for that."

"I see. What is happening on the ship and with the captain?"

"He be sober as a cold fish, missus. That he be," Pete said. "Since the captain lingered too long in the Canaries, we got to make time now to the islands." He gave a shudder.

"You don't like the islands?"

"No, too hot. Everybody gets sick from the bad humors. All us English, that is. Africans are used to it. 'Course you couldn't tell if they *were* turning yellow, 'cept their eyes." He laughed with a gurgle at his joke. "And then if the disease don't get you, them storms'll come and blow you to kingdom come." He scratched his chest, a familiar gesture in this flea-bitten place.

"Pete, before you go, will they let us up to the deck now while the captain is sober?" I asked.

"I think so, missus. Tell you the truth, I'll just do it while he *is* sober and the men sober too, since most weren't allowed off the ship." He looked around and lowered his voice. "I think Captain don't remember what he done to us, acts like him and me be great pals, doesn't speak of you. The good news is that Scully went ashore with me and didn't come back, so he's been left behind. One too many times, he got too drunk and disappeared."

Pete nodded with a satisfied look on his face. He even winked at me cheerfully. I peered at him closely, but he walked away. Could Pete have arranged for Scully to be delayed, or worse, could he have slit his throat and left him there? A chill ran through me. I had experienced more violence on this journey than I had ever seen before. And I would never know what even Pete was capable of. I finally just rejoiced that I'd not have to run into Scully for the rest of this trip. Thank the Goddess! Now, if I could just be sure he hadn't left me pregnant or infected.

Pete paused to speak in a low voice to Kate and Dougie. He seemed to have a way of soothing Kate that was hard to imagine in a man, but I thanked heaven for it.

I was glad that we could still go on deck. I had no idea what my future held; it seemed best to take each moment as it came. Margaret came up, and I turned to her. "Margaret, Pete will take us up to the deck."

Her sharp eyes were pinned on Pete. "All right, then." She turned to the other women. "We are going up. Be cautious!" Always good advice to the women of this world, I thought, as they prepared to go out.

Pete turned to Kate. Speaking quietly to her, he convinced her to go with him to the deck. He helped her up the stairs as she gripped Dougie. She came last and didn't stay long, but I blessed Pete again for his kindness to us.

I can't convey the happiness I felt to be in the air again. The sun glittered on a dark-blue sea, and fresh salt air filled the milky sails mightily. I filled my lungs with it and thought I might live after all. The captain did not come on deck. I let my shoulders relax and thanked the Goddess for small favors.

CHAPTER 51

December 1751
Ardath

THE COLONEL VISITED US many times in the few days after James returned, but after James had made his full report, the colonel came only occasionally. Though James continued to recuperate in our front room, with a fire always in the grate, we knew that other plans must be made. The colonel again offered to send the chaplain to us for a small marriage ceremony.

"James," I teased him one day, "I would not take advantage of you in your weakened state, but do you wish for us to be married so that we may spend the winter together without burning in hell?"

"Ardath, you know that I am already burning in hell without you lying beside me, so I may safely say yes to your brazen marriage proposal. I should like to stand without trembling for the ceremony, however," he said.

So we set about getting him up more each day, first to sit, and then to stand. He still couldn't walk far without assistance but grew stronger every day with all of us women doing his slightest bidding, plying him with food yet nagging at him to get up when he didn't feel like doing it.

"I don't really want a big ceremony," I said to him one day after we had walked the perimeter of the sitting room successfully. "I want the colonel and his wife, our shipmates, and our household, and maybe Franklin. Are there others you want to come? If we push back the curtain, we should have good room for all right here. Then we can get us both to our bed while the others revel below." I leered at him and waggled my eyebrows, whereupon he laughed and pulled me down on his lap in the biggest chair.

"I am the most fortunate man in the whole world!" he exclaimed. "You have just described my dream of a wedding, provided, of course, that you wear that light-green gown I saw you in at the colonel's ball." He grinned at me gleefully.

"As good as done," I said. And it was. Having him here after nearly losing him to the wilderness had removed my last doubts about whether we should marry. I decided that come what may, we would work it out.

We sent word to Smythe, who arrived with documents in hand to set up our marital agreement. He seemed so greatly happy to see us together that I thought he might split his narrow face with grinning. Gwyn greeted him in a subdued manner; I knew not why.

Gwyn brought us ale and biscuits, then left us to our private business. The three of us sat at the table near the kitchen hearth.

"I rejoice in your happiness," Gregory said to us. "I hope I may be ever helpful to your business and personal pursuits. Now to the business of agreements. This document," he said to James, as he spread a paper before us, "is a recognition of Ardath and her sister as the sole proprietors of the apothecary and of their house, grounds, and coin and the agreed profits therefrom in perpetuity." He paused.

"This," he said, spreading another official paper before us, "is the document that agrees to view your wife as the equivalent of a 'femme sole' in all her worldly dealings. That is, that she may conduct her business without interference or claim from her husband."

"As agreed, I will happily sign these," said James, reaching for the quill and inkpot.

"First, we must call a witness to the signature," said Gregory. "It should not be Gwyn, since she is a part of the document."

I rose and went to the front room for Mrs. Perry, who was busy with her sewing there. She leapt up to follow me. Her face, red from the fire, was lit with a broad smile. As we parted the curtain to the back room, she said, "I am pleased to be a small part of this! To be sure, it is about time you two made a plan for marriage," she joked, winking at James.

We explained the meaning of the papers to her, and all signed, then stood up from the table.

Gregory said, "Congratulations on your forthcoming marriage! I look forward to kissing the bride." He was teasing, of course, as we rose from the table. The others left for the front room. Turning more serious, he took my arm, steering me aside. "Where is Gwyn? I had hoped to see her before leaving," he murmured.

"I'll find her," I said. I was curious why she had left so quickly. I went into the storeroom and found Gwyn looking at the vegetables we had put up last summer. "Gwyn, what are you doing back here? Gregory wants to see you."

"Oh, uh, all right," she said. She studiously looked down, inching around me as she left. I was mystified. There was not much privacy in our small house in the winter; through the door I could hear her greet Gregory. "Gregory, how do you fare?"

He answered quietly, "I would know how *you* fare first, Gwyn."

"Well, there is much excitement here nowadays…" Her voice trailed off.

I pictured him tipping up her chin to look at him. "You are not happy. Have I done something to hurt you?"

"I, uh, I'm confused about a great many things."

"Hmmm. It used to be that you would tell me your feelings," said Gregory. "I feel a distance between us today."

"Well, I don't see you much anymore, really, since we left Aunt's house," she said.

"That is true. Did you think I thought less of you because I haven't been around much? It seems to me that you are avoiding me."

"I just don't know. I know I will always have this scar, inside and out."

"I don't love you less because of a scar so unfairly inflicted. You have never been more beautiful to me. I hate myself for the truth, though. I felt I must put a distance between us while those rumors swirled so violently. I was painted by your aunt as an opportunist. The business that I was struggling to build could have been destroyed by my appearing to take advantage of you. I came to the New World picturing such wonderful freedoms. In truth, many of the people here, especially the ladies, want to be more English than a London socialite. They are awful gossips and influence their husbands with it."

"I judge that there was more to your distance than you are telling me, Gregory," said Gwyn. I was proud of her for answering him calmly. I crept a little closer to the door between us.

"I should have talked with you. I am a coward. I feared your knowing that," said Gregory.

"I could have spoken as well. It seems that we both have been in some confusion lately, then," she said. She didn't sound any warmer.

Once again, I had been oblivious to the pain Gwyn was in. I vowed to pay more attention to her moods. I had been too involved in trying to make things right for her with the house. I hadn't realized that the scar affected her as it had, for example. Or that she had grown wary of Gregory.

"Will you let me try to win you again?" he asked.

"Let it be for now," she said. "We can talk more later."

I was torn over whether to make noise and announce my presence. I decided to wait it out in the storeroom. Soon I heard them move away to the front room. I sighed and came out to the hearth. I would protect Gwyn any way that I could, but I had no idea how to help in this circumstance. I wanted to go to Gregory and berate him for hurting my sister. I wanted to tear his hair out by the roots. But I was trying to learn some patience, in actions, if not in feelings. It felt unnatural, though.

*****

The wedding plans went apace. Gwyn and I decided that there was no need to make new dresses, as we had certainly not had many social occasions to be seen in the ones we had! Mrs. Perry insisted that we should do it in the already-joyful Christmas season, after we had hung the greens and purchased many beeswax candles for the house. Mrs. Perry and Isa had some wonderful dishes in mind for the feast to follow the wedding. Mrs. Perry knew how to make festive bows to hang about, on the greens. We had to calm her down about how *many* bows she planned or every log would have had a ribbon, or three! It was fun to give in to their plans and to spend time I had not had before, getting to know my husband-to-be.

"What do you think about the number of ribbons we will need to decorate for the wedding?" I asked James one day as the others bustled about us, making plans.

"I think it should be a number that will solve the political issues of the day, while changing the season from winter to summer," he said, smiling broadly.

I settled at his feet while he sat in the big chair. "I'm so glad that you feel better, so glad that you are back home," I said. "But I wonder what the Colonel has planned for you when you are fully recovered?"

"We are talking about what I can do in the spring, when I can get back to the wilderness."

"I anticipated that, but can you tell me more about the plans?" I asked, trying not to wrinkle my forehead.

"Well, the colonel understands that we will not find allies among the Iriquoian tribes I found to the west and north. They are firmly behind the French. Even to be recognized as English is dangerous there. However, the Cherokee tribes in the south have long raided their northern brothers by traveling the Warriors' Path along the mountain chain. They are likely allies to contact. The Warriors' Path is now in British hands, so we have had some contact already. More Scots traders work on the southern range of the mountains than do French. If it comes to war, we *must* have them on our side."

"So you might go south in the spring?" I asked with mounting excitement.

"You know I must go where the army sends me," he said, doubtless mistaking my excitement for apprehension. "I will be most sorry to leave you and this cozy home you have made here." He stroked my cheek with his still-bandaged hand.

I smiled at him; I longed to be touched everywhere and was distracted for a moment by the thought of it. "I knew that you would have to go out again. There is little for you to do here. You surely are not worried that we can't manage without you," I teased.

"Never that!" he said. "Never would I worry about that!" His blue eyes focused on mine. "You may be with child by then…"

"Hmmm, I have still known women to manage that, and even childbirth, without their men around." I did not intend to carry a child right away and had herbs ready to prevent that. Few men know what wiles women are capable of.

"True. You are safe here."

"You have never had the chance to tell me about your family. Would you take the opportunity now?"

"Yes. Though there isn't much to tell. My father is an earl. I have two older brothers and a younger sister. My brothers run the estate in England, which is the more extensive manor. We have a castellan in the estate in Wales. I like that countryside very well, and it usually does not contain my mother, which is a great advantage. I'm afraid that she is quite the tyrant when it comes to her children's lives. I suppose that you shall have to meet her one day. We shall try to avoid that as long as possible, for your sake."

"She sounds rather fearsome. Are you close with your brothers?"

"Not really. I am closest with my sister. I have written her of our marriage. I think she envies me since I have escaped, frankly. I do miss her."

"What is she like?"

"Well, she has the same coloring as I do, but she is dainty. She is kind yet strong in her way. She has learned to escape our mother by strength of mind, since she can't escape otherwise."

"Could she not marry?"

"Yes, she could, and you would imagine that our parents would push that on her, but my father clings to her somehow and thwarts the effort. Perhaps it really is his way to thwart my mother." He paused. "Do you still want to marry me after hearing this sordid story?"

"We are far from England *or* Wales here, but I wonder what you want to do if you are reassigned to England, oh, not because of what you tell me about your family," I hastened to add, "but because we all came here looking for a New World."

"I thought of this many times when I was in the wilderness. Ardath, it is so beautiful, so majestic, wild, full of life there. The trees, the rushing streams, the mountains. Even when I was starving, even when the elements conspired against me, it was a magical place. I felt at home as I have not anywhere else in the world—well, except for this cabin. I would try not to be reassigned to England, but if I were, I would resign my commission and find another way to stay here. Why, do you wish to return to Wales?" He raised his thick eyebrows; I don't think that question had occurred to him before.

"I want to see the forests and waters myself," I said. "I have no longing for Wales. I believe the wilderness will hold some of the same charm for me as it does for you."

His eyes had a peculiar glow in them. "We are indeed well suited!" he said.

CHAPTER 52

December 1751
Gwyn

THE DAY ARRIVED WHEN the wedding was upon us. Ardath and James had become especially close and devoted as he recuperated. They had spent many hours with heads together, going over plans, I imagined. All of us, even I, felt more comfortable with him in the house. We had learned to weave our days around each other so that it seemed natural to have him here.

Christmas Eve, so magical and hopeful, whatever your beliefs might be, saw us gathered in the decorated front room, surrounded by candles of golden beeswax. I stood up for Ardath in my blue dress; Colonel Ellis stood together with James. The two military men were handsome in their full dress uniforms. They wore the fancy red coats with long tails that fanned from gathers in the back, with gold braiding as decoration everywhere. The coats were lined and faced with a forest-green silk, and the breeches were of the same color, but slightly coarser material. The white shirts were pristine, with lace ruffles at neck and wrist. Brass gorgets gleamed in the candlelight. The colonel's was engraved with a royal coat of arms, James's was plain. Black riding boots completed the picture. If just any man had worn this outfit, he might have looked like a popinjay, but there was no mistaking the manliness of James or his superior! They were ready to fight for us and protect us come what may.

James did look very solemn as we waited for Ardath. I felt that he was sure of her, only perhaps a little nervous at the occasion. Of course, Gregory was there, dressed in his business finest, but I avoided looking at him. It was touching to see how Ibrahim and the Africans had decked themselves, Ibrahim in a very white turban, the Africans with brightly colored ribbons hanging from every piece of clothing. Mrs. Ellis was round and modest in a dark-blue gown that Mrs. Perry had made for her previously. Mrs. Perry attempted to look dignified while quietly crying into her handkerchief.

Franklin, in quiet but rich brown, walked Ardath down the "aisle." She was simply lovely, with flushed cheeks, her red hair shining, her smile brilliant, and her pale-green gown simple but fine. She looked excited; her delight spilled over to James, who looked at her as if she were the only person in the world.

"Dearly beloved, we are gathered here on this most sacred of nights to unite this man and this woman in holy matrimony," began the chaplain. My heart soared. I am a romantic person; I had begun to know that about myself. I enjoyed their triumphant day thoroughly. Only later did I feel the hole that this change left.

*****

We stayed downstairs after the wedding, but James and Ardath retired to their room rather quickly after our meal. By silent agreement, we all took our dessert to the front room, pulling the thick curtains closed behind us.

After the guests left, I sat up in the front room, pretending to sew. At least I had Christmas to look forward to. I had decided that I would go to Christ Church for the first time since leaving Aunt and Uncle's house. Surely, in the spirit of Christmas, my uncle would not slight me at church. After that, I was going to Mr. Franklin's house to pick up a puppy. The bitch was his dog, a terrier. He said that he couldn't be sure about the father, due to the wanton ways of the mother dog, but that the puppies were outstandingly adorable. I snuggled in my bed that night knowing it would be my last one alone, for I planned to keep my puppy right with me. Luckily, no sounds were coming from Ardath's room by the time I retired.

I was up early on Christmas, gathering all my warmest outer clothes for the walk to church. Mrs. Perry was coming with me. We banked the fire and left Ardath and James their privacy.

"I don't plan to speak to your uncle, you know," said Mrs. Perry. "I shall pass him with head held high."

"How will that help?" I asked.

"It will make me feel better," she said, tugging on her cloak and bonnet.

"Forgiveness, joy, love, Mrs. P.," I said but had to laugh. She had pulled herself up to her full height, which was now one inch less than mine, and she looked like a biddy hen ready to peck out the eyes of anyone who crossed her.

We trudged down the streets, for they had not been well-cleared of snow. When the church came into view, it was beautiful. Most of the tower had been completed and rose high above us over a snowy roof, which set off the red of the brick nicely. It was a more inspiring sight than the street, which had been trampled by many feet into a mucky trench. No wonder Franklin wanted to get more streets paved, and not just for the business. We had to lift our skirts indecently high to make it through.

Inside, the church was filled with greens, which made a wonderful smell, and candles that shed a warm light on the assembled. I found that I had missed church, especially the singing. I delighted in the music of the organ. I almost forgot to be on watch for my uncle, but there he was, amongst the other clergy, walking down the aisle. He looked not to the right or left but wore an expression of Christmas happiness. I actually missed him then. I really missed singing in the choir too, but sang the sweet hymns as loud as I wished from our pew.

The service was a joy. I walked out the door to greet the clergy with my head held high, sure that Mrs. Perry was doing the same. We happened to be in the line that pressed hands with my uncle. I told myself that nothing could destroy my spirit and forged ahead. I looked him in the blue eyes that so resembled mine. Instead of shaking my hand, he hugged me to his chest. "Oh, Gwyn, have a happy Christmas! I miss you!" he said.

I was overcome with feeling. "I miss you too, Uncle," I said, on the verge of tears.

"We must talk soon," he said, taking the hand of Mrs. Perry as he spoke.

To her credit, she did not sneer, merely shook his hand and moved on like a majestic ship passing a longboat.

Though I felt quite leavened by this experience, it was nothing compared to seeing those pups at Franklin's house. His wife, Deborah, let us in with a cheerful greeting. Though we had not met her before, she was as gracious as if she had known us forever. The pups were in a shed in the back garden, but she insisted that we take a hot toddy in the kitchen with her first.

"Perhaps I might convince you to take more than one pup," she joked. "At least three would be good." She laughed. "Franklin loves them all. He couldn't bear to see one go home with someone, but I don't want to be overcome with dogs."

"Should we wait for Mr. Franklin to return?" I asked.

"Oh, heavens no! He is out with Sally, so she won't see a pup leave either!"

The path to the shed was well-trod. I almost hated to take a pup away, until I saw the five of them gamboling about, playing at fighting with each other, a whirl of energy and motion. One immediately caught my eye. He was golden and white fluff with bright, dark eyes. He ran to me and began to bite my fingers with tiny sharp teeth. His eyes looked into mine. He whined to be picked up. When I did, he nestled against my breast with a sigh and went to sleep.

"It seems that the pup has picked you," said Mrs. Franklin. Mrs. Perry laughed.

I wrapped my shawl around my pup, and after thanking Mrs. Franklin, we were off home.

He was the best Christmas present ever! I had not had a dog before; we could not afford the extra mouth to feed in Wales. I called him Auri, from the Latin, for the many colors of gold in his fur, from amber near the skin to the ever-lighter layers that became almost white at the tips. He was my constant companion.

Ever underfoot, he caused Mrs. Perry to shriek not a few times when she stepped on him. I took to wearing him around my neck like a fur collar as I went about my work during the day and sewed at night. He slept up at my neck in bed, his little head cocked up on my pillow. His even breathing helped me not to hear the sounds that might be coming from across the hall.

It was a happy household, all in all, that winter. James and Ardath, of course, were practically ecstatic most of the time. I was happy to have Auri. Mrs. Perry was very happy with all the sewing work she got and the praise and tidy sums she received when she completed the orders. She was only unhappy when Auri peed on "her" floors. I waxed that floor many times in the process of teaching him to behave, but finally he became very reliable about going out, even about asking to go out.

We saw beauty in the snow and even believed that the wild winds that hit the house were simply cause to feel even cozier inside. Still, we did dream of spring.

"Mrs. P, what do you think we should have in the garden?" I asked her one day when I noticed the days were getting a tiny bit longer. "Herbs, of course," I answered myself.

"I do miss leeks," she said. "Do you think we could find some seed?"

"I think so. Remember we saw leeks for sale in the market? We never bought any because Aunt doesn't like them. With all the Welsh farmers around here, we should be able to beg for seed. Maybe some have kept leeks over the winter and will sell to us this spring. If you plant leeks all around your garden, our mother used to say that it keeps away some of the insects."

"Looks like we will have to put a fence around, too," she said, looking at Auri, who was trying to dig his way through the floor just then.

"Stop, Auri," I said. He pointed his little face at me, looked at the floor, and continued digging.

"He's a terrier, for sure," said Mrs. Perry as I scooped up the dog. He would soon be too large to ride around on my neck, but by then it would be spring and he could be put to work chasing rodents from around the house and yard. Come spring, we would all be put to our outside work. I couldn't wait, especially to air out the house and get into the garden.

I was learning much of worth that winter, apparently one of Philadelphia's worst. Without realizing it right away, I had learned to sew rather well. Mrs. Perry began to praise my cooking. I learned that patience was needed for training a dog. I learned that my shape was becoming more womanly; we had to remake some of my clothes. I even let out the breeches that Walt had given me on the ship. They certainly made more sense for working outside; they were very comfortable. After fixing the pants, I made a plain shirt such as a boy might wear. With a loose vest over it, I could still pass as a boy if need be. At least I should be as comfortable as a boy!

CHAPTER 53

July 1751
Carys

AFTER WE LEFT THE African coast, having moved to the middle hold and been given the right to go above decks, I found my life on board had changed greatly. The captain's "weather" remained calm. Surprisingly, he seemed not to be drinking at all. When I saw him, which was not often, he looked at me as if I were some pleasant passenger to whom he tipped his hat. The whole world was mad, or certainly, the captain was. Since he never spoke to me, Pete told me what the captain wanted me to do.

Two days' sail from Africa, after the women had had our time on deck, we again heard the chains clanking outside our door. Crew members herded the slaves up the stairs. A short time later, Pete came in, pulling me aside. "The captain has us cleaning the slaves up above. You are to come with me, to check 'em for any malady or whatever," he said. "They have been stripped bare so you can see all."

"Of course," I said, collecting my bag and pushing my hair under the mobcap. We walked onto a scene on deck that would have shocked me in former days. Now I was more used to seeing cruelty all around, but I still shuddered to see men, women, and children huddled in a circle, while seamen poured buckets of salt water over their completely naked bodies and laughed at their staring eyes.

"Ha, ha, jigaboos!" a sailor shouted. "We'll get you clean any way we can!" He spat at the nearest soul, a small black woman whose flashing eyes said that she was not to be trifled with.

"Enough, sailor!" I called. "Do your job in silence, please!" I was amazed when he shut his mouth, but then I had spoken in my old voice, which carried authority. The woman looked at me and straightened her slight back. Her dark, birdlike eyes seemed to pierce mine. I wondered why she was here. She was not tall and strong, as were most of the slaves, who were destined for rough work in the sugarcane fields.

I chose her to examine first. I thought she would not understand my words, so I put as much compassion in my tone as I could. I gave her a clean rag from those I had brought with me in my bag. "Here, dry yourself." She scrubbed at her arms and legs, blotted her torso, and handed back the rag, eyes still snapping. While she did this, I fashioned a loincloth from other cloths. I handed her this and helped tie it around her waist.

I pointed to myself. "Carys," I said.

She nodded. "Tionga. I know some devil tongue."

"English?" I asked, surprised.

"Yes, tongue of devil people," she said. "Jesus-man show me how."

"Ah. I need to look at you. Are you well?" I asked, indicating her body.

"Yes. Spirits with me. I the Loas for the people, for Vodun." She said this with some pride. Perhaps it meant that she was some sort of leader of the others. I found this fascinating.

"Are others able to speak the devil's tongue?" I asked, as it would make it much easier to examine them.

"I tink nobody," she said.

I straightened up, realizing that I had bent to hear her better above the sounds of the ship, the laughter of the crew, and the splash of water around us. I waved her to come with me, finding a shaded space nearby for examinations. She followed, dragging thick chains behind her.

"Watch out, miss!" shouted Mick. "Those devils can't be trusted."

I waved him over. "Mick, she speaks some English. I need her to help me question the others. Please bring them to me one at a time."

This he did, and Tionga proved very helpful. Not only could she speak their language, but the slaves all seemed to know her and hold her in respect.

Some even acknowledged her with a slight bow. For me, however, there was many a wary and hostile glance before the men, especially, submitted to my examination. After I had checked their legs, I handed them a cloth to place on their genitals, to give them at least a little privacy.

All in all, it was a hardy group. They had been inspected before purchase, Pete said, so the obviously ill and weak were left onshore. There were bruises and various other skin maladies, of course, but I spotted nothing major. The slaves were then herded back down the ladders to their hold.

"I think your sicknesses in Africa may be different from those we have farther north," I said to Tionga, after we had seen the last "patient."

"Umm, I know something of these sicknesses," she said. "Fevers. English say 'yellow jack,' for yellow skin. Kills English," she said, her lips curling in satisfaction.

Pete came to see to our progress. "Pete, this woman knows of the illnesses that we may encounter in the West Indies. I need to keep her with me to get more information."

"Yellow jack," she said to him, at which he promptly blanched. Her upper lip curled.

"Oh, missus, the yellow jack kills a great portion of all the English who try to live in them hellish islands to which we go, strong men as fast as the others. It seems only the Africans can get through it alive. Them that had it there," he said, pointing behind us to the African coast, "they don't seem to get it. Maybe you can find out how to stave it off. I think, if the women don't object, you could keep her with you part of today. In chains, though, mind you!"

"Thank you, Pete," I said. "Can you help her down the ladder?" This he did, a laborious process, but we finally were there. Pete opened the door and stood with Tionga while I went to ask Margaret if it was all right to bring Tionga in.

"Carys, I must talk with everyone first. Suspicions run high about the unfamiliar." I retreated outside the door, hearing only snatches of her speech to the women. Voices were raised, in protest, I thought. Maybe this had not been a good idea. Eventually, however, Margaret must have prevailed, because she opened the door and said, "Let us try this out. It would be better to keep her closer to the door, I think."

I turned to Tionga. Her eyes said that she understood. Pete sighed and said that he would check with us later. I slowly helped Tionga through the door, which Pete locked behind us. I made her a seat of sorts with pillows we had stuffed with rags. Since she was still naked except for the loincloth, Ann brought us a shift for her. We couldn't put the sleeves over the shackled hands, so we pulled the shift over her head and arms. She was so small that the shift reached almost to the floor. She looked like a child in a little tent this way, but it was better than nothing. She sank into the seat carefully, rubbing her hands together under her dress. Her back rested against the wall.

Ann brought food and water, at which she nodded. There was no way for her to hold it, so I put the cup to her full lips and broke the hard bread into bites. Ann stared at her, mouth open in wonderment. Tionga stared hard back at her, which caused Ann to squeal a bit and back away.

"She probably has not seen a black person before," I explained to Tionga.

"Hmmph," she said around her bread. As she sat, and I squatted there, gradually all the women came to peer at her.

I was amazed to see even Kate, who crept forward cautiously with Dougie in her arms. "It is all right, Kate. She is just a person with a different skin color," I said to her. Tionga closed her eyes while Kate stood there. "May I hold Dougie?" I asked her.

"No, I am going now," Kate said. "Keeping Dougie away from magic."

After Kate left, Tionga opened her eyes. "That not her child. She mad. No good can come of this in the end."

"Who told you these things?" I asked, feeling a chill run through me.

"The spirits speak loud around her," Tionga said.

"What else do you hear about her?" I couldn't help asking.

She looked at me. "You not his mother either," she said. "You worry like a mother, though. I am tired. Too many sprits here. Take me to my people, now."

I wanted to ask her more but thought she wouldn't say any more. In any event, Pete was at the door to take her to her hold. I bade her farewell with concern. She lifted her arms for me to take off the shift, which I did. "May the Goddess go with you," I said to her. She made no reply.

I turned to my own care. I had been taking douches to wash out the dirt and semen Scully had left in me. I was of an age when I still had my courses, but very irregularly, so I couldn't tell in that way if I were pregnant. No infection took hold in the first days after the rape. I stopped shaking and jumping at any surprise and was thankful, but still worried.

CHAPTER 54

Winter 1751–1752
Ardath

THE WEDDING WAS A lovely event and quickly over, thank the Goddess. Although the feast was magnificent, we were more hungry for each other and excused ourselves early for our bedchamber, ignoring the knowing smiles of the others. I climbed the stairs with James's hands cupped around my bottom.

"Ardath, you have the most voluptuous rump!" James exclaimed, but not too loudly. Though we both had had plenty of the sparkling wine the colonel brought, we tried to be somewhat discreet, as all the company still sat at the table below us.

"Oh, rump, is it? Am I a mere animal to you now?" I joked.

"Yes, you are my plump mare, my lovely piggy, my little hen, my—"

I stopped his silliness with a kiss that rooted him to the spot. We had not yet made it to the top of the stairs! With him two steps below, we were eye to eye. His deep-blue ones stared at me. They were suddenly very serious and intense. The rest of the journey to the bedchamber was swift.

He tore off all his army trappings, coat, shirt, gorget, and all, flinging them to the side. Then he started on me. "You are too slow," he said, breathless in my ear, as he roughly stripped off the dress, shift, and stays as if they were pieces of gauze. His hot breath singed my neck; his lips were causing chills. His hands ran over my body, tenderly lingering on my breasts, cupping them to kiss and suckle, plunging to my belly and teasing my bush lightly. I cried with wanting more of him. His cock was standing hard against my leg. I ducked to kiss it; it jumped up even higher, a live thing. He brought up my head. Kissing me fully on the mouth, he threw us onto the bed, wriggling out of his breeches. Now it was his hot skin against mine. He kissed his way down my body while the live thing danced against me, beating its own wild rhythm. Soon his tongue was in me, tickling and probing to my depths. I cried out and bucked against him, pulling his dancer into me. It hurt for one spare moment, and then we rocked in our own precious dance, waves of thrills running through me, my head thrown back in ecstasy. I bit a pillow to muffle my unstoppable cries.

After, we lay panting. It struck me as funny; we lay in a totally wrecked bed, both still wearing our shoes, and he with his breeches around his ankles.

"Why do you laugh?" he asked, rubbing my cheek with his thumb. His hair stood on end, and I could imagine mine kinking all around my face.

"Look at us. I do believe we were ready to be married. And I'm *sure* the bed ropes will have to be tightened," I said.

He laughed too. "Let's take off our shoes and be 'married' again," he said. And so we did. Our night together seemed timeless. In the light of day, we awoke, ravenous, this time for food.

Every night we took delight in each other's bodies. We shared sides of ourselves no one else had known. He told me more stories of his survival in the wilderness. He had eaten the inner bark from trees and even grass when he was unable to catch small animals or fish with his knife. At last he reached the first settlers' house and was able to borrow a gun. Thereafter, he could hunt. He might have stayed with the settlers, but he was eager to return to me and to report to the colonel.

These stories only made us cling the more to the pleasure we had together. Indeed, sometimes he seemed to need his body against mine more for the comfort it brought. In the spring, as soon as the roads were passable, he would be off again to the woods, with only a guide for company, and I? I knew not where I'd be. It was hard to imagine sitting around "the farm," as we called our little part of the city. Well, of course, no one would be *sitting*, but the work of the farm would not challenge me. I wondered if Ibrahim might advertise me as a midwife, if my marriage had made me respectable enough to assist in births. I wished I could put on a man's clothes and go with James. How much I might learn of the New World that way. But it was a military mission, and I knew that neither James nor the colonel would agree.

That winter of 1751–1752 was an extended honeymoon for James and me. Gwyn was safe, we all were safe in our little cabin in the woods, and I could relax my vigilance. James's health returned in full. He gained back his lost muscle. Mostly this was from toting wood for the ever-hungry fires and from performing the impromptu dances that we shared wherever and whenever the spirit moved us. He was teaching me steps I needed for balls we might attend if his army contacts required it. I cared little for the notion of balls; I liked dancing for the secure feeling of being held and swung in his strong arms. I was afraid we occasionally created confusion by sweeping too close to Gwyn as she worked in her chair, or by stepping on her excitable dog.

"As soon as we can get outside, I want you to teach me to shoot," I said to James one day, when the sun's rays gave us hope of warmer days.

"To shoot? You should have no need of that here," he said.

"Suppose war breaks out? The French will fight hard to keep the British out of the western frontier, especially the lush Ohio Valley you have described to me."

"Yes, but the fighting would be on that frontier and probably on the northern rivers and seaways they hold, not here."

"How can you be sure of that? And in the chaos of war, might not local men seize the opportunity to maraud and loot even in the city?" I had my head cocked to one side, a posture that I knew beguiled him.

"I would like to learn also," said Gwyn, to my great surprise. How often we forgot that she was nearby to hear us! She stood up from her chair to join in.

"Well, I can never say no to the two of you, or I should fear reprisal of the worst sort!" he said, smiling.

"No salt in your soup," I said.

"No extra desserts," said Gwyn. We had teased him about eating like a starving dog all the winter but were very glad when he did.

"Well, we can start now with how to load and to stand." He went to the storeroom, returning with a gleaming wooden box. In it, two matching pistols—"A brace of flintlocks," he called them—lay in all their glory.

"These look too pretty to touch," said Gwyn. The chestnut-colored wood glowed and the brass barrels shone against red satin lining. "They look new."

"In fact, I've never used them. They were a gift from my father before I left for the New World. Luckily, they weren't ruined on the ship."

Once again, I was reminded of James's privileged background and how much he had grown away from it, or had seemed to, at least. I knew that an earl was likely to be a very wealthy person, with much power, in the "old world." His son would be used to the best in equipment, really in every aspect of life. To marry me had been quite a comedown for someone of his class.

He showed us how to oil the pistols and clean the barrels. Next, he pulled out the ball and black powder they would be loaded with, including the bit of cloth that went in with the ball. "I show you all this, but I want you to be aware of how dangerous these guns are. They are as likely to flash and burn you as they are to fire. The powder must be dry, or they will fail to fire at all. They are not accurate past a very close range, but if you can startle your enemy or cut them down with the first shot, you have gained something. You must practice reloading to gain speed, or your foe will be on you while you try to load."

"Hmm," I said. "Wouldn't be very useful for hunting, then."

"That's correct," he said. "For that, a musket is better, but also harder to use. They have a kick that might knock you over. Since you must sight along the barrel, the explosion is deafening and a flash in the pan could blind or disfigure you. Also, you alert the enemy to your position if he can't otherwise see you."

"The Indians seem eager to get them, though, so there is an advantage over bows and arrows," I said.

"Ye-es," he said slowly, "the killing is more rapid. The Indians spend many hours learning both bows and muskets and become excellent shots with both, as well as their knives, of course." He frowned, stopped talking, and gazed at nothing. He did this whenever he was thinking about the fate of his guide and friend Manja.

The conversation was putting him into a wretched state, so I changed the subject. "You might be surprised to learn that Gwyn and I used to hunt small game with bows," I said. "We never had well-made bows, but I'll bet we could find or make some here."

"Let's do that!" said Gwyn.

Our next days, we practiced what we could with the pistols inside, as more sleet and rain poured down. When Omar came to check on us, we asked him to help us make bows and arrows.

"Many tribes in my country use dese in de forests, but we don't have de same trees as here. I will look for a small tree dat will bend," Omar said.

"I can show you what the Indians use, if you wish," said James. "Can you get sinew for the string?"

"Yes, I will ask Ahmed to get it, at de stable."

"How is your family and Ibrahim?" asked Gwyn.

"All well. We count Ibrahim as part of our family. He is very busy with de sick. Isa helps him, of course, but he hardly sleeps some days."

"I should be helping too," said Gwyn. I saw the look on her face. Sitting with her sewing all winter had not been enough. She was determined.

In fact, the next day, she asked James to walk her down to Ibrahim's, and she set in working with him. She took the pup with her. The pup loved to be out. The shop's yard was fenced in, and he could wander there happily. This arrangement suited James and me well, for we had some more privacy.

CHAPTER 55

February 1752
Gwyn

I HADN'T REALIZED HOW housebound I felt until I returned to helping Ibrahim at the shop. The days began to hurry by. I felt driven to learn everything I could about his useful remedies. For me, to help someone in pain or fear was like drinking a magic elixir. All thoughts of my own problems fled when I was able to help others.

Being out in the community gave me the courage and desire to talk with Uncle again. I had been encouraged by his kind greeting at Christmas. The opportunity arose one day when he came to the apothecary looking for a remedy for the rheumatism that bothered Aunt in the winter months. I was at the counter when he came in the door, shaking ice off his boots and snow off his cloak.

"Uncle, how good to see you," I said. I kept my eyes on his to read his mood. He looked both contrite and happy to see me, which I took as a very good sign.

"Gwyn, I hoped to find you here. How are you faring?" he asked.

"I am well, thank you, Uncle," I said. "We are happy in our new house. I suppose you heard that Ardath is married to Major James."

"Yes, of course, I was most delighted to hear of that union. I was glad to see you at Christmas church as well." He paused. I was proud that I did not get nervous and interrupt but instead was able to wait for him.

He cleared his throat, studying a knothole on the counter; he rubbed it with his thumb. "I must—I *want*, to apologize for the way I spoke to you when I came here in the fall. I disregarded your words for the very reason you guessed, that I felt I must defend my wife. However, since then I have watched her demeanor with Nancy and her delight in spreading rumors about you and Ardath, things which I knew to be untrue." He looked up at me, pain written on his face. "I see that she wronged you and"—he sighed, as if heavily burdened—"that I wronged you too, when you had no relations to turn to but us. I beg your forgiveness."

I came around the counter and, reaching up on tiptoe, took him in my arms as if he were the younger of us. "Uncle, I am sorry that you must face this. I have healed, but how will you?"

"With God's help, I swear to try my best. I am pledged to her for life, and that is that."

We stood for several minutes feeling this pain together. Then I moved back. "Uncle, come back to the hearth and have some tea with me."

"That would be most welcome," he said. He followed me back through the curtain. The doorbell would alert me to any customer, so I poured us both tea and set out biscuits at the high table near the hearth. We sat opposite each other. Uncle looked thin and more bent than I remembered him. He huddled over his tea and clasped the cup as if it could save him.

"Uncle, I forgive you and pray that you will forgive yourself," I said. "You are not to blame for Aunt's actions."

He took my chin in a gentle hand and turned my face to look at my scar. "Oh, Gwyn," he said. "What can I do to make it up to you?"

"We must find a way to be in each other's life," I said. We needed each other, and that was all that mattered now.

He nodded in agreement. His face lightened up. "I have heard from our son, David, in North Carolina. He wants to meet you whenever that could be arranged. He knows nothing of this other matter. He is working very hard, 'taming the wilderness,' as he puts it. He has two children and another on the way. His hands are full on the farm now, but he hopes to visit us someday. He lives in a lush land, very rich for farming, but still quite wild, not far from where some Moravians from Bethlehem have bought land for their own settlement. He met their Bishop Spangenberg recently when the bishop went to North Carolina to scout their land."

"That is an interesting idea. Is Pennsylvania already too small for the Moravians?"

"Oh, no, they are great missionaries. They go far afield to spread the Good Word."

"Especially since Ardath and I are his cousins, it would be good to meet him. You must miss him terribly."

"I do, but he lives in the New World, truly. Sometimes I think Philadelphia is too much like the old world. I think he agrees and likes his freedom down there, but we haven't even met our grandchildren."

At that moment, the doorbell rang. "I'll be right back to get Aunt's ointment," I said. When I had taken care of my customer and handed Uncle his package, I hugged him again.

"I will be back to see you soon, if that is all right."

"Of course. I look forward to it," I said, and I did.

*****

March 1751

Spring was trying to arrive! The days got longer, and my dreams turned to the garden. Ahmed had claimed old manure from the stable that he helped us spread out in the intended garden plot, so that our yard smelled like a barnyard, a good smell to my nose. I was excited about looking for chicks to raise, and little pigs, and perhaps a goat for the milk. We were *rich* in dreams!

The mud from snowmelt made mock of those dreams, though, or perhaps I should say made muck! My boots were continuously filthy. Walking to the shop, I must use two hands to pick up my long skirts. This was one time I didn't begrudge Auri the four feet he must put down, in mud. From a ball of fur, he had lengthened and grown into a proper dog, not a large one, but full of terrier spirit. The pen we made for him at the shop was thick with straw, so he could run around, playing to knock off the mud. Isa was very fond of him, unlike Mrs. Perry, who was only gradually forgiving him for "the messes."

Ardath was less excited to see spring come, as it meant that she would lose James soon to his wilderness trip. I believe that she was quite worried and would have liked to go with him, as if she could somehow protect him. And then there was her great curiosity about what lay beyond "civilization." But of course, her curiosity must be satisfied with stories from him later. He would not be in such hostile territory this time, we all hoped.

Ibrahim greeted me at the back door. "It's time to dig for ramps," he said. "Auri should stay here."

I smiled. "Ibrahim, please tell me what these ramps are for," I said.

"The wild, onion-like roots of ramps can be used for the coughs and colds that flourish this time of year. Since we will be digging, I'm afraid Auri would want to 'help,' to the complete destruction of everything in his path."

Isa put Auri in the pen. I went in to change to my breeches before we set off; we'd not be seeing anyone in the woods, so no skirts, thank goodness! I tucked the pants into my boots. Ibrahim brought a shovel and two sharp knives. As we walked, I noticed how healthy he looked. He had filled out with the good food Isa cooked.

"Ibrahim, you look quite well," I said.

He smiled at me. "As always, Gwyn, you notice things others might not. I feel very well also. Being on the sea was not the best place for me. I am so grateful to Allah, and to your sister and you, that we are so well set up here. I awake with a great desire to be useful, and I can be in many ways. You are also useful to me and to our patients in your growing knowledge and your infinite kindness. It is healing to be around you. Have you considered following your mother and Ardath into midwifery?"

"No, I haven't. They are both so much stronger than I am." I hesitated.

"I think that you underestimate yourself," he said. He stopped walking to gaze at me with those serious brown eyes. "In any case, there are many women expecting babies this spring and summer. We will need to refer them to a good midwife if they ask us."

"I'll think about it. I'd have to observe Ardath more first. Do you think Ardath's reputation is repaired enough by her marriage? She might want to work, especially when James leaves," I said.

He smiled, touching his gray beard. "Hmmm" was all he said

We began to walk again. The woods, though bare of leaves, were full of enough birdsong to bring spring out of its reluctance. The warming earth smelled rich, and the sun heated us as it rested on our shoulders.

Soon we reached the place where Ibrahim had marked the ramps the year before. Though the leaves didn't show yet, the roots would be at their best now. Ibrahim dug carefully from the edge of the plot. We loosened the rich earth, discovering the hard white shafts several inches belowground. Ibrahim showed me how to cut the shaft off just above the mass of roots so that the plant could produce again next year.

"Where did you learn about this?" I asked.

"At Bartram's garden. He has been very kind in showing me many things about plants that have medicinal qualities. I told Ardath about one that holds promise for our use, the ginseng plant. There are few left around here, but along the southern mountains they are reportedly plentiful. Their roots, when chewed, give a burst of invigoration to the entire body."

"You could show it to James," I said. "He could look for it when he explores."

"That is a good idea. We can only show him drawings now, as the plants are not visible until May, but also he will be talking with the Indians, who are surely using it already, according to Bartram."

*****

After that day in the woods, I asked Ardath about her desire to work. She was bending over the garden area, checking the ground. "Still too wet," she reported restlessly, as Auri helpfully dug the soil, sending it up in thick black clods.

"I know you want to work, and I doubt there will be enough for you to do here or at the apothecary," I said. "What do you think about being a midwife? Ibrahim says he needs one."

"Oh, now that I am a respectable married woman?" she asked with a faint sneer. "Control that dog, please."

I picked up a muddy Auri but had to laugh. "Is it *so* terrible being respectable? I know you never planned on respectability, but it seems to have overtaken you anyway."

She looked at me as if to offer a retort, then smiled herself. "What a strange turn of events, is it not, sister?" I had to agree!

So it came about, even before James left, that Ardath thought to pursue our mother's occupation in Philadelphia. But I didn't believe her heart was in it. I thought she wanted to go to the frontier, to be free, no matter what else fate offered.

CHAPTER 56

July 1751
Carys

THE WIND HELD. WE sped on our way. I talked with Kate each day, trying to prepare her for the future. "You know, Kate, that we will be coming to the West Indies soon. We do not know what lies ahead for any of us. We British women," I began.

"Not British, Scots!" she said proudly.

"Of course, I'm sorry. We women, I should say, were put on this ship to be sold to men in the West Indies. Soldiers, merchants, Spaniards, or Frenchmen, I don't know who, will claim us. They won't care about whom we have grown fond of, whose baby we hold in our arms, or anything that matters to us. Honestly, we will be at their mercy. I hate to sound so harsh, but we must all prepare ourselves. You must be a brave Scotswoman."

I felt guilty doing this to her, but it was better that she not be broadsided with the truth at the last minute. I felt she could not survive that. My guilt was not just for causing her pain now, though; it was for using her to help Dougie, when all along I intended to find some way to take him with *me*.

"'Tis not a matter of courage, nor fate neither. I'll claim my choice when it comes to it, that I will," Kate said stoutly.

I didn't like the sound of that. Images of Kate jumping overboard in her desperation, perhaps taking Dougie with her to their deaths, flashed, searing through my mind. "What choice do you mean?" I asked, but she just shook her head and lifted her chin. The Scots I had known were all the same, proud to the point of defying reality! I couldn't imagine how she would fare if sold to a man. The only man I had ever seen her converse with was Pete, who was extremely gentle with her.

I spent time now with Tionga as well, partly under the guise of getting information about tropical fevers. In truth, they all had about the same symptoms: fever, chills, vomiting, muscle pains, headaches. If the symptoms progressed, or returned with a vengeance, they seemed to destroy the liver, resulting in a yellow bile that spread throughout the body, a harbinger of death.

She confirmed Pete's thought, that those who had survived a certain fever did not get it again, although another kind often recurred repeatedly when a person's general health was poor. For this kind of fever, she had the bark of the cinchona tree. She drew me a rough sketch of this small tree, in case I should find it in the West Indies. She gave me some precious pieces of the bark as well. Over all, it seemed that little else could be done for someone with the fevers, other than prayer and some willow bark commonly used for any fever. I dreaded landing in the islands, which sounded like a hell on earth.

At last, I had my courses and finally knew I was not pregnant from Scully. I thanked the Goddess for that. I had been spared from looking at a babe and seeing Scully's scurrilous face looking back at me.

Pete spoke to me about the fate that awaited me in the islands. "Miz Rhys, the captain says he's going to give you to another captain, as a favor to him."

"Oh?" I said. We were in a corner of the above deck behind a longboat covered with canvas; even the high lookouts could not see us. "What purpose am I to serve with this other captain?" I looked very directly at Pete, who suddenly was backing up toward the longboat, as if he were ready to flee, a stricken look on his face.

"Err, can't say, missus," he said. "Shouldn't have said nothin'."

"Well," I said, resting my hand on his sunburned arm, "tell me about this man, or I'll just imagine the worst. Please, Pete." I cocked my head at him.

"You didn't hear this from me, ma'am." I nodded reassuringly. He cleared his throat and continued. "He's known as Captain Lazarus, or sometimes Jonah. 'Tis said that he was swallowed by the sea, drownded, and come up alive again. None saw if he was spit from a whale, but it's sure he had been dead a while, gray face and long white hair and wrapped in seaweed when he was found in the Sargasso. But then"—here, Pete's voice dropped to a hoarse whisper—"when they hauled him out and dropped him on the deck, he cried out and came alive again." Pete shivered in the bright sun.

"But he is in the West Indies now?" I was struggling to make sense of Pete's story.

"Yeh, the *Marilou* took him on with them and turned him in to the gov'ner of Jamaica. The gov'ner claimed he knew him and gave him a British ship. I say that the man must be a devil and took over the gov'ner to get what he wanted. So now he is a privateer against French and Spanish ships, but he raids what he wants and no one can stop him. He rules his men with fear. They all know his story, they do, and are feared to cross him. He has the very face of the devil, and if you look into his eyes, you turn to stone. They say he won't drink at all, but he's always hungry and the raw flesh of babies is his favorite meal. They know him to be a devil still!"

"Pete, don't worry about me! I have suffered worse, I'm sure. And perhaps Captain Smog will change his mind about what to do with me."

Pete looked doubtful of this, but he tugged his forelock and made his escape from me.

I had to take this story with a grain of salt. Turning people to stone and eating babies had the ring of a story well-embellished along its way, but it could be another frying-pan-into-the-fire situation for me and, of course, the delicious Dougie. I smiled to myself.

There was a real worry here, though, that maybe this man was cruel, hated children, and wouldn't let me bring Dougie. But that supposed that I had solved other problems first, such as what to do for Kate, and whether we might escape when we hit the islands.

*****

I was called to meet with the slaves in the hold to ascertain illness, and one of the men was ailing, so I happened to be there to see Tionga use her knowledge of the spirit world. She squatted on the floor. Arrayed before her were the instruments of her trade: dolls made from animal skins, shrunken to a leathery brown, with round dried peas for eyes; herbs I didn't recognize and whose purpose I couldn't fathom, in a bowl; sticks with odd shapes, some like the human form; several crooked bones, which rattled together when she spread them out. Apparently, Pete had let her bring her "medicine" aboard with her.

She peered at the "patient" in the lantern light. Raising her right hand, she felt his face, collecting some of the sweat pouring down it in the bowl containing herbs. Chanting in a piercing voice, she crushed the herbs, releasing a surprisingly sharp smell. She then took a leather bag, pouring some liquid from it in with the herbs and sweat. She drank deeply from the bowl. Then she sat back on her heels and went into a trance in which her eyes rolled back in her head. I kept quiet, though I worried for her. Apparently, she was speaking with the ancestors of this tribe for advice on a cure, for after a very long time, her voice rose louder. She swooped her arms through the air, sprang up, and pierced her audience with her fierce eyes.

"Open your spirit to the word of the ancestors. They bid you speak of your crime!" she said to the sick man. (This was in their language, of course; she told me later what was said.)

The man cried out, bowing to the floor in front of Tionga, wailing and confessing to stealing another man's bread. Tionga raised him by his hair, spit on his face, and rubbed the spit in. Immediately, his sweats stopped and he looked around, relieved of his pain. He then bowed before the man he had robbed, asking his forgiveness, which the other man gave readily.

What I had witnessed was called Vodun, or sometime later, I heard Voodoo. I never understood how Tionga knew the source of the man's pain was not physical. Instincts to cohere as a tribe, to put the good of the tribe over the individual, was a powerful strength in these people while they dwelt together. I knew, however, that they had no say in their fate, now solely in the hands of the white men who bought them. As were we all!

The clouds changed. We occasionally saw shorebirds as we passed by islands, many of them tiny rugged piles of rocks. As we progressed, the waters were sometimes a lovely aquamarine color. Apparently, the sandy bottom was not far below us there. I began to long to set my foot on solid land, though it be the place of devastating disease and storm the sailors thought it to be. It seemed nothing bad could come of the balmy air that blew sweetly around us, the glorious colors of sky and water.

All of us were on deck at every chance. Even Kate came up with Dougie, though still eyeing the sailors with every step she took. She had gradually relaxed in the company of the other women, who had mostly been very kind to her, especially Ann and Margaret.

As we stood one day on the deck together, I asked Kate how Dougie had eaten his pap today. "He is now about four months old, isn't he, Kate?" I asked.

"Yes. He eats his pap well, but it is my milk that makes him strong!" she said.

"Of course, it does, but he is such a big boy. He will be hard to feed as he grows heavier and even hungrier. Even now, he is quite the heavy load," I said, smiling at her. Dougie ground his mouth against his fist; he was getting his first tooth. "See how his teeth are coming in, so that he can have some more solid food now?"

She peered at the baby in her arms, as if seeing him more clearly. "Why, he *is* getting a tooth. I have felt it," she said, with wonder.

"You have done such a good job, but our babies grow and change. They need different things as they grow," I said.

She looked at me. "He won't need me so much anymore," she said. "I just wish my husband could have seen him." Tears brimmed in her eyes.

"I know you do. Kate, do you know what happened to your husband?" I said. This was the first time she had spoken as if she knew he was dead.

"I've been thinking so hard. It seems to me that Donald didn't come back…," she said.

"I'm so sorry, Kate," I said, and I really was. "You must have loved him very much."

She broke into tears, sobbing and holding Dougie against her, crying into his blanket. He held up a pudgy hand to her face as if to dash away her tears. My throat closed over in sympathy. She handed me Dougie, whom I held on my hip in order to put my other arm around her in comfort. Her beefy body felt damp and substantial against my own.

"He was a braw, braw fellow," she said. "He loved me too. We was going to live happy on our farm, we was. I would have borne him many babes." I nodded, holding my breath to see if she referred to Dougie as her baby. Oh, I was selfish, very selfish. But she said nothing further.

Pete had seen her crying and came over too. "Miz Kate, Miz Kate, now stop your cryin'. There be others here what care for you," he said with a tenderness in his voice. I thought now of all the times Pete had asked about Kate, how he had tried very hard to be of service to her, how he had made reasons to see her, even in her madness. I had assumed it was because he was a gentleman at heart and her story had touched him, but now I wondered if there was something more to his actions than simple kindness and a loyalty to his dead friend Donald.

"She's remembering that she has lost her husband," I said to him. He pursed his lips in sympathy.

"He was a brave lad. You remember that I knew him?" Pete said to Kate, gently touching her arm. She looked up at him. "He would want me to take care of you," he said.

"Oh, brave he was, and stubborn one, too," said Kate, actually smiling a little at him. "I told him, don't go back to fight them English. There's only more and more of them and less of us each day. But he didn't listen, did he? Oh, no, but he must go back with his mates and see the fight done."

"Aye, it's a bitter pill," said Pete. He stroked her hair, which had come undone in her distress. To my complete amazement, he took her aside to sit with him on a pile of canvas, talking to her intently and holding her hand.

I took Dougie to the other side. He gazed up at the taut sails and seemed to smell the salt wind. He pointed to the splashing water and looked at me, grinning. "Yes, Dougie, but don't get ideas about being a sailor now," I said. It was a wondrous moment.

CHAPTER 57

March to May 1752
Ardath

I COULD BE SUCH a fool at times! I could hardly imagine now why I hesitated over marrying James. He'd been a wonderful companion for me this winter. Our happiness had been far beyond my expectations. Before, I only saw the drawbacks that marriage could present. Now I could see that it could be managed like any other enterprise one would undertake. That included managing, really preventing, an unwanted child. James didn't know about my plan to prevent conception and kept asking if anything was happening.

James would be leaving soon. I shoved aside my apprehension. I dreaded not knowing that he was all right in the woods. Still, I could see and understand his restlessness. I privately envied him his adventure. I wanted to be ready to face the wilderness myself. He had taught us how to shoot. Next, I needed to know how to ride. Through Ahmed, I had found a riding teacher. Secretly, I had been to a tailor willing to make a leather split skirt for me that would make riding easier. I didn't see how women sat a horse tilted to the side as they were. Surely, they could hardly do more than walk the horse around. They must be dependent upon a man to rescue them if the horse should run. Anyway, they usually used a carriage when just a horse would do. If a carriage got bogged down, once again they must call upon a man. I could only assume they liked feeling helpless.

On the day of my first riding lesson, James had gone to get provisions for his trip. I hadn't told him about my plans, because I didn't want to argue with him. Though in many ways he had accepted my differences, I thought he might like to control my independence more than he realized. Perhaps learning to ride like a man would just be more than he could take.

I came downstairs to show Gwyn my leather skirt. She was by the hearth, tending to the fire. When she straightened up, the red light reflecting on her soft cheeks, she jumped with delight.

"Ardath, you have copied my breeches, but in a way that lets you look as if you were wearing a skirt. Clever! And scandalous, of course, as we expect of you. Has James seen it?"

"No," she said. "I am saving this as a surprise. I'll show it to him when I am ready to ride into the yard."

"Ride? What? When? Are we getting a horse?" Her dark eyebrows practically stretched up into her hair in excitement.

"No, silly, I'm going to ride a *cow* into the yard." I laughed. "Seriously, I don't know if we will get a horse. It may depend on how many times I fall off, but I am going to my lesson now."

"Oh, Ardath, can I come? Please?" she squeaked at me.

"Well, knowing how you can't stand animals, I had planned to leave you at home, but if you insist, well, come, then," I said. Gwyn tore off her apron, smoothed down her hair, and prepared to run out.

"How about wearing a hat? We must be proper ladies, you know," I said. I was happy to see her lighter in mood again. With James leaving, I was reminded of my responsibility to Gwyn and to our mother, to resume a larger search for her than we had ben able to mount previously.

"Oh, yes, good," she said, slamming her cap onto her silky black hair, which only dislodged her bun and left her looking more comical. We went out with her putting pins back into it, arms above her head as she hurried along.

I had consulted Ahmed about directions to Mr. Graham's corral, which was on the edge of town. More barnlike structures appeared as we got closer. This might have been a good place for us to build, since it seemed everyone wanted a full garden and animals, but Gregory had insisted it was too far out. I hadn't had time to look into it, so I followed his advice. Gregory generally gave good advice, though he had recommended putting our money into a bank.

Franklin advised against using the banks, as they seemed subject to the frailties of the humans who ran them. When we were building, I had slipped away from the group and buried the gold deep in an oilcloth bag not far from the stream. With earth and leaves tamped over it, it was completely hidden. No one but Gwyn knew where it was. The silver we still kept with us, under our skirts when necessary.

Mr. Graham was a respectable sort of man who, to my great surprise, wore formal black breeches and coat with a shiny white neckcloth. He hailed us as we arrived, with a slight bow and a tipping of his three-cornered hat. He showed us his corral. Inside was a mare who looked so old she could hardly stand. She was so short that my legs might graze the ground if I sat astride her. Despite the instructions I had sent ahead, she wore a sidesaddle.

Mr. Graham smiled as he gestured at her. I bit my tongue to remember my manners. "Mrs. James, it is a great honor to teach the major's wife in my humble corral. You will surely tell him of your satisfaction here, I hope?" He cocked his head to one side.

"I can see that you wish to please me, but you *did* get my instructions? This is a surprise for my husband. No one must know of it!"

"Oh, yes, yes, ma'am," he cooed. "Now, Nancy here is a safe horse to start with."

I wondered at that; she might collapse under my weight. "But you remember that I want to learn to ride astride. Perhaps you could saddle, oh, I don't know, a somewhat-taller horse, and with the other kind of saddle." I suppressed my grin. Gwyn tittered behind her hands.

He drew himself up to his full height, which reached my shoulder level. "Hmm, well, hmm. I suppose, uh. Hugh, bring us Molly with her usual saddle!" he shouted to a boy who stood in the barn door. The boy ran to do his bidding, while Graham fidgeted with his hands held behind his back and smiled tightly at us, occasionally looking at the sky and making comments about the weather.

Molly was soon presented by the barefoot Hugh. She was a chestnut color, sturdy and quiet; she stood peacefully and looked me in the eye, which I liked. I stroked her muzzle and talked to her softly as I had seen James do with his horse. I wouldn't be able to mount her without help, though.

Graham waved at Hugh, who bent down, making a stool with his back. Graham then gave me a hand to get up on her. His eyes went wide when he realized that my skirt allowed me to sit astride. "Ah, yes, I see, hmmm, yes, it may work, then," he said, mostly to himself.

I must say that he had my comfort and safety in mind. He adjusted the stirrup length. Showing me the correct way to hold the reins, he then led Molly around the corral slowly. I learned that I could influence her movements with pressure from my knees as well as hand signals through the reins. I was struck by how much I felt her shoulders roll beneath me. I wanted to go faster but disciplined myself to learn thoroughly, if slowly. I could already feel how much a horse's strength would add to my own. I chanced to glance at Gwyn. She looked like a girl in love. I knew she'd have to learn, too!

After I had rounded the corral many times, learning all the ways to signal the horse, I called to Gwyn. "Gwyn, would you come, please?"

She approached slowly. I turned to Mr. Graham. "I would like you to give the same lesson to my sister as well," I said. He seemed to have given up on us as the usual students. He didn't even protest, merely shrugged, as a sigh escaped him.

Gwyn came to Molly's head and spoke to her. Molly nuzzled her cheek in a horse-kiss. Not another word was spoken as I gingerly stepped on Hugh's young back to dismount. Gwyn took the reins with a quiet reverence and mounted with a fluid grace. She wore her pants beneath her skirt and looked natural astride. Like some maiden in a dream, she steered Molly around the corral, hardly listening to Mr. Graham's instructions. She instinctively knew what to do, as if in a slow dance with the horse. Gwyn could surprise me still!

When she dismounted after her turns around the corral, her eyes stayed dreamy. "That was truly wonderful," she whispered. "I can see things when I am on her back."

I assumed she meant that she could see farther into the distance, but her next statements left me wondering. As we walked away, Gwyn was at first silent.

Finally, she said, "You will want to go to the wilderness, and I will go with you." I heard prophecy in her voice but saw no chance that that would happen.

"Why, I thought we were settled in our splendid Philadelphia, Gwyn."

She said, "Something is happening; something is changing. Do you not feel it, sister?"

*****

March 1752

The time came for James to leave. I had steeled myself against the feelings of pain this separation might give me, so I remained dry-eyed.

Gwyn cried when he kissed her forehead and said, "Goodbye, sister. Take good care of Ardath for me."

I walked him out from the house to the street, wrapped him in my arms, and said, "Be safe, love."

"And you, my star," he said. He cleared his throat and mounted quickly. He once again looked like a trader in his buckskins, with saddlebags full of goods. The horse pranced to be off, but he held him in rein and looked longingly at me. "It will be better this time."

"May it be a quick return!" I said. With that, he took off at a trot, raising a puff of dust behind him.

I returned to the house and its routine with a slow tread, drained of energy and purpose. Mrs. Perry met me at the door with sympathetic eyes. "Ardath, let us check the garden together," she said.

The April sun grew ever warmer on our backs as we checked for sprouts, still shy about venturing out of the earth. "At least we are not so confined to the house now," I said to Mrs. Perry.

"Thank goodness for that, and look at that sun and blue skies! It is time to air the bedding. Let's go work on your bed first," she said. After that, it was the other bedding, to be hung on the line and beaten ferociously. Then the cooking chores and a general sweep of the floors. Wise Mrs. Perry knew to keep me busy all that long day!

In the following weeks, Gwyn no longer went to the apothecary shop as frequently. She was ecstatic just to be outside as much as possible. Fewer people were sick this late in the spring. Regardless of the mud, the city awoke again. The market buzzed. The ladies planted their herb gardens. Livestock, including the young, were again for sale. Gwyn got her beloved chickens, though we had to enclose them totally to keep the "watchdog" away. We continued our horseback lessons and soon felt at home with the animals we rode at Graham's. I put off Gwyn's questions about buying a horse. We hardly needed one in the city, after all.

Our books showed a good winter's income for the work everyone had done. Gregory had taken over management of the finances. He kept enough of our silver for purchases any of us needed. I wasn't really essential for that anymore.

And I, I was restless. Yes, Ibrahim wanted me for a midwife, but so far requests were not pouring in. I felt closed in, useless. Was I just supposed to wait at home for James?

*****

By May, I was missing James so much that it twisted my insides. I felt I had done everything of worth I could do in Philadelphia. Action was the only antidote for this malady!

On a fair day, I consulted Ibrahim about his trips to Bartram's garden. As we stood in front of the shop, he smiled at me.

"You must come with me. I'm going tomorrow to see more of the medicinal plants that may be out of the ground by now," he said. "Bartram will be packing one of his boxes for England as well. I would like to know how he prepares plants for shipment."

"Oh, yes, superb idea!" I said.

"Would Gwyn want to come too?" he asked. "I notice how she likes to see the beneficial plants we gather here. It is a rather long walk, though, for a young lady such as she." His eyes shone with a certain mischief.

"Well, actually, she and I have learned to ride," I said. "We could rent horses from Mr. Graham for the day…" I paused to look at him. His smile had broadened.

"But you *know* that," I said, as it dawned on me. "It was supposed to be a secret."

"To be fair, Gwyn thought I was trustworthy," he said.

"But of course you are," I blundered along. Ibrahim was *teasing* me.

So it came to be that the three of us set out on a misty morning, Gwyn and I riding, Ibrahim preferring to walk. As soon as we were on the horses, Gwyn's face took on that remote look that said she was in her own world. We'd hear little from her, I thought. The sun appeared and warmed our shoulders as we moved along.

"Ibrahim, you know that I gave James the picture you drew of a ginseng plant to show the Indians, so that he might trade for some plants if they can be found," I said.

"Yes, today we can hope to see some, perhaps even blooming."

"Does Bartram send those to England also?"

"I very much doubt it. I don't think he would have enough stock to spare," he replied. "The real market for it has been the Far East, where it is believed to be"—he stared at me for a moment, then shrugged—"it is believed to be a stimulant for sexual appetite."

"Hmmm." This set my mind to racing ahead. If indeed the plant caused a surge of energy *or* could be shipped to the Far East, it would be greatly valued by the common man and the noble alike.

"If we had a quantity of this plant, could we sell it from your shop?" I asked.

"Yes, it might be possible. We should test it, of course, to make sure it is safe."

I mused the rest of the way through the "city," which mostly consisted of a dirt track through trees, on the idea of growing and selling it, an enterprise I could get my teeth into.

At length, we came to a new river, much more narrow than the Delaware, with willows bending over it, a pretty scene. We had arrived at Gray's ferry, a flat raft that happily lay in the mud on *our* side of the river.

Gray, a young man with ragged trousers and bare, muddy feet, came out of a lean-to to help us across but shook his head when he saw the horses. "I'll not be taking those beasts over, but I'll be happy to tie them here in the grass," he said. "Going to Bartram's, I suppose."

"Yes, please," I answered. "How much to take three people and bring us back?"

"What do you have to trade?" he asked. He looked at our flat saddlebags. "Or if you have not, coin will do."

We gave him a piece of silver cut from a Spanish dollar, and he, seeming satisfied, turned to get the raft pulled across black mud and into the water. We all climbed aboard, and he began to pull us across by an overhead rope suspended from trees on both sides of the river. Ibrahim said this was the Schuylkyll, a name perhaps given by the Swedes, who had been in this area before the English. We came to shore above a large stone gristmill used by folks bringing grain by boat.

Up the hill we walked, through profusions of flowers, grasses, small blooming trees, all overarched in intervals by the large trees we usually saw in the Pennsylvania colony.

"Oh, Ardath, look at the colors!" Gwyn sang out as we climbed. "Pinks and orange, whites, purples, yellows, even reds, blooms at our feet, blooms in the bushes and trees. It is a marvel!"

"Indeed it is, sister! So many varieties of plants we have never seen," I replied.

"We could spend days here, just drifting about," she said.

I caught her eye. "Oh, but we are here for a purpose, of course," she said, as if she were focused on that, but her wandering gaze was not convincing me.

"Wander as you wish, then," I said to her, and the rest of us continued up the hill. At the top of a sweeping expanse, we saw a large stone house with three stone columns across the small entryway. A slate roof and several out-buildings added to the solidity of the settlement. Strange carvings adorned the pillars of the house.

As it happened, Mr. Bartram came to the front of the house, where we stood surrounded by barking dogs. "Quiet," he told them, and they slunk away. He was a slender man with a long nose, and spectacles, probably made by his friend Franklin. A long leather apron covered his clothes

"So good to see you, my friend Ibrahim!" he said.

"I have brought the Rhys sisters, Gwyn and Ardath, now Mrs. James, wife of Major James," he said. "Gwyn has stopped to admire the garden, which is so lovely today."

"Of course. There are many blooms to enjoy now. I am delighted to meet you," Mr. Bartram said to me. "I have heard much from Franklin of you and your adventures. What may I do for you today?"

"We wondered if you might talk with us about certain native plants you have found here in the New World, especially the ginseng you mentioned last time. I gave my drawing of it to Major James, who is on army business in the southern mountains," said Ibrahim.

"Ah, yes, I believe there may be good quantities of the plant there. The Indians say that the Cherokee chew the dried root to sustain themselves on long marches. I have not tried to use it, as I only have two plants that survived from those I gathered before our Indians became aggressive. It is not safe to go to these more northern woods anymore."

"Might we see the plants you have here?" I asked.

"Oh, certainly," he replied, calling out, "William, bring your sketch pad. My son can draw a quick sketch for you," he said.

Around the corner of the house ran an adolescent boy, with sketch pad and pencil in hand. He was slender and angular like his father and had inherited his long nose as well. He came to a stop before us. His father introduced us and gestured for us all to go with him, along the path we had walked before.

There, in the shade of a rock wall, we saw the ginseng, a five-leaved plant about five inches tall. In the center fork between its leaves sat greenish-white flowers in an umbel shape.

Pointing to the flower, Bartram said, "You are fortunate indeed to see the bloom, which does not last long. Soon tiny green seedpods will grow where each flower is now. In fall, the brilliant red pods are easy to see. They do not propagate well with any method I have tried, though. The roots are the valuable parts of the plant."

He turned to his son. "William, please draw the plant and the gnarled roots I have shown you before." This William did, with a deft hand amazing in one so young.

"If you had a quantity of these roots, would there be a market for them in England?" I asked.

"I believe so," he said slowly, "but I will not venture to the woods to find them. Perhaps your husband will bring some back with him. We had best go to the shed now, where I am packing my box, so that I can show you a little of how this is done. If ever you wish to collect plants, I can tell you some ways to preserve them. My wife will bring refreshment, and then I advise you to return home, as a storm is coming soon." At this he eyed the sky as a farmer does. "If you wish to look at other medicinal plants, we will need to do that another day."

We went to the shed, where a large wooden box was partly packed with seed pouches, plants in soil, and a few woody cuttings. Mrs. Bartram kindly brought us some ale. We sat on upended barrels a while to watch the process and quell the dust in our throats.

I gazed at the sky myself and saw the clouds had darkened. "We really should go," I said to Ibrahim, who nodded, thanked the Bartrams again, and led the way to the ferry. We rounded up a dreamy-eyed Gwyn, who was wandering in happy oblivion along garden paths. We made it home just before the skies opened up.

CHAPTER 58

May 1752
Ardath

MY RESTLESSNESS CONTINUED, ONE question burning in my mind: Could we do something more in our search for Mother? Our trip to Bartram's had only made me want to tell her of my excitement about medicinal herbs here in the New World. She would have gone straight to work on how to use such herbs as the ginseng we had investigated that day.

Although our trip to Bartram's was cut short by the weather, Franklin had told me of other herbs that Bartram had discovered and named in an appendix to the Philadelphia edition of Short's *Medicina Britannica*. Many of these were common plants here, though not available in England, such as bloodroot, Robin's plantain, puttyroot orchid, great blue lobelia, and butterfly weed.

In search of answers about Mother, I went one day to Uncle's office at the church. The secretary showed me into a small untidy study, where Uncle sat at a desk, writing his sermon.

"Ardath, how pleased I am to see you!" he said, jumping up with a kind smile. "May I get you some tea?" he asked. I accepted and looked around the room while I waited. No portrait of Aunt was to be seen, but a handsome young man who must be David stared out of a small frame on the mantel.

"I was just set to call for you," Uncle said, handing me a teacup, which I set on the tiny table beside me. "For two reasons, really, to apologize and to discuss the search for your mother."

"Oh?" I asked. "In fact, I came to talk about our mother also."

"Well, to start with, I haven't properly apologized to you. I assume Gwyn has told you of our conversations, but I have yet to see you, and I, uh, I treated you both in a heinous manner, and I…"

"Uncle, you are long since forgiven by us both. Our lives have moved on from that time."

His tense shoulders relaxed. His pushed his glasses up. "It brings me great relief to know this. Now, I can ask what I may do for you, in some way, to make up for not believing in you."

"We are well, but what prompted me to call on you is our mother. Have you any news from England?"

He lifted his spectacles again and rubbed at his nose. "Yes, but only that the Anglican churches have swept the countryside in and around Wales and England to no avail. The bishop of Wales suggests that she may have been abducted from the country. If so, the logical place she might have been sent would be one of these American colonies. That is if, well, I know Gwyn feels that she is still alive, but, uh, forgive me for bringing that in, *if* she is alive."

I gave a curt nod, picking up my tea with a shaking hand. "I have talked many times with Franklin. His postal contacts along the Eastern Seaboard have had no word of her. He has even advertised in his paper, which goes by ship as far as the West Indies. Still, if she is in another of Britain's colonies, I have no idea how we would find her." I stopped, threatened by unexpected feelings.

Uncle got up from his chair to stand beside mine. He rested his hand gently on my shoulder. "I'm so sorry that we have no word yet," he murmured. "I contacted your cousin David as well, because many new people are coming into his area of North Carolina from both North and South, just in case he may hear of something. I even spoke with Bishop Spangenberg, of the Moravian Brethren. A new expedition to their settlement in the North Carolina colony is setting out soon. The bishop purchased over ninety-eight thousand acres of good land there. They will go down the Wagon Road through the Great Valley to the Carolina frontier. Ah, if I were a younger man!"

"Would you join them?" I asked.

He smiled. "It would be a great temptation."

"That is the road James has taken on his way to the Cherokee," I said. "I

314

wish I could talk more with the bishop about it."

"Well, he is a kindly man, and you certainly could meet with him. He is in town from Bethlehem for business. I will send to his lodging to see if we could meet."

"Uncle, I would be most grateful to you!"

"I am just grateful to do something for you," he said. "I continue to pray for your mother and her brave girls."

I left the office with some disappointment but determined not to give up on my quest.

*****

Thus it came about that the next day, I met with Spangenberg at Uncle's office. He was indeed a kindly man, about the age of Franklin, I guessed, with an oval face, a precise mouth, dark, smiling eyes, and graying hair, of a portly build.

"I am most pleased to meet you," he greeted me. "Thomas has told me some of your extraordinary adventures."

"And I, you," I replied. "Your adventures have been no less extraordinary especially in seeking land in North Carolina"

"We are blessed by God to have found this rich land with its many opportunities for mission work among the natives," he said. "We have twelve Brethren who have settled last fall onto an abandoned farm there, preparing the land for the group of brothers and sisters who will leave shortly to make a more permanent plantation of Wachovia. The brothers' diary tells of the trip down the Wagon Road, which is a misnomer, certainly, for the southern part of the journey, as it was a process of following buffalo trails or carving their own path."

"What about the natives along the way?" I asked.

"They no longer dwell in the Valley of the Shenandoah River, perhaps because of tribal warfare. The Wagon Road was the Warriors' Path that tribes both North and South used to attack each other. That is a rich land also but is being surveyed and developed by landholders such as Lord Fairfax, who wants a pretty penny for it."

"Yes," Uncle volunteered. "The inexpensive property is why my son, David, purchased his land in North Carolina also."

"I hear that he does well with it," the bishop said. Uncle nodded proudly and offered more tea. Our cups clinked against saucers cheerfully as we took a pause.

"Major James, husband of Mrs. James," Uncle said, nodding to me, "has taken this same trail, we believe, on a trip to meet with the Cherokee."

"Ah, yes, the Cherokee are an important tribe, especially in the mountains to the west of our settlement. Their trading trails and those of other tribes are often the only way to travel in our frontier region."

"It sounds like such an adventure," I couldn't help saying.

The bishop gazed at me thoughtfully. "We must not be naive about the dangers of such a trail. The springtime rivers will be at flood in some cases. There is often little to eat and little protection from the weather. The wildlife includes wolves and panthers most eager to part men's flesh from their bones. Illness or accident may strike, as indeed it did in our party. And yet it is the closest way to that frontier from here."

"Could you please tell me where the Brethren are from originally? Uncle says that you speak German."

"Ah, yes. We are originally from Moravia in Bohemia, where the prophet Jan Hus was the first of the Protestant preachers, about three centuries ago. We were persecuted in Bohemia until a German lord, Count Nicholas Ludwig von Zindendorf of Saxony, welcomed us onto his land. We've been in the New World this past decade. We long to spread the Word of God's infinite love to all, especially to the poor and most-despised people, who have not heard the Good News. Here in Pennsylvania, we have grown and established the towns of Bethlehem and Nazareth. Now we look to carry our mission to new settlements and to the natives. We live in strict discipline and loving harmony to accomplish this."

"Thank you," I replied. He seemed a kind and well-meaning person, although I couldn't help but be suspicious of those who proselytized.

The bishop had other meetings to attend and left with many courtesies exchanged by us all. He promised to have his group ask about anyone who might have knowledge of our mother. I soon took my own leave and walked home slowly, thinking not of the dangers, I admit, but more of the complete freedom the frontier might offer, which caused a great stirring in my heart.

It was good to speak with Uncle and feel his kind regard, but I wanted to find Mother not only for my own sake, of course, but even more for Gwyn's. I told her of my trip to see Uncle and our reconciliation, but didn't mention our conversation about Mother.

Not three days later, a messenger came to our door with a note from Uncle, asking me to meet him at his office as soon as possible. I rushed out of the house, only stopping to take off my apron and don my hat, and hurried down the busy streets.

"Ardath," Uncle greeted me at his study door, "come in, come in. I can't believe that only days ago we met here to speak of your mother, and now!"

"Tell me, Uncle, quickly!"

"A messenger from David came by swift horse from Carolina," he said, his face beaming.

"Yes, yes," I breathed.

"A woman meeting your mother's description, tall, middle-aged, red-haired, a good herbal healer, able to read and write, came into North Carolina, probably through the port at Wilmington. She is an indentured servant serving as scribe to a westbound traveler in the next county east of David's. He has not been able to see her himself, as the spring planting confines him to his farm, and his wife is due to birth at any moment, so he can't leave her."

I stood, stunned by the news. "When did he hear? Is there any more news about her?"

"The messenger had been on the road for twelve days, stopping only at night. No, I have told you all he knew, and therefore"—his face grew serious—"we cannot be sure it really is your mother."

"Oh." I found my heart was pounding hard. "Uncle, excuse me. I must go to Gwyn. Oh, thank you!" I turned to leave, then threw myself into his arms and kissed his cheek.

"But we can't know for sure!" Uncle warned, but I dashed out of his office and heard no more.

CHAPTER 59

April/May 1752
Gwyn

My heart was full. I could hardly stand for trembling. I cried and paced. I clutched my arms tightly to my chest so that they would not fall off. It had been over a year! And what a year! Now Ardath said our mother was alive and *here*, on these shores. My head grew light, my ears rang, but I willed myself not to faint away.

Ardath was trying to say more to me. I drew in a sharp breath. I felt her warm arms on mine. "Gwyn, look into my eyes," she said and broke the spell.

As I gazed into her green eyes, so much like our mother's, I grew almost calm. It was as if I were already in Mother's arms, as I had so longed to be. "How can it be?" I asked.

"If she were abducted in Wales, she might have been sold as an indentured servant by her captors and transported to the American colonies. Apparently, this woman is an herbal healer and scribe for her master. I'm concerned that conditions may not be good for her. As we know, an indenture is close to slavery in many ways."

"But why? Why?" I asked. "Why would anyone take our mother?"

"I don't know, and, Gwyn, please listen. It might not be her," said Ardath. I would not believe that, could not. "We must prepare to seek her out. By sea would be the quickest way to go, if there is a ship available. Wilmington in North Carolina would be the nearest port," she continued. "Or we can wait and ask Franklin to look into it from here."

We looked at each other and shook our heads. We both knew that we could not wait. She had found me in the garden, where spring shoots were bursting out in the bright May sun. "Can you leave all this?" asked Ardath, waving her arm at the house and garden.

"Of course," I said. Mrs. Perry could keep the house going. She could postpone getting her shop if she had the whole house to work in. Without Ardath here to make the arrangements, Ahmed would have to wait for his shop, but he didn't seem unhappy at the stable. Isa could plant the rest of the garden and watch the chickens. Auri...Auri had to come with us. I'd be adamant about that.

It was early enough in the day for us to approach the harbormaster if we lifted our skirts to hurry, which we did. I had not met him before. Ardath had met him briefly through Franklin.

Mr. Brown had a rounded neck, probably caused by looking through his round glasses, down his nose on his papers, and apparently on his customers when needed. Indeed, he looked down on us as we arrived, somewhat out of breath. He was just closing the door of his gray clapboard office and had cane in hand.

"Please, sir, may we have a moment of your time?" said Ardath, introducing us quickly.

"Ah, Mrs. James, married to the major, I believe, and a friend of Franklin's," he said. His lined face tilted up. I hoped that meant that Ardath's credentials met with his approval, so that he would stay and help us. "I was just on my way out. Perhaps you could return in the morning?"

"Forgive me, sir, I don't want to inconvenience you," said Ardath with a brilliant smile, "but our question is urgent." She nodded at him, as if giving him the idea of a yes.

"Hmmm, if it is a quick one," he said, checking his pocket watch. He turned back to the door and ushered us in but remained standing. It hardly seemed that any business could be conducted in such a tiny room, which contained only one chair.

"Oh, thank you," Ardath gushed. "We must get to Wilmington, North Carolina, as expeditiously as possible. Have you a ship that can take us?"

"Well, as to quickly, no, I don't. The ship going south left today, I'm afraid. There won't be another through for several weeks now, and that one is purely a cargo ship, not suitable for ladies traveling," he said. He must have seen our faces fall, because he added, "So sorry, but the captain is insistent that he will not take women aboard."

"Thank you anyway, sir," Ardath said, the starch taken out of her voice for the moment.

We trudged away from the waterfront, momentarily disconcerted.

"We could stow away on board," I said. "Or you could talk the captain into it, or could we hire a ship?"

"I doubt it," said Ardath, "but there are other ways. We can ride horses now, so…after all, Cousin David took the Wagon Road, and so could we."

I groaned. "Not for such a long ride, surely!" Ardath picked up speed even as the hill became steeper. I hurried along after. "Ardath," I puffed, "we can't ride into the wilderness alone."

"Of course not. We'll take Omar," she said. Had she just said that on the spur of the moment, or had she thought this all out before? Perhaps she *had* thought about something like this, in her desire to get to the woods, I thought, remembering our trip to Bartram's farm.

"Omar can't ride," I said.

"Right, we'll need a wagon."

"Ardath, have you gone mad?"

She paused in the road, licking dry lips. "Omar can drive the wagon. We'll need supplies, anyway. I'll see to it posthaste." She hurried away, leaving my head spinning. I didn't see her the rest of the day.

I walked on to Ibrahim's. Luckily, he was in his shop, at the stillroom table. "Ibrahim, Ardath's gone mad. She wants us to set out on horseback for the North Carolina colony."

"What? Gwyn, take a breath, please. Sit and drink some tea."

I trailed after him to the hearth table. "She, our mother, I don't know what to do…"

"Your mother? She's in North Carolina?" He raised his shaggy eyebrows

321

in surprise.

I got my breath under control. "Uncle has heard from our cousin David that a woman who meets her description has been seen there. We couldn't get a ship from here for weeks. She wants to go by horseback." There, I had said something that made sense. Ibrahim's expression was unreadable, though. "I think she's already gone to buy a wagon, or horses, I don't know. She won't listen to me."

Ibrahim went to the door to the garden. "Isa, please send a boy for Mr. Smythe."

"Yes, right away," Isa said, hurrying off, as if this were a usual request.

"With good luck, we will help you make a plan," he said.

*****

Shortly thereafter, Ibrahim was waiting on a customer in the front. Gregory arrived in the hearth room. By then, I had washed my face with cold water and was somewhat composed. We looked at each other. I wondered if he wanted to rush into my arms as I did to his. He cleared his throat. "How may I assist you, Miss Rhys? The boy said it was urgent."

I had, without any thought, turned my unmarred profile to him. I put my hand over my damaged cheek. His eyes fell, as though that gesture saddened him.

"Please, we don't need to be so formal," I said.

"I had hoped perhaps that you would call for me, that we could resume our...friendship," he said, looking painfully eager.

"To be clear, Gregory, we will always be friends. I have not been able to sort out my confusion, but *that* I can be sure of."

He smiled then, that slightly crooked smile I had loved so much. "I am so glad. Please don't hide your beautiful face from me," he said, taking my hand in his.

"Not so beautiful now," I said, thinking of the red raised welt on my left cheek.

"Beautiful as your soul," he said simply.

We stood in a silence full of meaning and warmth. I sighed.

"I must tell you our news, our hopes," I said, filling him in on the day we had had.

"This is perhaps the best of news about your mother." He paused. "At least Ardath knows that you cannot attempt this alone," he said thoughtfully. "But, Gwyn, what about us? I want to have time with you, to make things right between us. I hope that isn't too selfish..."

My heart filled with turmoil. Here was a dream I had had, that Gregory would ask me outright to give him another chance, and that I would be ready to hear him.

"Oh, Gregory, of course, it isn't selfish. I have wanted that, too, have wished to make it so, but I wasn't ready. Now, if there is any chance that this is Mother, we must go to her, release her from her servitude. She may be in harsh conditions."

"Of course, you must. I wish I could go with you, but that cannot be."

"Oh, no, I wouldn't ask that. Ardath thinks Omar could go, as we need a man for his physical strength."

Ibrahim returned, bowed slightly to Gregory, and said, "I think we should call a meeting with Mr. Rhys and Franklin here, if they can come, in the morning. We'd then be able to look at your choices with the benefit of their knowledge and experience."

"I can ask Uncle to come," I offered.

"I am meeting with Franklin on another matter, so I can ask him," said Gregory. "Shall we say 8:00 a.m., then?"

Ibrahim and I nodded.

Off I went to Christ Church to talk to Uncle. He rose from his desk as I entered his office. "Gwyn, I am cautiously happy about this news that David sends," he said, taking both my hands in his.

I leaned into his shoulder and sighed. "I don't know what to do."

"Yes, it is so sudden that we are given this hope," he said.

I told him of Ardath's intention to go into the wilderness and the plan we had devised at the shop to have a meeting there in the morning.

"Of course, I will be there. I know something of that road from David and from the Moravians. And I know you and Ardath." He smiled gently.

Reassured, I went home.

*****

By the time I reached home, Ardath had two horses, with saddles, in the yard shelter. I recognized Molly and another mare, Sally, we had used in our riding lessons with Mr. Graham.

"Gwyn, I have our horses ready. We'll need saddlebags, of course…" She swung away from patting the mares to look at me. She was calmer than when I had last seen her; taking action always settled her. This time she really looked at my face. "Oh, what's the matter? Have you had bad news?"

"Ardath, this doesn't seem wise. Of course, I want to get to our mother as soon as possible, but we don't even know that this is our mother. We don't really know much of anything."

"That is why we must go, to find out," she said. "Don't tell me you don't want to go!" Without taking a breath, she continued. "Well, if you don't, then I will go on, of course."

"Ardath, please, I'm too tired to argue right now. Let's put the horses in the animal room tonight. It is growing too dark to do anything more." She agreed to that, since we could barely see our way to the back door. Mrs. Perry opened it so that a light shone our way. Of course, Auri rushed out to greet us. I scooped him up before he could bark and spook the horses. Ardath put them in the room with the dirt floor and gave them oats and water in a pail.

"Thank you, Mrs. Perry. Do you have something for us to eat? I haven't had anything since porridge," I said.

"Turnip soup, and it's hot," she said. Her arms went round my waist briefly as she gestured me and Auri back in the door.

I shuddered to think about the effect on her of our news. She, a great homebody, would be horrified to think of us traveling, anywhere, by any means. I settled at our table, waiting for Ardath. Mrs. P soon had two steaming bowls on the table with the bread she had baked this morning and yellow cheese slices beside them. Ardath slid into her place with a grateful sigh.

Mrs. Perry stood by the fire and watched us eat, her arms crossed on her ample breast. After she saw that we were slowing down, she asked, "So how is it that we have two great horses in our house tonight?"

I looked to Ardath to explain. "Um, well, you see, I bought those today. It is time we had means of transportation…," she said.

Mrs. Perry frowned. "Where is it you are needing transport *to*?" she asked in a suspicious tone. Mrs. Perry was no fool!

"Mrs. P, they may have found our mother in North Carolina!" she said, with enthusiasm.

"May have?" Her arms flew above her head. "That would be tremendous news, but…" She looked at me. "Hmm, what does Gwyn say? If anyone would have a feel for your mother's presence, I believe it would be Gwyn."

"I don't know," I said. "I don't get feelings about everything. I don't feel her closer, but we can't rely on that. If there is even a chance, we must find out."

"Horses?" Mrs. P swung around on Ardath again. "You would surely go by boat that far."

We explained that ships weren't available. Ardath said, "Even if we went by ship, it is a long and difficult journey to get to David's land from Wilmington. No rivers go into the interior far enough, and the paths are hardly passable."

Mrs. Perry sat down in a heap. "You are going to leave, aren't you? Just when we were getting our lives together here." I thought she might cry, but instead she rose and rushed from the room.

"Oh, dear," I said. "Perhaps we might reconsider waiting for a ship. Franklin could send an agent out from Wilmington to look for her. He could leave word at the Wilmington postal office…"

"We can't talk more tonight. We are too tired," said Ardath.

I took Auri up to my bed. I tried to review the events of the day but fell asleep straightaway with my little dog breathing steadily in my ear.

*****

Mrs. Perry actually burned the toast in the morning. She didn't look at us or say a thing, just flounced out the back after setting down our plates. I sighed.

"Ardath, we are having a meeting this morning at the shop to talk about our plans. Gregory and Ibrahim, Uncle, and I hope, Franklin can give us information about our choices.

"You mean talk us out of our plans!" she said.

I groaned inwardly but pressed on. It was becoming ever clearer to me how much Ardath mistrusted men.

"No, give us the benefit of their experience…"

"You don't have to go with me on this journey," she said, eyes blazing. "You know I shall do fine without you!" She rose from the table.

"Of course, I shall go with you," I said, knowing that I owed my mother and sister my complete loyalty. There wasn't a question of me not going. "Just come to this meeting for my sake," I said finally.

CHAPTER 60

May 1752
Gwyn

IN THE MORNING, ARDATH was still reluctant to meet with some of our friends about the choices we had. She compressed her lips and muttered angrily. Never before had I felt that I was in charge of a plan, which gave me some shivers. How had I not realized that Ardath so feared and hated having to trust in men, even her own husband? Perhaps our father's abandonment had hurt her more than either of us realized. At any rate, I was determined that we have a good idea of what was ahead in the wilderness, if we could.

It gave me a feeling of safety to enter the warm hearth room in the apothecary, where Ibrahim, Gregory, Uncle, and even Franklin had gathered in our behalf.

"Thank you all so much for coming," I said. Ardath said nothing. "We appreciate that you take the time to discuss our plans with us."

"There are big decisions to be made, but you are not alone in them," Uncle said.

I explained about the lack of ships. "But the Wagon Road seems daunting to me," I said.

"Smythe has told me the situation. I can send inquiries to the postmaster in Wilmington. He wouldn't know every indentured servant who comes through the area. There are many of them. He could send an agent to track her down, though, find out if this really is your mother," said Franklin.

"We don't know if she came through Wilmington. My son is of the impression that she could also have come through Charles Town. Further, we don't know exactly where she is now," said Uncle. "We could send money for David to hire an agent in his area to pursue the man who has her."

Gregory looked at me for approval. I nodded. "Money should not be a problem," he said. "We can have silver available."

"That seems preferable to letting two women travel down the Wagon Road, though women have certainly done it with their men. The Moravians are preparing to leave this very week with wives for the men at Bethabara, which is not far from David's land and is connected to it by an Indian trading trail," said Uncle.

I cleared my throat. "I very much appreciate your thoughts here, but I am afraid that Ardath and I want to go and see for ourselves," I said. I looked at the gathered company.

Every head swiveled toward Franklin. He studiously cleaned his glasses, to buy time, I suspected. "Well," he said, "you would send me to the lion's den, it appears."

Uncle smiled. "You are the eldest and the bravest man among us!" he exclaimed.

"Hmmm, flattery, the lowest form of persuasion, I'll warrant."

To Ardath, he explained, "We have gathered to see what we can do to help the Rhys sisters find out if this is your mother in NC. I know you may have your minds made up, but I think we should look at every option."

Uncle spoke up. "Would not the King's Road along the coastline be a better-settled route?"

"It is a well-established one, true, but the many rivers and swamps have to be bypassed," said Franklin. "It leads to Wilmington, but this woman has been seen somewhat to the west of there, has she not?"

Ardath stood straight, never having sat down. "Franklin, everyone, I appreciate what you are trying to do for us, but we feel it is urgent that we reach North Carolina as soon as possible. It appears that this woman, perhaps our mother, is with someone who is heading west, a traveler. Though I first thought to travel to Wilmington, that would leave us far behind her on a difficult overland trail. None of the rivers reach into the middle of the colony. The

Wagon Road, through the Great Valley of the Shenandoah, goes directly there and appears to be as safe as one can be in the wilderness, the Indians having abandoned its use several years ago."

"This sounds well-reasoned, but how can you know all this?" asked Franklin.

Ardath blushed. "It happens that I spoke with Bishop Spangenberg, out of curiosity about the settlement they are planning in North Carolina. He assures me that this trip can be done, was done last year, in fact, by the first men to claim the land they purchased there. Now, as Uncle has told us, they will be starting soon to move more settlers there, including wives for the men who went before. They can be there in time to plant crops this year."

Ah, I thought, Ardath *had* been busy secretly plotting a way to the wilderness, as I suspected.

"The bishop mentioned to me that that the first men went in November to avoid crossing the rivers after the spring rains," said Uncle, raising his eyebrows.

"Yes, but they probably think that warmer weather will offset the disadvantages of higher rivers," she said. Uncle still looked skeptical. "After all, David made this trip successfully."

"It is one thing for an adventurous young man to undertake the journey, another for two women," he said, his mouth in a grim line.

"Still, these are two extraordinary women," Gregory said, shaking his head as if wondering why he would say anything that seemed to support the idea.

"You know how I support spirit and adventure," said Franklin, "but well, I would never suggest you go without a man." He grimaced, as if he expected Ardath to rail at him.

"I would like to ask Omar if he would come," Ardath said, quite calmly. I wondered if she had already asked him!

"May I suggest this?" said Franklin. "Omar and the two sisters could travel to the Susquehanna, using a wagon packed with trading goods and supplies for the trip. If all goes well, they could stay with my friend Susannah

Wright at Wright's Ferry and decide what they want to do from there. At the same time, we could be making the inquiries around Wilmington and west of there to find out more about the woman we have heard about. It is possible that they would then have more information before setting out from the Wrights' house."

Ardath relaxed at this. "I think that making all efforts is the best plan," she said. "What about you, Gwyn?"

I almost fainted. Ardath was asking *my* opinion.

"I think this is good," I said. "But I must insist that we take Auri along with us."

CHAPTER 61

Jamaica, July 1751
Carys

As I STOOD ON deck with Dougie soft in my arms, I heard a familiar and unwelcome voice behind me. "Mrs. Rhys, where have you been keeping yourself?" Captain Smog said, oozing charm. I spun around to that greasy, hateful man. "I have hardly seen you lately!" He chuckled, as if he had made some tremendous joke. I hated him with a passion that burned in my breast.

"So," he continued, "are you looking forward to landfall?" He chucked Dougie under the chin.

"Captain," I said, inclining my head so that he could not see the rage in my face. "How I view landfall has much to do with where I will go next."

"Yes, wise, awaiting orders and all that, hmmm, hmmm," he said. "Well, considering that you have given good service to the ill upon the ship, I have a special 'berth,' shall we say, planned for you." I waited silently. "I have an esteemed colleague who is in need of a secretary, *and* whatever else he chooses, of course. You are still a good-looking woman," he said, casually raking his eyes over my body.

I held my gorge. Dougie was my main concern in this. "Captain, since you have been so kind as to look after me this way, I hope you have extended the courtesy to my child as well."

"Hmmm, quite forgot the child was yours. Hmmm, don't know if my colleague would want to take him on." His brow wrinkled as if in genuine concern; he pursed his lips in indecision. I didn't believe any of it; he simply wanted to torture me in any way that he could. "We will have to see about

331

that," he said. I groaned inwardly but only smiled at him. "Of course, if you were to arrive looking less of a street urchin and more of a lady, he might be more inclined," he said.

"Whatever you think wise, sir," I replied. He had me, and he knew it! I wondered if he could feel the flaming hatred brimming over in my heart.

"Well, let me see what clothes I can find lying about. Come to my cabin at supper. We shall see, hmmm." With that he strode off, looking the satisfied man that he undoubtedly was. I joggled Dougie on my hip and calmed my rapid breathing.

Kate and Pete came back, Kate reaching for Dougie, who squirmed toward her. Pete smiled down at them. "Well, back to work for me. Remember what I said," he said to Kate.

As soon as he was away, I asked her, "May I know what he said?" Her smile lit up her eyes but disappeared quickly. She fussed with Dougie's blanket.

"Well, miss, he says he loves me, but men ain't to be trusted, that's for sure!" she said.

A little hope crept into my heart. "I've trusted Pete this whole voyage," I said. "He seems an honest and kind man."

"Even so, that Smog is in charge, and he, for certain, can't be trusted." Kate had that right! There was nothing more to say. I couldn't see how Pete could manage to keep Kate out of whatever the captain had planned for her. She might be deluded when it came to Dougie, but she was strong, and the captain could probably sell her before anyone saw the delusion, provided Dougie went with her. After that, she would claim him as her own and no one would be the wiser. My heart sank. What a turmoil I had been through today! I felt exhausted. Perhaps it was better to let Dougie go with Kate, to give up my dream of a son to raise.

*****

I told Margaret the whole story once we were back in the hold and out of Kate's hearing. "Will wonders never cease!" she said. "Kate with a suitor? She has seemed more calm of late, but I hardly think she is no longer mad. Perhaps Pete is blinded by love and cannot see it."

"She realizes that her husband is dead," I said.

"How many times have you heard her say that? She might not know that tomorrow. We should listen for other signs. It is true that Ann has won her heart and she now speaks with most of us women, but to turn toward a man, after all she has been through, I don't know."

"I think you are right. Let us listen to her carefully," I said. I looked at Margaret's green eyes. "Captain Smog wants me to go to supper with him tonight."

She grimaced at that. "So are you to be his plaything again? What will you do?"

"You know I want to take Dougie with me when we arrive." She nodded. "So I will do whatever is necessary to curry favor with him."

I washed as best I could with seawater, which left a salty grit on me, no matter how I scrubbed at it. I combed out my hair, which was growing longer again, deciding to leave it out from under the cap. I used an extra cord to tie the shift at my waist so that I looked less like I was wearing a tent. I had to take many a deep breath to steel myself for the lion in his den. I walked like the good Christian I wasn't, to his door, screwing up my courage. As Tionga said, I must take the broom of anger and sweep away my fear.

Captain Smog opened his door with a gracious bow, gesturing to the bathtub that steamed in the middle of the room. I sighed to myself. We were to have the farce of the lady and her courtly lover again, I supposed. He handed me a towel and showed me the dress laid out on his bunk. "Perhaps you will enjoy a nice, freshwater bath and some lovely soap," he said.

I waited for him to smirk and watch me undress, but he said, "I will leave you to it, my dear lady." He left and closed the door quietly behind him. I shook my head. I never knew what tricks he was playing, but the bath looked like a piece of heaven. I quickly shed my smock and sank into it, lathering with soap that smelled like honey and glided smoothly over my skin. I curled my whole body under the water. I had lost weight on this voyage, but I thought my body was still attractive. The sensation of truly clean hair was the best of all, after the filth and sweat of this voyage. Freshly washed, it curled into tight dark-red ringlets that dripped water down my back. In the heat of the cabin, even the dripping water felt good. I scrubbed myself dry and sighed with contentment. How grateful I had become for any good sensation!

The dress was beautiful. It was of a lighter material, almost gauzy, with a cream background and red, purple, and yellow flowers embroidered all over it. It was maybe too youthful for someone my age, but I would not quibble over that!

As I finished dressing, a soft knock on the door warned me that Smog was back. I retrieved my mental broom of anger. I was no young girl, to be beguiled with a pretty frock.

"Ah, you look lovely," said Smog. A grin slipped across his face. In my mind, he rubbed his hands together in satisfaction, and perhaps greed?

"Thank you," I said, waiting to see what he wanted.

"I have asked for supper to be set for us on the deck," he said. Clasping my arm in his, he walked me to the door and waited while I ascended into the breeze and into the glow of an orange-and-lavender sunset. A small table was set with two places. Mick stood by in clean clothes to wait on us. Fresh fish and boiled potatoes with wine and fresh water, all followed by a custard dessert. I ate contentedly. Seize the moment, I said to myself. I noticed that the captain drank very little; I hoped that was a good sign.

"Mrs. Rhys, we have spoken before about my plans for you. You must be reminded of how to behave in society. The man you are promised to has strict standards. He is not a man to be taken lightly. He has become one of the most powerful men in the West Indies. It behooves any captain carrying cargo to be on his good side, as he is only technically a 'privateer.'"

"You mean to say that he is a pirate and you don't wish your cargo to be taken," I said calmly.

He smirked. "Ah, Mrs. Rhys, you are a woman of great intelligence. How I wish I could keep you for myself!" He practically drooled at me, wiping his mouth in haste. "However, you must report to him that I have used you with great courtesy and always had your best interests at heart. Can you promise me to do that?"

"One promise deserves another, I say. I can only do that if you promise me that the baby, Dougie, will go with me."

"Ummm, I believe the woman called Kate is his mother. You wouldn't ask me to separate a mother and babe, would you?"

"You don't remember paying John and Joe for the baby?" I asked, lifting my eyebrows. "Furthermore, I can't be helpful to this other captain if I am mourning for my baby."

"Hmmm, didn't King Solomon have this same problem?" he asked. "And don't you have any compassion for poor Kate?" His smile was evil.

My breast boiled yet again. "What about *your* compassion for Kate? Please tell me that you can guarantee a good home where she will be treated gently."

"Oh, you try to shame me!" he said in a low and menacing tone. "That is no way to get what you want."

"It seems neither of us may get what we want. That's a bad bargain," I said. We both reached for our wineglasses in an attempt to cool the conversation.

"Why would he not want me to take the child with me? Being a woman, I can't go on board with him, anyway, can I? Could I at least ask him for his permission?"

"You are not negotiating this deal, woman," he said.

"Of course," I said. He was right. I had no power here.

"Well, think on it, selfish woman. What are you willing to do to Kate?" he said. "In the meantime, I don't want that dress spoiled. Return to the medical cabin and change to your smock."

I was stunned. When not drunk, Smog was clever enough to manipulate me in this way. I walked back to don my smock, then took to my hammock among the women.

*****

The next day, I ate breakfast with Kate and Dougie. "We will be in a port soon,

I believe, Kate. How are you feeling today?"

"I think I remember Pete saying he loved me yesterday. Did I dream that?"

"No, I was nearby. That is what you told me then."

"Well, if he really does, I want to go with him," she said. "I don't think I'll find a kinder man."

"Did you talk about where you would stay, or any other plans?" I asked.

"He has a house in the Carolinas, he says. I could go with him there and wait for him to finish the last voyage he has promised the captain. But, Miz Rhys, he says we can't keep Dougie." She stopped suddenly, covering her mouth. "I can't leave Dougie, but the captain will sell him to someone else anyways, Pete says. He says I have to prepare for it. Dougie won't be mine." She sighed in a pitiable way. I touched her hand, and she put hers in mine. It comforted us both, although I was an evil person who deserved no comfort.

"How would Pete persuade the captain to let him have you?" I asked after a while.

"Why, he's already done it, said he had some money saved and told the captain he'd buy me. The captain needs him on this next trip and said he could."

"Land ho!" we heard shouted from above decks. We were allowed to go up briefly to see low-lying islands coming up on both sides. Then Pete escorted us down again. He came into the hold with us, closing the door behind him.

I moved aside a crush of women, all muttering together, to speak to him. "Pete, Kate believes that you want to take her with you...," I said.

He scrubbed at the stubble on his chin. "Yes, missus, I do. The captain will sell her to me if I promise to go the next trip with him, which I have. I'd rather not stay aboard, but for Kate I'll do it. She'll be a happy woman again, or I'm not a McCready!"

"Pete, that is so extraordinary of you, so kind."

"No need to call me a saint, ma'am. I love her. She is coming out of the madness, too, but don't tell the captain, or her price'll go up."

"But, Pete, what about Dougie?"

"I'll convince her she was a good wet nurse for him, and that's all." He smiled at me. "It's you brought him, and you should take him away."

"Oh, Pete, you are not only a saint, but my savior as well! I hope that someday I can repay you for this. Where is your house in the Carolinas?"

"Outside Wilmington in North Carolina. A shack, but it will serve until I can get land and do better."

"I wish you both the best, long and happy lives!"

He blushed and tugged at his forelock. "Wishing you the same in return. A lady should not have been treated as you were." With that, he went to stay with Kate and Dougie in their corner.

With a sigh, I slumped to the floor, back up against the solid wood of the door. No longer did I have to live with images of Kate in a frenzy, throwing Dougie or herself, or both, overboard. Or crying and clinging to my feet while I told her I had to take Dougie away from her. I allowed myself to cry with relief. The sobs racked my body, but my heart exulted.

After that, I had to take a deep breath and focus. If Dougie were to be mine, I must provide for his needs. Fortunately, he was taking to the pap as well as he had taken to the breast, so I would not need a wet nurse for him. I gave up the dream of escaping, though I would keep looking for a chance once we landed; escape with a babe likely would be too hard on both of us.

The pressing order of the day was to be sure Dougie could go with me. I needed the help of two men. One I knew to be cunning and vicious, the other reputedly the same. I knew some of Smog's weaknesses, but Lazarus was a mystery to me. And I had little time to make a plan.

We heard the usual sounds of the ship anchoring and furling sails, the crew running above our heads, orders shouted and repeated. Pete had told me that we would anchor first in Kingston, Jamaica, far enough offshore to prevent escape attempts.

Today the African slaves would be taken by longboat to be sold in the city. Pete let me out of our hold to say goodbye to Tionga down below. The tension and fear were palpable as soon as I entered their quarters, but Tionga had gathered them around her. Chanting, she calmed their fears, probably reminding them that their ancestors would go with them. Before I could talk to her, crewmen banged open the door and rounded them up. I moved aside, giving Tionga a nod that said "Best of luck." She returned the nod and lifted her head to stretch to her greatest height, which was still lower than anyone else's. She was a giant in spirit, though. I truly wished them all well and tried not to picture what was ahead for them in the blistering hot sugarcane fields.

The rest of us were allowed on deck after the slaves were gone. Jamaica was a tumble of green hills under a powder-blue sky. Tall masts of many kinds of ships stood before us, closer to shore, rocking at peaceful anchor. It looked more like a paradise today than the hell Pete had described, but then we were at a distance.

Kate stood next to me, with Dougie in her arms. She shyly held him out to me. I looked at her teary eyes. "You keep him for me today, Kate, please. I don't know when I'll be leaving the ship, but you have him for now, all right?"

She nodded, an errant tear creeping down her cheek. Once again, I was assailed with doubt. Would it be better for Dougie to go with Kate and Pete, if the captain would allow it? They would set up a home for him in North Carolina. But Smog had paid something for Dougie when he paid for me, so I doubted he'd let that happen.

I had to use whatever I could to bargain with Smog and Lazarus. The fact that I could read and write would help me with Lazarus, but how could Dougie help in that situation, except to be an expense and a distraction? Of course, I was prepared to use my body to bargain with, if it came to that. Lazarus could not be a worse partner than Smog, I supposed.

That night, Smog sent for me. He made me wipe down my body and don the flowered dress again to go to Lazarus. I combed my hair carefully; it was down to my shoulders now, enough to make a bun. Then he led me on deck. Pete and Mick took me to the longboat, and Smog followed. Away the crew rowed toward a ship in the harbor, which showed lights moving about on board. I could see no flag, even as we drew nearer. The night was soft and warm. It smelled of sea and flowers as we left our ship behind. Stars sparkled above us in a deep-velvet sky.

Of course, I was not at peace, since the rest of my life and Dougie's depended on the outcome of this meeting with Lazarus. I hoped it was not a trick that I had not been allowed to bring Dougie. Having Pete and Mick there helped me somewhat. I breathed in the night and prayed to the Goddess. Brigid would surely understand a woman's need to be with her child.

At last, we drew alongside Lazarus's ship, the *Dreadnaught*, and were hauled aboard. Smog spoke with the first mate, who escorted Smog and myself down to the captain's cabin. He knocked softly; Smog and I entered a darkened room, lit only by yellow glow of a lantern sitting on a large desk. Behind it sat a white-haired man whose skin, though brown and weather-beaten like rough leather, was that of a fairly young person. He did not look up from the paper he was scratching on with a quill pen.

Smog cleared his throat and announced, "Sir, this is the lady I have brought for your pleasure. She reads and writes well and, I hope, will be a great help in your labors."

"This cursed paperwork!" exclaimed Lazarus, squinting at the papers that littered his desk. Finally, he looked up enough for me to witness the ugliest man I had ever seen. His head, like a brown toad's, sloped into his thick neck. His eyes bulged out, bloodshot and weary. He had a bulbous nose. His face was gouged with pockmarks; his mouth was open just enough for me to see wildly crooked brown teeth between thick lips. If I hadn't had control of myself, I might have started or cried out—so shocking was his appearance. He peered at us, blinking his eyes. "Can't see you in this light. Come forward."

I braced myself and stepped into the circle of light. "Captain Whitsun, this is the lady I promised you, a Mrs. Rhys," began Smog.

As I stood before him, Captain Lazarus's mouth dropped open. He rose from his desk, reaching out to me as if he knew me. He rounded the desk and, blanching, slumped to the floor. The terror of the seven seas lay in a dead faint at my feet.

CHAPTER 62

July 1751
Carys

THE SCOURGE OF THE seven seas lay in a dead faint at my feet. I fell to my knees to help him. Rummaging through my bag for the smelling salts, I held them to his nose, causing him to sputter and shake his curly white head.

"What is happening?" said my captor of the last few months, Captain Smog, leaning over us.

"I don't know. Help me sit him up," I said. We rolled the notorious Lazarus into a more sitting position, though he still slumped in our arms, coughing and slightly retching. "Get him some water, or drink," I said. The captain did, with some alacrity. He really feared this man, even partly conscious, I noted.

"Ohhh," said the scourge pitifully.

"Here, take this drink," I told him, and he did, slopping some down the white linen shirt that lay sodden from sweat on his breast.

As he peered up at me, he looked as if he would faint again. "Oh, no, you don't," I said, mopping his face with a cloth from my bag. I bathed it in the drink, some kind of wine, to cool him down.

"Open that porthole," I ordered the captain. He did so, and immediately the tight cabin was blessed with some real air.

"Oh, curse me!" said Captain Smog. "Why can nothing go right for me? You have caused him to have a fit. Some lovely present you turned out to be!" He kicked at my skirts, banging the side of my leg.

I was having none of this. "Stop it. I caused nothing!" I growled at him, and he actually did desist. Somehow, now that we were off his ship, I couldn't hide my contempt for him, though he still held my life and Dougie's in his hands.

Lazarus was becoming more alert. "Do not address this lady in such a manner," he said, pointing his still-wobbling head toward the captain.

"Of course not, Captain Whitsun," Smog said, bowing to him. "A momentary lapse, forgive me."

"Hmmm," said Whitsun, as if reserving judgment about Smog. I was beginning to have some respect for him.

We got him righted and in a chair. His body felt all bones beneath his clothes, of which he wore too many, considering the heat. It was like lifting potatoes wrapped in multiple bags.

"I apologize," he said to me. "My sight is not what it used to be." Tears formed in his eyes, and he cleared his throat.

"Please," I started.

Smog interrupted me. "I am sorry this lady caused you such a shock! I had meant her to be a surprise gift for you, as she can read and write, to help you with the paperwork, you know, and all that." He paused. "But if she displeases you, I will remove her at once." He looked pained and undecided.

"No, please, I do need such help, and if the lady wishes to stay, I would be exceedingly glad." He looked at me, then glanced quickly away. "She could have no place on the ship, but I have quarters here in Kingston."

Smog's hand stroked my head. I couldn't stop myself from flinching away. Whitsun's eyes again flitted to my face.

"Please, sir, I wish to stay with you, but I must bring my babe with me. He will be no problem, I promise. I can watch him while I work for you," I said.

"A babe, you say?" He hesitated while my heart sank. He glanced at me quickly again. "Well," he added, rubbing his chin thoughtfully. "Hmmm."

I wanted to scream while we all waited for the other boot to fall. Suddenly, he grinned broadly, showing all the crooked brown teeth he possessed, his weathered round face split in two with a jolly thought.

"Of course, what a brilliant idea! My Marta would love to have a babe in the house. Beware, though, she will spoil him badly!"

"Are you sure your wife will not mind another woman in the house?" I asked this with some apprehension, but it was best to know if I might be tossed out onto the street because the lady of the house didn't want me.

"Oh, no, I am not married. Marta, a young Mestizo woman, keeps the house for me. She can serve as a chaperone."

He turned to Smog. "How much are you asking for her indenture?" he asked.

"Oh, for you, sir, nothing at all. I give her to you for five years' service as a token of my esteem. The babe is included. She also has healing skills and can be a midwife if you wish to lend her out," said Smog, at his most ingratiating. The nasty man!

"Ah, I see," said Whitsun. A thoughtful look crossed his face. "And what did you say the name of your ship is?"

"Why, the *Bellwether*, sir. A fine and honest passenger ship she is," said Smog, smiling in his oily way.

"Well, I shall keep an eye out for her, then," said Whitsun. I couldn't tell if this was good news for Smog or not, but he took it so, to my relief.

He broke into a big grin of his own. "Thank you, sir, thank you," he said to Whitsun.

Captain Whitsun then turned to me. "I was just completing my work for the night. You must be tired from the journey. Would you consent to coming to my house for supper and to get settled? All will be above board, I assure you. We can pick up your babe and your things with my boat, if that suits everyone?" he said, including Smog.

"Of course, as you say," Smog boomed at him. "I'll just return in my boat with the lady and you can follow."

*****

The next while passed as though in a dream. We were soon at the *Bellwether*, and after hasty goodbyes and good wishes, I took Dougie in my arms, wrapping him tightly in a sling. We descended the ladder to Captain Whitsun's boat and headed for the harbor. The rocking of the boat calmed Dougie. The fresh air and my apprehension kept me alert.

On the way to shore, I was able to sit close to Whitsun. I felt uneasy but had to ask. "Why did my appearance startle you so?"

"Ah, Mrs. Rhys, you reminded me of someone I once knew, but this is not the place to discuss it," he said and remained quiet the rest of the way to his house. Whitsun seemed a kind man as I had seen him so far, but somewhat peculiar. I groaned inwardly. Once again, my fate was tied to a man who had power over me, with little I could do to influence whatever was to happen.

He took me up the hill to a level place overlooking the harbor, to a lovely little wood-and-straw thatched house ringed with dark-leaved trees. The night was soft around us as we stepped onto his porch. From the house burst a pretty, young Hispanic woman, chattering away in her own language and waving her arms.

I gathered that we were late for supper, but she dropped her dance when she saw Dougie. "Ooooh, querido mio!" she cried, all thoughts of supper apparently gone. "Precioso," she cried, and nothing would do until she had him in her arms.

Captain Whitsun said, "I'll show you to your room." He took me to a small bedroom with a wide bed on the back of the one-story house, which was built on stilts above the ground. The room felt larger than it was because the ceilings were high, as in all the captain's house. A wide-open doorway led onto an enclosed porch covered with netting. It overlooked a garden at the back, which was filled with strange plants, many exuding sweet scents. It looked like a picture of paradise.

"We can have a bed made for Dougie soon," he said, standing still as I roamed the room in wonder. "Perhaps you would like to change."

"I'm afraid I have nothing else but a shift," I said. "But I would enjoy a wash."

"Of course. I will leave you, but Marta will come for you soon." He bowed slightly and left the room.

A basin of water sat on the table near the back door. I relished the feel of the water on my face but soon had done all I could to make myself presentable again. I straightened my gown. I rubbed the rough towel over my face, trying to make this circumstance feel more real. All the while, I burned with questions and tried to consider the place that fate had sent me. Captain Whitsun was kind and thoughtful, a shock of its own kind after Smog and the Lazarus rumors. He seemed determined to treat me as a lady, with himself the gentleman. I sighed. I must wait.

Marta appeared, carrying Dougie, who reached out to me. I took the heavy, sweet weight of him in my arms. We were to be together, after all. My heart brimmed over. Marta chattered at me in Spanish. I could see I'd have to learn the language, and quickly too.

Marta took us down the hall to another airy room, where a table was spread with many exotic fruits and a roast chicken swam in its juice on a platter. The bread was yellow and flat like a griddle cake. Thank the Goddess I was past the salt pork and hard bread from the ship! Drink awaited in a dark-green decanter. Captain Whitsun arrived and stationed himself behind a chair, which he pulled out for me. Marta again took Dougie, who gurgled and grabbed at her nose. They went away, I guessed toward the kitchen. Those two were certainly off to a good start!

To my surprise, Captain Whitsun bowed his head in a silent prayer. I followed suit and said "Amen" to whatever it was he had shared with God. He carved the chicken and served me with that and some orange potatoes. We began to eat rather ravenously.

"Captain, I thank you very kindly for your hospitality," I said. He nodded and poured punch for me. It was very good and tasted fresh.

"This punch is made here, not from grapes, but from fruit juices that I am just beginning to identify, very refreshing, I think."

"I agree. Captain—"

"Please call me Alex. When we are on the ship, it will be appropriate to call me Captain, but we need not stand on convention here."

"As you wish, sir," I said, a little disturbed by the informality. "I don't want to push you on a matter that is sensitive for you, but when may I learn why you seemed to know me at first sight?"

He sighed. "I am sorry for my outburst on the ship," he said. "I must tell you some of my history if my tale is to make any sense to you."

I nodded eagerly. "Please do!"

He smiled a closemouthed smile. "Perhaps you have heard stories of the creature known as Lazarus, or, sometimes, Jonah? Ah, I see by your expression that you have. Well, I started out this April as the first mate on a passenger ship from Liverpool bound to Philadelphia. We were beset by a terrible epidemic of the small pox. The captain fell ill and was killed by mutineers. I then became the captain, though by the end of the small pox, I had little crew left to run the ship. We were then beset by a storm, which blew us we knew not where but into sleet and snow. The remaining crew on deck were swept away by a huge wave. I had tied myself to the wheel, so I watched as we lost them all. The mast cracked and went down, severing the rope that held me on board. I flew in the wind and wet far from the ship but saw her go down beneath a mountainous wave with all passengers."

"What a terrible thing!" I said. "How did you survive?"

"I don't know how or why I survived. I know now that I pray every day of my life to know why I was spared, whether God perhaps has some plan for me." He stared at his drink for long moments. I kept myself from breaking his reverie. There is indeed great mystery in our lives at times, I thought, considering where I was also at this moment.

"I awoke to find myself alive and in the longboat that had been torn from the ship. How I got there, I have tried to remember but can't. Rainwater had collected in a bucket in the boat, which helped greatly. Two oars survived in the bottom, having slid under the seats. I shivered in the cold and wet but could see the sun trying to break through, so I rowed for the south. Providence had provided a net and some canvas as well. With the net, I caught fish at times. I held up the canvas if the wind was right, to serve as a pitiful sail, but thus I made some headway. After some time, I reached the Sargasso, where the boat was becalmed. I ate the little fishes, crabs, and even the seaweed there, but my water ran out.

"I was found by a ship headed to Jamaica. I remember that not, being near death at that time, but they revived me. Here I met with the governor, who knew my family. He needed a privateer to take over the ship I met you on, so here I am. I really have had only one expedition that garnered a large prize, but rumor has made that into a whole reputation for me. But you have no idea how much paperwork there is, reports and such on that ship." He smiled ruefully. "But I drift. Please eat more supper. It's better than you've had on the ship, I'll warrant."

"Yes, certainly true. You have a remarkable story to tell." I looked directly at his rather-bulging brown eyes. This time I saw them with sympathy.

"As do you, I am sure!" he said, drinking a big gulp of the punch. We ate in silence for a while. "But you want to know the important parts, the ones I hate to face and hate more to tell you." He cleared his throat.

"Yes," I whispered.

"On the *Gracious Anne*, we had the good fortune to have an excellent Moorish doctor. He and his helpers were the reason any of us survived the pox." He suddenly shuddered and swallowed, as if to keep back tears.

"I'm so sorry for all you have been through," I said. I wanted to comfort him with a touch, but of course I couldn't do that.

"You look so much like her, Mrs. Rhys," he said. Breaking into open sobs, he laid his head down on his arms. Now I did rise to pat him on the back. He straightened himself up, but tears still streamed from eyes. "Ardath and her sister, the sweetest little girl, Gwyn, all dead on that ship! And I didn't go down with her!"

"On the ship, but how?" I sank into the chair next to him. My girls, dead? No, not possible. I thought of the last time I had seen them, Gwyn singing us awake in the mornings, all eager to plant a spring garden, Ardath determined to start swimming in the pond, even in March, both so alive and so loved. But love can't always save people, I thought with a chill. If it could, my girls could never be gone. My mind refused the very thought.

Alex still shuddered, but strove to pull himself together. Sitting so close to him, I could feel his back straighten, feel him pull breath into his lungs. "I am so sorry, so sorry," he said.

"Alex, it wasn't your fault, but if you need forgiveness, I give it to you," I said slowly.

My words caused a fresh outbreak of shuddering, but then, something seemed to make sense to him. "I didn't have any control over it. I never would have wished it," he said in a wondering way, as if he might consider forgiving himself.

"I know," I said. "But *why*? *Why* were they on a ship to the New World?" As if knowing the whole story would somehow soothe me!

"It was after their mother disappeared. Everyone believed their mother had died, but you hadn't, had you?" His face was a mask of pain; he didn't look at me. "They concluded that they must call on their father for help. He wanted them to go with him to his brother in Philadelphia."

I felt another chill creep over me. "Alex, was their father on the ship also?" I asked.

He looked at me with reluctance. "Yes."

I rocked back in my chair. My whole family was gone. And they had thought *I* was dead before they died. I sat, stunned and shaking, beyond hope or sensibility.

CHAPTER 63

May 1752
Ardath

OF COURSE THEY THOUGHT I was mad to plan a trip down the Wagon Road into North Carolina, but I knew we were as ready as any pioneers who had done it before, maybe more so. We had reliable horses, abilities with guns and arrows, some money and trade goods, and most of all, determination to reach the destination. A determination to find our Mother if we could.

Mrs. Perry gave up her moping and helped us get food provisions together. Ahmed made us hoe, pitchfork, and shovel heads, pans and knives, even a plow and barrel rings to carry with us for trade, as coin did not mean much on the frontier. Omar, who had joined our party with joy, had seen the wagons to the frontier come through Philadelphia and made us a wagon in a matter of days that was like the new Conestogas, but smaller. Supposedly, these wagons were ship-like in water and could float while the horses swam them across rivers. He also made us extra bows and arrows in case we needed to hunt along the way. He packed a few of his most-useful carpentry tools.

Bishop Spangenberg gave us a letter to his missionaries, brave souls traveling the same route at a similar time. Isa took over our garden. Ibrahim gave us herbs for maladies we might run into along the way. Gwyn made this into a medical kit with bandages, sharp knives, scissors, soap, thread, and needle.

Gwyn went with Ibrahim to visit Mr. Bartram again. She obtained drawings of the medicinal plants we might collect along the way. He showed her how to pack them, first extracting a promise that we would bring particular ones back to him.

I put all our accounts into order, in readiness for Gregory to take them over. We would leave a small amount of the silver with him to help run the businesses, and take a small amount with us. I buried the rest of the silver close to where the gold rested.

Then I had the pleasure of meeting with Franklin. I found him at his office near Market Street.

"Ah, Ardath, please come in. It is a good time, as I have just concluded my business for today," he said with a genial smile, rising from his desk and shaking my hand.

I sank in a deep bow to him. It was our joke, because he abhorred obsequiousness.

His smile grew broader. "My dear! How I am going to miss you. Please don't let me forget to send along with you a package for Susanna Wright, the friend who lives at Wright's Ferry. You will enjoy each other. She is well educated and quite the natural philosopher. I promised her these books and a lively conversation with you and Gwyn."

"Certainly! It seems a long way to the Susquehanna, but if the weather is fine, we could be there in days."

"Umm, a horse can go three to four miles an hour for as much as six hours a day, so you may make as much as twenty miles per day. It has taken me about three to four days to go to Susanna's. How go the preparations for your journey?" He pulled the chair from behind his desk and gestured for me to sit in the other.

"It is going well. Our little company of friends has the skills to outfit us very well. Omar has made a rather-splendid wagon for us. Gwyn has been to Mr. Bartram's garden, learning which plants she should look for along the way. Ahmed has made many iron toolheads for our trade, or for David, if we don't use them on the trail."

That's all good news. You certainly have an industrious crew. I gather all are prospering."

"It seems a young city still, with much opportunity to be had. I hate to take Omar away from his prospects in carpentry here."

"Perhaps you would like to consider hiring a guide instead," he said.

"That could work, but..." I thought for a moment, rubbing my chin. "I don't think I'd like to go with someone I didn't know. The trail should be easy to follow through Pennsylvania and the Great Valley, and from what I've heard, no one is available who might know the trail well after that. However, the Moravians will be ahead of us, so we should be able to follow their trail."

"Umm. Well, we have talked about the dangers of wild animals, hostile Indians, floods, and other natural disasters. I know that these arguments do not persuade you toward having more protection."

I started to object, but he waved his hand in dismissal. "No, I know, I know, just reviewing out loud."

"You think me foolish," I said, exasperated. "But I know the risks are great. I'm not stupid."

"So sorry, my dear, an old man's caution," he said. "I will miss you *mightily*. We will send any news by fast horse." He rose from his chair.

I took the package he proffered, and we hugged each other well. His body was solid and pleasant like himself.

"It has been an honor," I said, and I meant it, leaning back with my hand still clasped in his and meeting his hazel eyes, perhaps for the last time.

I walked home under a threatening sky. We were undaunted by rain, though used to gentler showers in Wales than we saw here. Everything about this continent seemed somehow more dramatic and certainly wilder than we had been used to. I realized as I walked how little my mind had dwelled on finding Mother and how much more on the journey itself. Perhaps that was natural, considering how hard we had worked to be ready, but truly it seemed unreal that we would find her in all this vast territory.

Gwyn stood on the porch as I came up. She definitely looked like a young woman now, wearing her dark hair in a bun on her neck and a pretty blue-sprigged muslin dress. Her womanly figure seemed to glow with excitement.

I was proud of her, that she had led us in meeting about the trip with our gentlemen friends, none of whom had tried to bend us to their will as I suspected they would but had offered us help where they could. In fact, when she had asked me later about my suspicions of them, I admitted that I must stop feeling the anger toward all men that I had toward our father for his abandonment. That painted all men with the same brush, which was inherently unfair. Though the men around us had been reared in the societal expectation that women were inferior and weak, these friends had accepted us and our ideas on their merit. My own husband was willing for me to keep charge of the money Gwyn and I had. I respected all this greatly. But it didn't mean that we didn't need to be alert and keep our minds as keen as a knife's edge around the other sex.

I rejoiced that Gwyn and Gregory had rekindled their relationship as well. Perhaps this journey would give her enough time to be ready for more when we returned.

"Ardath," she said, with eyes gleaming, "I believe all is in readiness."

"Then," I said, "shall we leave after breakfast?"

"We shall," she said, clasping her hands together before her in anticipation.

CHAPTER 64

May 1752
Gwyn

GOODNESS, WE WERE REALLY going! I found myself eager to be on the road, though wishing at the same time that I didn't have to leave Gregory. He came to supper the night before we left. I ate sparingly; the excitement of the trip and of him left my stomach aquiver.

We excused ourselves early and went to walk the town. Well, not the rough parts down by the public houses and wharves, of course, but the lamplit, sweet-smelling, tree-lined streets abloom with the whites and greens of chestnuts, tulip poplar, and locust.

I curled into his warm, protective arm. "I wish I didn't have to leave you," I said, reaching up to brush his feathery hair out of his eyes, letting my fingers linger on his dear face. I felt his breath catch.

"I feel the same, you know, you *know*," he said, turning to face me, lifting my chin, gazing into my eyes, suddenly kissing me hard, then tenderly. "There is a stone where my heart should be. I want to cherish every moment we are together."

I had no need to reply, just disappeared into the kisses. Peace dropped around us like a warm cloud. Holding him, I felt I had been in exile, in a desert, a strange and unwelcoming land, for those months without him. He caressed my face with his long fingers. I tried not to startle when he brushed my scar, but he felt my response.

"Oh, how I hate her!" he said. "I hate her for hurting you!"

"No, don't let her come into this," I said. I managed a smile.

"Well, I understand, but secretly I shall continue to picture her falling into the river mud headfirst, with her ugly feet kicking vainly in the air like the witch she is," he said.

"Well, if it pleases your funny bone, I shall not interfere with your fantasy," I said, really smiling this time. I pulled my shawl back onto my shoulders. "Or perhaps she goes to the garden and is attacked by a roaming wolf who bites but then spits her bad-tasting leg right out again."

"Hmmm, I like it. I shall add it to my private imaginings immediately!" he said.

"Seriously, Gwyn, please be careful on this trip. Ardath is fearless, but there are times when your more thoughtful approach may help the two of you more. I hope you won't hesitate to speak up to her when she leaves you out of decisions or ignores dangers you can see but she can't."

This stopped me in my tracks. I felt my brow furrow as if I didn't know what he meant, but I *did*. Ardath often left me out of decisions as if I were too young, or incapable. At this thought, I felt a flash of anger.

"You are right," I said. "I haven't always noticed, because it has always been this way with us, but I can see things she can't sometimes, and I should be speaking up more." Now my brow furrowed again with this revelation, which ran deep for me.

"It would mean confronting her. She can be angry and dismissive of me if I confront her. I would have to pay the consequences for giving voice…," I said.

"You are every bit her equal, though younger," said Gregory. "You are a strong person in your own right."

Many thoughts flew through my head then. I remembered Ibrahim praising my healing skills. I remembered knowing that poor Alex had fallen in love with Ardath when she hadn't seen it. I thought of my affinity with horses, how I seemed to communicate well with animals. Mrs. Perry praising my sewing. My understanding of plants and their effects that Mr. Bartram had shown me. I recognized that I could never grow into myself if I didn't look at myself apart from who I was to Ardath, how she saw me. It was as if doors opened all around me, with a bewildering array of choices I could refuse or take up as *I*, not Ardath nor anyone else, judged them worthy.

"Oh my!" I said.

"All right?" asked Gregory. "You look rather stunned." His chin was down, head tilted, as he studied me.

"Yes, somewhat stunned. You have given me so much to think about..."

"Uh-oh, when thinking starts, kissing stops," he said with a crooked grin.

I laughed outright then and twirled in his arms, drawing him to dance with me beneath the lamp. "I can think while on the trail. Now's the time for kissing!" I said and commenced to show him what I meant by that. It was a beautiful night.

*****

Ardath and I awoke to a different day the next morning. Rain poured down in sheets, reminding me of our great storm on the Atlantic. Ardath appeared at my bedroom door.

"Oh, dear, I think I hear a hard rain," I said, shoving Auri off the bed, to his evident disgust. He rewarded me with a sharp growl.

"Well, we can't let the weather stop us," said Ardath. "Why aren't you dressed?"

"Ummm, because it is insanity to go out in this?" I ventured.

"I'm sure this will stop soon. Will you wear britches for this part of the trip? It should be relatively safe, but at the same time, comfort—"

I interrupted her. "Ardath, I shall be comfortable by the fire while this continues." I got up, slipping on my slippers, thudding down the stairs, and opening the door for Auri, who poked a nose out into the flashing lights, thunder, and torrents of rain and dodged past me, running up the stairs and back to bed.

"See, even the dog knows better!" I said. Ardath grimaced, returning to the hearth fire as I followed her. I dished myself some porridge and rashers of bacon, which Mrs. Perry had made for special, and settled on the wooden bench. Today I could eat, and it might be a while before a hot breakfast came our way again. Ardath paced like a caged animal.

"Hello, my ladies," Omar called in a cheerful voice as he entered the back door. "Good weather for da ducks, in't it?"

I smiled at him. Ardath looked up but said nothing.

"Omar, it is good to see you. We're so happy you want to come on this journey with us," I said. "You are a ray of sunshine."

"Da only one, doh," he said, showing the gap between his teeth as his round face split in a grin. "We see if da wagon float before river even. All packed and waiting under da roof. Let up soon, I tink."

"I certainly hope so," said Ardath. She had been strangely subdued since we met with our friends to discuss the trip. She hadn't lost her capacity for bad humor, however.

"Well, I, for one, am excited to be going. Have some porridge, Omar," I said. I gazed at him as he slid onto the bench and tucked into the bowl I served him. His skin was so black it had a glow of its own, a somewhat-bluish tinge. He seemed the picture of health and strength. And his humor was always light and happy. We were fortunate that he was along.

Auri barked from the back to be let out. This time he dashed into the rain, lifted his leg against a tree, and dashed back inside, where I waited with a dry towel to scrub his muddy feet. His long curly hair dripped into his eyes as he looked at me with devotion. I reached for scissors to trim it. "You must be able to see to be our stalwart watchdog," I said to him, at which he grinned happily. I gave him a bone, which he brought to the fire, wagging his curled-up tail. Except for Ardath, we were a happy group.

Mrs. Perry came in from the other room, proceeding to fix us parcels of food, corn pone, dried venison, and pickles to take. She even petted the dog, whom she had begun to like once he became well-trained.

"I hate to see you go," she said for the thirty-third time, but she didn't sound so lost this time, more accepting. She had already fixed up her work-room in the front room. Her spring frocks were in high demand as warmer weather came on.

"I know." I walked to the back door. "I think it's letting up," I said, looking out. Water dripped from the tree limbs and ran down the fresh green leaves. In the quiet I could hear the horses chomping their hay as they shifted their weight beneath the shed roof. I was glad to be wearing canvas today, as it would dry faster than wool or leather. We were bound to be wet no matter what else the day held.

"You ladies could ride in da wagon," said Omar, coming up behind me.

"I think I'd rather ride Molly and wear my oilcloth cloak instead, unless it starts to pour again," I said.

"Yes, let's ride," said Ardath from behind Omar's solid body.

We hugged Mrs. Perry. We had said goodbye to everyone else the night before. "I hope you find her. Be careful," she said, but not a tear escaped her eyes.

"We will," Ardath and I said together. Then we tightened our boots and ran for the shed, with Auri close behind us. I tried to get him to ride in the wagon, but he jumped out and ran in circles around us, causing even Ardath to laugh.

"You'll want to ride later, you little fool," she said to him.

We followed a now-familiar path toward the Schuylkill River and down to Gray's Ferry. The river was somewhat high from the rain, but Gray liked our coin and agreed to swim the horses over, taking the draft horses first, then Molly and our other mare, Sally. His raft was just large enough to take the wagon on the next trip and then the three of us on the next. We rocked on the raft, and water sloshed over our feet, but I reminded myself that we had had much worse on the ocean! For these four trips, Ardath gave him a whole Spanish dollar.

We trudged up the road beside Bartram's farm. He and his sons were away, so we moved on, after turning toward the last view of the city to the northeast, where the Christ Church's steeple rose above the trees.

We had gotten a late start and wanted to make more distance before night fell. This was the first time we had been this far into Pennsylvania. The land was beautiful, with greening fields and pale-green leaves on the trees.

Sparkling white of dogwood blooms peeked through the trees beside the road. We passed many prosperous-looking farms, mostly English and Welsh, with lilacs beside the houses sending up their sweet scent. The road was fair, though muddy from the morning's rain. Omar showed us the two wire brushes that he and Ahmed had made. With these we scraped the worse of the mud off the wagon wheels. Even wearing aprons, we would clearly spend much of our journey quite dirty.

At regular intervals, as we traveled west, we saw the stone road markers, which read "King's Road" and our distance from Philadelphia. We pushed on, eating our provisions on horseback.

We would be leaving the King's Road after Lancaster, but we didn't get that far the first day. When dusk came, we pulled the wagon over to a flat roadside to make camp.

Benches that let down on chains from the inside walls of the wagon would serve as our beds, covered with pallets Mrs. Perry had made. "But where will you sleep, Omar?" I asked.

"Oh, it's good. I have oilcloth, bedroll, and my blanket for da ground. I sleep under da wagon," he said.

I started, "Oh, dear, I don't think—"

"It will be fine, Gwyn," said Ardath. She had busied herself making a fire, with which we boiled our pot of water for tea. We had a fine dinner of venison, greens, and corn pone. The air became cool, so we sat at the fire, pulling our cloaks around us. I sang my favorite ballad, "Elen Fwyn," but we didn't linger. Our wagon beds were very different from the rope beds at home, but I nestled in mine and was soon fast asleep, Auri curled beside me.

We reached Milltown by the end of the following day. It was a small but bustling village, and we were able to find a room in an inn that night, with hot stew and beer provided in the downstairs. Omar slept across our doorway for protection.

CHAPTER 65

August 1751
Carys

THE NEWS OF MY family's deaths would have rendered me paralyzed, but for the need to attend to others. Dougie had to be cared for and eased into a new routine at the house and with Marta. Captain Whitsun and I had much to do; he was preparing his ship for another trip. Before he could leave, he had to finish his paperwork from the last one. I saw he had great need of a secretary. Not only was his eyesight quite poor, but the ordeal on the ocean had also left him with a tremor in his hands that made writing difficult. It was an arduous undertaking to read his records; his captain's log looked like a nest of snakes.

As we worked the first day at the huge desk in his parlor, he showed me his notes and said, "I know what a task this sets for you, but I must have legible notes for the governor. Can you transcribe it?"

"I can become more used to the writing over time, but perhaps we can make it easier on both of us. I notice that the beginning of each report starts about the same. Perhaps we could have a shorthand for that and for other repetitive phrases," I said.

"Ah, good idea." He beamed at me, exposing his unfortunate teeth.

"For these notes here, perhaps you could draw a circle around the repeated parts so I may recognize them more easily. I will then ask you about what I still can't read."

Here I smiled kindly at him so that he would know I wasn't criticizing his efforts.

"Yes, yes, that could work," he said in a very relieved tone. His face looked younger immediately. This had been weighing on him, so simple a thing.

Thus we worked together. He had bills of lading and prizes that must be recorded and accounted for. In time, I did recognize the symbols he wrote more easily. I was good at figures as well, so the accounting began to smooth out.

At the same time, Dougie had to get used to his new surroundings. In this, Marta was a great help. She somehow managed her considerable work-load of running the house and yet always had time for him. Alex kept a nanny goat, whose milk Marta used for her wonderful cooking. She milked the goat for Dougie's food, and it agreed with his stomach, thank the Goddess! After a few days, we added mashed fruits to meals. He especially liked the sweet little bananas that grew in the yard. He ate flat wheat bread softened in the goat milk as well. I began to relax about his prospering here in this strange land.

While Alex and I concentrated at his desk, Dougie would play with his own feet and reach for a little doll Marta had made him. Lying on his back on the floor, cushioned by the pallet we had set down, he entertained himself well. His happy gurgling lightened our mood as we struggled over the paperwork.

If I had not been so busy, it would not have gone well for me. In moments alone, a dark-gray veil closed around me. My family was gone. I struggled to accept this, but it never seemed real, yet the stone in my heart told me it was. I had to keep myself from despair.

Unexpectedly, Alex helped me. As we sat quietly on the porch after a day of hard work, I began to talk. "Alex, my heart says, 'What's the point? If we live only to suffer the pain of losing our children, to whom we have given everything worth giving, for whom we have worked and worried and planned, done the best we could, gone on when we couldn't have gone on for ourselves, what's the point?'"

"Umm," he said, listening intently. "It must be the greatest suffering."

"I have no family anymore…"

"Are your parents gone also?" he asked, handing me his handkerchief and leaning forward a little in his chair.

"They might as well be. They disowned me for marrying Jacob. And Jacob's family disowned *him* for marrying me. We used to laugh about it, how we could be two black sheep together, but that was long ago, before he left."

"He *left* you?"

"Yes, with two young children. He felt he'd been called by God to be a minister, perhaps more of a monk at first, as he went into retreat and I heard nothing of him most years. Oh, he'd come home occasionally, looking gaunt and unhappy yet saying he had found God and I should be happy for him. Finally, I heard only news of him, mostly through his cousins' servants at the Manor House."

"Manor House?" Alex asked.

"Yes, his family was a prominent one in that area. Their ancestor was the Lord Rhys, who ruled all of southern Wales in the twelfth century, built castles nearby to fend off the Normans. We were the poor relations. After Ardath was born, we were allowed to live in the castle woods in an abandoned gamekeeper's house. My family never contacted us at all. They were also nobles, but from farther north in Wales."

"You haven't had an easy life," Alex said. "How did you support your children when Jacob was gone?"

"I was a midwife and healer," I said, sitting back in my chair. "Fortunately, Jacob was a good carpenter and a handyman and had made our stone house secure and comfortable before he was 'called.' My patients usually paid us with food or goods. Occasionally, I went to treat the Rhys's staff—only they called themselves Rice, for the benefit of the English court—or wealthy guests and received some coin in return, which I kept for things we had to buy. The Rices also allowed us to fish in the river and to use nets when the salmon ran, and to shoot rabbits using our bow, at which both Ardath and Gwyn became skilled. We lived a simple but good life.

"The lord of a neighboring manor, Lord Harleigh, whom I treated for gout, allowed us to borrow books. I taught the girls to read, including Latin and Greek, though I don't know how they would have used it…" I was suddenly stricken through the heart with my loss and could not go on.

"Mrs. Rhys, I tire you with all these questions," said Alex, concern for me written on his face. "I am sorry and so very sorry for your losses. I feel responsible."

Now it was my turn to comfort. "Please, Alex, don't blame yourself. I can tell you did everything in your power to keep that ship afloat. We are not gods, to make the impossible happen through our wills."

At this moment, Marta came in with a very sleepy Dougie in her arms. "I believe the prince is ready for bed," she said, grinning at us.

I stood up, feeling how tired I was, and gratefully took his warmth into my arms. "I'll say good night," I said softly to Marta and Alex, who looked at each other with contented smiles.

Dougie had his own bed now and slept on his stomach with the loose abandon of babies. I thought I might not sleep because my mourning paralyzed me with wakefulness at night, but I was able to drift off. Merciful Goddess, how I needed it!

In the morning, I found Alex on the floor of the dining area, teaching Dougie how to clap. It was a game that had both of them giggling with laughter, as Alex pretended to miss his own hands the way Dougie did. I thought what a fine father he would be, if ever he married.

"Do you think of having a child of your own?" I asked as he looked up at me.

"That would be a wonderful dream, but really now, what lovely young miss would want me, ugly as I am?" he asked, smiling as he pushed off the floor and swung Dougie in the air, to the baby's delight.

"Why, a woman of intelligence and taste!" I replied. It was true. Alex continually showed his kindness, intelligence, good humor, and steadfastness. Of course, what he said was also true; sadly, most young women would not see past his appearance. Marta clearly adored him, but he might not consider her opinion valid, since she was of a servant class.

He bowed formally to me. "Thank you very kindly. I must be off to the docks today, to interview the scum of the earth for my crew. With your help, I have been liberated from the ghastly paperwork and can get on with the real business of taking prizes for the Crown."

"I will finish the bills today," I promised. "I hope we can talk more tonight. I have told my story and want to hear more of yours."

He smiled, took his hat off the hook, and left the house with Dougie and myself waving goodbye to him.

His figures were easier to read than his longhand. I finished my work early. Dougie was napping on his pallet. Marta came in quietly, smiling, with a finger up to her mouth. We went to my room, where she had a surprise for me, a new dress in the same style she wore, including the vibrant colors that matched the colors of this bright world. I was both grateful and taken aback.

"Marta, how kind of you!"

"You try it on!" she insisted.

I hadn't the heart to tell her that bright colors weren't appropriate for me, as I was in mourning. I took off the ship's shift, which I wore when Alex was gone, to keep cool. She slid the new dress over my head. To my surprise, it was soft and yet wonderfully cool. Instead of the completely loose style she wore, this had tucks between my breasts and waist, making my figure stand out.

"You wear for Captain Alex," she said with a coy smile. "He a good man. A kind heart," she said, putting her hand to her breast. "Needs a good woman. This is cotton."

What could I say? My shoulders were exposed, but my breasts more modestly covered than fine ladies' gowns in England. Cotton was an expensive material, costing much more work than flax or even wool. I shrugged; I wasn't in England anymore.

"Thank you. It feels wonderful," I said, hugging her. She hugged right back. She was exuberant with her feelings. I said nothing about the disquieting feeling that she might want Alex and myself to have more than a business relationship. Alex couldn't be more than twenty-six. At forty-two, I was old enough to be his mother.

That evening, we sat on the porch after supper again, as had become our habit. I urged him to tell me about himself. "The only past I know about is your ordeals on the ocean this past spring."

"Well, I never want to bore you," he said, looking down into the red wine he swirled in his glass.

"You won't," I said.

"I come from Southern England, along the Cornish coast. I've never been to Wales, but I imagine it must look somewhat like the coast there, with high cliffs, rocky, dramatic shorelines, and rolling hills of grass and heather."

"Yes," I said. "I once went to the coast near St. David's in Wales, and it is like that there. What of your family?"

"My father made his fortune in his copper mines. My mother wished us to be raised as if noble children, so we were all formally educated, taught to dance, etc. I was an embarrassment to my father, though. I did not reach his ideals of young manhood as my handsome and well-formed brothers did. I think he was vastly relieved when I went off to sea. I think my mother was sad for me to leave. She kept me close after I survived the small pox as a young child." He smiled wryly. "My father only tolerated me. My brothers constantly made fun of me. She's the one person I miss."

"Does she know that you are alive?"

"Yes, she would by now. The governor sent my letter to her, so it got there as fast as anyone could expect."

"Good."

"The copper mines seem to be running out, but my family's fortunes are made. They have bought an estate and live a high life. One of my brothers is an MP, even."

"Ummm. What did you see ahead of you when you went to sea?"

"Seriously, I was more running away from than toward something, but the life has agreed with me. I rose to a mate's rank quite quickly, but there I stayed for many years. My appearance still made a difference to the merchant owners. They didn't take me seriously, so I was never captain. Until I survived the small pox on the *Bellwether*. Then I was captain by default, and I was in love, two things I never thought would happen."

He stopped there, his mouth turning down, chin held firm against the threatened wobble.

"Ardath?" I asked gently.

"Yes. She was a Goddess to me, brilliant, beautiful, statuesque, commanding. I couldn't help myself. I asked her to marry me. She, of course, refused." He looked down, shamefaced.

"I'm sorry," I said.

"Well, and then I acted the child, shunning her when formerly we had been friends, or at least so I imagined."

"Ardath could be difficult, I know. I'm not sure she ever would have married. She liked her own way too much," I said. "I was training her to follow me in my healing work, but…" I paused, thinking of my drowned hopes for my poor, dead children

Immediately, Alex said, "Perhaps we shouldn't talk of your daughters yet. It is perhaps too painful."

"No, I think it would help. You are the last person alive who knew them. We have much to share. Don't mind my watery eyes."

"Of course not. Please tell me more about your daughters, if you will."

"Ardath would go swimming in the oxbow lake below our house, even in March. I know she did it when I wasn't looking, because I'd come home to find her hair kinked. Often I didn't bother to fight about it. She was a strong swimmer, sometimes startling the swans that came in summer. Then we'd hear the racket they made, flapping heavily across the water before they could lift off, honking indignantly."

"I can imagine that. She was very interested in the workings of the ship also, always wanted to know more! She and Gwyn worked very hard with the small pox sufferers as well. Gwyn particularly showed great compassion."

"Yes, I can believe it. She was always tenderhearted. As a young child, she would bring home injured animals for us to tend." I paused. "The girls didn't get the pox?" I asked.

"No. They had had the ship's doctor variolate them before we left Liverpool, as it was rampant there."

"And Jacob didn't."

"No. Thought variolation was the devil's work." He paused, glancing at me. "Some of us had the pox as children, so we didn't get it. Most others died."

"Horrible!"

"Yes. It was a nightmare in broad daylight." He paused again, as if remembering those days. We drank our pineapple wine in silence.

"That was a cursed voyage," he continued, "but I remember some good times on it, Ardath's intense pleasure in mastering aspects of sailing, Gwyn wearing the cabin boy's pants so that she could run the deck and even some of the rigging. She thought that no one noticed. Eventually, one of the ladies reined her in, of course. There was an army major whom I admired, a tall fellow, a noble, and somewhat aloof, but he didn't mind lending a hand after we lost so many crew. He was a natural leader. I thought he might have an eye for Ardath, but then, what man wouldn't?" He sighed. "Well, enough of that! Have you seen the beauty of the stars here?" he asked.

"Yes, every clear night they amaze me."

He chuckled. "There are stars in the grass as well."

I craned my neck toward him to see if he was serious. He arose, grabbed a lantern, and gestured for me to follow him the few steps to the yard. A cool breeze stirred the leaves. He held the lantern high, and the grass suddenly sparkled with lights, thousands of them all around us. I drew in my breath sharply. "What is that?"

"Spider eyes! Every grass blade has its own spider."

"Oh my! I never suspected," I said. I paused as the lights twinkled before us. "Perhaps every fearsome thing has an aspect of beauty to it."

CHAPTER 66

May 1752
Ardath

WHEN WE TRAVELED OVER the green rolling hills and began to see well-built stone barns, fences, and houses, we knew we had reached the Dutch, really German, settlements of Pennsylvania. Sure enough, we spotted an austerely dressed man in a shiny black buggy pulled by matching bay horses. He had a white flyaway beard and a stern expression as he flipped the reins and pulled over to the side to let us pass. Otherwise, he did not acknowledge our presence.

"We must be in Lancaster County now," I said to Gwyn as we rode before the wagon. "Sometime today or tomorrow, we should reach Wright's Ferry, where Franklin's friend Susanna lives."

"I can't wait to meet her, if she is as interesting a person as Franklin says," Gwyn answered. Looking to the dark-gray sky, she shook her head. "I doubt we'll be there before the rain breaks, though. We'll probably arrive resembling drowned rats."

We unfurled our dark-green cloaks from the back of our saddles. We had tried rubbing oil into the wool in repeated applications, hoping to render them more waterproof. It had repelled the water we threw on it, but the real test would be a hard downpour. The storms of this new world were unlike those we had in Wales. Like the trees and spaces, the weather here was huge and wild.

We soon had our answer concerning the cloaks. The wind roared; the trees around us whipped as if in a frenzy, throwing wild heads almost to the ground. The rain fell in buckets. The scent of wet earth blew through our opened lips. Nothing was keeping this storm from soaking us to the skin, head to toe.

Omar stood up on the wagon seat, waving both arms and shouting at us. He was just yards away, but we couldn't hear him well. He gestured for us to come to the wagon. "Ladies, you must get in the wagon. We must stop and protect you!"

I shouted back, "No, we must go on! The roads will be getting worse if we wait."

He looked vastly unhappy but laid the reins on the wagon horses' backs, a signal to pull on. Fortunately, they had on blinders and could not see the thrashing trees well.

We moved on, but at a slower speed than I liked. It seemed like night-time, although it could not be more than four in the afternoon, when the storm started. After several hours, thank the Goddess, we began to see more frequent buildings and pulled into a small settlement, which I fervently hoped was Wright's Ferry.

A swinging lantern shone from a two-story log building ahead. The mud dashed up on our legs, our horses blew out exhausted breaths, heading straight for the building, which had a stable behind it. Omar got out, lunging through the downpour to a back door.

"Help my mistresses, please," I heard him say to the burly man in the lit doorway.

"Of course! Davy, get these horses into the stable for a rubdown," he said to a boy who came up beside him. He donned his cloak while the boy ran out in his shirtsleeves, taking the reins from Omar to lead the draft horses away. He and Omar maneuvered them and the whole wagon into the stable, including Auri. Meanwhile, the man helped us down into the muddy yard and guided us to the door.

The warmth and noise hit us as we entered a hallway leading to a large common room. While we stood, making puddles on the worn wooden floor, the man said, "Welcome to Wright's Tavern. I am James Wright, at thy service."

"Ah, Mr. Wright, we have traveled here to meet your sister, Susanna," I said. "I am Ardath James, and this is my sister, Gwyn Rhys."

"Splendid! I invite thee to stay here tonight if thee can. My sister's house is a short distance away, but the storm seems destined to continue a while. I can provide thee with a clean and private room and some clean tunics for thee to wear in the room while thy clothes dry. Thy man is welcome to bed down in the stable. Davy can take him dry clothes and a bowl of stew. I shall have ale and bowls sent to thy room also, of course."

"That would all be most welcome, sir," I said. We followed Mr. Wright up the stairs to a spacious room with a large bed. He provided dry shifts from the wardrobe and left us to change. We stripped off our cold, soaking clothes, rubbed ourselves red with towels, and gratefully sank to the bed in the shifts. Moments later, there was a knock on the door. I covered myself with a blanket and, opening the door, found a hot toddy, stew, and fresh bread and butter left there. Never had food or drink been more gratefully received.

We awoke following a good sleep. Our clothes were tolerably dry from the fire. Mr. Wright greeted us warmly and handed us a hearty loaf and cheese for breakfast.

"We are very grateful to you for your hospitality," I said when we had finished eating, "but if you will point out the way, we will pay and go on to your sister's house now."

"Oh, thee does not owe us anything. A friend of our sister's is always a welcome guest. I'll bet thee have some news of Franklin and some packages, too, with which she will educate us all." He winked at us, smiling broadly. "From the front of the tavern, turn left up the hill to the stone house overlooking the river. She expects thee."

So we loaded up, dried out the rain that had blown into the wagon, and were on our way. Susanna truly lived in a mansion; closely mortared gray stone gave a solidity and a feeling of timelessness. Dark-red shutters adorned the top floor windows, each of nine panes. The lower windows peeked from under the full-length porch's roof. Trees framed the house on each side. Red and yellow flowers rioted from the baskets lining the front walk.

Susanna's nephew John greeted us at the front door. "Aunt Susanna is working in the silk shed," he explained as he guided us through a foyer and main hall to the rear. The upper walls were paneled in a glowing reddish wood, perhaps cherry or walnut, while the lower walls were a creamy white. Crown molding adorned every part of the cornice; molded medallions graced the ceilings. It reminded me of the Newtown Manor House of the Rhyses (or Rices, as they called themselves). It was truly a gentlewoman's house, here on what most would consider the frontier of Pennsylvania. It was not that far from the large town, by colonial standards, of Philadelphia, I reminded myself. I smiled at Gwyn's gaping mouth. She said not a word, taking it all in.

Susanna Wright was tall and agile, her gold hair shot with gray. She smiled at us as she straightened from a wooden spinner. Filaments of shiny thread stretched and unwound as a servant cranked a handle at the end of the frame.

"Ah, you see me at one of my favorite things. Always seems a miracle that such thread can come from these little tight white cocoons," she said, pointing to the bucket where many inch-long oval cocoons floated. She rubbed her hands on her apron. "This is my best weaver, Frolly, who has a skilled hand with the loom." We nodded to the black woman. "You, I found out from brother James, are the friends of Franklin, who happens to be one of my dearest companions, by way of correspondence, of course."

"Yes, we have brought you packages from him." I introduced us.

"Delighted to meet you! Come, it is time for me to take a break. We shall all have tea."

She led us through a room at the back of the house, but detached from it, which had red tile floors and a large stone fireplace. "Franklin always says I should use his stove, but I like an open fire myself," she said.

"We do, too," said Gwyn. "This is wonderful. Your home is so beautiful."

"Thank you. Well, then, since it is a rather-nippy morning, shall we be informal and take our tea here?" She bustled about with preparations as we seated ourselves at the long kitchen table. She brought out shortbread cookies, which made me hungry, despite the solid breakfast her brother had given us. The tea was exceptionally hot and fragrant. I sighed with contentment.

"You have had some hard travel as you neared our settlement," she said.

"Very stormy," I said. "I hope it won't make the passage over the river too difficult."

"We are used to it in the spring, but this is the best passage across. Higher and lower on the river, the banks are steep and the river deeper, with stronger currents."

"Franklin told me that you are quite a serious natural philosopher, especially as pertains to plants and even medicines, as well as a lawyer and judge for settlers and natives alike," I said.

"Yes, I keep myself busy with many things, but my personal favorite thing is writing poetry. We have a circle of women writers who share with one another by post, very rewarding. Here is one I wrote that I think you might like. It's about the rule of inequality of women's rights in marriage," she said, handing me a piece of paper from her apron pocket.

> *But womankind call reason to their aid*
> *And question when or where that law was made*
> *That law divine (a plausible pretense)*
> *Oft urg'd with none or little sense.*

I laughed out loud. Susanna pursed her lips in amusement, her eyes gleaming. I did really like this woman, leading a frontier life but giving up none of her pleasures or her agile mind. In different circumstances, I thought we could have been close friends, a relationship quite lacking in my world.

"You have been preparing for us!" I said.

"Well, Franklin is a good correspondent. He told me about some of your adventures on the high seas, but I want to hear it all straight from both of you! First, let's get you settled in. Then let me ask if you have sufficient boots and an interest in seeing my fields."

When we told her that we did, she showed us to two lovely guest rooms upstairs. Omar unloaded our cases and went to the servants' quarters with Auri.

Susanna's hundred-acre farm had an unusual assortment of crops. There were hops for making beer, hemp, indigo, flax, and of course, the silkworms, mostly for the local silk and linen production. She had an herbal garden, with medicinal plants, and a kitchen garden with vegetables. Gwyn was in heaven!

When we returned to the house, we walked on her wide floorboards to the parlor. The doors leading in were curved and carved of the same polished wood we had seen in her foyer. The mantel was made of it and had a large mirror above. A brisk fire burned on the hearth, welcome this late in the day.

"Tomorrow, if you wish, we shall return to the silk shed so that you may see the many stages of silk production," she said.

"Oh, yes!" Gwyn and I said together, then smiled at each other, having enjoyed the day.

"We want to show you what Franklin sent," I said, pulling out the well-wrapped package we had brought. In truth, I was curious myself what books Susanna might have ordered.

"Oh, wonderful!" she said, tearing into the package while a maid served us tea. There was Ovid's poetry, in the Latin; a title in French, which I could not read; and several pamphlets, probably published by Franklin, as well as a lavender sachet. "Oh, Franklin! Such a romantic," she said, fingering the sachet. "I hope he behaved honorably with you," she said to me, looking me firmly in the eye. "He does love beautiful young women, especially clever ones."

"He was always completely chivalrous," I said, remembering the night we had first met and talked behind the governor's window curtains.

"Good, then! Now, we shall soon go in to dinner, and you shall tell me of your every adventure on the high seas. But first, there is one more item to see. Aha! I was hoping he would have it." She reached into the sack and unrolled a rectangular piece of vellum, which she showed to us. "It is a map of the Wagon Road made just last year for several lords by Fry and Jefferson. Now I shall be able, starting tonight with you, to show the way that lies before travelers on the Great Wagon Road."

"That's wonderful!" Gwyn responded.

"That will be a major help to us," I said. "May I make a copy?"

"Of course," Susanna said. "But it's time to go in to dinner now."

For dinner, we enjoyed fresh Susquehanna salmon, really a local fish of the walleye family. It was crisp and juicy, having been cooked on a griddle and topped with several herbs in butter. We spent the rest of the evening drinking wine and telling our stories, in which Susanna openly delighted.

"Please tell me what costume you wear in order to ride as you do," Susanna asked.

I showed her the leather divided "skirt" I had had made in Philadelphia, and Gwyn showed her the canvas pants she had from the ship.

Susanna looked at me askance. "You do know that as you move south, these leathers will become very hot to wear," she said.

"I admit I hadn't thought of that. I should have had some made of canvas too," I said.

"Don't worry, Frolly can make those for you tomorrow. I have canvas to hand. She can use these leathers as a pattern."

"Susanna, you are uncommonly kind to us," I said. How I admired her cleverness!

While we talked that night, I made a makeshift copy of the map. Mine at least showed the named major rivers all the way to North Carolina. Our stay at Susanna's was a great help and an inspiration to me.

CHAPTER 67

May 1752
Gwyn

AFTER A SECOND COMFORTABLE night at Susanna's, I found her and Ardath standing in the dining room, simultaneously quoting and throwing their arms out like actors.

"Arma virumque cano, Trojae qui primus ab oris Italiam, fato profugus."

Even I, though I had not Ardath's facility with languages, recognized the start of Virgil's *Aeneid*, Aeneas's journey to Italy. Appropriate for the trip ahead, I supposed.

"Shouldn't we be making haste to the ferry?" I said. I could hear the irritation in my voice. In just two days these two were such fast friends that I felt a little jealous. "Since we haven't heard any more news of Mother, we should be moving on as quickly as possible."

"Oh, but you have time for breakfast," said Susanna. "James will be making the ferry ready while we eat."

We had a full breakfast of eggs and bacon from her farm. I couldn't resist Susanna's good spirits and was soon laughing with the others.

When we stepped outside to meet Omar and mount our horses, I gazed at the broad, rippling river, which shone a pearly gray in the morning light. I expected to see a large barge-type ferry, but none was in sight.

Susanna saw my face and smiled. "The ferry is composed of two canoes, which James lashes together side by side. One side of your wagon and its wheels will go in one canoe, the other in the second canoe. The draft horses can remain hitched. Omar can go over with them. Then the men will take you

373

and your riding horses on the next trip. Because of the rain, there are many wagons waiting, but on my behalf, he has given you priority."

"That is very kind of you both," I said. I wiped my nervous hands on my canvas pants and adjusted my broad-brimmed straw hat. The sun glinted on the swells of the river. Swallows flitted and zoomed around the water, chasing the big black gnats that swarmed around us. Seagulls soared above us with raucous cries. From the wagon, which was closer to the water, Auri raced toward me, almost knocking me off my feet on the muddy slope of the riverbank. "You want to go with *me*, Auri?" A silly question, as I stroked his wiggling body. We had not allowed him in Susanna's immaculate house, so he had missed me.

Ardath came beside me to watch the men drawing the canoes farther onto the bank. The ends were flat, so that they shoved right into the mud, making an easy access to them. Side by side, they allowed room for the horses and wagon to be drawn directly onto the canoes.

Omar did a fine job of coaxing the horses and wheels into place while the ferrymen waved arms and shouted, "Draw 'em in! Draw 'em in! That's right." Traces jingled, the water rushed, and I was frankly glad that the wagon was going first.

Fascinated, we saw the ferrymen, two in the water in front and two from the bank in back, jump aboard with poles and paddles. Pushing the canoes off the bank, they grunted, muscles standing out from arms shiny with sweat. Once in the stream, they poled, then paddled hard upstream for quite a way. Auri jumped from my arms and ran, barking, along the bank paralleling the ferry.

"What are they doing?" I asked Susanna.

"They have to get farther upstream before they can catch the current that will pull the boats to the far side," she said. "I know that it looks perilous, but they have been doing this for twenty years now."

I noted that she didn't say how many passengers, horses, or wagons had been swept away during that time, but I felt a strange trepidation looking at the scene. This was a civilized crossing of our first major river. How would it be as we got farther south to wilder rivers with the three of us on our own? I shuddered.

I turned to Ardath. She put her arm around my shoulders. "All will be well, sister," she said. I gnawed on my thumb anyway.

A shout went up from the ferry. The men had paddled into midstream, turning the prows to their left. A swift current picked them up, jerking the boats rapidly downstream while the draft horses neighed in terror. My heart beat wildly, but in moments the boats lurched to the bank across from us.

A cheer went up from our side. A long line of wagons, horses, and individual people had gathered behind us. All of them must be relieved to see the first trip of the day end successfully!

After a laborious return, the ferrymen appeared below us again. We hugged Susanna and led our horses down the bank. I had Auri fixed to my chest in a tight sling. The horses entered the rocking boats with anxious looks. Ardath and I each settled next to the front ferrymen on plank seats. Out they poled and paddled. Green water splashed around us. I talked to Molly the whole time. At least that soothed *me*.

The last of the trip, when we were snatched by the current, was not as rough as I had feared. Still, I sighed with relief as the boats juddered to a stop on the far bank. All of us alighted with due speed. Omar had settled the draft horses down.

"Are my ladies ready to go on?" he asked.

"Oh, yes," Ardath and I replied, almost in unison.

The weather held as we traveled toward York, where Susanna had recommended the Golden Plough Tavern as a stop. In less than fifteen miles, we entered another small village with rough, muddy streets, which was more of a way-stop than a town, filled with the industry of men who shouted in Scotch and German accents. The farther west we went, the more primitive the settlements were, and we were just getting started. I liked to think that I had developed courage through all the adventures we had had, but now I thought maybe I had just been swept along, flopping through them like a fish stranded in a shallows.

"Well, that's enough of that!" said Ardath as we pulled out of York the next morning. "I'd rather be on the road than sleeping in a tavern." She rolled her shoulders as we rode into peaceful woods.

"The road is less well-traveled here," I said, "and not so well-maintained."

I looked back at Omar, whose wide lips were pursed, concentrating on taking care with the wagon. It tilted from side to side and bounced along behind us, slowing our journey.

According to the map Susanna had showed us, the next town would be in Virginia, about five days from York. Meanwhile, we had many stream crossings. The land would begin to slope down. At the bottom, a small stream of maybe four feet across presented no problem for our horses, but we all dismounted and guided the wagon down the slippery bank, across the water and, with a push, up the next bank. It seemed no time of riding the next hill up before we had to repeat the process on the next branch. Then the land rose constantly as we headed to a mountain pass. We reached the end of several days, exhausted.

"Let's stop and make a real camp," I pleaded to Ardath. Omar's face split into a broad grin.

"I like dat!" he said.

Stopping with good daylight was a real treat. After we rubbed down and hobbled the horses, Ardath got out the copy of the map she had made from Susanna's. We looked at the hills and streams ahead of us. We sat close by the fire; the air had cooled as we climbed.

Ardath sighed. "It's too slow," she said.

"Hmm," I said, my heart sinking.

"Look at the size of the rivers ahead of us as we go south. Most of these won't have ferries. How will we get the wagon across these? Furthermore, when the roads are rough, the wagon is slowing us down. I can imagine they will mostly be rougher as we get farther along," she said.

"What are you thinking? That we would leave the wagon behind? What would we do for shelter from wild animals?"

She grimaced. "Don't be a ninny. We'll have a fire."

"But Omar," I said, nodding toward the wagon where he rummaged around for his sleeping pallet. "He doesn't know how to ride."

"Of course, he couldn't come with us," she said.

"No, Ardath! We can't do it without a man," I said. I stopped suddenly because I had said exactly the wrong thing.

"Oh, can't do it without a man, huh! We will just see about *that*."

I remembered what Gregory had said to me about speaking up. "*No*, Ardath," I said. "I won't even consider it!"

Ardath sprang up and began pacing around the fire. She glared at me, green eyes flashing; I tried to hold her gaze calmly. She sighed. "All right, but we have to do something different."

What that could be, I didn't know.

In the morning we explored around the camp. Rushing, rocky streams hurtled past us on either side of the trail. The soggy black soil around them was green with the luxurious foliage of what we found out later was "skunk cabbage." So far on the trip, we had not found any of the plants Bartram told us to watch for. Perhaps it was just too early in spring.

While we prepared to leave, I took a moment to lean into Molly's warm neck, to whisper in her ear and feed her some oats by hand. The bond we had before had only increased over the time riding her. She nuzzled me back, looking with calm brown eyes through her long black eyelashes. "Don't worry," she seemed to say.

Today we would reach the pass and start down the other side toward Virginia. Auri ran alongside us, at times running off the trail in pursuit of squirrels or other creatures we did not see. Something about this land made me homesick for Wales.

Of course our mother was on my mind when we weren't dealing with some problem with the trail or streams. I wish I could say that thoughts of her uplifted my spirits. The truth was that I had a very uneasy feeling about this trip. The worst of it was that I became more and more convinced that the woman we sought in North Carolina was *not* our mother. My soul did not feel her any closer than before. I had my best visions while rocking along on Molly, but no visions of Mother had come to me.

Late in the day, we came to the crossing of the Patowmack River, where we boarded the Watkins Ferry, endured another haphazard crossing, and spotted ahead of us the mountains that formed to the west of the Great Valley. We were on the plateau that led to the town of Winchester, with the Shenandoah River looping to our southeast. This river meant the trail had to go to the northwest so that crossings could be reduced. We would be getting closer to those mountains near Winchester. I struggled about whether to tell Ardath and Omar of my forebodings about the dangers of the trail and the doubts I had about finding Mother.

We were at yet another creek crossing when a draft horse slipped in the mud as we tried to push the wagon up the bank. With an ominous creaking and swaying, the wagon teetered, then plunged back down the hill. Omar had been on that side, pushing. His leg caught under the iron-bound wheel, he screamed as the wagon rolled over him, dragging the horses over as well. They lay struggling and kicking in the mud and water while we somehow managed to pull Omar out from under them and the wagon. While I held Omar, Ardath unhitched the horses from the wagon so they could get to their feet. They clambered up the bank. All of us shook with the shock.

Omar was conscious, his mouth in a grimace, his skin turning gray. White bone had torn through the britches on his right leg.

"Omar, can you tell me where else you are injured? I see your leg is hurt. How is your chest?" I asked, but his eyes rolled back and he fainted away before he could reply.

Ardath appeared beside me. "I see the leg," she said. "Do you know if the horses stepped on him?"

"It happened so fast I couldn't tell. I don't think anything hit his head or neck. It would be best if we didn't move him, but we can't leave him in this cold water."

"Agreed. While he is out, we have to pull him up the bank. Wait a minute." She examined his neck, which seemed to lie straight, and unbuttoned his shirt. "Because his skin is so black, it's hard to tell if his chest was bruised, but I don't see cuts from the hooves."

"All right, then, I think we must move him. I can hold the leg, if you can get him under the arms." We were able to hoist him farther up the bank and into a patch of sunlight. Looking up, I said, "Ardath, it is just a little farther to the top. Do you think we can get him to level ground?"

I heard her take a deep breath, blowing out through her mouth. "Yes, good idea."

So we again hefted his inert body, this time over the lip of the bank. I slipped in the mud and let go of his legs for a moment, cursing to myself and straightening his leg, hearing and feeling that awful pop from the bones as I did so.

We stood, panting and shaking, but out of the hole, dripping mud and creek water. Ardath went back down to the wagon, which lay canted over the water. I smoothed Omar's brow and checked his breathing. It was steady. His pulse was rapid, but regular. I carefully felt his neck. No bones were out of place. His head was intact. As far as I could tell, his upper body had not been injured, thank God!

Ardath came back with a bucket of water, cloths, and scissors. We cut open the britches on his right leg. Carefully wiping around the break, we removed as much mud as we could. The break was mostly clean, a few small bones scattered around the wound.

"We have to boil this water," I said. Ardath nodded and got materials for a dry fire from the wagon. We would have to camp here, which was fortunately a fairly level spot. She soon had a good fire going, water boiling in the pot. She brought up a pallet for Omar. I looked at the sky, clear, thank God!

We poured the home-brewed alcohol Susanna had given us on the wound. Bits of bone washed away. "There's nothing we can do about those," I said. Ardath mopped blood from the wound while I stitched the major blood vessels.

"I agree, but we must try to save the major bones," Ardath said.

"Whatever we put in his body is there to stay, so we can't use gauze as a binder. I suggest we use spiderwebs," I said. Ardath nodded. I went in search of new-spun webs. There were many in the bushes around us, glistening in the sun. "Thank you, Goddess," I said to the nature that provided for us.

We pulled the bones into place and wound the webs around the break. I sewed the flesh together in layers as smooth as I could manage. Then we wound the gauze around both the leg and the boards we used to keep it straight.

"Good job, sister," said Ardath.

I almost cried, then, with relief that it was over. We had done the best we could. I lay back on a patch of grass and let the sun bless me, breathing deeply of the fresh air, once again aware of birdsong and blue sky.

Of course, it wasn't over, really. The wagon still lay in the ditch. The horses needed tending. Omar would soon be waking in pain. We had a very limited supply of laudanum, but I thought he should have it, as his pain would be severe.

While I was pondering this and Ardath was examining the draft horses' legs for injury, we heard the rumble of hoofbeats coming from the southwest, beyond the hill just ahead of us. Auri placed himself at my feet, growling. I stood and drew my surgical knife. Ardath straightened and ran to the wagon, emerging with the guns.

CHAPTER 68

October 1751
Carys

IT HAD BEEN ALMOST four months since we arrived in Jamaica. Alex had been gone on his expedition three of those months, leaving me with little to do here except care for Dougie and learn the Spanish language. Both the caretaking and the learning were a delight to me.

Marta also wanted to speak better English for her Captain Alex, so she was learning English as I learned Spanish. Alex had explained to me that Marta, her family, and a few other Spanish-speaking mestizos had come to Jamaica, which was largely filled with English settlers, from Santo Domingo when she was a baby. The mestizos were the offspring of Spanish settlers and the native Indians they found living in the islands.

We spoke often of Alex, of course. I tried to teach Dougie to call him LehLeh, which were the closest sounds to *Alex* that he could make.

The weather was consistent here, rain every day, then sun, not awfully hot because of the breeze we got on our hill. Marta showed me the way to the nearby stream, which poured down from the mountain over rounded rocks, making its own sweet music as it went. Dougie delighted in sitting in the shallow water, splashing it with his hands for long periods at a time, or playing with rocks that flashed gold on its bottom.

As long as I could stay in the moment, I was secure and content. Then the night came, hot and twisting, with the dreams of my daughters drowning, my husband writhing in illness. These visions stayed to haunt me. Sometimes I could sleep in the day, when Dougie took a nap, and be free of the dreams, not always.

Sometimes, too, I thought of my old country, so different from here. The stream reminded me of those in the northwestern part of Wales, where I was born, but of course, those were misty and full of greens, moss and fern, like faerie havens.

Here grew fabulous trees covered with fernlike leaves and bright-red blossoms so thick you could hardly get a hand between them, strange lizards with crests and bizarre eyes, birds with many-colored beaks larger than their bodies, palms with huge green coconuts, and other wonders I could hardly describe.

Alex had asked me if I wanted to go back to Wales. Being a gentleman, he didn't take seriously Smog's offer of my services for five years. I couldn't see taking a baby back onto a sailing ship for that long journey. Nor was there anything left for me there without my girls. My heart pained me. I turned my gaze to Dougie, who was joyfully splatting his hands on the floor as he crawled.

*****

"Mistress Rhys," Marta called one evening, as I watched the sun make its way to the western horizon. "Someone here to see you."

I followed her voice to the back veranda. I was astonished to see before me a face I had thought never to see again, that of Tionga from Smog's slaves. Her tiny frame stood proudly, but she gestured for me with both arms to come quickly. The tropical sun had disappeared in an instant. I grabbed a lantern and ran to her.

"Marta, can you please take care of Dougie?" I called behind me as I followed Tionga into the bush.

"Tionga, how are you? Where are we going?" I asked, panting.

She clamped an iron grip onto my arm to guide me with her. We hurried over rock and cactus, sending lizards skittering for shelter and birds rising with raucous cries. I gasped in air to keep going. It seemed an urgent mission.

In a short time, we came to a grove of bushes where Tionga stopped. I lit

382

my lantern; its reflection showed a semicircle of golden light on dark leaves. Gazing around me, I looked to Tionga for an explanation.

"Look, lady. You will need dis. Dese da cinchona bush. You make medicine for the shaking sickness."

All around stood the treasure of these plants. They were so close to the house that they might even be on Alex's property. If not, they just belonged to the English Crown. With these I could help others from the old countries survive here. I had used very little of my medical skills in the last months, not being familiar with the local plants except the few that Marta knew about, such as a cactus called aloe that was good for burns, and Chaney root for building good blood and enhancing a man's sexual nature.

"Thank you! Thank you! Such a gift!" I said to Tionga.

"Now not owe you anyting," Tionga said.

"Of course, you don't owe me anything," I said. "But how are you able to be here? I thought you and the others would be working on sugar plantations inland."

"Hush, lady, we not be slaves. We go to mountains, be Maroons. They never find us!" She grinned, showing short white teeth.

I gave her my lantern, insisting she take it, though she tried to give it back to me. "I say goodbye now," she said, and with that, she melted into the bush.

In the distance, I saw other lights join hers. It seemed that many of the slaves were with her in this escape. She had trusted me to be on their side, not to report what I had seen. And she left me with a gift worth more than gold. Swallowing a lump in my throat, I marked the spot with my handkerchief so that I could find it easily on tomorrow and felt my way back to the lights of the house.

Next day, I could not wait to go up the hill to the cinchona grove. In the better light, I saw that some bushes had reached the height of small trees, while others looked more compact. The leaves were oblong and a dark green, with a waxy sheen; the flowers were tubes of waxy pinkish red with a white star at the end. I determined to collect the bark off the larger specimens, and then only off the branches, since I feared harming the tree. With a sharp knife,

I carefully peeled off the bark of a lower branch. As I walked back, I noticed more of the bushes, made distinctive by their blooms. They grew all around Alex's property, so many that they looked like planted groves. I was puzzled; why had I not noticed them before?

Wondering about Tionga's plan, I asked Marta, "Who are the Maroons?"

"Oh, they slaves when the Spanish lived here. Spanish had to leave. They freed those slaves before English come. Now live by selves in the mountains. Stay free."

"Oh," I said. I guessed there were too many black people for the Spanish to take away. I shook my head at this strange place.

I enlisted Marta in my project. First, we boiled the bark in iron kettles for many hours, some in water and some in wine, to see which might make the best decoction. We wore bright blue, red, and yellow bandanas around our foreheads to keep the sweat from running into our eyes. Sometimes we sang to make the work seem lighter. I also tried sun-drying the thinner pieces of bark, laying them out on a log in the middle of the clearing behind the house. That took a long time, but we were then able to grind the dried bark into a powder, a way to keep the medicine longer.

"Marta," I said after a few days, "how will we know that we have made it correctly?"

"Bueno! I know a man in our settlement who has the sickness. I will ask him to try it for us."

"But I will try it first to know that we have not made a poison," I said. With a deep breath and a secret prayer to the Goddess, I drank the wine decoction, a good sip or two.

We stared at each other. "It is bitter, but I don't notice any change," I said.

"Gracias a Dios!" Marta said. "I will ask Jose if he wants to try it."

While we had worked, I took time to wonder. How had Tionga known where to find me? How had she known the cinchona groves were here? Had they even been there before she showed them to me? A shiver ran up my back. I never expected to see her again, so I couldn't ask her. She had knowledge that could only come from an extraordinary spiritual ability. There truly was a world of mystery beyond our own world.

Marta took the decoction to Jose, who suffered from the sickness. After several days, she reported that he was much better. Truly, this medication seemed a miracle. I wondered if it was available to people in Kingston. I still didn't feel able to go down our hill, with its hideous road and the fearful unknown that lurked before me in the city streets. I hoped Alex would be home soon so that I could ask him what he knew about this medicine. In the meantime, I made more of the powder to have ready, hoping that it would keep its potency.

CHAPTER 69

May 1752
Ardath

WE WAITED, HEARTS THUDDING, while hoofbeats thundered up the hill beyond us, the rider hidden from view. I took a deep breath. We were as vulnerable as we could be, our horses hobbled, our wagon in a trough, Omar unconscious on the ground, just two of us, and a knife and two pistols with which to defend ourselves.

Above the hilltop appeared a head with tricorn hat, the face of a young man, only one, thank the Goddess! He rode a big dun horse, and he must have been over six feet tall. He pulled back sharply on the reins as he saw us, causing his horse to twist away. A skilled horseman, he didn't lose his dignity in the process but calmed his mount and alighted gracefully.

"Ladies, are you in need of help?" he asked, doffing his hat. He was even taller than he had appeared on horseback. I still viewed him with suspicion. He might be pretending courtesy, to catch us off guard. Perhaps his thieving fellows awaited us just over the hill.

While we stared at him and that silly dog growled at Gwyn's feet, he bowed to us. "George Washington, at your service. I am surveyor in these parts to Thomas, Lord Fairfax."

This could be true, as Susanna had mentioned that Fairfax owned most of the land around the Winchester area. I fixed my eye on his blue-gray ones, which were deep-set under a strong brow. He had a long nose and well-shaven chin, with deep-brown hair pulled into a queue at the back. His face showed no deception, only a polite desire to help. I relaxed.

Seeing this, he smiled. "I would be most honored if you would lower those pistols," he said.

I did so. Auri ran at him and, I suspected, might bite at his ankles. "Auri!" I yelled, but the pup was throwing himself on the man's boots with delight.

"So sorry, sir," said Gwyn, who hastened to retrieve the dog.

"No bother," he said.

I introduced us and explained our predicament, although it was pretty plain to see.

The stranger knelt beside Omar, checking his wounded leg without touching.

"Umm, a bad break. It was fortunate that I was exercising my horse in this direction."

"Are we near Winchester?" I asked.

"Yes, but there are no quarters there that I could recommend to ladies, or to a man recovering from such a wound. We are closer to Greenway Court. Fairfax is not at home right now but I am sure would want me to help travelers such as yourselves."

With that, he slid down the muddy bank to the stream. Lifting the wagon easily with his large hands, he called up to us.

"Could you please steady the tongue for me?"

We hurried to guide the wagon as he lifted it up the bank. When he had it at the top, he smiled again, wiped his hands together, and bent over to examine the wheels and undercarriage, while I unashamedly admired his undercarriage, which was fine. He banged on the left wheels with the base of his palm and nodded.

"This will do to get us to the house, I believe," he said.

Omar was awake and groaning. Gwyn hurried to give him some laudanum, holding his muddy head with careful hands.

"My ladies, are you all right?" he asked, trying to lift his head.

"We are fine, Omar. A gentleman is here to help us. We will lift you into the wagon, which will pain your leg, but first we will let you rest a moment while we harness the horses again," said Gwyn.

"No, I can help," Omar began.

"Your slave is most solicitous," said Washington. To Omar, he said, "You must rest so that you may again serve your ladies." While Gwyn was speaking with Omar, he had already harnessed the horses.

"He is a freedman who rides with us at his own volition," I said. I supposed that from this place and south of here, everyone would think Omar was a slave.

"Ah, well, a good man he is. I am ready to lift him into the wagon, if you can hold his leg as still as possible." Washington gazed at me thoughtfully. "I do believe you can do this," he said. "You ladies look strong, if I may say so."

"You may," I said. "We must be fit for our journey down the Wagon Road."

With this, Gwyn jumped into the wagon, preparing a place for Omar to lie flat on his pallet. We pulled down the back gate. Washington lifted Omar as if he were a handful of straw while we held his leg as straight as possible. The poor man fainted again in the process. We tied Molly and Sally to the wagon. Gwyn rode with Omar to help him stay still. I drove the wagon with as much care as the road allowed.

Washington rode slowly off to the left of the wagon. "So you are headed down the Wagon Road through the Great Valley?" he asked.

"Yes, we are on our way to North Carolina, where we hope to find our mother. We stopped with Susanna Wright at the ferry on the Susquehanna, and she showed us a map of the way."

"All the way to Carolina?" he asked. "Do you know someone there?"

"Yes, our cousin lives in Anson County."

"Well, perhaps I can be of some assistance to you, having surveyed in the Valley of the Shenandoah. I must say that it is hardly a road fit for wagons, more a footpath in some areas. Not meaning to discourage you."

My heart did sink a little at hearing him say this; he exuded a sense of competence and confidence. I put this away to be considered later.

Even at a slow pace, we were able to reach Greenway Manor before dark. The wooden house had dormer windows above, which looked out over the roof covering the long veranda. When Washington stopped beside the wagon, he said, "Not so luxurious as the final house will be, but very comfortable. You can lodge here. I will be in the land office there." He pointed to a small stone building closer to another road. "Mrs. Dickens will probably put your man in the travelers' room at the back of the house. Ah, here she is."

A long thin woman with a severe bun came from the front porch to greet us. She agreed with the accommodations Washington had proposed and invited us to eat dinner shortly. I took the wagon around back. Omar's skin looked very gray as we lifted him out, but he didn't call out or complain. We got him settled in a narrow but clean bed. Gwyn stayed to tend to him.

"Please go on, Mrs. James," Washington said, handing my valise to Mrs. Dickens. "I will tend to the horses and wagon."

Mrs. Dickens showed me to one of the dormer rooms above the front porch. I sank to the bed with a sigh.

"Thank you so much!" I said. After she left, I got up to refresh myself with the bowl of water and towel she had brought. I rummaged in my valise. A fresh dress seemed a heavenly idea after this muddy, tiring day. Besides, my leather pants were a mess; they would have to be scraped and oiled. They were already stiffening. I should have worn the canvas ones Susanna had given me. Gwyn had worn her canvas pants; she could wash them out, and they would be dry in less than a day. Our mud-caked boots, we had left outside the kitchen.

We soon were at supper with Washington in fresh clothes also. In some ways, he reminded me of James, with his heavy brow, his height, his coloring, and his competent manner. He seemed less experienced than James, though, and younger. His eyes did not shine when he looked at me, of course. In fact, he was quite diffident toward us. I felt a painful stab of loneliness, of missing James.

"How did your mother come to be in the Carolinas?" he asked, after we had been served some pasties as a first course.

My mind was on James still, but Gwyn answered carefully. "Well, we don't know that it is our mother, but the woman meets her description. We have been hoping to find her since she disappeared in Wales over a year ago. Some assume she is dead, but we hope not…"

Here Gwyn's chin began to quiver, so I jumped in, explaining how we had come to Philadelphia with our father and settled there, sending out requests for news of her in the Old and New Worlds, until finally we had heard she might be in North Carolina.

"My husband traveled this road south earlier in the spring. I hope that we may find him also. When spring advances further, we hope to collect plants that may have medicinal properties, as both our mother and we have studied herbal medicine in Wales."

"You know herbal medicine?" he asked. "You will be most valuable members of whatever community you settle in! On the frontier, we must all fend for ourselves, sometimes entirely *too* much." With this, he rubbed his left jaw, where I had noticed some bad teeth. "Would you happen to have a remedy for toothache?" he asked.

"We have oil of cloves for the immediate pain," I said. "It heals as well, but not if the tooth is crumbling."

"Ah, well, if you could spare some of that precious oil, I would be very grateful," he said.

"Yes, of course, you must have it. It is easier to get here than in Wales, where we were more isolated," I said.

"Thank you. By the way, what do you think of the New World?" he asked.

Gwyn put down her pasty, shedding, flaky crumbs. "It is a most wonderful place, so wild and full of beauty. I feel the awe of God in every tree, flower, breeze, and in the warm earth."

Washington nodded. "The wilderness inspires awe indeed. Beyond us are the mountains and spaces where few white men have set foot, rushing waterfalls, clear streams, people of amazing beauty, unknown plants, soaring trees."

He paused. He and Gwyn looked into each other's eyes. Did I imagine a spark flew between them?

"About halfway down the valley, there is a natural bridge of rock spanning a gorge many hundreds of feet below it. The road goes right over the top, and the views are sublime."

Washington and Gwyn again stared at each other. I cleared my throat.

"Well," I said. "We have many decisions to make concerning our journey. If you are free, Washington, I wish you would tell us what you know about the road to the south."

"I would be pleased to do so," he said, rising from his chair and bowing to us. We retired to a cozy library where a bright fire burned, with padded chairs placed around it.

We showed Washington the map we had traced from Susanna's.

"Ah, yes, Fry and Jefferson," he said. "I had heard of this." He examined it carefully. "It does look like a fair representation of the route." He pulled over a small table so that we could all look at it together.

"You see how the route is fixed to the northwest of the Shenandoah River, because of its many loops. Most of the valley is fairly flat, with rolling hills at times and the Blue Ridge to the west. It is quite lovely but wild territory. Homesteaders have mostly built right beside the road, so you should be able to purchase corn and feed for the horses along the way," he said. "There are a few small settlements as well. One could hardly call them towns."

"Tell us about the river crossings, please," said Gwyn. Her high voice showed the tension she had about that part of the journey.

"You will be crossing many creeks about the size of the one I found you near, but there are also major rivers, a branch of the Shenandoah, here," he said pointing to the map. "Then the James, the Dan, and finally in North Carolina, the Yadkin." As he pointed to the rivers, I thought I saw Gwyn shiver.

"Perhaps we can continue this tomorrow, Mr. Washington, as I see my sister tires now." Gwyn's lips tightened, but she stood.

"I must go to Omar to dress his wound," she said.

"Of course, ladies." Washington rose and bowed. "Might I have use of this map a little longer?" he asked.

"Of course," I said. "Good night to you, and thank you."

CHAPTER 70

May 1752
Gwyn

I STAYED WITH OMAR until his body was relaxed and he was breathing evenly, then went to my bed in the dormer room with Ardath. When I peeled off my clothes and burrowed under the soft covers, a lassitude came over me. It had been quite a day. I couldn't even think about tomorrow. Tomorrow, when we had to decide what to do about our journey.

I dreamed about our mother, rising with the sun, warm, and exuding a lovely scent. The ancient Welsh lore says that we are all made of the seven elements, calm and tempestuous air, fresh and salt water, then earth, fire, and flowers, but she, she, was made of flowers only, bright hues that made the earth glow, bees humming around her, birds singing above her head. Her eyes were the green centers of white daisies, which spread cool petals across her brow; her cheeks were opened roses, her lips red tubular honeysuckle, her ears of pink rose of Sharon, her hair made of fragrant dark-red curls of bark. She wore a cloak of brilliant green leaves; her dress was strand after strand of reddish-purple foxglove flowing to the ground. Her lips moved. She was telling me something important. I awoke still breathing fragrant, earthy smells, longing to stay with her. But she was gone. All that remained was the morning sun streaming in our window. We faced another real day.

"Ardath, I dreamed of Mother last night," I said over breakfast. "She was made all of flowers, and she was trying to tell me something."

"What do you make of it?" asked Ardath. I wondered if she was also looking for guidance about what to do next, but dismissed that thought straight out.

"I don't know what to make of it. Perhaps she is telling us about where she is. It felt like somewhere tropical. I know I smelled cinnamon. Maybe she is saying to continue south. Maybe she is saying that she has passed beyond earthly concerns." I paused to take a breath. "Ardath, I have to tell you honestly that I have had a foreboding lately that we are not going to find her, that the woman in North Carolina is not our mother." I glanced at her. "I'm sorry."

"Well," she said crisply, "as you say, we don't know what these feelings and the dream really mean. We must make our decisions based on whatever actual information we can glean. Or perhaps you just don't want to go on?" She asked this looking sideways at me, not with anger, but as if she could understand.

I searched myself honestly, looking down at my folded hands, scratched and bruised from yesterday's ordeal. I felt a great pull toward Philadelphia and the life we knew there. I wanted to go back to the hearth, to stay where I belonged. I wished I had Gregory to talk to, or, better yet, some sort of divine adviser.

In the face of not knowing, I had always followed Mother or Ardath. Now I didn't have Mother and I was trying to be more independent of Ardath, more centered in my own judgment. Mother might have prayed either to the God of the little gray stone church at the bottom of our hill in Wales, or to a vision of the Goddess from earlier times. Father had believed in the faith of Christ; I had no doubt where his prayers would be sent. Ardath? Well, she believed in herself; the power of action worked for her. Sometimes she invoked the Goddess, but I thought that might only be in imitation of Mother.

"Well?" Ardath asked, her tone this time becoming impatient.

"I don't know. Omar can't go on, or go back either, until he heals, which will take weeks, perhaps months. Riding in the wagon would be torture for him and probably dislocate the break, rendering his leg useless for the remainder of his life," I said.

"Umm, true. We can't go on with Omar, as much as he will urge us to," said Ardath.

At this point, Washington entered the warm kitchen, where we sat at an old table. Mrs. Dickens served him breakfast and left. The cook had made tall biscuits, which we ate with fresh butter and honey.

"Mary, we are lucky to have you as our cook," he said to the red-faced woman near the fire. She beamed with satisfaction.

"Always want something good for you, Mr. Washington," she said.

"I'm afraid I have interrupted you in your discussion," he said to us. "Please continue as if I were not here."

I smiled at him. "Actually, we would welcome another viewpoint in our debate about what to do. Omar can't be moved without grave consequences to his leg."

"True. He must stay here until he heals. If you decide to continue your journey, I will take responsibility for his care. He is obviously very important to you."

"Oh, but we can't ask you to do that!" I said, blushing for some silly reason.

"But you aren't asking. I am offering. Here on the frontier, we must help one another. I sent our servant Gabriel to sit with Omar last night. He physics for all the workers here and would take tender care of a fellow African."

"We have silver. We could pay for his expenses," Ardath said. Washington nodded.

"We must decide whether to go on or to go back and travel by ship," I said.

"We *must* go on. There is no question of going back," said Ardath. She now had that set to her chin that bespoke the danger, and the futility, of confronting her.

"I don't know, Ardath," I said slowly. "I'm worried about what we will find on the trail. Past Winchester, as Washington has said, there are scattered farms but no towns worthy of the name. You know that we can't manage the wagon without help, especially as the road, or path, narrows and the rivers grow bigger in the spring rains."

Her face took on a dangerous red hue, her lips set in a thin line, but she drew a breath to say, "Sister, we *cannot* go back."

I stared at her. The silence in the room grew heavy. Washington cleared his throat. "Well, if you *do* go on, perhaps you could travel south with the Moravians. You are only a day or so behind them. They keep their sexes separate until marriage, but there are women among them, so they would probably accept you."

"In fact, we have a letter of introduction to them from their bishop," said Ardath quickly.

My heart sank. The Moravians were moving slowly, having set out a week or more ahead of us. Ardath would grow impatient with their lack of progress and pressure me to leave them, I felt sure of that. But now I was caught. I could not argue that we would be alone on the road.

"How I wish that I could go with you, to ensure your safety," Washington said, his brow wrinkled as if he had failed us somehow. "However, Fairfax is due back tomorrow and has another mission he will send me on."

"We understand, of course, sir," said Ardath.

"I am quite sure I can delay that mission long enough to escort you to the Moravians, though," he said.

"Many thanks to you!" said Ardath.

My goose was thoroughly cooked.

CHAPTER 71

October 1751
Carys

"MARTA, I'M HOME," ALEX'S cheerful voice called from the path beside the house.

"Alex!" I cried from the back deck, rushing down the steps to greet him. "Marta has taken Dougie to the stream to wash. Let me see you!" I caught his arms at the elbow. He looked more weary than he had sounded, with dark circles under his eyes, but a happy expression on his face. He bowed, laying down his seaman's bag and grinning at me.

"Success?" I guessed.

"Aye, we've had good fortune, I'd say."

"Nothing to do with skill, then," I teased, grinning back.

"A fine prize that makes the governor happy and me somewhat the richer. I could drink a good flagon of sweet wine and be even happier," he said.

"Of course, come in. We have some chilled. Marta had planned a jungle hen supper tonight, anyway. We are celebrating an end to some work we've been doing, but we shall have an even better reason to celebrate now," I said.

It didn't occur to me that I was inviting him into his own house. It had become so much my own home in the last months.

Just the walk up that hill had left him sweaty and covered in red dust. I handed him a basin of cool water and a cloth, which he took into his room.

I worked in the kitchen, slicing bananas and pineapple. The sweet smell added to my happiness. The out-of-doors oven had been heating all day, making it ready to roast hens wrapped in huge tropical leaves. It was best to leave

cooking heat outside, especially today. It seemed a particularly sultry afternoon. I could almost see the leaves droop on the trees; not a breeze stirred
them. The sky looked different, too, strangely colored, almost yellowish. I
shrugged. I lived in a very curious place.

Marta was soon back from the stream with Dougie and elated that Alex
was home. She ran to find him with Dougie still in her arms, but Alex was
closed in his room. She ran back to the kitchen, where I wiped my hands and
took Dougie from her.

"Ooooh! I must get those hens in the oven! We will have potatoes too, si?
All good for Captain Alex."

"Yes, I'll be getting those ready now," I said, putting Dougie down. He
looked up at me with big blue eyes, sensing our excitement. He crawled well
now and could even go down a few steps backward; Marta and I were very
proud. He crawled off toward the parlor, where he had a basket of toys. I sliced
potatoes and pondered my happiness at having Alex home. It seemed we had a
domestic relationship, a curious one, to be sure. What if this was my life now,
to live in a curious place curiously related to a man and a child? Once I might
have predicted a future for myself, but it would never have been this one.

The next thing I heard was a crow of delight, then babbling from Dougie.
Alex laughed in the next room. I wiped white potato starch from my hands and
went to see them. Alex was on the floor with Dougie. They were taking turns
putting Alex's hat on each other's heads, with limited success. Dougie giggled
from under the black tricorn, which sat on his forehead and down his nose. He
turned his head, hat and all, and pointed toward Alex.

"DaDa," he said in a definite tone. From the mouths of babes, I thought!
Alex smiled. "Words already!" he said into an awkward silence.

Marta came to the door. "The hens are in…Captain Alex, so happy you
are home!" she said, wringing her hands with delight. She rushed to shake and
shake his hand.

He rose, smiling at her. "It is good to be home, Marta. You grow more
beautiful and accomplished every time I return. I understand you were ready
to celebrate without me. Come, sit, you two. I want news. What were you

celebrating?"

I sat in a big cushioned chair. Dougie pulled himself up on my skirts. Lifting him in beside me, I watched Alex and Marta sit close together on the sofa.

With all her white teeth showing against a lovely light-brown skin, Marta laughed. "We have surprises for you, most ricos, most maravillosos! You tell," she said to me.

"Well, for one thing, we have our own chickens now. We have built a henhouse so that their eggs will be safe. Hens come in at night because we feed them in the nesting box. We even have our own jungle rooster, all shiny feathers and proud as a peacock. He had a broken wing, so we have penned him and the chickens in for their safety. Fresh eggs are forthcoming every morning. Soon Dougie will be able to feed the chickens, won't you, Dougie?"

Dougie grinned up at me. He was a smart boy. I thought he followed many of our conversations. "Dickys," he said.

"That is wonderful news!" said Alex.

"I bring the wine," said Marta.

We sat together, drinking the pineapple wine I loved so much, talking several hours, until the hens and potatoes were done. Then we moved to the table for a lovely meal.

Alex told us about the prize he caught. "So, we flew our right colors all the time, yet one day a Frenchie decided that we were ripe for the taking, colors or no. She bore down on us, but we were ready for her and turned to chase. We rolled out the guns and fired a warning shot across her bow, but she was committed to having us by then. Our next shots tore into her rigging somewhat fierce. We came to and boarded her. Hand to hand it was then, and they fought hard, I'll say that. Turns out she was loaded with rich trade goods, gold, rough jewels, spices, on their way back to France. Why she came after us, I'll never know. Those Frenchies are in the stockade now and will bring a good price themselves."

"Wonderful!" I said. "I do hope you will have some time to rest now, Alex."

Before he could reply, the roar of a sudden wind came through the house, where the breezes usually blew gently. None of us had been paying any attention to the weather as we caught up on news.

Marta looked up in alarm, dropping her napkin and running to the back of the house. "Dios Mio! It is the big storm!" she shouted, her words caught and flung away in the gusts that followed. She ran for the yard, dragging the goat up the hill.

Alex grabbed a blanket from his chair. Wrapping Dougie securely in his arms, he gestured for me to follow him out the door. I snatched up my shawl, running behind him. The clouds were dark as night, though it was only late afternoon. The wind began to howl. In seconds it would pour on us, but both Marta and Alex ran away from the house. I picked up a lantern. I could only follow them in confusion. No voices could be heard above the wind and the thrashing of the trees. They ran up and up the hill while I gasped for breath that the wind snatched away. Sure enough, the skies opened on us, rain needled our hunched backs and necks, and we were soaked and shivering. Still they ran, farther away from the house. Alex looked back to make sure I followed. Where were we going? Then they disappeared into thick brush that crowded up against a rocky hillside. I crashed my way through the brush, ignoring the scrapes of voracious limbs.

Before me lay the answer to my questions. A black opening in the hillside from which Alex's arm reached out to me. I lowered my head and stumbled into a shallow cavern. It was cool but dry in the cave. The others sat around; we'd not be able to stand. Alex struck a flint against his knife, producing a small flame he used to light a lantern. Dougie, undisturbed by all the rush, clapped his fat hands. The goat had to stay outside the cave, her head lowered, eyes shut against the rain.

When we had all reassured each other that we were all right, despite dripping clothes and a few scrapes, I looked around. To my surprise, the cave had been supplied at an earlier time, with a lantern, the flint, a knife, a pot, several dry cloths, blankets, and firewood. A dusty bucket lay on its side in the cave. Crouching, I put it out in the storm to catch water. No doubt it would fill quickly!

Alex noticed that I was shaking. "We'll need a fire to dry out and run the chill off," he said. His face was clear in the golden light of the lantern, full of concern.

"Thank you," I said. "But why have we left the shelter of the house?"

"Because this is not just a thunderstorm. It is called a hurricane."

"After that evil god!" said Marta.

"Yes, hurricanes send worse winds than you can imagine. The rain will be so hard that the river will flood. In the harbor, the waves will be so high that many ships and buildings may be washed away. Right now, I am thanking God that I am not on my ship in this. I would be a dead man."

I shivered again, this time not just from the chill. Alex turned toward the cave entrance. With agile brown hands, he stacked the firewood into a pyramid, striking his flint to light it. We soon had a nice blaze and even had to shove ourselves back from the heat.

Dougie clapped his hands again.

"So," said Alex, "tell me more about your work around here."

I nodded. We needed the diversion from the roars and the flashes of lightning without.

"We fashioned a well house in the stream to keep our goat milk and cheese cool." I didn't mention that it would probably be washed away in the storm. "We also planted a garden, which has mainly been eaten by the wildlife. Marta had some seeds of a fruit the Spanish know, called watermelon, that we are trying out. So far it is taking over the garden space from other plants, so it must be doing well."

"And Miss Carys, she has found a miraculous cure for the shaking sickness, right here on your land!" said Marta.

"Oh," he said, turning to me. "That is remarkable! What is it?"

"The bark of a bush or small tree called the cinchona, but it really isn't a cure. It helps when the sickness attacks," I said. "We have been trying to find the most effective preparation for it."

Alex looked in my eyes. Admiration shone from his. He turned to include

Marta in his appreciation. "You are amazing women. You have done so much," he said, then lowered his head and began to adjust the fire. He smiled again at Marta as she laid out blankets and rearranged our living space.

I called Dougie, who was playing with the sand in the cave, to come to my lap. His drooping eyelids quickly claimed my attention. I rocked that precious boy, smelling his clean boy-smell, putting my warm cheek on his curly brown hair until both he and I were nodding off. Marta laid a blanket down for us. Dougie and I curled up together on it and were gone to dreams.

It was a long night of storm, but we were fed and warm and dry. The rain provided us with water, and the Goddess sent us sleep.

Morning dawned clear and quiet in the cave. When we emerged, the world was greatly changed. Trees lay uprooted, vegetation lay broken around us, the river roared almost like the wind had yesterday. We could see clearly all the way to the house, or where the house had been, now a pile of rubble sticking up jaggedly toward a blue sky.

"Oh my God!" said Alex, hurrying downhill to the scene of destruction.

"Dios Mio!" echoed Marta as she led the goat slowly down the hill.

Taking Dougie in my arms, I picked my way down the littered hillside to the house. The cinchona bushes had lost some limbs but were mainly intact. To my amazement, the chickens were strutting around the pen, scurrying away from the rooster, who pranced after one and then another. The raging winds had somehow missed their shelter entirely. The garden was strewn with wreckage. That would take some time to repair, but we had better plans for it, anyway. The house, well, that was a complete wreck.

Alex looked over his property slowly. He walked up the steps toward the shattered timbers and heaps of thatch from the roof. Hauling up a shattered beam, he threw it aside and kicked at the piles around him. He was standing on a solid floor at that point, which gave me some hope. I set Dougie down among palm fronds and went to Alex.

"I'm so sorry for this loss," I said. "Now I know what the sailors were telling me about the storms here."

"Umm, thank you. I believe the floorboards may be intact under all this," he said slowly. "Carys, I need to go to the harbor to see to the ship. I'll get some of the crew up here to do repairs if I can. Perhaps you and Marta can clear the smaller debris while I am gone. If rain threatens, we will have to sleep another night in the cave. I'm sorry."

"Of course, Alex. We will salvage what we can here. We can certainly get the smaller limbs off the house materials."

He studied his hands. "Please be careful. Don't lift anything too heavy. I hope to be back soon."

"Of course. Don't worry. We will be fine here."

After he left, taking along a walking stick to help him down the muddy path, Marta and I set to work. There was much we could do here, carrying the debris to an area we didn't use for anything else. We felt better in action than sitting by. Dougie entertained himself, sweet boy!

Anything that had been covered by house materials actually survived pretty well. We found pots and pans a little dented, but usable. My cotton dress had survived, though filthy from debris. Dougie's blocks and other wooden toys were still in his toy box. I breathed deeply. Thanks to the quick action of Alex and Marta, we were all alive. I also said a prayer of thanks to all of nature and the Mother Goddess for sparing us.

For hours I lifted more debris off the floor of the house. The glass bottles of cinchona bark that we had spent many painstaking hours drying and grinding into powder lay shattered in glass and dust on the stone floor of our workroom.

It was as if the splinters of our efforts struck me in the breast. Suddenly, I was down the dark hole where my children grieved and drowned, my husband died in misery, where I'd lost my homeland, and I was dragged into a helpless slavery. I don't know how long I dwelt in that darkness before Marta shook me, repeatedly calling, "Miss Carys, Miss Carys!"

"Oh, oh, I…I'm sorry, Marta."

"You scare me! You scare Dougie!"

I looked around to see my precious boy kneeling in the dirt, wailing, rubbing grubby hands across his teary eyes. "Oh, Dougie, Mama is all right.

Here I come," I said. I stumbled across wreckage to his forlorn little figure, wrapping him in my arms, wiping his reddened face with my dress. "So sorry, Mama is all right. You are all right. Here, let us get a drink in the shade." I picked him up, then settled with him under a cinchona tree. He was soon sobbing quietly while I combed through his brown curls with my fingers. "What a brave boy you are, Dougie. Mama loves you."

Looking up, I saw that Alex had returned. I didn't know how much of this he had witnessed, but his face was filled with a deep sadness. He came to sit beside us. Marta brought us cool water from the well.

"I'm sorry, Alex, I fell into a hole in my mind..."

"You don't have to explain anything. It has made me think even more, this storm, my work in a dangerous sea. Marta always has her family to go to. You and Dougie have become *my* family, but I am leaving you vulnerable. I want to offer you the best protection I can in our uncertain situation. I want to marry you, adopt Dougie, give you both the protection of my name. It would, of course, be marriage in name only, not for bedding together." He sighed. "I have grown to love you both so much. You are the richest part of my world."

I saw the sincerity shine from his eyes, the crease of concern in his brow.

"Alex, what a good man you are, but this would not be a fair arrangement for you! Suppose you find a woman who could give it all to you, perhaps even bring you a dowry and likely produce children of your own? We would then be a burden to you."

"Never a burden!" he assured me, patting the arm I had wrapped around Dougie.

"I deeply appreciate your kindness, and I have been very happy here with you. Dougie has too." I smiled as Dougie reached up to Alex's face to tug on his nose. "But don't give up on having a woman of your own age to love."

He looked down at his hands, tanned and tough from hard work. "Well, I will find some way to make things better for you by legal means. I promise you that."

At this moment, several hardy-looking men walked up the track from town, carrying large bundles. Alex hailed them, rising to his feet. "These are men from the ship. The ship and town mostly fared better than we did. They have come to help us."

With Alex and the three crewmen hard at work, Marta and I were amazed at how quickly the rest of the rubble was cleared and a canvas tent covered in mosquito netting set on the wooden platform for us for the night. We had set our bed pallets over bushes to dry earlier in the day. The bright sun worked wonders on these, and we soon had a camp worthy of the name. The men left us with provisions from town when they departed. This night's dinner was served on the floor of yesterday's house, but just as gratefully received.

CHAPTER 72

May 1752
Ardath

IT WAS DECIDED. WASHINGTON was to take us to the Moravians today. Gwyn and I went to see Omar.

"My ladies, my ladies, I have failed you," he said, trying to raise himself on his elbows.

"No, Omar, you have not failed us," I said in my firmest voice. "Accidents happen. We are sorry this has happened to you."

"Omar, please don't worry. You have been so devoted to us! You must rest now and get well. We are the ones who fail you! We wish that we could stay with you while you are healing, but we must hurry to see if we can find our mother. Otherwise, we would never leave you. Mr. Washington will see to your care. Gabriel"—Gwyn nodded to the black man standing by—"will be with you for whatever you need. Remember to rest for at least the next six weeks. Don't get up too soon, or you will suffer further damage to your leg."

Omar grinned at her. "Miss Gwyn, I will not disobey you, I promise, but I am so sorry not to go on. How will you handle dat wagon?"

"We are going with a group of people, the Moravians, who are making a similar journey," I explained. "We can all help one another."

Omar visibly relaxed at that and lay down with a sigh. "Dat is better. Den I will send up prayers for safe journey."

Gwyn stroked his head and kissed him on the forehead. I could see Gabriel's look of surprise. I took Omar's hand in farewell.

Washington had the wagon and horses ready. I drove the wagon; Gwyn rode Molly. Sally was hitched on behind. Auri ran in circles in his usual helpful way. Washington rode his dun horse in advance of us all, directing us through small paths in the woods that we never would have found on our own.

Within a few hours, we caught up with the Moravians. They were taking a rest stop on the road. I really didn't relish spending time with these people of strange beliefs, but they were now part of our plan to reach North Carolina. I did respect their determination to go through the difficulties this trip presented. They were all dressed very conservatively, most of the men in workman's clothes of brown and gray, the women in similar colors.

Washington led us to the probable leader, a tall man with a gray beard, dressed all in black, who was accepting a ladle of water from a woman of a comparable age. A bonnet shielded her face from our view.

"Brother," Washington hailed him. "I have brought these ladies here to present to you. They are known to your Bishop Spangenberg and have a letter from him. I am Washington. Do you speak English?"

"Yes," said the man, looking up at Washington. "I am Brother Aaron. What can I do to help?"

"The ladies' escort has become incapacitated, and they have not a guide to take them to Anson County, south of your Wachovia Tract, where they seek their mother," said Washington.

I took the letter from Spangenberg out of my saddlebags. Dismounting, I handed it to Brother Aaron, who accepted it with a nod.

"Please come, take some refreshment with us," he said, turning to the woman beside him. "My wife, Rachel."

"These are Mrs. James and Miss Rhys," said Washington. Not knowing what else to do, we bobbed a curtsy to the two Moravians.

"Rachel speaks English too," Aaron said. She smiled at us and gestured for us to sit on a bench beside the road. She offered us water and journey cakes, which we were happy to receive. All around us, women glanced at us and chattered in German, a language I didn't know well. The men stood apart in their own group, stretching and conversing in a lower register. I could hear that some words were similar to English, but not enough to follow a conversation.

I vowed to learn this language as quickly as I could.

Auri was behaving himself today, thank goodness! Maybe the running he had done on the way was enough to calm him down. Of course, he was at our feet, begging for crumbs. I caught Gwyn "accidentally" dropping some of her cake to him.

"Well, Rachel, how has the journey been so far?" I asked her. She lifted a weathered face to me, pale-blue eyes smiling.

"The Lord has provided for us. We have traveled in his care."

"Ah," I said. Inwardly, my heart sank. Afraid I would get only sanctimonious platitudes for answers, I still forged ahead. "Have the river crossings been very perilous for you?" I looked at the three huge wagons and the teams of six horses hitched to each one, trying to imagine the spectacle of their crossings.

"Every difficulty has been seen to by our Lord, who is with us at every moment, as we go to our new Canaan Land," she said.

"We have the highest respect for your courage in setting forth on this road," said Gwyn, nudging my foot with hers to remind me to remain polite. "I have certainly had my worries about how we would fare out here. If your husband agrees, we will be most grateful to travel with you."

"We always want to help other pilgrims in need," said Rachel. Gwyn smiled, at her most charming, while I reined in the wild horses of my impatience with all this syrupy patter.

Aaron soon returned to us, nodding. "We would be most glad to have you join us on our journey through this great valley. Brother Washington has been most helpful with his knowledge of the trail farther south. I believe he wishes to take leave of you now."

Washington approached us and, bowing, held out his hand, taking each of ours in turn. "Ladies, it has been a pleasure meeting you. I wish you every success in your journey and your search. You may depend on me to see to your man Omar. May we meet soon again."

"Thank you for all your help," I said.

"We really appreciate your kindness," said Gwyn.

"My pleasure," he said. Mounting his horse, he cantered away. I was sorry to see him go. Though still young, he was a gentleman, and very straightforward in his manner. I respected that.

They placed our wagon in line behind their first two. It looked like a toy compared with theirs. Of course, they were carrying all they needed for setting up a permanent colony. I was glad that they seemed willing to leave us to our own devices, managing our own wagon and horses as we saw fit. For a while, we hitched both mares to the back of the wagon and sat on the driver's bench together.

"Well, we're on our way again," Gwyn said.

"Umm," I said.

"Ardath, you will keep your temper with these kind folk, won't you?"

"In all honesty, Gwyn, I will try, but what I see behind their innocent faces is the 'Christian' cruelty our father wielded over our mother and the 'Christian' hatred Aunt showed as she kicked you, the hypocrites! And I fear the Moravians will move very slowly."

"But not all people nor all Christians misuse their beliefs like that!" she said.

"Hmmpf," I said, effectively closing the subject.

*****

After a long pause, Gwyn asked, "What do you think happens after we die?"

"What makes you ask that? Is being among religious folk bringing out strains of madness in you?" I turned my head to look at her closely.

"No, I have been thinking of this lately anyway. If this isn't our mother in North Carolina, it doesn't mean she is dead, of course."

"But...," I said.

"But if she were dead, where would she be? I don't know if she was a real Christian, as such. I know she fervently believed that the Goddess Brigid looks after women, especially those in transitions of life. Do you know if she believed we go to a heaven where we might meet up with one another again, or whether we simply dissolve into the earth or sea?"

"Gwyn, for goodness' sake, why *are* you on this morbid track? Leave it be!" It irritated me to have her go on this way, spreading doubt when we had so many practical matters to face.

To my surprise, she didn't back down, but continued, "Ardath, do not try to shut me up. This is important. Besides, what else have we to talk about on this lovely day?"

She was right about the day. Blue sky and billowing cloud rolled overhead, birds called, and I swear, the sun was warmer since we left Winchester.

"It is a beautiful day, I'll give you that," I replied. "So let's not spoil it. After all, what use is it to speculate on what we can't know?"

"Well, many wise men across the ages have asked these questions," Gwyn said, sighing.

"Yes, but what kind of answers did they get? And meanwhile their wives were making them supper." I grinned.

She laughed, as I had hoped she would. "You won't get me off this subject so easily, Ardath."

"To be serious, I just don't know. It might be comforting to think we would meet loved ones in another life after this, but even that seems unlikely to me. I say we can make the most of this life we have. Mother will always live in our hearts, no matter what."

"I have to agree with both those last ideas," Gwyn said. Her thoughtful face showed that this concern wasn't over for her.

Dear Gwyn, with her deep thoughts and her growing spirit. I felt a sweep of love for her, and taking one hand off the reins, I enveloped her cold little fingers in my warm ones.

We looked up as the spatter of rain on the canvas caught our attention. How suddenly the weather changed here! We pulled the covering further over the roof of our bench, feeling the cold drops on our bare arms. I was glad Omar had thought of providing a roof for the driver. Our wagon train plodded on, with the Moravians stoically covering themselves against the elements. Gwyn crawled into the wagon for our shawls. She came back with a yawning Auri.

"He has been fast asleep on the sacks in the back," Gwyn said. "Such a hard life, right, Auri?" In response, he yawned so widely we could see down his throat.

Oh, please don't talk to him as if he were your baby, I thought. Fortunately, she was too distracted, wiggling to get them comfortable, as the rain began to blow sideways.

"Gwyn, go on into the back. No sense in both of us being wet," I said.

"I hate to leave you out here," she said.

"I mean it. Get in the back and warm yourself up." I gave her a one-armed hug, and she argued no more but scurried with Auri into the interior. In truth, I liked being in the rain with my own thoughts.

CHAPTER 73

May 1752
Gwyn

IN OUR FIRST NIGHT with the wagon train, I made a friend. One of the Single Sisters approached me shyly as we looked for a fairly level place for the wagon.

"Sprechen Sie Deutsch?" she asked. I shook my head and looked at her, curious. She wore a brown homespun dress, remarkable in its ugliness, with her blondish braids tucked under a large white bonnet that tied in the back. She had hazel eyes and a pug nose in a broad face. It was perhaps the most innocent face I had ever seen.

"I speak some little English," she said. "I like to practice, yes?"

"Yes," I said, relieved.

"Good dog," she said to Auri, who was, of course, jumping up to get her attention. She knelt down to let him lick her on the face as she giggled. "I hope get a dog in North Carolina, maybe good big dog, or small dog is good too." Her *good* sounded like *goot*.

"What will you do when you get there?" I asked.

"Marry a good Brother, whoever the lottery picks."

I looked down so that I wouldn't stare at her. She appeared to be about twelve years old. And she seemed perfectly happy that her husband would be chosen for her by chance in a lottery. I marveled at the devotion to discipline that showed.

"I will make a good home for him. I will tend his garden. I like to grow vegetables," she said.

"Oh, so do I. Leeks and salad greens, beets and squash, beans, cucumbers for pickles, onions, garlics, herbs."

"In the south, I have heard you can grow corn such as the Indians use, flax for cloth, even cotton," she said.

"In Philadelphia, I used to sew with my friend Mrs. Perry. We used some cotton, but mostly linen and the heavier silks and velvets, even brocade, for colder weather."

"Those were costly clothes, then."

"Yes, but the ladies brought their own materials. We just sewed them."

"I was born on our farm. I have not see fancy lady clothes," she said, looking a little wistful.

"Some are very beautiful, but they are too delicate to use on a farm or trail. Honestly, they cost too much money to make sense to me," I admitted. "My favorite clothes are pants and shirts such as the boys wear. When we were on the ship, I loved to go barefoot and wear the cabin boy's clothes."

She looked shocked. "You came from old world on a ship?" she asked. "You wore pants?" Then she threw questions at me as fast as I could answer about the voyage and our time in Philadelphia.

Before we knew it, Ardath came for me, and Brother Aaron and Sister Rachel for Hannah.

"So you have met our niece," said Rachel. Then to Hannah, she said, "The Sisters are waiting for you; Please hurry!" Hannah waved at me and ran off toward a group of young women.

"The Sisters will be singing for the service tonight," said Brother Aaron. "We ask you to join, if you wish."

"Thank you," I said. Ardath stood by in silence.

"Gwyn, we need some kindling for the fire," Ardath said. "I have our camp set up, but we also need some more water from the stream." Her mouth was a thin line. Obviously, she felt I had been shirking my duties to talk with Hannah.

"I'm sorry. I'll get some wood first," I said, grabbing the hatchet and heading for the nearby forest. By now, the leaves were full on the trees. The silence of the forest muffled my footsteps, and its cool shade fell over me. I felt the magic of the Goddess of Nature here. These were old trees, with pale green lichens hanging from the rough branches and the huge deeply grooved trunks. I trod carefully over the bright-green mossy mounds and hollows. Most trees were hardwood, with some pines mixed in. The pines had lower branches of gray deadwood. I grasped one of these, and by swinging on the branches with all my weight, I was able to break it off. Fine firewood, I thought with satisfaction.

By continuing to swing and break, I soon had a good pile of choice sticks and was ready to go back to camp. As I turned to go, I saw ahead of me an ugly black dog. His hindquarters were taller than his fore, and he moved with an awkward sway that worried me. What was this poor creature doing out in the woods by itself?

I approached, calling softly to it, "Here, doggie dog, what is wrong with you?"

It turned its head to me. I realized that this was no dog, but a little black bear with a pointed brown nose and rounded ears, who rose on his hind legs to look at me.

Behind me, a deep-throated growl rumbled. The little bear scrambled up a tree, but I was stuck between that tree and a protective mother bear. I turned slowly to face her. She was huge, probably three hundred pounds, deep black, with her lips drawn back from her red mouth. The growl deepened. She stood, towering over me, waving her arms. Her rows of nipples dripped milk.

I had no idea what to do, but if she wanted to look big, I would look small. I slowly backed away from the baby's tree toward a large oak I could see from the corner of my eye. When I felt the rough wood against my back, I slid to the ground, hiding my face in the leaves, covering my neck and face with my arms. I could just see her. She dropped to all fours, lumbering over to me. I prayed to nature that the mother would know I meant no harm. I tried to send a sense of peace out to her.

Her wet nose snuffled over my ear, pushing at it while my heart beat hard, but I stayed as still as I could. She smelled rank, like rotted meat. I wondered if she could smell my fear. With a huff, she turned from me toward her baby, calling to him. He clambered down the tree. She touched her nose to his, and off they lumbered toward the thick forest.

I sighed and rose, cramped and damp from the leaves. My sticks still lay nearby in their pile. With a prayer of gratitude, I picked them up. As I went back toward the wagon train, I heard scrambling in the woods before me. I prepared to drop to the ground again, but soon Auri's bright black eyes and welcoming bark greeted me.

Now I worried that he would chase the bear. The bear would not be patient with him! He stood still, scenting the air. "No, Auri, to me," I called. If he decided to follow the bear, it would take only a swing of that massive paw to wipe him out of existence. Thank goodness he obeyed me this time.

"What took you so long?" asked Ardath when I dumped the branches down near the fireside. I had to laugh; in truth, it was a rather-crazed laugh. Ardath just looked at me. I never replied to her but, still giggling wildly, hauled up the bucket and headed for the stream.

That night at the Moravian service, Hannah pulled me from the sidelines to the Single Sisters choir. They sang in full joy, in German, but I was able to catch the tunes and could hum along at least. I could tell that the men, from the other side of the "aisle," spoke of thanksgiving for their journey. All the congregation exuded a solid peacefulness that I envied. For the moment, I was caught in it too.

We bedded down early. The wagon's shelf-beds had become like a home to me. Auri was a comfort always. I spared a moment for my own thanksgiving, but where the gratitude was directed, I didn't know.

CHAPTER 74

December 1751 and January 1752
Carys

IN THE MONTHS FOLLOWING the hurricane, we were busy rebuilding. Work crews headed by the ship's carpenter remade the house as it had been. Alex said it was pointless to build a sturdier house on a hill such as this. If a hurricane came, any structure would fall.

"Don't worry, though," he said, as the hammers rang at the house, "hurricanes are actually very rare here. After this, we must see to the ship, which, thank heavens, requires fewer repairs than I feared to be seaworthy again." He smiled at me. "How are you doing?" he asked. "Do you feel able to help with the paperwork from my last trip?"

"I am really fine, and very ready to work," I said, somewhat surprised that it was the truth. Alex had been like a grown son to me, showing a touching strength and tenderness. Dougie, bless his soul, had bounced back so quickly that he cheered the rest of us up. It was a full-time job to keep him out of the workers' way. At ten months, he toddled around, holding on to piles of lumber and attempting to carry little sticks over his shoulder in imitation of the men carrying timbers, even copying their grunts as they picked the heavy wood up. He had a "hammer" Alex had carved for him, with which he sat and pounded away on a block for happy hours.

With one eye on Dougie, Marta and I had repaired the garden area and replanted parts that weren't doing well after the storm. To enrich the soil, she brought guano from the small mestizo community where she and her mother lived. Whether from that, or the climate, which changed little as the months

415

rolled by, plants sprang from the ground almost overnight. Alex gave us a new plant, called ginger, which had been brought in by merchant ship. It prospered under our care too. I began to experiment with it for cooking and in medicine as well. I had already found that a tea of ginger helped soothe the stomach.

The chickens prospered also. Dougie delighted in throwing our food scraps over their fence to them and watching them scurry over to peck them up. He clapped his hands and turned to us, forgetting to hold the fence. He plopped down on his bottom while we called "Boom." He giggled, turned onto hands and knees, and was up again in no time.

Alex and I got the paperwork done in record time. After that, he helped the men with the building, but some days he went to the port to make plans for his next journey. On those days, he brought back fresh fish, and sometimes spiny lobsters. Fish marinated in lemon juice and cooked on our outside fire was a fresh delicacy. We would never go hungry here!

The river had gone back to its banks within days. We remade Dougie's pool, which had filled with tumbled rocks of all sizes. By midday, we all used the cool stream for relief from the heat. That was the best time to rebuild the cool box, which had washed away in the torrent caused by the heavy rains.

The day we had moved fully back into the house, I noticed that Alex was sweating abnormally and his eyes were glazed over. I went to him as he lifted the box he had remade for Dougie's toys.

"Alex?" I said. He looked at me vaguely, then crashed to the floor on top of the box.

"Marta, help!" I called. She was there in an instant. We helped Alex to the couch, where he slumped, his dead weight on us as we swung his legs over to lay him down. Marta ran for cloths and water while I examined him. When he began to shiver violently, I realized he had caught the shaking sickness. Marta and I had not had time to replace the medicine from the cinchona that was destroyed in the storm. The best we could do was to cool him with the cloths while I brewed a decoction.

"Marta, keep wiping him down as best you can while I get some bark ready. Where is Dougie?"

"By the chickens," she sobbed.

"Marta, you must stay calm. I'll get Dougie and make the medicine." She still sobbed over Alex; I knew her well enough by now to see how utterly devoted she was to him. "Marta." I turned her to face me, hand on her chin, eye on eye. "I have to leave Dougie here with you. Don't let him see you like this!"

She breathed in and set her shoulders.

I grabbed a knife and headed outside. Thank the Goddess, Dougie was still down by the chicken coop. I grabbed him up as if it were a game and took him to the main room. "Stay with Marta now. Don't leave her, promise?"

Dougie solemnly nodded and peered at Alex.

"Alex will be all right. I need to make him some medicine, then I'll be back. Be good!" I said.

I ran to the yard. The coals still burned from the morning's breakfast. I carefully stirred them and put small sticks on to revive the fire. Next, I put the cast-iron pot on to heat and ran for the cinchona grove. My hands shook enough to make the knife slip, causing blood's red bloom to swell across my palm. I ignored it and labored away to get enough bark for the decoction. Wine was actually a better carrier of the medicine, but it took too long. I'd make it with water and add the wine to make it more palatable.

It seemed forever waiting for the water to extract the cinchona essence. I went inside, where the scene was much as I had left it. Dougie played quietly on the floor. Marta mopped the sweat from Alex, who tried to rise when he saw me.

"No, Alex, please relax. We will take care of you."

"But I don't want you to get sick," he said.

"We will not. This sickness is not like the plague or the small pox, where a person catches it from another. You will not harm us. Be at peace."

I lifted his moist shoulders to give him a drink. He shook his head, but I insisted. "You will feel worse if you don't drink. You are losing much body fluid through the sweating. Remember, I am a healer."

He smiled ruefully and drank several mouthfuls.

"That's it," I said. "Marta, make him drink whenever he wakes," I said.

She nodded.

"Alex, have you had this sickness before?" I asked.

"No," he replied, clenching his teeth against a shiver.

"All right. Marta, I'm going back to check the decoction. Come for me if you need me."

I reached down to hug Dougie. Concern flared in his eyes. "LecLec?" he asked.

"We are going to make him better," I answered. How I hoped that was true!

In hours of hanging over the pot and stoking the flames, my eyes stung from the smoke, but this was one fire I had to keep going strong. The tedium left me too much time to think. Most people recovered from this illness, but I didn't know if Alex, his constitution weakened by his ordeal at sea, would be that fortunate. I had been living day to day without anxiety about my future and Dougie's. But if Alex were to die from illness, or in a storm, or fighting at sea, what would become of us? Alex was the linchpin of our lives here. Maybe I could be a midwife and healer in the Kingston community, but I doubted I'd ever feel at home there. Marta, it seemed, might be in love with him and never get over his loss.

Finally, I judged the medicine to be ready. Cooling off the pot in the stream, I strained the contents through a cheesecloth and went to the main room. Dougie had fallen asleep on a blanket on the floor. Marta dozed, lying across Alex's arm as he slept.

Alex shivered and jumped in his sleep, looking waxy beneath his tan. I touched his shoulder gently. "Whaa?" he called, waking Marta. She slid away when she saw me.

"Marta, please find the Madeira," I whispered. When she returned, I added the wine to the cinchona and convinced him to drink.

The first sip dribbled down his chin. "Alex, you must focus on the drink," I said. "It will help you!" He shook his wobbling head, but I forced the cup to his mouth again. "Alex," I said more sharply, "you *must* drink!"

Bleary eyes peered at me, but something about my tone must have convinced him. "All right, Mother, don't shout," he said in a little-boy voice.

"That's it," I said when he drank. "Good boy!"

At this, Dougie stirred and began to whimper. His little plump mouth turned down. With a start, I realized that none of us had eaten since breakfast, especially hard on a baby.

"I'm sorry, darling. Let's get a banana and then I'll make you some eggs." He smiled, and every fear vanished from his face. The responsibility of keeping him from harm and making him feel as loved as he was overwhelmed me for a moment. Then it gave me strength. There was nothing I wouldn't do for my last remaining child!

*****

Marta and I nursed Alex for several worrisome weeks. The cinchona bark helped greatly, according to Marta, who had seen more of the illness than I had.

"Alex, how are you feeling?" I asked on a day when he seemed improved. His prominent eyes had sunk into his face and his cheeks were gaunt, but he was calm. He lay back on his pillow, which was still wet with his sweat.

"Ah, Carys, I have been better, but I have been worse as well," he said with an attempt at a smile.

"You do seem better, fewer chills, and you are more alert," I said.

"I feel weak." He looked around to make sure Marta wasn't in the room. "Don't tell Marta. I know she has been crying over me. I didn't like leaving you all unprotected while I was so feeble."

"We are fine," I said. "We are even fine when you are on a voyage."

He groaned and raised himself on the bed. "Oh my God! Does the governor know? How long have I been down?"

"Not long for such an illness as this. The governor has been keeping track of you and even offered to take you into his house, but we thought it better to keep you here. He has often sent gifts of fruit and fish and even bread, since he knows we are busy here."

"I know that you or Marta has been here every time I was awake, any time of day or night," he said. "You both must be exhausted! And Dougie?" he asked with a sudden concern.

"Dougie is fine. We have kept him busy outside. He has 'his' part of the garden in which he happily digs by the hour."

"I would like to see him, but I must look and smell a fright!"

"How about a wipe-down and some broth?"

He blushed when I took off his shirt to wash him, but I said, "Remember, I am a healer. There is not a part of the body that I haven't seen!" I smiled at him.

"Of course, it's just that…"

"Please let me know if you feel a chill when I do this. I have heated the water, but I want to be careful," I said. He nodded.

Alex was able to tolerate his bath in bed, which I thought was a very good sign. He lay without protest while I moved him around to do it. It was pitiable to see how shrunk his body was. When he also drank chicken broth and tea, I was encouraged.

"You should rest now," I said. "Marta will be awake soon, and she will be happy to see you feeling better!"

"Carys, how is Marta?" he asked, a certain pleading in his eyes.

"She cares for you very much. She was very afraid for you, but I told her that you are strong and have survived worse than this. She is sleeping now because she watched you through the night."

"I care for her too. She is not just some servant to me…"

"Ah," I said, quietly, understanding how much affection had bloomed between them during his illness.

"I don't need to rest. I want to see Dougie now," he said, with some spirit.

"I will need to wash him down, too, before he can be presentable!"

With that, I left to find Dougie in the fenced-in garden, where he had happily smeared himself with black mud. He looked like a native of some foreign land, with streaks of dirt down both chubby cheeks and a dollop over one ear. His big blue eyes shone with mischief. "Dut!" he said.

"Yes, yes, wonderful dirt, but Alex wants to see you," I said, scooping him up. "You, young sir, are not going into the house like that!"

I plunked him into the stream, the only thing he liked better than dirt. He bent to blow bubbles in the water, thus easily cleaning his own face. I washed him all over, making a game of it, blowing my own bubbles on his plump tummy. He thought this process quite merry. Into the house we went, letting him drip-dry.

His diaper on for the occasion, he toddled in to see Alex, who sat up higher in bed, applauding his walking skills. Dougie applauded too. "LecLec."

"Yes, LecLec is good," said Alex with tears in his eyes. "Let your mama put you up in my bed."

"Alex, are you sure?" I asked, but Dougie was already trying to climb up, so I helped him.

Dougie put his small hand on Alex's forehead. He nodded, imitating Marta and myself, with his mouth pursed.

Marta had appeared in the doorway, and we all laughed together in our relief.

*****

After the day when he appeared so much better, Alex recovered apace. He must have had a strong constitution, but I really believed the cinchona decoction had helped as well.

"Alex," I said to him as we relaxed on the screened porch one evening, "you have a fortune in cinchona on this hillside. Marta and I could make medicine that you could sell in Kingston for a profit. You could even export it to the other islands here and to the Southern American colonies, where, I understand, the shaking sickness attacks many people. You could make yourself wealthy while helping English people survive."

"Hmm, I had no thought to use it thus, but I see your point." He reached for his cup to take more wine. "If I were a merchant captain, it would be a small matter to include it in my stores of goods. But I am a privateer now."

He paused and sighed. "The prizes can be very rewarding, but I actually hate privateering." He looked down. "Oh, I love being on the sea. Yes, certainly that! But I hate killing men just for gain. We're pirates by another name."

He looked up, I thought appealing to me to understand. "I do understand, Alex. In fact, I'm glad you don't like it."

"I respect your opinion, but other men would call me coward."

"Do you care so greatly what other men say?" I asked.

"Hmm, I cared what my father thought of me and always sought to please him, which I never could, but now? No, I have had too many close scrapes with death. My father will never respect me anyway. I might as well be my own man, take this chance in the New World to do as *I* believe right." He straightened on the bench.

"My dear Carys, I believe that you have helped me to a truth that makes me quite *cheerful*." He actually grinned from ear to ear, and we clinked glasses in a toast. "I will make more prize money, retire as a privateer, and work as a merchant instead."

"'To thine own self be true,'" I quoted. I was happy for Alex.

CHAPTER 75

May 1752
Ardath

I MUST SAY, THE Moravians were an industrious people, nothing lax about them at all. Of course, they wasted a lot of time on religious pursuits, but that seemed to give them a great sense of contentment and harmony with one another. Otherwise, they were tidy, hardworking, and endlessly polite. The Single Brothers stayed away from us assiduously, but married men were allowed to help us with heavy tasks.

Hannah, Gwyn's new friend, came to see us this morning even before the wagon train left. I was making a last survey of the wagon before climbing into the driver's seat.

"Oh, Mistress Ardath, you have the prettiest little wagon," she said. "Your draft horses are so big and handsome and of a good nature too. I'm a good driver. Will you let me take the wagon on the road for a while?" All this she said at top speed, while gazing up at me with an appealing grin on her street-urchin face.

"Well, let us give it a try," I said, to my own amazement.

She clambered up beside me on the seat and took the reins with practiced ease.

Gwyn rode up on Molly. "Oh, hello, Hannah," she said in a warm voice. "Are you driving us today?"

"Oh, yes," she said. "Will you ride with us?"

"I'll be on Molly. Sally is hitched to the back rail," she said, looking at me.

I nodded but climbed back into the wagon. Suddenly, I felt quite ill. I had no fever and hadn't had bowel troubles, so I didn't take it very seriously. All I wanted to do was sleep, though, and this was not usual for me. I made myself a pallet on the rocking floor of the wagon and lay down to rest for a minute.

The next I knew, Gwyn was calling me from the rear of the wagon. "Ardath, are you all right? You've almost slept through dinnertime!"

I looked out into bright midday sunshine. We were stopped on the road. A breeze tugged at Gwyn's hair. Hannah appeared beside her, eager eyes bright, grinning. "I gave you a smooth ride, didn't I?" she said. "I'm a good driver!" Suddenly, her face clouded over. "But it is wrong to brag about your talents, of course."

"Don't worry. It is fine with us," Gwyn said.

"And I am fine also, just sleepy," I said. I sat up and climbed out of the wagon. Gwyn handed me some waybread and cheese and a flask of fresh water. I only wanted the water but made myself eat the food also, to prevent myself from falling back asleep, still a danger.

"Mrs. Ardath, may I please drive your horses some more? I would like to help out," she said. "We will be moving in a moment."

"Why, if you wish to, that would be good," I said. I could then walk beside the slow-moving wagons and survey the countryside more.

So that was what we did. Gwyn dismounted and tied Molly to the wagon. She and I walked to the side. We happened to be on a low ridge that gave us good views for a short way. Usually, we had had dense forest beside us. The breeze felt cool. We could see other low hills and hear birds twittering in the trees below us.

"This is so beautiful, isn't it, Ardath?" said Gwyn. A small herd of cattle lowed from a distance, so we were passing a farm.

"Hmmm, yes. This would be our chance to look for herbs that need sun," I said. Our mother had been trained by a doctor in the herbal Myddfai tradition, so we were used to looking for Welsh herbs in our Twy Valley.

Now we proceeded to look for both familiar and new plants around us. The dandelion was a plant we found in abundance, good for a stimulant; choler, or yellow bile; passing urine; or better bowel movement. We found these beside the road and knelt to trowel up the whole plant. The young leaves and dark-brown roots would be good for spring tonics. The roots were most often used for urinary problems. The earth was dark and rich; it smelled of aged leaves and the nurture of growing things.

We also found plantain, called by the Indians "white-man footprints," since it appeared where the English had settled. "Look, Gwyn, these do look very much like footprints," I said.

"I remember that it is good for making a lotion to soothe inflammation," said Gwyn, with some excitement.

We found an American feverfew here, too, which mixed with plantain, sage, and bugle, or ajuga, and steeped in butter, will help heal bruises. If warmed, it will ease the bites and stings of insects. We were happy with our brief but productive plant search.

"Ardath, look," called Gwyn. "I have found heal-all, or as some call it, heart of the earth."

The purple blooms were all around us, like the earth's gift to us. We gathered all we could, though now our basket was quite full.

We ran to catch up with the jingling, thumping wagon train, passing the cows, pigs, and geese as the drovers guided them along the road, passing the stoic oxen and horses that pulled the long wagons, finally leaving their dust behind, until we found ourselves back at our own small wagon.

"Hello, Hannah, and thank you for driving for us," said Gwyn. "Look at the rich store of plants we were able to gather because of your help." Gwyn climbed up on the wagon seat, showing our collection basket to her.

"Ooooh!" said Hannah. "There is a doctor in Bethabara, where we are bound, that would like to know how you use them."

She and Gwyn chattered together happily. I hauled myself up on the back of our wagon again, feeling sleep press in on me from all sides. Now that the excitement and, yes, contentment of gathering herbs was over, I sank into my own mind again. We were going at a snail's pace traveling with the Moravians. Our purpose was not the same as theirs. They had to have many things to take with them into the wilderness, but we needed to move quickly for our purpose of finding Mother.

I found myself longing to talk this over with James. He listened to me well. I could not take that for granted, certainly in a man. He had been willing to let me be independent in many things, especially in affairs of money and business. I missed his strong arms and calm demeanor. I could see myself in a business with him, should he ever leave the military and settle in this New World permanently. Finally, I had to acknowledge it. I felt a need for him, not that I couldn't do everything for myself, of course, but that I wanted a partner in it all. I was often alone, but now I was lonely.

And then I was asleep.

CHAPTER 76

May 1752
Gwyn

I WAS WORRIED ABOUT Ardath. If she wasn't walking or riding Sally, she fell asleep. She said she didn't have a fever and I shouldn't worry, that she was just catching up on her rest, but this wasn't normal for her. She didn't even take the time to complain about how slow the wagon train was traveling.

"Hannah," I said as I rode beside our wagon, watching the steady manner in which she managed the horses, "how did you learn to drive horses so well?"

She smiled at me, which tilted her little nose even farther up. "You are a girl from the city. But *I* must know how to drive horses, hoe the fields, harvest, make haystacks, tend the animals, milk the cows, churn the butter, haul the water, muck the stalls, sew, cook, care for babies, anything."

We were both laughing before she finished her long list. "Is that all?" I asked.

"And that's not all," she said at the same time. We both giggled again.

"But what does that leave for the poor men to do?" I asked, loving her good humor.

"Please believe me, they have plenty of hard work to do!" she said. "I'll tell you a secret. My aunt and uncle have allowed me to learn most things that a man can do, because of going to the frontier."

"How did you decide to come on this journey, where the work will be even harder?" I asked.

"Some are here because they have a certain job, like a blacksmith or a gunsmith. Others, like me, because they have relatives who are going, or maybe they were picked by the lottery. I am happy because it is an adventure in a new land. God will provide for us, and we will have a mission with the Indians."

I fell silent then, because I never thought it was a good idea to push your own beliefs on another. Mother never liked it, and she hated knowing that Father was doing just that when he preached that people should come to God out of fear of eternal damnation. Fear didn't seem a good path to the spiritual world for me. I had a very different feeling, one of awe. The beauty, even the sometime violence, of the earth could not have been made by chance. More creatures of knowing lived here besides us too. I could see it in Molly's and Auri's eyes. I could feel it in the mother bear, who somehow sensed that I was not a threat to her baby.

I said goodbye to Hannah and rode by myself for a while. As it sometimes did, the measured sway of Molly's walk eased me into a waking dream. This time it had nothing to do with Mother, but with James. He appeared dressed in his "trader" clothes, among natives. I could feel their mutual respect. He appeared to be listening to one who might be a chief of some sort. A long curved pipe was passed among the group. I could almost smell the smoke that puffed from it.

I snapped back to my present state, drawing a deep breath. This vision seemed a good omen for James's work with the Cherokee. Perhaps he had completed a treaty with them to help the English in the upcoming war. I wished he were here. A great deal had happened since he left Philadelphia in March! I realized I could use his help with Ardath. If she became ill, she would be a difficult patient.

Listening to Hannah, who had the enthusiasm of a child, and considering what I could do for Ardath made me feel older than my years, but I was no longer that scared girl who had left Wales hardly more than a year before. I would do what I had to do.

*****

Over the following days, Ardath gradually returned to her old self. She still took naps at unexpected times, but she was again caustic and impatient with our progress.

The end came when we camped one evening beside a loop of the roaring Shenandoah River. The rains had left it so swollen that the wagon train stopped to camp and wait for the river to subside.

We knew that we were at the correct crossing, because last year's settlers had left marks in nearby trees. Apparently, they had wandered on old buffalo trails and wasted time until they finally found this flatter ford. The Moravians kept detailed journals of their days. Those journals and markings from the first settlers now guided our way.

"This is unbearable!" said Ardath as we sat on a small rise on our wagon seat. "They are setting up a quite-permanent camp. We could wait for days or weeks here. We'll only have more rains. The river could get even worse before it gets better. We don't have weeks to spare."

"But, Ardath, consider, what choice do we have? We are safe here."

"Safe, bah! Nowhere in the wilderness is safe. Don't be craven! With only Sally and Molly, we could swim that river and be gone from this tedious place!"

"Or more likely, we could be swept away and drowned!" I said. My heart sank. Her eyes were blazing, her body tense beside me. I felt she might jump onto Sally and be off without further plans. "Listen, Ardath, let's rest and think about this. We are still in the middle of the valley. Washington, and the map you copied, told us we have at least three more large rivers to cross. And...I must rest here tonight or I can't go on at all." I thought if *I* made the plea, if *I* appeared weak, she would be convinced.

"Well, we must accommodate you, I suppose," she said with a grudging tone. Muttering to herself, she leapt from the wagon seat and stomped off into the trees.

I had foreseen this long ago yet wasn't prepared in my heart. With a false sense of security, I had relied on the comfort of traveling with the others. I shook my head to forestall any tears.

Looking at the raging waves, white caps on muddy green water, I shook my head again. Was Ardath's impatience bordering on madness? Was this a time I should follow my own instincts for safety? Yet I could understand Ardath's impatience also. We were going so much more slowly than we could.

Auri curled into my lap on the wagon seat, a welcome comfort. I stroked his tangled fur. He was no more a city dog. In fact, he was often out in the woods, hunting small game, occasionally bringing home a squirrel or even a rabbit, with great pride.

Ardath was back in a short time, patting down her hair and looking more sane.

"Ardath, we must be reasonable, consider *all* our choices, consider the danger," I said.

She sighed impatiently but sat down on the wagon seat beside me. "I know you want to stay until the water goes down. And you don't want to go by ourselves, I can see." She flicked away a gnat that flew at her face. "But, Gwyn, I am worried about our mother. We can't dally while she may be in distress, or leaving the area where David lives. We might never find her if we go so slowly."

"I know," I said. I wondered if Ardath sought to bend me to her will by voicing my own worries.

"Can we at least wait to see how the water looks in the morning?" I asked.

"Of course," she said. "Right now, I can see that there is a strong current in the middle, but rocky shallows on each side. The crossing might not be as difficult as it first seems. The strongest currents can't be more than eight feet wide."

"Still," I said. "I don't want to do this today *or* tomorrow!"

"Let's look at it again in the morning," she said

I wasn't happy with this, but I thought more discussion now wouldn't help. "Well, Hannah has asked us to supper with her family. Will you go?"

"Hmmm, yes. That's good," she said in a distracted manner.

With Hannah bustling about to help her, Rachel already had a meal prepared at their campfire. After a prayer from Aaron, we had some small talk about the day's journey. Hannah was still enthusiastic about driving our wagon, which I had thought she might tire of by now.

Ardath took this chance to bring up our possible departure from the wagon train. "I believe we must leave your kind company and travel on horseback soon," she said, "to our cousin David Reese's home in North Carolina."

Rachel's blue eyes widened in shock. She set aside her plate and began to wring her work-worn hands but waited for her husband to speak first.

"Mrs. James, I appreciate your need for hurry, but this is a dangerous season. I cannot advise you to separate from our party so soon," said Aaron, with a solemn countenance.

"I mean no insult, Mr. Schutz, and we are very grateful for your help and kindness to us. But we are called to find our mother and could travel more quickly by ourselves," said Ardath.

"Oh, no, dear girls, you mustn't put your lives in danger this way," said Rachel. I could hear the tears in her voice.

"But what would you do with your wagon?" asked Hannah.

"Why, you could drive it to Bethabara for us, if you would," said Ardath. "We could pick it up when we find our mother and return to the north."

Aaron gazed at the fire in silence. He might have been praying. "God calls you to do this?" he asked, looking up.

"I believe so," said Ardath, folding her hands demurely into her lap.

Anger flashed through me. These people genuinely cared about us, and Ardath didn't mind lying to them. "God" had no more figured in her plan than had Auri. It was her will alone that moved her to this.

"Well," he said slowly, "if God calls you, then we must help you do it." Aaron paused. "Hannah can drive the wagon, if Rachel agrees." He looked toward Rachel, who simply nodded. We sat in silence for a while.

Aaron stroked his beard. "We can tie our longest rope to a tree on this side to pull you out if you wash away. Otherwise, you must stay on the horses no matter what. Would you promise that? With the rope, you could help us, too, by fastening it to a tree on the other side."

"Yes, of course," said Ardath. I was still too angry to reply.

Aaron continued, "You will only be able to take the greatest necessities. Along the trail you can find a few farms where you may be able to buy corn for the horses. You must take our extra dried meat and all the cornmeal you can."

"I believe we can take small bedrolls as well and an oilcloth to sleep under at night," said Ardath.

"Take your weapons and keep them dry, especially the gunpowder," Aaron said. "Remember to look for the markings our Brethren have left, especially for river crossings." He sighed. "I will pray on this and think how else we may aid you." He tugged at his beard again, thinking, or perhaps worrying.

"You are so very kind to us, as you have been since we met. We will hate to leave you," I said.

Hannah startled me by rushing to hug me around the neck. "I will take good care of your horses and your wagon!" she said. "While you shall have a great adventure."

"Thank you, all of you," Ardath said, with some grace and, I hope, sincerity.

We stood to leave, pleading the necessity of sorting and packing. It wasn't really an excuse. Figuring out what we could take and what we had to leave was hard work, but finally we had everything but our bedrolls ready for a departure.

"We have to give up the notion of taking plants back to Bartram from here on out," I said.

"True, but surely he will understand. If we find something truly odd, we could take it back dried, though," Ardath said.

"All right," I said.

I still hoped that departure was several days ahead, but I gave up being angry with Ardath. It was like being angry at leaves for being green. She had always had a willful nature and, I supposed, always would.

CHAPTER 77

January through April 1752
Carys

WITH ALEX QUITE RECOVERED, we brought Marta into our plan to sell the cinchona decoctions in Kingston and to make more of the powder to sell in any ports Alex might reach on his ship.

"I feel that I must give the governor notice that I want to leave the privateering trade and work toward becoming a merchant," he said to us one night at supper.

"That seems right, for he has treated you generously," I said.

"Leave the fighting, Alex," Marta pleaded. He smiled at her.

"But then I might be around here more," he teased.

She smiled broadly and tilted her head at him. "Si, si!" was all she said.

He left us the next day, to be gone for how many months, we didn't know. But we had a task now. We stripped as much bark as we dared from the bushes. The water and wine decoctions steeped while we left the bark to dry in the hot sun. Toddling around in his straw hat, Dougie helped us smooth out the bark. He patted the strips proudly.

After getting thoroughly roasted by the sun, we usually went to the stream to swim. He swam in a small pool between me and Marta, cheering with excitement as we pulled him up. He was a healthy boy, not something we could take for granted. His complexion was very fair, but we watched him closely and put coconut oil on his tanning skin whenever he was out. His blue eyes shone with merriment and made our days pass quickly.

In several months, we had enough medicine to send to Kingston. I wrote a note to the governor explaining our purpose and asking his help to sell it. Marta took the bottles down to the town. Using Alex's name, she was able to get the bottles and my note to the governor.

Marta returned in high spirits. "Mistress Carys!" she called as she puffed the last steps up the hill. "He talked to me! The governor talked to *me*!" She stopped to catch her breath.

"You talked to the governor himself?" I said.

"Himself! And he want all we can make. He have a man can sell it for us. Call the shaking sickness malaria." In Marta's excitement, some of her English was lost.

I hugged her tightly. Dougie came out of the house to see what the commotion was about.

"Mahta, Mahta," he called. Forgetting to hold the rail, he tumbled down the stairs to get to her. Rubbing his sore knees, he ran to her and hugged her legs.

"My Dougie, the best boy!"

"Mahta happy?" he asked, looking up at her.

"Yes, si, very happy!" she said.

That led to an impromptu dance for us all. How Alex would have laughed to see it!

*****

Of course, we worried about Alex. His work was dangerous. Also, I wasn't sure, despite his protests, that he felt fully strong after his sickness. As was the custom of those sent out by the crown on business, he had a will, in which he had previously left his worldly goods to his mother. A new will now left them to me, with a provision that I take care of Marta and Dougie. That had assured me that I would not be penniless should he die in his duty, but the loss of Alex as a person would be very hard for any of us to bear.

*****

Dougie was over a year old when we heard Alex's cheerful whistle on the hill in April. He walked with a light step and grinned when he saw us rushing to him.

"Who is this giant boy?" he asked Dougie, holding him out to look him over. "Is it Daniel? Is it Darryl? Is it Donovan?"

"No, Dougie!" he said.

"Oh, yes, Mr. Dougie, I remember you!"

"No, no, just Dougie!"

"Just Dougie! How do ye do?"

Laughing, Dougie finally reached out to Alex and was folded into his arms, sublime expressions on both faces.

Alex carried him to me and hugged the two of us together. Marta stood on one foot, beaming. His hug for her was the longest of all.

"Dear Marta, how I have longed to see you...all of you," he quickly amended, blushing a little under his tan.

"Alex, tell us of your adventures on the sea," I urged him as we headed for the shade of the house.

"Yes, Alex, tell us," said Marta.

"Well, we got our prizes. Both the governor and I are very pleased. We had our share of misfortune. We lost some men in the fighting, and that's all I want to say about the voyage. My heart was home with all of you, and my thoughts were all of the future."

Alex rested in his room for the afternoon. Dougie even took a nap with him.

We resumed our routine with a late supper and had the pleasure of sitting on the porch together in the sweet-scented night. "I feel I have met my duty to the governor," Alex said. "I have to say that we had good success, but my mind is made up. My mother sent me a generous amount of banknotes. With that and the riches from our prizes, I can buy a merchant vessel."

"Alex, that is very good news!" I said. "I'm excited that your dream is coming true."

"Aye, it is a safer occupation but has its problems and perils also. Now I have to find, or have built, a ship that meets my needs."

"Hmm," said Marta. "Where can that be done?"

"The governor recommends the port of Charles Town in South Carolina or Wilmington on the coast of North Carolina," he said. "But first, I have many things to attend to here."

"You must rest first," I said. "Have you had any recurrences of the shaking sickness?"

"Only a minor spell, which I quickly quelled with your magic medicine!" he said.

"That is good news, indeed!" I said. He did look healthier than I had ever seen him, despite the white hair.

"Alex," Marta spoke up. "Did the governor tell you of our success with the malaria medicine in Kingston?"

"Oh, yes, I meant to say that he is very pleased with it. I gather he has sent some funds your way already, and I carry even more silver from him with me. It is most wonderful that you have provided that medicine to his men and others in the town. The governor sent his regards to you, Marta." He looked at her fondly. She was sitting beside him on the bench. He reached over to squeeze her hand.

I excused myself from the company. "I need to put Dougie to bed. He is nodding in my lap. I look forward to hearing more in the morning," I said. "I bid you good night!"

It was true that Dougie needed to go to bed, and I did also, but mostly, I wanted Alex and Marta to have some time alone together. I smiled to myself. How my noble mother would have shuddered at our lack of chaperoning!

Alex was gone the next day to Kingston again, to bring back the paperwork from his expedition. That night, we began our fair copy to present to the governor. The next few days went well, despite interruptions from Dougie, who thought Alex had come home just to play with him. Marta was as happy as usual to distract our boy with other tasks or play.

In fact, Marta looked happy all the time, happier than I'd ever seen her, and that said volumes, because she had always been quite cheerful.

"Alex," I said as we stretched from our cramped writing positions, "do you notice that Marta is even more cheerful than usual?"

He blushed and cleared his throat. "Ahem, well, you see, we are both very happy." He paused to look at me. "I hope this is well with you, dear Carys. I have asked Marta to marry me!"

"Why, Alex! This is the best of news! I'm so glad for you both." I took his hand in both of mine. The thought of my dear friends' happiness made my heart warm with joy.

He grinned at me somewhat sheepishly. "I should have told you about it first, since we had, ahem, discussed the question before…"

"And you remember what I said, I presume. I am too old for you. With Marta you can have a full life, children. You know she adores you!"

"Well, it is a mutual attraction. She seems to genuinely care for me, knowing well who I really am." His eyes became shiny with unshed tears. "I only hope I can make her a good husband."

"I have no doubt of that at all," I said. I suspect he saw the tears of happiness in *my* eyes.

"Carys, this in no way lessens the deep admiration I have for you. You are a remarkable woman in so *many* ways. You have helped me know that I am worthy of good things, that I have choices, can do what is right for myself. I might have spent my life in an abyss of my own making if not for you."

"Alex, no one deserves a good life more than you."

"It won't be a life in England. I know Marta would never be accepted there. Thank God for the freedom the New World gives us, freedom from the strictures of society."

"Would you live here, in the islands?"

"Most likely, or in the colonies on the Atlantic Seaboard, perhaps. Marta and I both want you and Dougie to stay with us, wherever we may settle. You are part of our family."

"Thank you, Alex. That warms my heart. In truth, Dougie and I have no other family to call our own." I looked down at my hands, reminded of all I had lost.

"Then it is settled. Let's finish this wretched paperwork so that we can get on with our lives!" he said.

CHAPTER 78

May 1752
Ardath

THE NIGHT AFTER WE talked with the Schutz family, I expected to be sleepless, as I planned our trip across the river, but instead I collapsed with that strange lethargy I had felt lately, much more than I had let Gwyn know. I wouldn't let it conquer me, though. I maintained an image of myself as one who could not be held back by circumstance, concealing what it cost me to rise from my bed the next morning.

"Ardath, are you sure this is what we should do?" whispered Gwyn as she rose also.

"Of course, I'm sure," I snapped at her but did not apologize. I felt ashamed to lose my self-control, but if I were pleasant, she would notice I was not myself.

She sighed in exasperation. "Well, you promised we could look at the river carefully this morning," she said.

"And so we will," I replied. Standing by the riverside, we gazed intently out over water that was still surging but seemed calmer. "Look, no whitecaps. No branches rushing past. It's gone down. The edges are shallow for several yards out from each beach. The horses will only have to swim a few feet in the middle. We can go."

Gwyn's lips were compressed into a grim line, but she went about the business of rolling our beds into compact bundles to be strapped to our saddles.

Hannah brought us hot tea as we left the wagon for the last time. "I see you are making ready. Come to our fire," she said. "We have porridge this morning to line your stomachs well for the trip."

We had a quiet last breakfast with the Schutz family. Even Auri seemed subdued. Aaron gave us supplies of journey food. But then it was time to say goodbye. Aaron showed us a goodly rope tied to a tree. I took up its other end and tied it to the pommel of the saddle. Along the bank, clusters of the Brethren stood, men in one and women in another. They said nothing but watched with solemn faces.

"I will go first on Sally. Watch closely to see how the current pulls me in case you need to alter your course over," I said to Gwyn. She shivered in her boots, and I knew it wasn't caused by the cool fog of morning. Nevertheless, her chin was high.

We both mounted at the river's edge. It definitely ran less viciously than the night before. I patted Sally, solid between my thighs, her warmth a comfort.

When I urged Sally into the swirling current, the cold shocked me into a high alertness. The water was much stronger than I had anticipated, but I urged Sally on. She still had a footing on the bottom until we were several yards out, but then began to swim, her eyes showing the whites of fear. The current pulled us strongly downstream despite her best efforts. She struggled to keep her head above water.

The rope rubbed at my waist but still had some slack in it. I could see it looping out into the current like a dark water snake. Sally bobbed and dipped; muddy waves splashed into my mouth as she strove to push past the current. I spit and fervently hoped we were at least in the middle of the river, but I didn't dare raise my head high enough to see. Sally drifted farther and farther downstream, but she was keeping up the swimming that moved us toward the shore.

I don't remember passing out, but suddenly I emerged from blackness and could feel Sally's feet slipping on rocks. I struggled to dismount, pulling Sally a few more yards, grabbing a downed log that stood out from the shore. Dragging myself along its slimy surface, I followed the log to a muddy bank, where I lay panting, burping water and exhausted.

Next, I encouraged Sally through the next few feet of rocks to the beach, soothed her with soft voice, and tugged her to open ground. She limped ashore and puffed out her sides, but when I inspected her legs, they were whole, though muddy and scraped.

I felt for the rope, untying it from the pommel with shaking fingers. It slipped off into the water, dancing away downstream of us, but not far from shore. Gwyn needed it for support coming over. That is, *if* I could grab it from the current before it rushed farther away.

Once more into the chilling waters, I swam for the rope. Each time I reached for it, the perverse current whipped it away from me. I saw black dots crowding my vision. Emerging from under the waves, I drew a deep breath, pushing back the blackness. The next lunge brought me my prize. I hung on to it, drifting with it until my arms almost gave way, finally righting myself in shallower water. Once again, I dragged my unwilling body to shore. I found myself close to a still-puffing Sally.

The rope tugged me back toward the river. I would have to anchor it well and very close to shore. It was a miracle that it had extended this far. I thought of the Brethren on the far shore praying intensely for our safety. Well, that couldn't hurt, I suppose.

I fastened the rope to the nearest tree of any size. It would mostly be a guide for Gwyn, but an important one. I was afraid my crossing had not inspired confidence in Gwyn and the others on the opposite shore, but I had made it!

I waved at the group across the river. As the sun rose higher, we were more visible to one another. I made large gestures toward the rope to show that I had it secured. That done, I stood in the shallows and waved for Gwyn to come over.

I saw her enter the water on Molly. She held the rope in her left hand, and while Molly's body fell into the deeper currents, Gwyn pulled herself along with it, river water slapping at her body. I realized that I was holding my breath, and sighed it out. I had to keep strong and alert in case I needed to go in after her or Molly. Molly's head strained to keep out of the waves, her body jerking in the currents as she struggled toward me. I closed my eyes in a brief prayer. When I looked again, Gwyn was out of the saddle, clinging to the rope to pull herself across.

Finally, Gwyn drew next to me, spluttering, bedraggled, and dirty. I pulled her waterlogged body farther up the shore.

We both were wheezing and choking out water. A small figure jumped up and down on the far shore's beach. Hannah. Again, we waved as if all were well.

Auri struggled from the pouch on Gwyn's back, sneezing. Gwyn coughed and didn't try to speak. I looked around for Molly. How she had managed it, I don't know; she was actually on the beach a few feet upstream of us, her head hanging, her chestnut coat turned mud-brown.

Exhausted, we forced our quivering limbs up the bank until we were on flatter land. We tightened the rope until it was well out of the water. The Brethren could use it to haul goods over the river. I built a fire using my flint and knife and the driest leaves and twigs I could find. I unsaddled the horses and saw to Gwyn. Miserable and muddy, she still flashed me a game grin. I felt ashamed of pushing her; by all rights, she should have been angry with me, or afraid. But she had moved beyond the timid little girl who had left Wales over a year ago. How I admired her courage!

"Well," I said. "I doubt we have any possession that isn't soaked." Gwyn just nodded and got up to help me unload the saddles, bedrolls, and our bags. The river had penetrated even the oilcloth-wrapped bundles. Our bedrolls were a sodden mess. We spread those out on nearby bushes.

The sun warmed us all as steam rose from the horses' coats. Auri was busy washing himself down with his tongue, spitting out the mud clots on his legs. We curried the horses as best we could. They were still tired. After all, they had carried the largest burdens. But after a cursory brushing, they moved off slowly to crop grass.

Gwyn spotted my scored hands and the red welts on my arm from tugging on the rope. "Oh, Ardath, you need ointment on that," she said, grabbing the wet tin that held the calendula salve.

"I didn't even notice," I said. But as soon as I did, fire leapt up my arm and both hands closed in pain.

"You'll notice it soon!" Gwyn replied. She coughed and rubbed her face, leaving a streak of brown down her cheek. "Let's hope this won't be the usual river-crossing!"

"Agreed," I answered.

Finally, we flopped on the ground on our backs. There was no use pretending we'd have clean clothes anytime soon, but at least we wore our canvas pants, which would dry as we rode. We broke out wet bread, and Gwyn made a silly show of wringing it out. The cheese Rachel had given us was in good shape, and we ate some for strength.

"We'll have to find water soon," I said. We looked at each other and laughed. "Not river water, though," I said.

"We should try to make some progress, if only walking on," said Gwyn.

We loaded up the horses. The brushing had helped dry them, but we had to put wet saddles on them and draped the bedrolls over their backs to dry further. Thank the Goddess, we were into June and traveling south, so we were not tormented by cold. We hefted our bags, walking slowly down the trail. As we left the river area, the trail began to narrow into more of a path, with vegetation pressing close in. At least it was fairly flat here. Gwyn started to sing a simple song. I joined in, though I wasn't much of a singer. In this way, time seemed to pass more quickly, and we kept up our pace, at last mounting the horses, who took us on without protest.

By the time the sun began to lower, we had reached a clear spot in the never-ending woods. A blackened fire circle and smoothed ground showed us that people had camped there before. We might have pressed on farther if we had the wagon, but this was our first night out by ourselves. We had to do our best with the oilcloth cover, a good fire, and the hope that wild animals would leave us be.

I had meant to keep watch for the first hours, but leaning back against a tree, I slept. The horses' nervous shifting and a low growl from Auri woke me. The fire had burned low. Soft footsteps sounded off in the woods. I jumped up, pulling a firebrand from the embers, and faced the sound.

CHAPTER 79

May 1752
Gwyn

I AWOKE TO AURI'S deep growl as he stood at stiff attention next to my bed-roll. In the low firelight, I could see Ardath, a tense figure holding a blazing firebrand before her. She faced the woods farthest from the path. I could feel animals out there, ones we could not see and barely heard. I rolled up, grab-bing sticks for the fire. They lay on top, not catching from the coals. I threw myself to my knees to blow on the fire. Flames licked up. The night was dark, but the flames made a large circle of light. Beyond Ardath's torch, yellow eyes flashed at us through the darkness. As she turned her light, the eyes formed a disembodied ring around us.

Auri had begun to whine, lowering his head as if to charge. "Auri," I whispered frantically, edging in his direction, but before I could reach him, he rushed off toward the nearest eyes. My heart sank. I couldn't go after him without risking myself. Our only hope was to stay near the fire. I heard a low howl from a distance and an answering one just feet away from us.

Lunging for my bow and arrows, for our gunpowder still needed to dry, I nocked and waited, turning and straining my ears. The way they had sur-rounded us could only mean a wolf pack. I willed the beasts to go away. I fed the blaze even more.

Growling, snapping, and scuffling, the sounds of Auri engaging them, made my heart thud. Wild yelping of an animal in pain followed, then loud whimpering. Gritting my teeth in pain for him, I steeled myself not run to the sound. That poor little dog against a whole pack of his wild, vicious cousins!

After a few minutes of tension, in which Ardath came and put her arm around me, he dragged his bloody rear legs and a sagging tail behind him from the woods into the firelight. His golden muzzle was red with gore, but his eyes were clear and adoring as he gazed at me, and he held his head proudly.

"Good dog, good dog," I cried into his fur.

Ardath knelt to examine his legs. "Sister, I'm going to pour some warm water over his fur. I think this blood makes the injury look worse than it is." She bathed his legs, tail, and his muzzle while he lay against me without protesting her attentions.

"How is it? Can you tell?" I whispered.

She was turning him with careful hands and wiping him with the gentlest strokes. "I can't see any punctures in the legs. They got his tail pretty good, though. I think we should just give him some water and let him rest by the fire to keep warm," she said. She got her blanket, wrapping him in it to pull his body the short distance, then covered him up. He lay on his side with a grateful sigh.

We had never seen the wolves. I sensed that they had gone, moving away as silently as they had come.

Auri had relaxed. The horses had resumed cropping grass. "Ardath, they're gone," I said. "Auri is asleep. Thank you for helping him so gently."

"Well, of course. I *will* say he's a plucky dog, or maybe just foolhardy," she said, smiling. "By the way, sister, well done. Building up the fire probably scared them away. We'll have to make sure to keep it bright tonight." She looked at the ground with a shake of her head. "It was my fault. I fell asleep on watch, but I'm awake now. Rest, and I'll keep the fire."

My turn to smile at her *almost* apology. "Oh, no, it's my turn, and besides, I am wide-awake," I said, no words ever truer!

She went back to sleep almost instantly. I sat on a log, thankful we had survived for a second time today.

I actually started to enjoy the darkness. Stars lit the night; a tiny crescent moon rose white in the sky. Owls hooted and night birds twittered. A breeze swept through our camp, the air incredibly sweet. I let my thoughts dwell on my beautiful childhood in Wales, where the rivers didn't rage, no wolves roamed the woods, and rains dropped gently into our green valley. Most of all, we were loved. Mother and Ardath protected me. I didn't miss Father, not really having known him. Our little house was filled with song. I awoke with the joy of each day and had no fears.

But I was here now. This world had its own face and a wild beauty of its own. It was never dull, and the possibilities seemed endless. Well, of course, that included the possibility of being eaten by savage beasts. I shrugged. I just hoped Auri would come out of this all right. I'd protect him with all my heart as he had protected us.

I wondered how it would be to see Mother again. Would she be terribly scarred by her life? It didn't matter, in a way, because I had so much love to give her and I was convinced that love could heal.

I shifted my position on the log and felt the stickiness that meant my courses had come. This no longer meant to me what it once had, that I was proud to be a woman and so forth. Now I wondered if it ever could come at a good time. Cursing to myself, I found my belt and rags and was glad to see that the blood had not stained my pants, that small blessing at least.

After settling myself again, I looked to Ardath, rosy-faced and sleeping fast in the firelight. Like a flash of lightning, it came to me. I hadn't seen her use her rags lately, in fact, since our journey started. Could this be the reason she fell asleep so often? Could she have been so concerned with other matters that she hadn't noticed?

I knew how little she wanted to be with child so soon in the marriage. I could imagine how much more she wouldn't want it, in our situation now. James had left in March. I counted up the weeks, including all of April, then May. Yes, it could be around two months. Goddess preserve us!

I didn't wake her the rest of the night while I contemplated how this might change her mind, how we should think differently about our plans. Should we wait for the Moravians? I feared Ardath would never agree to that.

We should get to North Carolina before the pregnancy was far advanced. Would we have to stay there until she delivered? What about James? Would he find us? Now more fervently than ever, I hoped Mother would be there. If she were not, I would be in charge of Ardath's care, especially daunting if the pregnancy should become difficult. I shuddered to think what Ardath would be like as a patient, but that was the least of our worries, of *my* worries. The change in our roles would not be smooth, though, I felt sure of that.

The sky began to gray, then pink light spread across us. Whatever our situation, the beauty of the morning could not be denied!

First, I checked on Auri, who wiggled to get out of the blanket he was wrapped in. He stood on all four legs and shook his body, staggering a little afterward. His former upright and jaunty curled tail now leaned at a severe angle to the right, but the miracle was that he could use his legs. They were stiff, but he stretched and walked off to his morning toilette with little difficulty. A grin lit my face, and I gave a little hop of happiness.

I stoked the coals to boil our water. The Moravians often used oats instead of cornmeal to break their fast. When I ate oatmeal, it gave me extra energy, so I made some porridge for us while Ardath slept on.

The sun was well up before I waked her. She arose, hair tousled and sticking out from her braid almost comically.

"What are you smiling at?" she asked in an ill-tempered voice.

"Oh, nothing. Auri seems to be all right." I paused. "And good morning to you, too!" I said. "We have porridge."

"I could eat a rat this morning!" she said.

"No need, fortunately," I said. She sat herself down on the log and held out her hand. I gave her a bowl of porridge; she grunted her thanks.

"Why didn't you wake me for watch?" she complained.

"I hoped you could get more rest," I said.

"Humpf," she said.

It was going to be a really good day, I thought with irony.

After we finished striking camp and were mounted, with Auri in my pack, she said, "We need to make good time today. We have rested enough."

She urged Sally on at a good pace. We spoke no more until we reached a rest spot beside a small stream.

"Could you imagine the work it would take to get the wagon over this stream?" she asked. "We have done right to leave it and the other people behind!"

"I need to rest a few minutes, though. My courses came on in the night," I said. I unloaded Auri and stretched out, enjoying the light of the sun filtering through the leaves. Auri ran off as if uninjured. "By the way, Ardath, have you had your courses lately?"

"Hmm. It has been a while. I'm sure the strain of traveling has set them aside for now."

"Oh, for how long?" I asked in an innocent voice.

"So Miss Nosey, what is it to you?"

I said nothing, just busied myself with laying out some cheese for us. The stream was clear, providing us with good water to take on. I went to fill the water bags.

When I returned, Ardath looked at me. I thought I saw a glint of fear in her eyes that was immediately replaced by a look of indifference.

"Gwyn, I have not had my courses since before we left Philadelphia," she said. "Do you think I could be with child?" Despite herself, her face twisted with worry.

"It would certainly explain the sleepiness," I said.

"But I was so careful. I took all the herbs. I took all precautions." She seemed baffled. "It just can't be!"

"Sometimes, nature will out," I said quietly. I took her hand, but she wrenched it away.

"No, no, I won't have it!" she said, jerking herself to her feet.

I hoped this didn't mean she would harm her child. I waited, examining my nails, which were a pitiful sight, cracked, filthy, and torn off short. I wanted to say, "Perhaps if you stamp your feet, it will go away." Instead, I breathed.

She did stamp around the camp in distraction. Auri scurried to my feet, watching her movements. I stroked him. No need to look at *my* feet. I knew they were rubbed raw and blistered from walking in wet leather. Probably shriveled too. We couldn't let our boots dry in the sun, or they would stiffen and lose the shape of our feet. I sighed. This afternoon, though, I would ride Molly barefoot and take my chances.

"Well, get up. It's time to move on," said Ardath, breaking my reverie. I eyed her carefully. Her mouth curved down; she was not well pleased, nor was she mad with despair. We got going soon after. I spoke not a word to her, just let her stew.

Thank the Goddess, our next nights and days were uneventful. The trail was narrow, but obvious. We were making fast progress, although where we were exactly was not clear. We would know that when we came to the next big river, the James. We were very watchful at night but didn't have a recurrence of nighttime visitors. The rain had let up. I took this with good cheer. Maybe the spring deluges were over.

We shed clothing as we went south and into summer, until we wore only a linen shirt and canvas knee pants and broad-brimmed hats as we rode. There wasn't much chance of meeting folk on the road, so our attire had become rather informal. Ardath's belly began to swell a little; in the firelight one night, I made a panel in the front of her pants that would allow me to let them out gradually.

We came across evidence of some farms along the way but saw no habitation next to the road until the day we spotted a small building made mainly of red mud and short logs. It leaned to the side as if it might topple over at any moment. A thin cow cropped grass in a meadow nearby.

"That must be the poor animal's home," I said to Ardath.

Just then, a woman as thin as the cow emerged from the shed, followed closely by three young fair-haired children. She carried a yoke on her shoulders, from which hung two buckets. Her brown hair was dull, her eyes weary.

"Just goin' to the crick. You'ins don't have to foller me everwheres," she snapped at the children.

They all stopped dead when they saw us. The youngest began to cry. "Hush up!" the mother said. She put down her yoke. "Well, mistresses, what may we do for you?" she asked, shading her eyes from the sun with both hands as she looked up at us.

"We are looking for some corn to feed our horses, if you have any to spare," said Ardath.

"And what have you in trade?" the woman asked.

"We have a few iron tools and some woolen cloaks, if you need such," Ardath said.

"Why, iffen you have a good hoe head, you may have some corn. I've broken my hoe, and the weeds are a-comin' on."

"We do have one for you," I said. I dismounted and rummaged in my saddlebags for it.

"Let me see, then," the woman said. "Name's Nancy."

"I am Gwyn, and this is my sister, Ardath."

I showed her the hoe, which she appraised closely.

"Seems good to me. Corn's here. Got a sack?"

"Yes, thank you," I said. She took us to a corncrib, where we filled a sack. I didn't want to take too much, as it looked like they needed all they had.

"My man's back soon, 'e'll make me a good hoe with this." She smiled, showing us she had no front teeth. "He's gone hunting. That durn cow quit giving us milk. Hunting's good here, though, and the cabbage and potatoes comin' in soon." She proudly showed us her cabbage patch, where a few stringy hens scratched about in the dirt. At least the cabbage looked healthy.

The children had disappeared. As we remounted, they peeked at us from the doorway of the shed. *Their* house, then.

We rode away, waving at the little faces. "There's a hard life, I'd say!" said Ardath.

"True," I said. Even in Wales, we'd never been as poor as that. We'd always had the river for fish and rabbits for meat. Gardens grew well in the Twyi River bottomland.

Thinking of meat, I knew Ardath needed to have some to nourish herself and the baby, as we'd mostly been eating meal and porridge and the greens we scavenged along the trailside.

I went out in the twilight with my bow and a pistol. I made Auri stay at camp. In a patch of open ground, I startled a rabbit and brought it down with my arrow. I thanked the rabbit and Mother Nature for providing for us, wrapping the poor beast in cloth. Ardath would have to skin and cook it, as I was never able to stomach that part.

Ardath was pleased and had little problem preparing the rabbit, only heaving once. I ate some, too, and had to confess it tasted good. We gave the hide to Auri, who had a good time wrestling with it and eating what he could of the bloody skin. In the morning, another rabbit, one he had caught, lay by the fire.

CHAPTER 80

May 1752
Carys

WHEN ALEX AND I had finished the paperwork for the governor, he delivered it, then spent some time at home with us, working in the garden, repairing a wall of the house, playing with Dougie.

We spent our evenings on the porch, after Dougie went to bed, discussing what the future might bring.

"It's spring in the continental colonies," said Alex. He sat very close to Marta on the bench, his arm around her shoulder. She gazed at him with a radiant smile. "It's a likely time to set sail for the mainland, to see about a ship. A merchant vessel may be landing here soon. If we can get cabins on board her, it would serve to see how she is run, as well as get us to a shipyard where we might commence building, or buying, whichever works out. It is a good time for a honeymoon, do you not think so, Marta?"

"A honey's moon? What is that?" she asked. We laughed.

"Why, that is the time spent looking at the surroundings by a newlywed couple," said Alex, smiling broadly. I hid my grin behind my hand.

"Married? Now? Casado? Ahora?" she asked.

"Yes, my lovely, we should be married first, don't you think?" said Alex. "Before we share a cabin…"

Marta's shriek threatened to wake Dougie, although he usually slept through anything. She muffled her mouth with a quick hand, then unashamedly kissed Alex on the cheek.

"Yes, yes, si, si, mi madre, mi madre!" she said.

"Of course, your mother will be there, and anyone else you wish," he said. He smiled indulgently while she listed off other relatives she wanted to invite.

"Is all right, Alex, we have a priest?" she asked.

"Whatever you wish!" he said. So the plans for a wedding went on apace. Marta's mother was a good seamstress, in fact, had taught Marta how to be one herself. Mama sewed the wedding dress of whites and reds. Marta made a darling blue suit for Dougie, as he was to be the ring bearer. I had a fresh frock of green and yellow, which made me look rather like a tree in bloom. Alex planned to wear a set of clothes he used in his interviews with the governor, who was invited as well.

Edward Trelawny, whose Cornwall family had known Alex's, had been governor for many years, a just and equitable ruler of the island. He was originally a military man but proved a good administrator as well. Marta, though, was mainly impressed that he would come to the wedding. We planned it to be at our house, to be more comfortable for Marta's relatives and friends, who were certainly not the governor's social equals.

It was beautiful, and no one deserved their unrestrained happiness more than these two people I had come to love. There were flowers, flowers everywhere, in all the brilliant yellows, purples, reds, pinks, oranges, and whites of that tropical place. And food, such as had yet to be seen, a whole roasted pig with a lemon in his mouth, all kinds of corn dishes and flat breads, sweets to make your mouth water, and spice dishes to make your eyes water.

The couple stood together under an arbor of green palm fronds. Morning sun shone on the happy scene. Alex looked splendid in his cream-colored suit and cocked hat. He had no need to powder his hair, as it was whiter than the linen he wore. Marta's dress, in mostly white, was flounced from waist to ground, with all edges trimmed in a merry red. Her rosy brown neck rose gracefully from a tight square bodice. Pearls sang a lovely circle above the neckline. Her greatest adornment, though, was a smile of such radiance that I had never seen its equal. The bridegroom beamed his joy almost as widely as Marta hung on his arm.

As the ring bearer, Dougie stood solemnly between Marta and Alex with a small pillow. I had helped him toddle into place and kneeled behind him to prevent mishaps. It was I who actually carried the rings, of course.

Since it was a Catholic Mass, this wedding took longer than the usual Protestant service, yet all seemed to pass quickly, as in a dream.

It was all put together in time for the arrival of the merchant ship. In fact, that was where the honeymoon was to take place. Alex reported that the ship had two rather-spacious passenger cabins, which he had engaged for us through the captain's agent.

I had been impressed with the things Marta and Alex had said about the governor. When the wedding was over and he stood looking rather alone near the laden tables, I noticed he gazed at me closely, as if he were trying to remember something. His color was not good, and I wondered if he was ill.

"Governor, how pleasant to meet you in person," I said. "I'm Mrs. Rhys, a friend of the couple."

"Mrs. Rhys, I am delighted to meet you," he said with a bow. "I have been very impressed with Alex and his masterful victories at sea. His reports have been very clear, largely due to your help, he says. He has told me of your expertise in medicine, and it has been my pleasure to meet his lovely wife when she brought your decoctions to help my household and others in the town. Several of my staff have been greatly aided by these draughts."

"We have been grateful to help others in this way," I said.

"Alex tells me that these decoctions will be among the goods he plans to trade when he becomes a merchant."

"Yes, so he plans. There are also other plants he could take to the North American colonies, eatables such as ginger, pineapple, and lemons, and medicinals such as the cinchona and the aloe vera."

"Well, you are very knowledgeable and talented! And I shall not find a captain of Alex's ilk again, but I truly wish him prosperity and happiness in his new estate. It has been one of the pleasures of my command here to give mutually beneficial help to my old family friend. Of my other goals, well, I fear my health shall require me to retire to England before I can see my greatest ambition made real in Jamaica, to free slaves from their shackles."

"Alex told me that you made a treaty with the Maroons here, that they should be free, as the Spaniards had meant them to be when they gave over the island to the English." I picked at some fruits on the table.

He nodded. "Yes, the new landowners would have liked to enslave them again, but that we couldn't allow! In exchange for their freedom, the Maroons promised to turn in runaway slaves that came to them," Trelawny said.

My scalp prickled, thinking of Tionga and her group. "But *do* they turn in runaways?" I asked, ceasing to eat my fruit.

He smiled, causing his face to show the wrinkles due to his years. "In truth, I haven't seen that happen. I believe some slaves do escape, but we don't mention that."

"Ah," I said. I felt sure then that if anyone had made it to freedom, Tionga had. "The ship on which I came to Jamaica carried many of those unfortunates here to work in the sugar fields. It was a sad sight." I didn't tell him I had been a slave myself.

"Someday, we may hope to see that cruel practice at an end everywhere we English rule," he said, nodding at me in a somber way. "Meanwhile, the planters insist they must have slaves to survive."

"We can hope for a better day," I said.

We were interrupted by Marta's brother, who pulled me into a celebratory dance. Merry and energetic like so much of the day, it was a felicitous blend of old and new worlds, with Spanish foot-stomping and Indian circle dance. I was pulled along, helpless to keep up, but so happy!

CHAPTER 81

May 1752
Ardath

WHAT A MUDDLE I had made for myself! Pregnant, regardless of trying every way not to be, in the middle of wilderness without physical help, no decent place to lay my head. And I was still sleepy, as if I didn't need to be alert to danger at all times. I stopped in sudden shame. All my thoughts were of myself! I could hear my mother's strong voice saying, "Ardath, you must take care of your sister." How was I to protect my sister while *she* endured these hardships too? Well, I would *not* feel sorry for myself! There was nothing for it but to forge on.

By the map, it looked like the next large river was the James, where Washington said there was a ferry crossing. The creeks and smaller rivers we crossed were still engorged, so the ferry would seem a necessity, not a luxury.

We reached Looney's Ferry that morning, but it was not on our side, for us lunatics who came this way. The James was large and muddy. I felt weak; Gwyn would have to be in charge for now. I lay down in the shade of a lofty tree. Immediately a swarm of gnats dived for me. I shooed them away and put my straw hat over my face, falling fast asleep.

I awoke to Gwyn's voice. "Wake up, Ardath, the ferry is almost here."

Sure enough, a slight figure was poling his barge across the waters. "How is he doing that, and how can one man get us all across that?" I muttered as he bobbed toward us.

"Good afternoon, ladies," said the rather-cheerful boy, for he couldn't have been over sixteen. "I'm Gabe. Be ye ready to travel across? What have ye for pay?"

"We have iron tools," Gwyn replied.

"I've no need for that," he said. "Have ye silver?"

"A little," I answered, for I thought he might want to rob us.

"Two bits, then, for you ladies. We can tie the horses to the raft, but they'll have to swim it."

I readily agreed. At least we knew the horses could make it across without drifting away from the barge. We all joined in to unpack the horses, a tedious process, but better than dealing with wet baggage. When we were finished unloading our goods onto the raft, Gwyn and I were moist with sweat, but the boy looked as fresh as new daylight. We tied the horses to the raft and set off from shore. They looked at the wide water and came in reluctantly. I couldn't blame them. Gabe somehow managed the rocking craft easily. He might be young, but wiry muscles stood out from his arms. The trip was blessedly swift.

When we reached the far side, I paid Gabe from the small purse I brought out with only a few coins in it. The money belt was too small for me now, but Gwyn wore it securely around her waist.

The wet horses rolled in the grass above the riverbank, hooves beating the air. I sucked in a breath. Now we had only two major rivers to cross, the Dan and the Yadkin. Soon we should be coming to Big Lick, where the animals, especially buffalo, came to get their salt. That meant we weren't far from the area where the road to North Carolina turned south and another Indian trail turned west.

The weather had held for some days now, but we had entered the season for lightning storms. In early afternoon, the lightning flashed, thunder rolled, and a furious rain threatened. We could see the gray veil of it stalking us across the plain. It hit with shocking force. We sank deep into our oilcloths and searched for better shelter. This *would* be a place where we traveled open fields, giving us nowhere to run. Then bruising hail, the size of hen's eggs, flew at us from all sides.

"Gwyn," I shouted over the violence, "I can see a grove of river cane ahead. It might save us from the sideways blow, at least!"

She nodded and urged Molly forward. We were drenched and cold by the time we reached our hoped-for shelter. We saw a small break in the cane and pushed our way through. In a few steps, it became a wider path. In the middle of the green stalks, we suddenly came into a small clearing. To our amazement, groups of people stood there, mostly under crude wooden shelters held up by some of the larger canes.

It was like the backstage of a theater company. They were arrayed in all sorts of costumes, from English ladies in long skirts, to raggedly field-hand clothes, to loincloths. The "English ladies" carried parasols but were swarthy like Indians. Many of the people were black, some seemed to be Scots or English, while a few were definitely Indians. Their gazes toward us were not friendly. We had stopped, but a giant of a man with a great black beard gestured for us to come forward and helped us tuck ourselves into his shelter. The horses had to stand in the rain and hail but at least were sheltered from the worst of the wind.

Nothing could be heard over the storm, so Gwyn and I didn't try to speak but looked around us. As well as we could see, it seemed to be a more or less permanent camp. There were no horses, so wherever the people had come from, they had walked here. Most of the faces were lean, as if they had little to eat, and I saw no evidence of possessions other than one iron pot swinging over a smoking firepit.

Since we were in river cane, there must be a stream just beyond the grove. That and the seclusion of the cane must be the reasons they had picked this site. In hiding, then, I guessed.

My neck prickled as the hair stood up. They would not want us to report their hideout. Would they even let us go? And if they were starving, our horses must look like good eating.

The hail drummed on the wooden roof of our shed; the rain leaked through as we huddled together. Gwyn shivered beside me. Though we had a form of shelter, we were amongst desperate people. No one would ever find us if they decided to take our horses and meager possessions and leave our bodies here.

Nobody made a move until the hail and rain stopped. I heard a collective sigh as everyone moved out into the clearing. The women drew long knives from their belts. I watched them carefully. Gwyn stood so close to me that I could feel her quickened breath.

Behind me, Blackbeard began to shift. I flinched, and he laughed. He was speaking, not English, but something I felt I should know. Ah, a form of French. I turned to him. He was asking a question, something about ladies. Gwyn merely stared at him.

I could see from the corner of my eye that several men walked to the edge of the clearing, perhaps to fetch weapons? They were speaking some patois of English, hardly more understandable than the French, but embellished by gestures they all seemed to understand.

I tried my academic French with Blackbeard. He looked puzzled at first, then appeared to recognize the language. He seemed a little too jovial. Perhaps it was his role to distract us while the others planned our capture. I concentrated on understanding him. He seemed to be asking us to eat. What? Our horses?

Meanwhile the men came back, two with rifles. Gwyn stood with chin erect but still shook. The men had retrieved a soggy deer carcass, which they pulled to the firepit. The women rushed to it with their skinning knives out and made quick work of skinning and butchering the deer.

Gwyn and I looked at each other with relief. The knives were not meant for us, at least not then. Blackbeard introduced himself as Bernard. His eyes had become wary, whether of us or his companions, I didn't know. He gestured to us to stay close to him and muttered in French again.

"Gwyn, I think he is asking us to dinner!"

She smiled, a little tremulously, I thought. She also watched the group carefully. They were either staring at us or picking their way through the piles of hail with due caution.

I asked Bernard what we could give to the meal. I brought out our saddlebags and showed our store of cornmeal. He nodded eagerly. It must be hard to buy supplies for themselves when they must stay hidden.

He gestured for a young black boy, who led me to the woman in charge of the cooking. She was one of those dressed in "English lady" clothes.

"We would like to give you this meal," I said, presenting the whole bag.

"Thank you," she said in perfect English, with only a small lilt to her voice to make it seem unusual. She had the beautiful brown eyes of an Indian, and the blue-black hair, tied back in a queue. I longed to ask her for her story, but she was busy.

When I picked my way back to the shelter, I saw Gwyn had let Auri out of his sling. He stayed close by her, with only an occasional growl. I saw she had not relaxed, nor had Bernard. Anyone who looked our way still exuded wariness, if not hostility.

By snatches of conversations overheard and painstaking attempts with Bernard, I was able to gather that this was a community of mélange, a melting pot of several races, some slaves who had escaped by following the James River west, some Indians who had not joined other tribes when theirs died of the small pox or other white man's diseases, some others who had no home elsewhere and down on their luck white men.

Bernard was vague about his own past, other than to say he had been a trapper in lands west of there. Although there were few authorities in these unsettled parts, I suspected he might be a fugitive from the law or from the ire of some Indian tribe he had wronged.

Gwyn ventured to the cook fire and spoke with Sara, the main cook, helping her roast pieces of venison on a spit over the fire. Later, she told me that Sara and the other woman so attired had been kidnapped from their tribe and raised as "white Indians," a novelty to be paraded out by their master as objects of curiosity. They had escaped but had no idea where their original tribe lived. They belonged nowhere, like the rest of the people here.

Eventually, the group seemed to relax in our presence, but we still kept a close eye on our horses and on anyone who approached us. We clustered at the cook fire near the other women in hopes that we would stand out less.

I said to Sara, "Please assure everyone that we will not tell anyone about your presence here." Gwyn nodded as well.

"I will, indeed," Sara said. "Many among us are in hiding or have been forced into unsavory lives. I don't fully trust them all myself. Be very careful of yourselves and your horses after you leave here."

"We will," said Gwyn. "Thank you for sheltering and feeding us."

"Bernard has a soft heart. It is good he welcomed you. That protects you for now. He is showing us how to get to the west, as he knows the Indian trails very well, so he is the closest thing we have to a leader," Sara said.

We had a surprisingly good meal and left wishing there were more we could do for them. We did leave Sara a skillet. It was small, but she was delighted with it just the same. We promised again that we would not reveal their hiding place and wished them good fortune. They planned to travel to a less-settled place beyond the mountains to make a town of their own.

When we left, we still carefully watched the trail behind us and listened when we entered woods for any disturbance that might show we were being followed. The goose bumps on my arms were not entirely due to the misty air.

Night was coming on fast at that point, but the horses were rested, so we rode quickly. The Melungeons, as I heard them called later, had told us there was an inn ahead named the Black Horse Tavern. We reached it before full dark, as the days were long now. It was the biggest building we had seen for a long time, made of painted board, with two chimneys toward the middle of the shake roof. We presented ourselves at the front door, but a barmaid told us the inn had no rooms available. That was fine with me, as the place smelled of dirty clothes, old tobacco, and spoiled ale.

Not that we ourselves smelled much better than the inn, but we were happy to sleep in the stable loft's straw, where the horse sweat smelled some-how cleaner than the inn. At least we were out of any rain and our horses had good oats to eat.

In the morning, we paid for our stay, bought some cornmeal to take and two bowls of last night's stew, which was actually good. We sat on the front porch to eat from steaming bowls. I had noticed that my sense of smell was especially acute now. I didn't think I could hold my gorge if eating inside.

The barmaid was friendly and told us we'd have some uphill riding to do ahead until we reached Mag-i-dee Gap, known by the locals as Maggoty

Gap. From their rest and good food, our hearty horses were ready to go. The day was beautiful, sunny and bright with a fine breeze, as we made our way on the trail. It was a shady, steep climb, with the horses' heads swinging back and forth as they clopped their way to the top. When we emerged from the trees, we overlooked a wildflower meadow, green leaves on all sides, a dancing creek flashing in the sun, with long mountains showing blue in the distance. Why someone had not put a house right there, I couldn't understand, though I guessed this valley was too narrow for extensive farming. I am not one for flowery phrases, but I was enchanted with our surroundings.

We rode on, my mind ranging ahead to Big Lick, which might be more settled and have some supplies we would need to get to North Carolina.

CHAPTER 82

June 1752
Gwyn

WE HAD MADE GOOD progress the day we left the Black Horse Inn, camping in a wooded glen that night. The next morning revealed a beautiful dawn. Ardath was still abed, so I made my way to the stream nearby. Sunlight flashed gold on the droplets that fell from the sweet green leaves of our forest glade. The air smelled of fresh moss. Soon I heard the murmuring of the creek, and more! The sounds of a quiet flute curled around the music of the water.

As in a dream, I pushed through a screen of bushes. There was a light-brown man playing a flute as he sat relaxed on a rounded rock by a little waterfall, for all the world, like the "little people" said to inhabit Welsh glades when no one was watching. He was, however, a full-grown man, dressed in worn buckskins, with a reddish-brown scarf around his neck.

He didn't look up but said in a gentle voice, "Hello, young miss."

Somehow, I felt no alarm, or even surprise, at seeing him there, but was merely curious. "Hello, I am Gwyn. Are you camping near here?"

"I am on a spirit journey for my village. No need to camp." He raised his rounded face, showing deep-brown eyes that seemed to look both at me and beyond this world. With a warm thrill, I recognized a fellow seer. My heart thumped with excitement.

"I see you have come for water. I have come seeking white man's knowledge," he said, making no move from his perch.

"I see. What kind of knowledge?" I asked, breathing deeply and dipping my bucket into the clear creek. I tried not to stare at him, as I had heard the natives thought this was impolite. But I glanced at him every chance I got.

"My people suffer from a white man's disease. I have heard it called the small pox. Are you acquainted with it?" He asked this with a knowing smile.

"I think you can sense that we are," I said, amazed.

"I have been told to search for two women healers who can help us," he said.

I felt sure that he knew both where our camp was and that another woman waited there.

"Well, of course, we will try to," I said. I gestured for him to follow me back to our clearing, where I found Ardath stirring around. Her hair was loose as she brushed it out. Blazing in the rays of sun that struck it, it bloomed around her face like a corona.

I turned to my new friend. His mouth hung open as he gazed at her, murmuring with reverence in his own language.

"What are you saying?" I asked him.

"I called her 'Hair is burning' in my language, what you call the Cherokee tongue."

I nodded. Ardath looked up, startled, at our voices.

"Ardath, he is from the Cherokee, come to ask our help," I said quickly.

"Well, that is sudden! Where did you find him?" she asked me. I heard her suspicion.

"By the stream, but I just know we can trust him," I said, my tone pleading with her, for her face had that hard look that portended an outburst.

"Hmm," she said, eyeing him carefully.

"Really, it's all right," I said, setting down the bucket. "He needs some advice about treating the small pox, and…" I grasped at a straw. "Maybe he has seen James," I said.

"Well, all right," she said, sweeping her hair back into a quick bun. "Let's see what he knows."

"He understands and speaks English well," I noted.

"So sit and eat with us," said Ardath, proffering a bowl of porridge to him.

He bowed his head quietly in acknowledgment. We all sat to eat on logs around the fire.

"I am called Fox," our guest said. "You have a question for me concerning James?" he asked Ardath.

"My husband is a trader who left this spring to meet with the Cherokee peoples in the mountains near *here*, I think. He is tall, with brown hair and blue eyes. He was riding a large black horse when he left Pennsylvania."

"Hmmm. He has not been to my village but I believe is at Kituwah with the chief there, not far from my village. I have heard it said that he is a good man, but is more than a trader, I believe." He smiled at that, showing he knew quite a bit about James's mission.

"The tribes are mostly inclined to join with the English. Your husband has made good words and promises," he continued.

Ardath's voice cracked, betraying her anxiety. "Is he well?" she asked.

"Oh, yes, very well. I should have said that first of all!" he said. "They call him Curlyhead. He has become a favorite of our people."

Ardath's shoulders relaxed. She took a deep breath. "Your news has relieved me greatly," she said.

"I will soon return to my village, where I am a healer. I can send a runner to him if you have a message," he said.

"I can tell it to you, but it is a long message," she said.

"I will not forget," he said.

Ardath explained where our cousin lived and that we were going there in search of our mother, asking James to come and find us if he could. Fox repeated it verbatim.

"Good," she said.

"Now tell us how we can help your tribe with the small pox," I said.

"We are doing everything to help them. Each morning when we go to water, we take them with us. We set them in the sweat lodges as often as we can. We gather around them to hold them and pray for their recovery." His face saddened. "So few survive, and they are so ugly, so marked by the disease, that they wish to die."

"Ah," I said. "I see that your people care very much when their fellows are afflicted." I could tell that Ardath wanted to shout at him. "You idiot! You are doing all the wrong things for them!" Thank goodness she held her tongue and stepped away instead.

She made herself busy readying the horses for our journey, but she was near enough to hear me explaining what to do. I quelled my excitement about James. I could only imagine what Ardath might be feeling! I tried not to leap to a hope that he could somehow find us in this wilderness.

"First, you will benefit by doing some of these loving things you do, differently," I said. "We had an outbreak on the ship in which we sailed and found that keeping the sick person dry and at a constant temperature helped them the most. Isolating them from others, no matter how caring those others are, will keep the disease from spreading. Physical contact with the sick person will often lead to sickness for those who touch them. It would be better to let family and friends encourage them from outside the enclosure where you keep the sick." I watched Fox carefully to see if he understood.

I could see that Fox was upset by these ideas. "But," he said, "my people will think these things are all wrong, all against the closeness of the tribe and our most cherished customs."

"These are hard changes for you to make," I said with sympathy, "I know."

Fox dropped his head into his hands. We were silent together for long minutes, both, I think, mourning the ravages the disease was making on their population and their customs, the difficulty of unasked-for change. I could understand that, having been ravaged by the loss of our mother and our unex-pected journeys since then.

I cleared my throat to speak, but Fox started again.

"I must be on my way back. I came seeking the white man's knowledge of the white man's disease. Of course, we cannot treat this in our old ways, or we would have been more successful before now. Still, it makes me sad. I have much work to do, to honor our spirit but, to give the sick a better care."

"Fox, I must say, even if you do all these things as I have told you, it does not cure the sickness. It may forestall the spread and make the sick ones more comfortable for a time, but each person must fight it off as best they can with their fellows' support," I said. "I wish I could come with you to help out, but our way is urgent and is in the other direction."

"I understand, and I will get your message to Curlyhead as soon as I am able."

"Thank you," Ardath and I said, almost in unison.

"And, Fox, we are looking for a plant you might know, that we call ginseng. Let me get a picture of it for you," I said. Reaching into my saddlebag, I brought out Bartram's son's drawing.

Fox smiled. "Yes, a very good plant, but you will need to look on higher ground for it. We nurture it where we live and carry it on journeys to keep up our strength."

I thought about that, how it might keep Ardath more alert. When I explained her sleepiness, Fox nodded. "Here. You must take what I have. It will help. Chew it as you go." He handed me a leather bag of dried brown roots, twisted and quite unappetizing in their looks, reserving only one root for himself.

"Forgive my curiosity," I said, "but how is it that you speak our language so well?"

"It is quite the story, but I will say it simply so that we may all be on our way. Perhaps someday you will come to our village and I will tell you the whole. Once when I was a child, an Englishman came to our people. He was a writer with pen and paper. He wanted to learn our language, come to know us, and set down our customs and sayings. He was particularly interested in the skills of our orators, for it is known far and wide that the Ani-Kituwah speak eloquently. So I learned from him how to say in English what our speakers said in our language. We taught each other very much." He stopped suddenly, as if overcome. "He became a 'beloved man' among us. When he left, the orators spoke of him in ways he would have approved."

"That is a beautiful story," I said. "I wish we had more time to learn from you about your plants and medicines."

"I wish it so as well. Ask Curlyhead how to find us and come to visit. You will be welcomed." He nodded, straightened himself, and turned. With a ground-covering lope, he ran off toward the west.

I felt grim. "I wish there were more we could do. We know not how Indian bodies might differ from ours, so I couldn't recommend variolation. It might kill all who received it."

"It does seem, from what Bartram and others told us, that Indians have died in much greater numbers than the white people do," Ardath said.

"I've prepared the horses," Ardath said to me. "Do you feel ready to press on?"

"What, oh, yes…and isn't it wonderful that old Curlyhead is doing well in his mission?" I said with a smile.

"You have no idea how that has lifted my spirits," Ardath said. She even blushed, she who had always maintained that she didn't need a man. If we didn't have to get to Mother in North Carolina so desperately, I wondered if she would have followed Fox back to James.

"Well, I might have *some* idea," I teased, wrapping Auri in his carrier.

CHAPTER 83

June 1752
Carys

ONCE WE KNEW WE were going, it took us little time to settle the house and prepare to take ship. I was so eager to begin a new adventure that I hardly paused to say goodbye to the lovely spot where we had spent many happy hours. But it was also the place where I'd learned about my family's deaths, a past that only made me want to press on toward the future.

Dougie felt our excitement and asked continually, "Go now; go now?" at which we had to laugh. It was how we all felt.

Marta's family came to the house to see us off. They hugged and laughed and cried in a touching way. Their love for Marta now extended to us, it seemed, so Alex and I, and especially Dougie, were the recipients of many a generous hug as well. Marta's sweet mother had promised to care for our animals and gardens while we were gone. Dougie said his own goodbye to the goat and chickens.

I even endured the walk through Kingston stoically, but then Alex was right there with us. Somehow I had associated the town with the rough treatment I'd had on the slave ship. Of course, it was a seaport with all the clamor, the stink of tar, dead fish, and unwashed men, the sun too bright and unavoidable in the hot streets, the colors assailing us in oranges and reds and hot purple. The docks were busy that day, the merchant's goods being loaded for transport, cranes and ropes and barrels swinging wildly above our heads, men shouting in several languages, and ropes creaking, cargo banging against the hull.

We ducked onto the ship in a hurry. Alex was dressed in his best dark clothes. From here on out, his mission was to portray a successful merchant about his business, with family in tow. Earlier, Marta and I had made faces when we donned our "English women of dignity" clothes, as we called them. Once we were sailing, I planned to wear simpler garments, but first impressions were important to Alex's position. Even Dougie, riding along in Alex's arms, was dressed as a young noble, his fawn-colored hair cut short and firmly combed. No looking like an urchin for him! In fact, he looked the part of a noble-born child, though perhaps not so haughty as he should have been. His eyes, as they turned from one scene to another, were huge. He was stunned into silence.

We had luxurious cabins by shipboard standards, still quite tight with hardly space to stand, but each had a good-sized porthole. Alex had requested hammocks for us to sleep in since we might hit rough seas. Dougie even had his own, where I could tie him in securely. There were bunks as well, with actual mattresses on them, though I mistrusted what vermin might inhabit them, even on the cleanest ship. The meager belongings we had brought with us stowed well under the bunks. The precious cochina bark and decoctions had been carefully packed and loaded in the hold several days before.

Dougie needed a nap after the morning's excitement, so I fastened him into his hammock, where he fell fast asleep, fat fist on red cheek. I went to explore the ship with Marta, who had knocked on our door. The loading occupied one side of the ship, so we lingered on the other. Alex was already deep in conversation with the merchant captain. Around us a breeze had come up, wiping away some of the tar, fish, and other smells of the port. The water rippled a beautiful aquamarine blue, with white sand under it.

"Will you miss the island?" I asked Marta.

"Oh, yes, it is the only place I have been," she said. "In fact, this is the most far I have been from my home already." She didn't look at all sad about it, though. "But I have my Alex, and he is my home now." She smiled happily.

My heart sank a little. Marta was innocent of the hard ways of the world. I hoped she never had to face some of the trials I had been through. I knew she wouldn't, if Alex could help it. Still, I didn't know how the people we would meet in the American colonies would treat her, a mestizo, though her coloring was a light brown, not black as the slaves were.

My concerns were demonstrated very soon when Alex brought Captain Jones to meet us. Jones was a rather-beefy man with a large mustache, young for his position, I thought, but amiable.

"Captain, may I introduce my wife, Marta," Alex began.

The captain turned to me and bowed. "Mrs. Whitsun, delighted to meet you. I look forward to meeting your young son as well."

"Oh, no, this is our family friend, Mrs. Rhys, and it is her son, Dougie, to whom you refer."

The captain flushed. "Forgive me!"

Alex took Marta gently by the arm. "This is Mrs. Whitsun."

Marta now bowed, and the captain took a breath to overcome his embarrassment. "Delighted. Please let me know if you have any questions, or if I can make your stay aboard more comfortable in any way. I hope you will join me for dinner tonight."

Alex replied, "Of course. It would be our pleasure."

The captain moved away to supervise the last of the loading. "We will be in port tonight and sail with the morning tide," said Alex. He seemed not to notice that Marta stood mute before him, for he turned away to examine the rest of the ship in detail.

After Alex moved away, she said, "Oh, Carys, he think me the serving girl and you la esposa." Dear Marta, almost in tears.

"Well, he was wrong, wasn't he? Don't let him spoil your day," I said firmly. "Let's look overboard to see if any fish come in this close to shore."

As it chanced, Captain Jones had overcome his embarrassment and, it seemed, any prejudice he might have felt toward Marta by the time we dined at his table that evening. His quarters were not palatial, not even as well-appointed as Smog's, but very clean. His manner was charming. He pressed delicacies on Marta as if to make up for his mistake earlier in the day.

He turned to me as we dined on fresh fish and local fruit and bread.

"Mrs. Rhys, please accept my condolences on the loss of your late husband." I nodded. "Your name is a fine one in Wales, particularly in the south. Was your husband a descendent of the Great Rhys of Carmarthenshire?"

"Yes, he was, but it was his cousins who lived in the Manor House." I smiled. If people only knew how humble our situation had been, they would have been less impressed.

"My own people lived in Pembrokeshire, closer to St. David's," he said. "The beauty of the sea there made me want to explore it more widely."

"A lovely area!" I replied. I sipped my fine wine, which I suspected the captain had brought out especially for the occasion.

"It is so generous of you to allow us to ride as passengers on your vessel," said Alex, and the conversation turned to the merchant business.

Jones said, "Trade is booming in the American colonies, thanks to further settlement of the colonial coastline. Even the interior is becoming settled quite quickly, which makes for more demand when I dock in Charles Town and Wilmington."

"Which would you say is the bigger port?" asked Alex.

"Oh, Charles Town, most definitely. It is a bustling place. And, ladies, a place to shop for all the finest in fashion from the continent, even French designs, so I hear." We smiled politely.

"In the case of searching for a ship to buy, which port do you think is the better?" asked Alex. He was picking at his nails, a sure sign that he was tiring of the small talk.

"That is hard to say, but we will lay in at Charles Town for several weeks' trade. During that time, you may search for a ship there. I will give you the names of captains and shipbuilders likely to know the market. Some may have news of the market for ships in Wilmington as well."

"Captain Jones, I could not have asked for a kinder or better-informed host than you," said Alex.

After that, small talk about the route and probable weather ensued until we excused ourselves for bed.

The next day, Alex made a harness for Dougie. It was one thing to watch him career around a ship lying at harbor and quite another to keep up with his toddling runs when we were at sea. We certainly couldn't keep him in the cabin unless we were forced there by bad weather. However, tied to the mast or to one of us by a short line, he had as much freedom as was safe for him. We didn't want him disturbing the sailors at their work, but they seemed to love him and took turns showing him things about the ship or the sea around us. It wasn't uncommon to see him riding on the shoulders of an off-duty sailor while Dougie jabbered away, mad with excitement.

"I believe Dougie may be destined for a life at sea," said Alex as we stood by the rail.

"Well, if you think about it, he was accustomed to the motion of a ship for his first months," I said. "I do wonder if that makes him feel at home here. But surely not."

"What *do* you picture for his future?" asked Alex.

"I have pictured no future as yet, but now you make me wonder. I can certainly claim that he is my legitimate son in this part of the world, and no one would know differently. That entitles him to exactly nothing but at least doesn't leave him with a stain," I said.

"It does not, and he doesn't deserve one, of course. No man can choose the circumstance of his own birth."

"Truly said!" I agreed.

"But whatever you decide to do, my promise holds. I will not see you or Dougie in want. I plan to be a very successful merchant, you know, looks be damned! Wealth makes any man comely," he said with the grin I had come to love.

I smiled at him. "But, Alex," I said gently, "we need to talk about Marta in this regard. When the captain thought I was your wife, she felt that he saw her as a servant girl because of her brown skin."

"She did? She should have told me. I am proud that Marta is my wife. I would never let her be hurt by such a prejudice." He rubbed his hand across his brow in perplexity. "Surely, it was a simple mistake on Captain Jones's part!"

"I wish we could know that for sure, but even if it were, we still don't know how Marta will be seen when we reach the Eastern Seaboard cities. I fear that the ladies there will be proud Englishwomen who will do anything to keep the prized pallor of their skin. They might judge any lady by her color. I'm sorry to bring you pain, Alex, but I think we should have a plan."

He groaned in reply, and I left him with his thoughts. "I'll not disavow her in any way!" he said finally.

"Nor should you!" I said. "We have all relaxed in this island atmosphere, but I know you must project a certain image to get your business started. Perhaps you could refer to Marta as your Spanish wife. That is true enough, and if she should speak any Spanish words, that would be natural."

"I hate anything that smacks of deceit," he said, turning on me, face red with frustration.

"I understand," I said.

"I hear your concern," he said. "We will wait and watch." He touched my hand briefly, and his eyes smiled at me, to show he didn't have any hard feelings.

I still felt guilty that I had mentioned a future problem when he had so much on his mind. "So sorry," I said.

*****

Regardless of what might lie ahead, we were all happy, and the weather reflected our mood. Being on a ship in these circumstances was almost fun, but eventually the confinement was wearing and we were glad when Captain Jones announced that we should be in Charles Town on the morrow.

Charles Town was a place unlike any I had seen. Of course, all seaports shared some likeness, mainly the smells and the busyness. Clearly, black slaves did all the menial work of the harbor and the town. The town itself showed some planning, a distinctive architecture adapted to its sultry weather, brick or cobblestone streets, at least in the better parts, and formal dress such as one might see in London. It was fascinating, but I didn't like either the weather or the society here.

Our clothing wasn't suited to the climate. Marta and I were not accustomed to a wet blanket of heat without a breeze, combined with constrictive attire. Whenever we could, we sneaked out our cotton island dresses and sat on our private veranda in the shade of vines. Dougie commonly wore only short pants and a light shirt now that he no longer needed diapers. Not dealing with diapers gave us some freedom from toil, but he needed to be moving all the time, forcing us to don our "dignity" clothes and take him out.

It was on one of our trips out that my worst worry happened. We had taken Dougie with us to the market, where he loved to point to treats like bananas that reminded him of Jamaica. Seeing a booth of colorful toys, he dashed in front of Marta, causing her to fall onto a booth filled with fruit. The fall upset the baskets of the vendor, who jumped up and cursed at her.

A crowd of women gathered while Marta said, "I'm sorry." She bent to pick up fruit, meaning to return it to the baskets.

"Don't touch my fruit, nasty nigger woman," said the vendor, a white man.

Marta drew back from him in alarm. White women with angry pale faces turned to me. "How can you let your slave behave like this?" said one.

"She isn't my slave. She is a Spanish friend," I said.

"A likely story! She should be beaten with a hard stick!" said another woman.

I grabbed Dougie, who was looking at us with wide eyes, and took Marta's arm gently to lead her away. Several people followed us.

"She should not be allowed near your child. Don't you know any better?" one shouted.

Poor Marta! We made haste through the hard, hot streets back to the inn, where she broke into uncontrollable sobs. Dougie was beside himself with concern. He kept patting her, trying to comfort his friend. My sorrow lodged deep in my throat. It would be easy to be bitter in such a world.

Alex arrived before Marta had finished crying. He was aghast, of course, and took her away to their room. I put Dougie in the bed for his nap, wiping away his own teardrops before he settled down to a story about a magical rabbit.

Alex knocked lightly. When I let him in, he sighed. "Marta is calm and resting now." He paused. "So you were right, then."

"How I wish I had been wrong," I said.

"Marta has asked me to not take her out in public, not to claim her as my wife here."

Tears leaked from his weary eyes. I put my hand on his shoulder. Agitated heat came off him in waves. "I regret exposing her to the market, Alex."

"You are not to blame for this. I learned that there have been slave rebellions here recently. Everyone is overwrought. I hate what she saw today, and I hate even more not presenting her proudly everywhere, but I have to get my business done. It will take social contacts, merchants, and government officials. Apparently, most of them are as sensitive to skin color as those you saw today. I don't know what the best course might be, but I must protect her. Then we must get out of this hellish place."

"Alex, it may be wise to honor Marta's request for now," I said sadly.

*****

Now, as Alex's new acquaintances began to invite him to their homes for supper, Marta asked me to go as his companion. She rightly worried about being judged for her rosy brown skin color in this town where color meant class.

These acquaintances were prosperous merchants and shipbuilders for the most part. However, soon we received an invitation from the colonial governor, James Glen, for an evening's entertainment. Marta once again asked me to go in her stead.

Glen's house was impressive, lit by many candles and manned by slaves in formal attire. The governor wore a wig of curled white hair and a padded red jacket, which I thought must be a prison in the heat. I noticed that he didn't move much and had a slave fanning him.

I had seen that slaves were a large part of the society here and did most of the heavy work. I had also been privy to the conditions in which they were brought here and knew intimately their miserable lack of freedom. I couldn't be as impressed as these wealthy Charles Town men were with the advantages of the slave system!

I was seated next to the governor at table, a great honor, I assumed. He was sweating, patting his cheeks delicately with a lace handkerchief. A terrible bodily smell issued from his fancy clothes. Nevertheless, for Alex's sake, I made polite conversation and complimented him on his lovely house, as we sipped our wine.

"Ah, yes, thank you, my dear. If only the slaves did not get ideas about running off and trying to promote rebellion, all would be well here in Charles Town and we could live as we were meant to."

"Oh, I see. It is a large problem, then?" I asked innocently.

"Hmm, you are lately arrived, I believe. Well, you shall hear more of the problems raised by these rascals," he said, taking a serving of cherries from the black hands that held the dish. "It is necessary to squash these rebellious creatures, as one would squash an insect." He illustrated his point by grinding his thumb into the tablecloth and twisting it with a heavy hand. I took a deep breath behind my fan to conceal my revulsion, wondering what he would think of beautiful, loving Marta.

"In fact," he continued, "it is only with the help of native tribes that we can feel secure in our tenure here, outnumbered as we are. Still, with indigo in one season and rice in the other, slaves can be constantly employed and thus quite profitable.

"But enough of this. Tell me about you. You must have had quite the adventure coming here from Wales, is it?"

I gave him the standard story we had concocted, about sailing here, losing my husband to the small pox and having a young child in arms. How Captain Whitson had rescued me from my ship, how I had helped him with his accounting in Jamaica.

"Hmmm, Rhys is it? Are you by chance an herbal healer and midwife?"

"Why, yes, I am," I said, wondering.

"My dear, someone is looking for you. A Reverend Rhys in Philadelphia sent out a notice through a gazette some months ago, asking government officials to tell him if we knew of your whereabouts. Some relation, I expect?"

"My husband's brother! Oh, I didn't know he was looking for me." I was overcome. Some family, if only by marriage, wanted to find me.

"Well, I can see that you are very moved by this information. The notice is in the, uh, I believe, the *Pennsylvania Gazette*. I'm sure it would reach your brother-in-law if you wrote to that publication."

"Oh, thank you. You are so kind to pass this on to me. Oh, dear, I fear I am faint from this unexpected news," I said, fanning myself with the paper fan they had given us upon arrival.

Turning to his other side, the governor whispered to his wife, who arose to help me. I teetered on my feet, but Alex was up in an instant to assist me. They took me to an adjoining room, where, to my embarrassment, I broke into tears.

"What is it, Mrs. Rhys?" asked Alex, being proper because Mrs. Glen was there.

"Why, the governor has just told me that my husband's brother in Philadelphia is looking for me," I sobbed. "Jacob's brother Thomas must have heard that the ship went down. He knows that Jacob and our daughters are gone, but he still hopes to find me. Good news really, sorry for...I just thought that he would not care." I wept, overwhelmed with the tender knowledge that I still had a relative, the vestige of a family, who was concerned about me.

CHAPTER 84

June 1752
Ardath

IT WAS AS FOX said. The ginseng worked miracles on my lassitude, returning me almost to the energetic state I used to have. The gnarled, dry brown root certainly didn't look appealing, but I persevered in grinding away on it with my back teeth until I could feel the stimulating effects. It was a good thing, too, for not long into our ride that morning, Gwyn unexpectedly dismounted from Molly. I saw her bend to pull up a front foot.

"Ardath, I think Molly may have a stone bruise on her hoof. I'm going to walk her for a while to see if she stops limping."

"Yes, but let's see if we can keep a reasonable pace nonetheless," I said. "We shouldn't get lazy just because we are closer."

"That's true. I even *want* to see the North Carolina's wilderness," said Gwyn.

"I thought you didn't want to see more wilderness." I teased her because we were both in good spirits, having passed beyond the long ridge of a mountain that had appeared on our left several days ago. Somehow, coming into the wider spaces made us feel our progress again. That lighter mood wasn't to last, though.

After we had gone on for another hour, Gwyn stopped suddenly behind me. "Ardath," she whispered, "something is following us."

I looked all around the thick forest on both sides of the trail and could neither see nor sense any presence there. Auri had been ranging ahead of us for several hours now, so we didn't even hear him. "Let's push on a little faster. Do you think you could ride Molly now?" I asked.

"No, but I still feel something. Go quietly," she said. She continued leading Molly down the trail, but the horse began pulling back on the reins restlessly, her eyes wide open, lips fluttering in an uneasy whicker.

"Ardath, get the pistols," Gwyn said.

With that tone in her voice, there was no hesitation on my part. Since the meeting with the Melungeons, we had carried the loaded pistols in the top of my saddlebags. While I got them out, Gwyn unslung her bow, slipped her quiver over her shoulder, and nocked an arrow. She stood intent on the ground, near Molly's neck, then crept off the path a ways and peered into the woods behind us. We heard no sound, not even the normal chirps of the birds.

When the scream came, it seemed to come from all directions at once. Like the sound of a woman in the throes of agony, it burst upon us. Despite myself, I shook at the sound. And then the great cat was flying at us, almost quicker than we could see. Claws flaring, it landed on Molly's back, raking her flank as she reared and screamed, twisting and kicking to get the monster off her.

The mountain lion lurched forward; its claws clutched Molly around the haunches, red mouth cruelly open to bite through her spine. Gwyn was too close to shoot an arrow; she backed up, at the same time straining to get out her long knife. Sally had threatened to bolt with me; I struggled, wrenching on the reins to keep her in check so I could aim the pistol. But Gwyn was too close. If I shot now, I might well hit her.

Abandoning Sally, I leapt from the saddle and slapped her rump. Sally took off down the path. Gwyn was trying to stab the cat, who hung on to Molly's twisting body as the horse screamed in pain.

"Gwyn, get back!" I yelled. She jumped just in time. I took aim with both trembling hands, squeezing the trigger as James had taught us. The cat turned toward me, hissing, fangs bared. I aimed at its mouth. I missed.

Gwyn gave a wild-hearted shriek and struck at the cat with her knife. At this point, the cat turned toward Gwyn, bleeding a little from a gash on its shoulder. Molly was loose and limped away as fast as she could.

I pulled the second pistol out. No time to reload either pistol. I had to make this shot finish it. The mountain lion crouched to leap onto Gwyn. I drew a breath and fired. Now it truly bellowed. I had hit its face, but it didn't die. I had no other weapon and searched about me for a stick or *anything*.

I heard a thump, of arrow hitting target. Gwyn was standing back from the lion with tears streaming down her cheeks. The cat fell with a thud, Gwyn's arrow protruding from its neck, which gushed bright blood.

"Sister, are you hurt?" she cried. Just like Gwyn to think of me first!

"No, are you?" I asked, as I hurried to her.

"No," she said, sobbing. "But we have killed a beautiful thing." Her gaze fell on the tawny creature lying at her feet, still twitching.

I sighed, bending toward her, tilting her face up to mine. Thank God I had not been half-asleep. "You did a necessary thing to save us."

"I know," she said.

We embraced, our bodies shaking hard as we held each other up, almost staggering in our misery. We both took deep breaths to steady ourselves.

"I am most fortunate to have you as my sister," I said, feeling her light bones, knowing what courage lay within that fragile cage.

"Well, we must see if we can find those horses!" I said at last. "Molly will be hurt."

"We'll be in a dire way if we *don't* find them," Gwyn said.

We smiled grimly at that, picked up our various discarded weapons, and walked down the road. As far as I could tell on the damp earth, both horses had stuck to the path, the clearest route for them in the forest. Molly's blood trail was clear as well, with drops entirely too close together.

We were weary from walking and the aftermath of our fight with the mountain lion when we finally dragged ourselves into a meadow and found the horses. Sally grazed the grass almost as if nothing had happened. Auri ran up to us from the edge of the field, so he was well found too. He stopped short when he got near Molly, sniffing her suspiciously, crooked tail held stiffly.

"Thank the Goddess," I said.

Gwyn approached Molly slowly, making soothing sounds to reassure her.

The horse stood, legs splayed, head down, breath puffing while flies swarmed around her bleeding rump. "Oh, Ardath, she really is hurt."

I went to help take off the tack. The lion had not been able to sink in its teeth, but the claw marks on her flanks were running red. Mercifully, the cat's claws had jerked the heavy saddle blanket partway over Molly's back, which had deflected some of the blows.

"Let's boil some water and get those cleaned up," I said. "The flies must be driving her mad." I set to work on the fire-building while Gwyn looked more closely for cuts on both mares. Other than scratches from their flight through the woods and Molly's gouges from the ordeal with the cat, they had no further wounds. Molly's saddle had deep scores on it. She had been saved from the most serious injuries by the thick leather.

"Well! I'll have a fine story to tell about the saddle after Molly is healed," Gwyn said.

"That you will!" I said. We were both more cheerful while doing something to repair the damage.

Molly was patient with our ministrations. Her wounds should perhaps have been stitched, but I didn't think we could get through her hide with the needles we had. Gwyn held her head and stroked her shoulders while I swiftly washed up the slashes, then applied calendula and numbing powder made from pepper, cloves, garlic, and herbs to her coarse coat.

"Thank you," Gwyn said, sighing now that the worst of Molly's treatment was over. I saw her ready her bow and was reminded to load our pistols. From now on, I would be very aware of where these were at every moment.

Since the day was still young, we walked and rode along at a reasonable pace, taking turns on Sally to let Molly's rump heal. We came to a brick house, where we asked to buy corn or oats. The Scot who greeted us had a stringy beard and was not very clean, but then neither were we. He sold us corn and told us we were only a few miles from Big Salt Lick.

We had sufficient feed and didn't stop in the town, if the collection of wood shacks there could be called such, but walked on toward the Dan River. Thank goodness for the regular marks the Moravians had left! Otherwise, the "trail" just looked like a goat track. It certainly didn't resemble a path that a woods buffalo would find comfortable, though it must have been a buffalo track originally. We saw not a one of those creatures, even right near the cliff containing the lick. Perhaps they had learned that they would be hunted there.

When we reached the Dan, we would be in North Carolina, *finally*! But it took us several more days of walking the most primitive of trails to get there. Fortunately, we had no further animal or human threats on the way. Gwyn was quiet, though, almost sullen, spending her time attending to Molly and Auri.

CHAPTER 85

June 1752
Gwyn

I<small>T WAS UNFAIR OF</small> me, I admit that, but I blamed Ardath for the whole situation, for pushing us to come on this godforsaken path, for letting Molly get hurt, for resenting Auri, who still regularly brought us small game every morning, for taking me away from Gregory. She might be relishing the wilderness, but I was sick to death of it. I wanted nothing more than to crawl into a soft bed at night and sleep without worry, sleep late into the day if I wanted. I wanted decent food. I wanted the safety of a town. I wanted loving arms around me.

Then I would stop chewing on my resentment and remember our mother's loving arms, the reason for this trip. After a moment, though, I'd be back to blaming Ardath. Mother wasn't waiting for us in North Carolina. I'd tried to tell her, but Ardath never listened to me. What did await us there, I didn't know, and that just made me feel more frustrated.

The anger boiled over like a steaming pot when we reached the wide Dan River and found it running high, great coppery waves two feet tall with white caps. There was no ferry, no one to help us. Molly's wounds were still fresh, and I was exhausted.

Ardath turned to me, bright anticipation on her face. "We can get across tonight before the sun sets and be in North Carolina!" she exclaimed.

"Ardath, by God, I'll not do it!" I said, facing her down. "Can't you see that we have to wait for the water to calm? Molly and I are exhausted. I will *not* go tonight."

She stared at me in wonder, as if I were a two-headed monster, some changeling in place of her sister. "Now, Gwyn, you know we need to push on."

Her reasonable tone infuriated me further. "No, I'll not!" I said. "Would you risk yourself and your child here? Haven't you some responsibility to him?"

"Gwyn, all right," she said, face red with anger. "Then I'll go on by myself." She jerked Sally's reins toward the water. "Since you are such a baby!" She threw the last comment over her shoulder at me.

"Then you *will* go by yourself, not with me!" I replied. I stood my ground, allowing Auri to run about in confusion as he saw Ardath enter the river without us. Molly nuzzled my neck as if in support.

I tried to go about setting up a camp for myself, but of course, I couldn't ignore the figure of Ardath urging Sally into the water. She slung the saddle-bags containing our pistols around her neck and climbed into the saddle as Sally plodded into the roiling stream.

Sally soon whinnied her protest, to no avail. Ardath was caught in her own determination and anger. How many times had I gone along, as Sally had to now, goaded by my sister's mad ideas!

I watched in horrible fascination as the river swept around them, swifter and swifter while they tried to ford it. Soon Sally was swimming for her life, Ardath bent over her head, fierce resolve shown in the angle of her receding back.

My fury forgotten, my breath came in sharp gasps. I found I was praying with all my heart to any God or Goddess that might listen. "May they make it, please. Let three lives not end here."

But the reply came from nature, merciless nature, who must make her own way. They were half-across. They were two-thirds across. Then the current took them, Sally twisting sideways in the rushing waters, Ardath bending upstream to try to right them. Now Ardath was washed off Sally, pushing toward the bank on her own, then rammed by the river inexorably downstream. Sally's head disappeared, then Ardath's. I strained my eyes to see them, but there were only the copper waves crashing.

Nothing. And no way for me to help them. I was too terrified to think or feel. I have no idea how long I stood frozen to the spot. Finally, I stared at the river's side to my left. I could look farther downstream for any sight of Ardath or Sally. I started pushing through the brush in that direction, scraping my arms and stumbling in the dense growth. Soon I came to an utterly impassable log-jam left by the flood. I could only get around it by entering the river. I stopped to listen and heard only the water's roar.

Auri whimpered at my feet. I saw that night was rapidly closing in on us. We struggled our way back to the strip of beach where Molly waited. Auri began jumping on my legs, and Molly pushed at my neck. I sighed; the animals must be cared for. I took the packs and saddle off Molly, shaking, still too stunned to cry. I rubbed her down briefly and set her to graze some grass on the bank. To Auri, I gave the bone I had carried with us since the morning. I drank some water and paced on the shore, hoping to see some movement on the other side. Nothing. The last of daylight left us as night moved in. I could see nothing, hear nothing, do nothing.

Eventually, I was beyond exhaustion. Throwing my bedroll on the ground, I dropped into it, wrapping the blanket of darkness around me.

I arose in the gray light of morning, sick with horror, the memories of yesterday crowding back. The river was back within its banks, only a light brownish color recalling the flood. I could actually see rocks above the water. We would be able to walk across, to search for Ardath's body.

As I glumly saddled Molly for the trip across, I heard a distant gun-shot. I'd cared little for my own safety the night before, having neither fire nor weapons prepared, but now I dashed to my bow and quiver. The sound seemed to have come from across the river. I tucked Auri into his sling and watched carefully from behind the cover of willows. As the sun peeked out of the clouds, I saw movement on the other side of the brown water, a flare of red-orange light. Perhaps a trick of the sunlight flashing on the water as it filtered through the trees.

Or Ardath? I hardly dared hope! But yes, it was Ardath, dragging herself along that shore, hauling a saddle. She dropped her burden to wave with both arms toward my side. She was alive! I hurried to the water line, waving my arms as well. That was when I wept, hands on knees, unstoppable sobs.

Trembling, I hastily struck camp and turned Molly toward the river. I rode her across carefully and felt her slipping on the rocks, but the water was never higher than the top of the stirrups.

Ardath was a sight as we slipped up the muddy slope to her side. Her hair was wild and tangled, full of sticks and debris, her clothes in shreds, her hands raw and bloody. She held a pistol.

"Ardath? Are you hurt?" I asked, standing back a little to inspect her.

"Oh, sister," she said. Her face crumbled. I held her in my arms. She laid her head on my neck and wept like a lost soul. We stood that way, with me murmuring small kindnesses to her, until her weight fell fully on me and I had to pull her over to a log, where we sat down in a clumsy heap.

"Ardath, we are alive. All will be well. Nothing can stop us when we are together!" I said, smoothing her hair, easing the pistol from her cold fingers, holding her tight with one arm. Though she was badly scraped, I could see no part of her bleeding greatly, and her arms and legs seemed whole as I patted her shaking body.

When she calmed enough to speak, she said, "I have been such a fool. Can you ever forgive me?"

"Of course, you are forgiven, of course!" I said, wondering at the *apology*, words I had thought I'd never hear from her.

"But," she said, straightening away from me. "You don't know it all." She looked at my face, her eyes bleary, then looked away. "I had to shoot Sally."

It struck me then, the thoughts I had avoided. That was why Ardath dragged the saddle. That was what the gunshot was. We were alone in the wilderness with one injured horse to our name.

"Oh," I said, my heart sinking, picturing Sally broken and suffering. It seemed unreal that we had lost her, who had carried us so faithfully on this cursed trip. I heaved a quivering sigh.

After a long while, I continued. "Well, we are both wet and cold. I need to start a fire." I covered Ardath with the one blanket I had left, only a little moist.

I had let Auri out of his sling as soon as I reached that shore. He was gone, hunting, I presumed. I rubbed Molly down quickly and gathered wood that wasn't too damp. With some effort, I got a small blaze going. Fortunately, I had been carrying the oats, so I was able to feed Molly and make porridge for us. Hot food and hot water to drink would help us all.

The coffee and tea had been torn off Sally in the flood, along with the corn, salt, and other provisions. Ardath had only the saddle, of little use to us unless we could find another horse quickly. Thank goodness I had had the silver with me. She had salvaged her saddlebags with the pistols in them, but her bedroll and extra clothes were gone.

Faithful Auri returned, dragging a rabbit between his legs. I had had much experience recently in skinning and roasting small animals. I no longer had the luxury of great pity for the animals. We wasted no time in cooking and making a meal of it, with Auri enjoying the hunter's share.

Ardath's posture improved visibly as she ate and drank. She was able to walk again, but when she stood, the blanket had slipped from her shoulders. Linen scraps hung across her ample breasts. Her pants parted to show her alabaster skin. Her tattered clothes would have been ludicrous if it hadn't been such a serious problem. The only fabric we had was the blanket. I still had my needle and thread, so I fashioned a dress of sorts for her, which opened down the back to her waist. I made ties from strips of her linen shirt to fasten it.

It emphasized her growing belly. I cupped that lightly, as if to smooth the dress, but she knew what I was doing.

"The baby is all right, I think," she said curtly. She must be better if she could be snappish again, I thought.

She went to the river to wash her hands. I put some ointment on them, which she rubbed in slowly. She picked at the debris in her hair with her thumb and forefinger. Her long locks shook like injured snakes.

"Do you want to rest today?" I asked.

"No, let us walk on, now that I have made a thorough shambles of everything!" she said.

I knew better than to reply to that.

CHAPTER 86

June 1752
Ardath

IN TRUTH, I MISSED Sally on the trail, and not just for the convenience of riding her. I had been fond of her. And when I had awoken, coughing up rotten river water on that far bank, I heard her screaming in pain but could not find her in the absolute blackness. I had to wait for hours, torn and bleeding myself, sore, thick of head and sick of heart, hearing her agony, until a gray light slowly spread over the sky, to see my way toward where she lay entangled in logs, legs askew and obviously broken, to relieve her pain. I thanked the Goddess that one of the pistols was dry enough to shoot her. Hell couldn't be worse than that night.

I never told Gwyn how the horse had suffered, not wanting Gwyn to feel the pain, and being ashamed that I had so misjudged the situation at the Dan and caused that good mare's death. We left her saddle beside the path, carving "Moravians" on a piece of wood to place with it, in case it might be found by the Brethren as they came through.

Our slow process through the woods gave me time to think about other responsibilities I had shirked with that decision. First, I had broken my promise to Mother to take care of Gwyn. Thank the Goddess she had not followed me into that water!

Second, I was a married woman now, and though I still had the freedom to make decisions (bad or good), I had pledged to have regard for the person of my husband and hence of our child. It wasn't because of any paper we had signed but because I had discovered on this trip how my love for James had grown. I truly wanted to be bound to him and to believe his promise that he would help me with my burdens. I had survived. I had a new appreciation for my own life and the life inside me. James would be so excited to know we would have a child. He could have lost us both in those treacherous waters.

I shuddered. I must somehow learn to think through my actions. What I thought to be strength had proven in this instance to be weakness!

*****

My blanket, a true state of "undress," was hot. I had to cut it far shorter than fashion dictated in order to walk along the narrow path. We took turns riding Molly. I know Gwyn wanted to do most of the walking to help me, but I tried to do my share. After all, I was pregnant, not sick!

"Ardath, we may find some settlement soon, since we are in North Carolina, maybe some farms," Gwyn said hopefully.

"Even the Moravians didn't know much from this point on, to their settlement at Bethabara," I said. "We shall just have to hope that we can replace some of our lost supplies, perhaps find other clothes for me," I said. "Not that this 'gown' isn't a miracle of sewing," I hastened to add. More each day, it was becoming clear how much she gave to me and to our effort. I was ashamed of how I had taken her for granted.

She just looked at me with a wry twist of her mouth. "Sorry we had no silk with us!" she said.

We had made do with worse rations in the ship across the Atlantic. We weren't starving. Molly had sweet grass to eat when we stopped. I even had to appreciate what that stupid dog brought in, with local game apparently plentiful. We didn't take time to hunt as we could have, because with one of us walking, we were slowed down once again.

Still we made our progress as we could, until, one day, we were pleased to see the next river, the Yadkin. We were even more pleased to see a young man in homespun fishing from the bank.

"Hallo!" I called.

He turned to us, a thin, gawky-looking boy with a hooked nose and large eyes. "Ladies!" he said and gave an awkward bow. "Are ya lost, then?"

"On our way to Bethabara, land of the Moravians," said Gwyn. "Do you have a house near here?"

"Yes, ma'am. Please come along with me and we'll do all we can ta help ya," he said. He led the way down a path along the river to a house on a small knoll above it.

It was a frontier house, but better appointed than most others we had seen.

"We ben hereabouts for two years now. Still plenty ta do, o' course," he said, pointing up to the house. An older man appeared on the porch. "Pa, we got company," he called out.

The man scrambled down the knoll, quite agile for his seeming age. "Squire Boone, at yer service," he said and looked to his son for explanation.

"Pa, these ladies are a-traveling ta the Moravians."

"I see," said Mr. Boone. He gazed at us, thready beard bobbing on his chin. "Please be our guests for some refreshment. Dan'l, see ta the horse. Looks like it has met with an angry critter."

We introduced ourselves and followed him up to the house. Since it was fine weather, we sat on stools outside under a spreading tree while he brought us elderberry wine and fresh bread. "Most of my family's gone taday, gatherin' herbs," he explained. "Normally not so quiet here!"

"Thank you so much for your hospitality," Gwyn said. "It is kind of you."

"Well, glad you stopped. We don't get too many visitors here. We've come down from Pennsylvania looking fer a fresh start. The land's good here."

He told us the story of his formerly Quaker family, who had been dismissed from the congregation because two of their children had married "worldlings," people not of the Friends' faith.

"Well, we can do jest fine on our own here, no church ta dictate ta us," he said. Suddenly, it seemed to occur to him that we might not find his sentiments agreeable. "Well, no matter. Tell me what you search fer in this wild country."

We told him about the journey to find our cousin and our mother. I included the loss of my horse and much of our goods. "We need to buy another, if you have a saddle horse to trade," I said.

"No, sorry, no riding horse ta spare, but Dan'l can get ya across the river and started on yer way ta the Moravians. I've got an old gown of my daughter's that was goin' for rags, but since ya lost yers, ya might find it acceptable."

"Thank you. I'd like to try it, please," I said. Boone showed us to a girls' bedroom and brought out a white muslin ensemble. He excused himself and closed the door. Of course, it was too small for me, but at least it had a full skirt. If I hitched it up, I'd have room for my belly and could pull the material around my legs to ride. The jacket could be forced to fit over my breast.

"Thank you for this," I told Boone when we found him on the font porch. "We would like to buy the clothes from you, and some corn or oats if you could spare them."

"Nah, that outfit's a gift, but we have some o' last year's corn for yer horse and some oats laid back that we can trade ya," he said. "And some cheese for yer travels."

He smiled crookedly when we brought out some silver coins. "Well, now, I don't have much use fer silver here, so might be best if ya keep that for yerself. Might be helpful in finding yer mother."

In the end, he would let us pay for nothing. "Got girls myself," he said with a shy shrug.

Daniel asked if we would cross the river in their wagon. Boone smiled. "He's always after usin' that wagon. Wants ta be a wagoner!"

We planned to sit on the wagon bench with him and tie Molly on the back. The river looked too deep for wagon wheels, though I hesitated to say so. They surely knew their own territory.

"It seems awfully deep," said Gwyn as we waved to Squire Boone and rambled down the path to the river, where sturdy draft horses began pulling the wagon along the bank.

"Oh, yes, ma'am, up here it is, but there's a ford lower down," said Daniel with confidence. Sure enough, we had the easiest crossing of our trip. The ford was a wide swath of rock less than two feet under the water. It ran across the river at an angle; we never would have found it on our own. Molly walked it with no trouble. On the other shore, Daniel took us farther inland and pointed out the markings the Moravians had made the year before.

"We thank you, Daniel. I know you will be a great wagoner," said Gwyn.

He blushed and grinned and, like his father, would take no pay.

*****

In another day, we were at Bethabara. The path opened up suddenly into a large clearing where men in straw hats hoed in a field. They looked up in surprise. A man holding his hat in hand came to greet us.

"Sisters, well come to Bethabara."

"Thank you. You speak English?" I asked, for at the moment I couldn't remember a word of German.

"Yes, I am Hans Martin Kalberhahn, the physician. How come you here? Alone?"

"We bring word from Jacob and Rachel Schutz," I said.

His face brightened. "You have met the Brethren on your way?"

"Yes, they are coming, we hope not far behind us," Gwyn said.

"Are they well?"

"When we left them, they were very well," she said.

"Ah, blessed news!"

We explained that we were on our way to Anson County to find our cousin, David Reese, and had needed to travel faster than the Brethren's wagons could go.

"Yes, big wagons! Very good news. We work to be ready for them," he said, gesturing around him. On the small rise above the garden, several long timber houses had been started, having stone foundations with wooden platforms above, and the start of some walls. The gardens, though, were well along, showing fine medicinal herbs, lettuces, and onions. A farther garden had corn sprouts eight inches high. The earth was a rich reddish hue.

"We sleep there," he said, pointing to a tiny cabin farther from the garden made of red mud and chunks of wood. It resembled a sty for pigs. The pigs, though, were apparently out foraging in the woods. A nearby corral held several horses and cows.

"You are tired," he said kindly. "Will you rest with us this night? We can put a tent on the floor of yonder Sisters' house, where we have at least some walls built up. Wolves are little threat this time of the year."

Nothing sounded more wonderful to me. "Thank you. That would be most welcome," I said. We proceeded to the partially built house, its walls about four feet tall.

Gwyn looked happy. When we had moved on from the working men, she said, "I feel safer here. At least there are some people around."

"I agree. We can put down our burdens for a time today."

Even our animals seemed happy. It was a day of sun and blue skies. I was disappointed to feel drowsiness sweep over me as I sat on the stone steps. I reached for the ginseng and stopped. I'd let myself have this one afternoon. I spread out our one bedroll on the wooden floor and fell asleep.

When I awoke, Gwyn was at the garden, talking with the doctor, no doubt comparing herbal remedies. She wore her wide hat and gestured with animation.

That evening, the doctor brought our meal to us. Fresh salad and onions and a roast of venison.

"Forgive us that we cannot sup with you. Our sisters and brothers do not mingle until marriage," he explained.

"We understand," Gwyn replied. "Thank you for this food."

"We thank the Lord," said the doctor. He bowed briefly and turned away.

"Excuse me," said Gwyn. "How far do we have to travel to reach Anson County? And do you know of our cousin's farm?"

"No one here knows him, but I think you would have a few days' journey south to go," he said. "We can put you on the trader's path in the morning."

"Thank you, again," I said.

So it was that after several good meals and a good rest, we continued on yet another primitive trail south. These were the only "roads," so there wasn't much way we could get lost, providing we always faced the sun most of the day. We saw only a few men, mostly leading mules with packs. Finally, we found a trader who knew of our cousin and gave us directions to his home.

CHAPTER 87

June 1752
Gwyn

WE WALKED IN THE hot green woods until our hearts lifted at the sight of our cousin's board house. It was one and a half stories tall, with dormers above the front porch and trees on each end. Beyond stretched miles of open fields with outbuildings and a large barn.

I took a deep breath. "Ardath, this is where we find out more!" I exclaimed, hoping against hope that we might find our mother within.

As we approached the house, we could hear children wailing, especially the cry of a young infant. Hesitantly, I knocked.

We had waited for a long time when the door jerked open before us. Our cousin David stood there, black hair spiking up from his head, his black eyes staring at us wildly. He smelled strongly of sour whiskey, and black stubble marred his handsome face. He blocked our way into the house.

"What, what is it?" he yelled, eyes darting between us. He stared at me. I must have blanched, showing up my scar. "Good Lord, woman, what happened to your face?"

I covered my scar in dismay. I had forgotten its mark on our journey.

Ardath straightened and spoke for us. "David, we are your cousins, come from Philadelphia."

"Oh, ho! My cousins the healers! Well, it is too late. She is already dead!"

I felt myself grow faint. Our mother, dead? Black spots rushed toward my eyes. My knees began to buckle.

Ardath's firm hand clasped my arm. From behind David, the wailing of children and a nasty smell swelled around us like a poison fog.

"David, gain control of yourself!" Ardath barked at him. She let go of my arm and grabbed both of his. "Who has died?'

His face crumbled into a weeping mass. "My Rose, she died these three nights past and us with three boys, one a babe in arms!"

I gasped in a breath. Thank God! Not our mother. *She wasn't dead!* I let go a sob of grief, though. She wasn't here. And a poor woman *was* dead. Beside me, Ardath shuddered.

"You must let us in. We will help you tend to the children," Ardath said, steering him to the side.

I breathed deeply, unpacking Auri from the sling and letting him down on the porch. I ran toward the sound of the wailing baby. In the back bedroom, I found a small infant lying in a cradle, soiled by his own filth, flailing legs and arms against his hunger and pain. I spoke to him quietly and stroked his belly. Wrapping him in a nearby cloth, I lifted him into my arms. I found napkins to clean him. He was the main source of the fetid smell in the house, but once I had taken him to the kitchen, cleaned him, and thrown the nasty cloths out the kitchen door, I noticed two more small faces looking up at me with both fear and hope from just outside the door. Their bodies didn't smell very good either.

"Boys, come in," I said. "I am your cousin. I can help you, but I need your help too."

They both nodded solemnly at me. "What does the baby eat?" I asked.

The larger one, probably about five, with black curls and dark-blue eyes, pointed at a bin containing cornmeal. "He eats pap?" I asked. They nodded. I built up the smoldering fire and soon had a pot of water heating, while I jiggled the baby in my arms and smiled at the older boys.

Auri appeared in the doorway, which brought murmurs of delight from the boys. After they leaned down to pet him, they again looked toward me.

"Are you hungry?" I asked. They nodded again, the younger a small blond boy about three, with his finger in his mouth. "All right. Who knows where the salt is?" They pointed together toward a small wooden box. "Very good, boys! We shall soon have something to eat! But I must feed the baby.

Can you feed yourselves?" I asked, to which they nodded vigorously.

A hint of a smile creased the corner of the older one's mouth. "We are big boys, not babies! Of course, we feed ourselves!" he proclaimed.

"Of course!" I said, smiling at them as all our spirits rose.

The baby sucked with all his might at the spoon of pap I held for him. His little face was gaunt, his limbs weak. He was soon too tired to try any more, falling asleep in my arms. Pap was not enough to nourish him fully. He was too young for it, needed milk.

"Boys, my name is Gwyn." Turning to the older one, I said, "You must be Alphonse." I grinned.

"No, my name is David!" he said.

"Well," I gestured to the younger, "then *you* must be Alphonse."

"No, we have no one called Afons here," said David. "He is Solomon."

"Oh," I said in mock dismay.

"Gwyn, you play the fool," said David. Still not a word from Solomon.

"Do you have a goat?" I asked.

"Yes, Mildred milks her," he said. "I think she is afraid and hiding in the barn, though."

"Could you run to the barn and tell Mildred that help is here? She should milk the goat and bring me the fresh milk as soon as she can."

"Yes, ma'am," said David. He ran off eagerly while Solomon stared at me from beneath wispy bangs.

"Solomon, does the baby have a bottle?" He nodded, swiveled on his feet, and pointed toward a shelf I hadn't noticed before.

"You are very bright, aren't you?" I asked him. He nodded again. I decided his name was really descriptive, "solemn man." He must be terribly scared and confused about his mother's death. It made me ache for him.

Ardath came into the kitchen, her apron splotched with water. "I dunked his head in the water barrel," she said. "I'll make coffee, if he has some, and try to get some sense out of him. Obviously, Mother isn't here, but maybe he knows something more. We can hope," she said, but she didn't look hopeful.

She stirred around the kitchen while I washed the bottle, that action made more difficult by the sleeping baby on my arm.

"I hold him," Solomon's first words to me, from the corner where he had stood after his brother left.

"Ardath, this is Solomon. He is the middle boy. The older, David, is looking for the maid."

"Ah, good," Ardath said.

I stowed Solomon securely in the corner, with pillows behind him, and lowered the baby into his arms. He held him gently and carefully. They must have had a good mother, I thought, with a sharp stab of sadness.

Mildred entered with a bucket of goat's milk. The bucket looked none too clean, so I strained the milk and put it in a kettle to boil over the fire.

Ardath had made a mug of coffee for our "host." She disappeared after we introduced ourselves to Mildred, a pale, undernourished girl of about fifteen years old.

"Mistress Gwyn, I am so happy that you are here. He has been out of his head these last days, with the death of the lady," Mildred whispered. "I am under indenture to him, but I have been in fear of my life lately!"

I sighed. "It is a hard situation. How long has Mrs. Reese been ill? Have you been feeding the boys?"

"Oh, yes, ma'am, whenever I can feed them without seeing him. Mrs. Reese has not been good since little Charlie was born, fevers and such. But she was took bad three days ago and never woke."

"Well, we are here now, and we will take care of Mr. Reese and the children. How about you? Have you eaten?"

"Oh, not for some time now," she said in a weak voice. I sat her down at the small table and gave her the remaining mush from the boys' meal. "Oh, thank you. You are an angel from God above!"

In came little David, his fingers red with juice from the handful of cherries he had gathered.

"Why, David, look at what you found!" I said with genuine delight.

He rewarded me with a smile. "I got what I could reach," he said.

Ardath appeared in the doorway, signaling for me to come out of the kitchen. "I have him somewhat settled. Can you come with me?" she asked.

I turned back to Mildred. "Can you watch the children?" I asked.

She nodded. We went toward the front of the house. Ardath stopped in the narrow hallway.

"He's sobering up, but he's still in a bad way," she said.

"I'm ready," I said.

We found David bent over on the front steps. I approached him cautiously. "Cousin," I said, "we are here to help you in any way we can."

He looked up at us with tortured eyes but answered calmly. "I'm so sorry for the way I greeted you. I am ashamed." He ran a hand over the bristles on his chin.

I sat beside him. "It's all right. I have taken care of the children, and Mildred is with them."

"Thank you!" he said, with both his mouth and his eyes. "To repay cruelty with kindness is the greatest gift."

"David, you know that we have come in search of our mother. Have you had any more news of her?" I asked, my heart in my mouth.

He groaned and held his head. "Oh, my cousins, I am afraid you have come for nothing. I am so sorry."

Ardath and I looked at each other in alarm. Red rage came into her face. I was afraid she'd loose her bile on him. I shook my head at her. "No, Ardath!"

She took a deep breath and contained herself, at least for the moment. I did the same.

"David, what has happened?" I asked. He mumbled into his hands. "What?" I asked, a little more sharply.

He raised his head. "That scoundrel, that scoundrel! He wanted the reward, that's all. I caught up with him, the liar, and dragged the truth from him."

"Caught up with him? Who?" Ardath asked.

"That liar, Jesse Fairchild! He told me of your mother coming through, but she hadn't. He did it for the coin, that's all."

"You mean, the man who said he had seen our mother was lying? We came all this way for her and she was never here?" asked Ardath.

"Yes, that's the way of it. I found out just before my Rose died, and too late to let you know. This was my fault, to believe him!" he said, in apparent misery. He buried his head in his hands once more.

Ardath and I stared at each other in our own misery. "I thought your premonitions were wrong," she said to me, the extent of her apology. I was greatly bereft, but not really surprised by the news.

We said no more to him but left him on the steps and returned to the house. "Ardath, this is terrible for us, and we must make plans, but first we must straighten out this pitiable household."

She seemed more disappointed and stunned by the revelation that our mother hadn't been here than I was. She pursed her mouth and nodded. She had no more words than Solomon.

"It doesn't mean she's dead, just that we haven't found her yet," I said. "I really feel sure she is alive!"

"But where could she be? What else can we try that we haven't already?" Tears of pain appeared in her eyes.

"We shall just have to take one thing at a time. We can, we *must*, have hope," I said, reaching for her hand. She shook herself as if to throw off her suffering.

"First, we must find out if Rose has been prepared for burial," I said. "Something is terribly wrong in this house."

In apprehension, we explored the house. In front of one door, we found a chair propped to prevent entrance. We opened it to find, to our horror, that Rose lay in the bed where she had died. The smell of decay in the house was explained by her moldering body. Blue eyes stared at the ceiling, mouth set in a grimace. I could only pray the children had not seen her. We opened the window and set to work, washing her body and carrying away the soiled sheets, smoothing her face into peaceful lines, closing her eyes. Our cousin had truly been distraught to leave her thus; he must have loved her very much. We went to the yard to have a breath of clean air.

"A fine way to take care of his darling wife and family!" said Ardath, spitting on the grass in contempt.

"He was very affected by her death, I think," I said. "Perhaps you could be generous with your mercy. He seems a kind man."

She blew out a breath. "Oh, Gwyn, I'll never understand you!"

"Ardath, you look tired. Let's find you a bed. I'll see to the children."

I tucked her up in a large bed that probably held all the children. Lucky woman, she fell asleep.

In the kitchen, Mildred looked better for having eaten. Little David smiled at me. Solomon leaned against my leg. The baby was stirring in the corner among the pillows.

"I washed the bottle, ma'am, and the milk is ready for little Charlie," said Mildred.

"Good, Mildred. Will you take the boys outside for a while? I will feed Charlie some more."

"Yes, ma'am, thank you, ma'am." She bobbed a curtsy.

"And take Auri out with you. The boys might like to play with him," I said.

I picked up Charlie, holding his warm body against mine. "Would you like some milk, little one?" I asked. He burrowed into my chest. His mother had probably still been nursing him, then. I gently pushed at his lips to guide the bottle's nipple into his mouth. Thank the Mother Goddess, he had a strong suck. I had to slow him down so that he would not make himself sick, poor starveling!

I wondered at the tenderness I felt for him. Could it happen that fast? What more would I feel if this were my own child? Although I had physically become a woman while we sailed, I understood that I really *was* a woman now, in my heart.

Charlie fell asleep in my arms again. I nestled him in the corner pillows once more. He needed the protection of his own cradle, though. I went to clean that out, no small feat. I also opened every window in the house, hoping that soon the place might smell more like a home.

When I went to open the front door, I found David still on his steps. I sat beside him in silence.

"How are the children?" he asked after a long while.

"They are fed, clean, and at peace, as much as they can be. Little Charlie has taken a bottle of goat's milk and fallen asleep. They are sweet boys."

"They had a sweet mother. I loved her more than I had thought possible! I am lost without her," he said.

"The boys need you now, you know."

"Of course, but they need a woman's touch too. I can't give them that." He shrugged his shoulders as if to dislodge off a heavy weight.

"No, but you can give them a loving father."

"Aye, I've not been that. Not been anything." He turned to me. "Gwyn, do you think you might stay a while, even though your mother isn't here?"

"We don't know yet. We will certainly stay until we get word from Ardath's husband, Major James. He may be coming this way. In the meantime, we can help Mildred care for the children. She seems quite fond of them."

"Ah, yes, Mildred. I think I have scared her out of her wits," he said, shaking his head with regret.

I smiled. "Well, she will recover, I believe."

He gazed at me then. "You are not much older than Mildred yourself, are you? But you seem much more settled somehow."

"It is probably because of all I have seen and done in the past two years."

"My father has written to me about you, about some of the misfortunes you have faced so bravely. I admire you and your sister greatly. I am sorry to have added to your sorrows."

I drew a deep breath. "I have been convinced for some time that Mother was not here, but we had to know."

"Of course. Again, I—"

"Please don't apologize. It is not your fault," I said. In truth, I wanted to be alone to absorb my feelings about Mother's absence.

As if he understood, he said, "Excuse me. I must clean up. I don't want to scare my boys."

"Of course," I said.

He wandered off to a well, drawing up water to shave and wash with. He had a fine, manly figure when he took off the dirty shirt and squared his shoulders. I felt a definite spark in my heart when I saw his body.

*****

As for not finding Mother, I tried to let the disappointment flow over me without hurting too much. Despite my intuition, I had never thought through what would happen if we didn't find her. I sighed, a heavy feeling pressing on my chest.

I assumed we would go back to Philadelphia. I wanted to know how Omar's leg was and if Washington had gotten him back home, how Ibrahim and the apothecary were faring, whether Mrs. Perry had become a mantua maker, whether Ahmed had his own smithy yet, how Isa and Uncle Thomas were. If, I hoped, all were in good health.

Of course, Gregory was on my mind. When I dreamed of him, I didn't feel the excitement I thought I should, if I were to marry him. He seemed more like a very beloved older brother and friend. He certainly made me laugh. But I had changed, grown more mature. I understood now that I had no need to compare myself with Ardath. She had her own kind of weakness, and I had my own kind of strength.

As much as being back in Philadelphia had appealed to me when we were on the trail, it now seemed like the defeat of our dearest dreams. And the thought of slogging our way back up that trail was more than I could bear.

Auri ran up and sat close to me, as if thoughtful himself. I smiled. He was a good dog, but I no longer needed him for comfort as desperately as I had before. He had become a different, more fully grown creature on this trip, though still loveable and comic, with his twisted tail awry.

I put on my hat, which had lain this whole time on the porch railing. Auri and I would walk David's gardens to quiet my mind. Surely, there would be some lavender or rosemary to sweeten the rooms as well.

CHAPTER 88

July 1752
Ardath

IN THE NEXT TWO weeks, we had that house and farm put to rights.

First, I found the manager skulking about in the barn. "Mr. Prentiss, I assume you know where the workers are?" I said. He had wisps of hay in his hair, stubble on his chin, and probably slept in the barn.

"Yes, ma'am," he said in a sullen voice.

"Well, get them to work. This tobacco crop won't weed itself, and clean yourself up. There is no reason to be slovenly," I said.

"Yes, ma'am." He scurried away like the rat he resembled. I knew nothing about raising tobacco, but anyone could see that the weeds were winning.

Gwyn concentrated on the house. She soon had the boys in hand. They clung to her as if she were their new mother. And Gwyn, oh my! She seemed to have fallen in love with them at first sight, and maybe their father as well. She had spent hours in close conversation with him, trying to keep the worst of his grief at bay, I supposed. I watched with concern. I had never seen her look at anyone but Gregory the way she looked at David, and she often touched him with sympathy.

Of course, there was the practical matter of getting Rose buried, which had to be done soonest. Mr. Prentiss sent word to the neighbors, who brought food and came to sit with David. There wasn't a preacher in the area, but a tall man in a black hat was more than willing to read the Bible over her grave. The boys clustered around Gwyn's skirts at the service. No one but little David cried, and he at least did not lose control. This handful of folks were neighbors, true, but so far apart and so new to this wilderness as to hardly know one another. This would be a lonely life.

Many days after the service, I sat on a bench under a tree. I didn't know what we were going to do next. Gwyn was teaching the maid how to care for the boys, but would she be ready to leave them? What if she fell in love with David and wanted to stay?

There was a hollow place in me where the hope for Mother had been. I couldn't see what else we could do to find her, if, indeed, she still lived. It would not be many months before *I* would be a mother in the flesh, not just standing in the place of one, as I had with Gwyn. Mother wouldn't be here to help me with the birth, a comfort I had hoped to have. Who would I have in my life, if Gwyn stayed here? I couldn't know where James would go next, where his orders would take him.

I assumed we would all go back to Philadelphia. We had a community there, of sorts. Like so many other women, I pictured raising our child on my own, perhaps in wartime, if James was right about a war coming. I thought Mrs. Perry would help, though, and Ibrahim could deliver the babe if we got back in time. Well! I seemed to be catching Gwyn's habit of deep thinking, but I couldn't see that it was doing me much good.

I got up to see to the workers. They were not slaves, as David didn't believe in that institution, but they were indentured workers, the next thing to slaves. No day off for them. They had stood at Rose's grave, of course, but then seemed to melt away. The farm needed tending, and I had to check on them every day thereafter. Where was that damned weasel Prentiss? I asked myself.

As I walked toward the house, I saw dust rise and heard hoofbeats in the little lane that led from the woods. A large black horse, a man's figure astride it. My heart beat faster as he approached. With a happy bounce, I ran to him, for it was James! I had no other thought now but to be in his arms at last.

"Oh, James! You have found us!" I called. He swung down from the saddle before the horse had stopped, running to gather me up.

"My love, my love!" he said, joy in his voice.

Unembarrassed, I buried my face into his neck, tears rolling down his collar, holding tight to him. He smelled of woodsmoke and man-sweat.

He held me out from him. "Let me see you. Ah, as beautiful as always, more so, I think." He grinned and kissed me, as thorough a kiss as I had hoped for. He was browner than his buckskins, making his white teeth and blue eyes stand out.

One of the farmhands ran up to us. "May I tend to your horse, sir?" he asked.

"Yes, please, and give him oats," said James, turning over the reins. To me he said, "I am filthy. I should wash up before we talk more."

I smiled and led him to the outside washing area. "How I have missed you! I will bring you some warm water," I said, but he shook his head.

"You will find me more like a wild Indian," he said. "They wash every morning, no matter how cold the water."

I helped him strip down to the skin. We poured cold water over him, and I offered a sliver of soap. His body was hard with muscle and almost as brown as his face. True to his word, he didn't shiver under the water but did seem to enjoy the soap and the rough towel I dried him with. I dried him very thoroughly *all over*.

Before we knew it, we were in the woods, on a bed of pine needles. "You are cleaner than I," I said around his kiss. There was no comment to this, but only the lovemaking I would never forget.

As if in a dream, he leaned over me, kissing, undressing, caressing, rough hands over all my body until he found the tender parts, wet and swollen for him. He eased in gently, then groaned and quickened his pace until we were both beyond reason in our pleasure.

"Sorry," he said as he came in one jerking burst, but it was good.

God, how had I lived without this! I'd never live without it again, I promised myself, even if it meant going into battle with him.

His hands roved over my body, giving me tingles of delight. He gently cupped my breasts. He smoothed over my stomach. I looked up at his intent face.

"So when is the baby due?" he asked, suppressing his grin. "And when was it you were planning to tell me?"

I laughed. "The baby flew out of my mind along with everything else when I saw *you*," I said. "Let's see. You left in March, so it must have been that last night, umm, remember?"

"I do remember. It has kept the Cherokee women off me all these months, and they are very handsome and willing," he teased. I swatted at him, but he caught my hand. "Ah, I see how you have missed me!" he said, ducking my next blow.

"Scoundrel!" I replied.

Off in the distance, I heard Gwyn calling me. I hurried into my clothes. James's were back at the washing stand. "I'll get yours," I whispered.

Before I reached the washing stand, Gwyn came along the path, holding James's clothes. I startled her, but not before she had seen James in his nakedness. She swung around from the scene, her face reddening. A small "Oh!" escaped her as she flung the clothes at me and hurried back toward the house.

"We've embarrassed her," I said. "I'll go to her."

When I pushed through the bushes, she was breathing deeply.

"I'm sorry," I said, to her stiff back.

She turned to me. "Ardath, I was afraid for you. It looked like you had been dragged into the woods by a stranger without any of us hearing!"

"Oh, I didn't think anyone would notice, but I *am* sorry."

She heaved one more sigh. "It's all right. I know you were eager to be alone together." She cleared her throat, staring at the ground. "Supper is ready."

*****

Before James and I appeared at the table, Gwyn had told them about James's arrival. Even with him there, it started as a somber meal. It was still so soon after their mother's death. However, the little boys wanted stories about the Indians, which James told, lightening the mood. I wondered at how genuine he was with them. It seemed he would be a naturally good father.

I sat back, watching the gazes around the table. James looked at the boys, seated opposite him with their fingers still twined in Gwyn's skirts. Gwyn looked at James and, at times, at the silent David. Her face softened distinctly when she looked at our host, but her expression toward James was unreadable. Once, she looked at me and was surprised to see me staring back. She dropped her eyes to her plate and ate with deliberate motions from then on, except when attending to the boys.

"James, how did you reach us so quickly? We've been here less than two weeks," Gwyn said.

His smile was tired. "Let's just say I didn't sleep much and I wore out my poor horse, Augustus." He turned to me. "I chanced to meet Fox on the trail when I was heading for the Wagon Road to report back to the colonel in Philadelphia. When he told me you were on this road, I diverted in this direction."

"Your work with the Cherokee is finished, then?" I asked.

"Yes, for now at least." He paused. "David, what more have you found out about the sisters' mother?"

"Oh, I thought Ardath might have told you. Mrs. Rhys was never here. I just discovered that the man lied to me for the reward I offered. I truly regret the trouble that caused! I have heard nothing else concerning her."

"That is bad news! An honest mistake, though," James said. "I hope you will let me repay you for the money lost."

"Oh, no, sir! This is for family," said David. "And even if not for family, it would be more than repaid by the help my cousins have given me since they arrived."

Gwyn blushed, and I merely nodded.

"We should speak at some length about your overseer, Prentiss," I said.

"Thank you. Let's discuss it tomorrow morning," David said. "Now I will take my boys to their bed and sleep with them, so that you may have my bed. Now you must have family business you would like to discuss in private." He gathered the baby in his arms and gestured for the children to follow him out of the room. He seemed much calmer than when we arrived. Gwyn had given him a tincture of lemon balm to take each day and valerian to help him sleep. I do believe we had helped him regain himself in other ways as well.

"Well, now we have to decide where our future lies," I said.

"I can hardly face that trail again," said Gwyn.

"I can understand that! It was very brave of you to come all this way. I greatly admire your devotion to your mother, although she definitely seems worthy of it," James said. He cleared his throat. "You must forgive me, but my road is clear. I need to get to Philadelphia to report to the colonel, by the quickest way. Fox told me of a guide we can hire here who will take us to the coast at Wilmington, whence we can get a ship."

"Oh, a ship!" I exclaimed. "I thought the trails to the coast were too rough."

"They would be without a guide. They are worse than the Wagon Road for having no markings. Only the natives can see their paths, but the rivers flow the way we want to go!"

"Well, I suppose we should be on our way, then, as soon as we can," I said, looking at Gwyn from the corner of my eyes. She appeared rather doubtful, I thought.

"Please excuse me," she said, leaving the table abruptly.

My fears returned, that, even though we now had a way out, she would want to stay. Well, we'd have to see, but in the morning.

"David has given us a bed big enough for us to sleep in together," I said to James.

"Again, please forgive me, for this night I shall truly need to sleep," he said, smiling down at me. So we did.

CHAPTER 89

July 1752
Gwyn

Just when I had decided I was ready to be a grown woman, I had to see James's beautiful body, his love for Ardath, his good way with David's boys. It tortured me. I might be ready for a man like that, but it was Ardath who had him. That these were unworthy thoughts was not lost on me; I struggled to keep down my jealousy.

At the same time, I found myself drawn to David without wanting to be. Something about those snapping black eyes told me he'd normally be a man of spirit and humor, as well as one who was to be reckoned with. Since the search for Mother was at an end for now, I could see myself staying with him and his darling boys, a ready-made family.

Then, guilt on guilt, I remembered that Gregory waited for me in Philadelphia. And that I wanted to go home, to be amongst people who had long loved me, in a familiar place. I longed to learn more of herbal and other kinds of healing alongside Ibrahim. I wanted to be a doctor.

David approached me as I ruminated on the garden bench. "Gwyn, I don't want to disturb you."

"Oh, no, you won't," I said, smiling at him. I felt my heart lift, just seeing him.

"Ardath and Major James are telling me that you must be on your way to the coast as soon as they find the guide."

"Oh, yes, I know," I said. The breeze stirred a lock of his black hair, which he brushed away. The veins standing out on his strong young hands sent waves of desire and tenderness over me. He took my hand in his, gazing first at our hands together, and then directly into my eyes.

"You may think me highly inappropriate for saying this." He hesitated. "But this is not a normal time for me in any way, so I will just say what is in my heart." He very gently trailed his fingers across my wrist. "In the short time you have been here, I have come to admire you very much, your kindness, your competence, your beauty, your steadfastness. I want you to stay here with us, to be my wife and a mother to my boys. I have no doubt we will grow to love each other even more deeply over time."

"Oh, David, I am so glad you can see me in this way, for I am drawn to you as well." It hurt to see the hope leap into his eyes, so I hurried on. "But I want to go home. I'm sorry. It has nothing to do with you. I want to explore my life there, to get my feet under me, to learn to live without our mother."

His gaze again fell to our hands, twisted together on our knees. "I only know that I want you to stay," he said.

All against my better judgment, I took his chin in my hands, turned his face toward mine, and kissed him full on the lips. Aroused, we kissed deeply, hungering for the touch, the comfort, the joining of spirits and bodies.

"Daddy," we heard little David say from the back of the house, "can you come to help me?"

David sighed. "Children have a way, don't they?"

I breathed deeply and tried to control my racing heart. Was this what a true love was supposed to feel like?

As I sat there, Ardath came to join me. "Sister, we'll have to leave soon. What are you thinking about all this?" She waved her hands around vaguely.

"You mean, what do I think about leaving?" I asked.

"Yes, and about going back to Philadelphia, about not finding Mother, any of it?"

"Well, not finding Mother makes me feel aimless, a purpose gone, sad. I guess I want to go back to Philadelphia…"

"You don't sound so sure about that," Ardath said.

"Why wouldn't I be?" I answered, too sharply.

She looked up at the leaves above us, still as green as early summer.

"It's just, well, I see how you look at David. I don't think it's just pity in your eyes," she said.

"It's not. He wants me to stay, to marry him."

"Oh?" Her brow knitted. "But that's what *he* wants. What about you?"

"Oh, it's so clear," I said sarcastically. I threw out my arms. "I want to stay and I want to go. There!" I said.

"Well, David will be here. I doubt he'll find someone very soon. You could come back with us and see if your heart grows fonder with distance."

My sister, the impulsive one, suddenly giving me sage advice. Would wonders never cease?

"I feel tired," I said.

We stood to go when we heard James calling.

"Ladies, please sit again," he said when he reached us. "I have found the guide. He will be ready to leave here in two days. Does that give you enough time to prepare?"

"But…but," I said and caught myself. "But what about the horses?"

"Ah, we shall have to leave our horses with David. They deserve the rest! The guide will take us on his mounts on the long trails to the river, whence we shall board canoes to get to the coast. It is the fastest way to go in this direction. I believe you haven't many things to carry?"

I smiled. No truer words! "But what about our wagon, at Bethabara?"

"Hopefully, the Moravians can make good use of it, a sort of payment for their help," said Ardath. "You could send a letter to Kalberhahn."

"Oh, yes, good," I said. "Ardath, what about clothes for you?" I answered myself. "Perhaps we can make over one of Rose's gowns. It will be too short, but I can make a ruffle from Mr. Boone's gown to lengthen it."

"Excellent!" said James, all business now that a plan was in place.

"Gwyn, I'll go look at Rose's gowns again. Can you ask David if we can have one?"

"Yes, I'll speak to him," I said.

I first went to see Molly. How steadfast she had been, and how loving!

I looked into her deep-brown eyes, stroked her nose, and gave her a carrot. I whispered, "Thank you. Rest now, you good girl."

Then I dragged myself back to the house, dreading what I'd tell David, yet somehow cheered by the idea of moving along. I found him in the kitchen, shooing little David out the back.

He smiled happily. "Ah, just the person I wanted to see." He stopped. "What's wrong?" he said, gazing at my face.

"Well, James has just told us that we leave in two days," I said.

"We? You are going with them?" he asked. His mouth settled into a line.

"I'm sorry. I have to go back. We need time to understand how we feel about each other, don't you think?" I said, my heart pleading with him to understand.

"I don't need time, but"—he paused—"I want you to have the time. You are several years younger than I. We must not rush you. May I hold you?" he said.

We stood, comforted, in each other's arms for a long while.

Finally, I pushed away. "Ardath needs a gown for the journey. Would you let us take one of Rose's? I'll understand if you don't want us to," I said.

"No, that's fine. If you would, take the rest and get rid of them, please." He turned, leaving through the back.

I looked after him with longing. Had I just closed the door on my best chance at happiness?

Rose had ample sewing supplies. It was not too difficult to make over a yellow dress with an extra panel and flounces from Boone's muslin gown. Ardath actually looked quite good in it, since her cheeks were so round and pink from the pregnancy. She never wore it in front of David, of course. We reverted to breeches for the journey, anyway, which left the little boys giggling.

Since we had been at David's, Auri had deserted me in favor of the children, who ran and played with him all day. He truly belonged here more than with me, and I no longer depended on his companionship as I once had. When David and I told the boys that I was leaving, they looked very sad. But when I told them Auri could stay, they cheered up immediately.

"I know you will take very good care of him, won't you?" I asked.

"Yes, yes, Gwyn," they said and called for Auri, who came at a run. I rubbed his ears and said, "You be a good boy now."

"Wuv you, Gwyn," said Solomon, and he and little David threw themselves at me for a hug. I held their moist bodies tightly, smiling through tears. Then they ran off to chase Auri to the barn.

"Thank you, for so many things. Please come back to me," said David, wiping his eyes.

"I will if I can," I promised. "Will you write to me?"

"Of course, and I'll be thinking of you always!" he said. We held each other again, then kept our feelings to ourselves.

*****

Of our journey, I have little to say. I felt safe with James and our guide, Three Deer, and sank into my own thoughts while Ardath and James told each other stories of their separate adventures. All I wanted, now that it was decided, was to reach Wilmington and start home.

CHAPTER 90

July 1752
Carys

I WAS THROWN INTO confusion by the news from the South Carolina governor that my brother-in-law, Thomas, was looking for me. Alex and Marta were most solicitous about it. What did I want to do? I could stay with them always, they said, but did I want to go to family? I remembered Thomas Rhys as a kind man but had thought his wife shrewish. What would I tell them about Dougie? Could I convince those who knew Jacob so well that Dougie was his son? Or should I tell them I had adopted him from a family who didn't want him; it was true enough. I was undecided what to do next.

In any event, Alex was not able to find the ship he wanted in Charles Town, so we embarked again, next traveling to the Wilmington shipyards. If I wanted to take a ship going on to Philadelphia, I'd be going the right direction at least. Also, I wondered if I might see Kate or Pete, since they would have settled near there.

We stayed at first in the inn, where we were comfortable, although Wilmington felt just as hot and wet as Charles Town.

Alex spoke to Marta and me at supper after we had been there several days. "It seems there is no ship for sale that meets my needs. We will have to stay while a ship is built. The shipbuilder says that he can begin immediately. It should take him two or three months to complete it. If it takes three, we would be going to the Indies at the worst time for storms, but..."

"Then what should we do in the meantime?" asked Marta.

"Be a lady of leisure, my dear." He smiled; I saw that thought made him happy.

Neither of us women was happy with leisure, though, so Alex rented a small house with a garden, where Marta, Dougie, and I spent all hours except the hottest ones in the flower and vegetable beds. When Alex wasn't working with the shipbuilder or talking with merchants about buying his wares in the next year, we all drove in a carriage to a nearby beach, where Dougie got to play in the ocean. He loved it, chased the birds, leaned over the shells and sand crabs in fascination, and came home entirely covered in sand. He had to go into the dunking barrel, where we rinsed him off, usually every day. He thought it great fun!

Before he went off to the shipyard one day, I asked Alex, "Would it be possible for me to take ship to Philadelphia and return while you are still here?"

He smiled at me. "That might be a good idea. You could meet with your brother-in-law and consider a life there. If you decided to stay, you could send notice to us here." He tilted his head. "Of course, I selfishly wish you would return to the islands with us," he said.

"It is so kind of you to wish it, and that may well be the best plan," I said. "I do feel I should respond to Thomas in *some* way, though." In the end, I wrote to my brother-in-law, sending the letter by packet boat. Alex thought the packet trip might take two weeks or so.

In the meantime, I left Dougie with Marta at times to walk past the few houses and establishments that constituted little Wilmington. Most were modest board houses, but two were in a pleasing pinkish brick. A grand palace was planned for the governor there, but Governor Johnston was never seen, perhaps too ill to stir from his house. I heard later that he died while we were still there.

Near the small store, I thought I saw Kate and Pete, but when I approached, it was not them. No one that I talked to knew of a Pete McCready.

The most bustling places were the public houses, two of those to serve the roustabouts and shipwrights who worked the docks and shipyards. It was not prudent to go near those working areas or drinking spots at any time of day or night.

For a woman, a full walk around Wilmington made for a short excursion, since the docks were no place for any woman, except maybe the fishwives. As for the rivers, the Cape Fear near town was filled with shipyards and docks, and the Brunswick River of no consequence to us.

*****

It seemed I was destined to see ghosts in Wilmington. One day, I must have been too tired to be out walking. From a distance, I thought I saw Ardath's shining hair, but the woman was in a canoe with an Indian. I couldn't get any closer without venturing onto the wharf. I had found that I couldn't be alone among rough men without reliving my time with Smog.

Of course, it couldn't be her anyway, just some trick of my tired eyes and yearning heart. It sent me to a horrible nightmare place, where I again saw my girls drowning. I hurried home to Dougie and my kind Marta.

When I told her about it, Marta said, "Mi Querida, do not think about their passing. Think instead of the happy times you had together, the brave and kind girls you raised. Be proud that you had them with you in their beauty and that you all helped so many people around you."

"Marta, you are right, of course. We never know how much or little time we have with the ones we love. It should make us more cautious in giving our hearts, I suppose, but instead it just seems to make those people more precious."

Alex walked in as I was saying this. I looked up briefly. Marta spoke. "She thought she saw Ardath."

Alex hastened to my side. Marta moved over so that he could hold me. I wished I could cry, but I was suspended in my own world.

"What did you see?" Alex asked.

I took a breath. "I saw a woman with red hair in a canoe with an Indian." I gave a mad laugh. Only in the wilds of America could one hear such a strange statement!

"What did they do?" he asked.

"They drifted under the wharf, and I lost sight of them," I said. "I would have followed, but I don't like to be near there."

"Nor should you. I will go down there tomorrow to see if I can find out more," he said.

"Would you, Alex? I have such a strong feeling of my daughters' presence, yet it could just be my longing for them to be alive in this world."

"Ummm," he said, looking sad, but he gave a hearty reply. "Of course, we must investigate! Don't worry." He hugged my shoulders and turned to Dougie, who had crept in and now stood in front of us with a guilty expression on his face. "Young man," he said with mock sternness, "are you not supposed to be in bed for your nap?"

Dougie pretended to look hurt, pushing out his lower lip dramatically. "Noooo?" he said, then burst into laughter.

Alex swung him over his shoulder and returned him to bed, while Marta and I shared a smile. "Such a good boy," she said. "I only hope mine is so sweet!"

"Marta! You have something to tell me?" I asked.

"Shh, I haven't told Alex yet," she said. "I tell him when he returns."

"Oh, happy day! That is wonderful news," I whispered. Marta's happiness buoyed me up so that I went about my chores with a lightened heart.

CHAPTER 91

July 1752
Ardath

I WOULDN'T WANT TO repeat the horseback journey we took across the North Carolina countryside, nor the canoe trip on a slow-moving blackwater river called the Cape Fear. Mosquitos and dark water were the order of each day as we moved into sandy territory. We smeared bear grease on us as Three Deer told us to. It helped prevent bites, but the whine of those bloodthirsty beasts drove me mad.

On the other hand, I was with James, and I believe I have never been so happy. As we sat together in the canoe, we laughed, told stories, and teased each other shamelessly, until I noticed how subdued Gwyn was.

At our camp by the river that night, I asked James quietly, "Could we be a little less jubilant? Gwyn seems sad, having left David so recently. I believe our happiness must emphasize her lack of a love to enjoy."

"Ah, Ardath, you have grown in your sensitivity toward your sister, and I admire that greatly. Of course, we must be more considerate of her."

"Thank you. I found on the journey to North Carolina that she is a person who deserves my respect in every way. Her exceptional courage and good sense showed itself and saved us many a time."

He nodded and looked thoughtful. "Do you suppose she doesn't want to marry Gregory anymore?"

"I don't think anyone knows that, even Gwyn," I said.

"Ummm. I would like to see her settled with someone to support her."

"There's no need for financial support. She can do whatever she wishes,"

I reminded him.

"I forget how I married into money," he said. He cleared his throat. "As for us, I hope we can make all haste to Philadelphia, so we can make plans for our future. There is some possibility that the colonel would want me to be an agent to the Cherokee, as most of the chiefs agreed to be on the English side in the coming war. It will be important to keep their goodwill. Honestly, I was afraid of going to the Indians after what I experienced coming from the Ohio Valley, but these people I respect."

"What of me and the child?"

"It seems unlikely that the fighting will be so far to the south. If it is possible, I would like to take you with me." He held my hand. "I could also serve as a trader to them, to give goods at a fair exchange, which some traders do not. They are a noble and proud people, clever in the ways of the forest, great warriors, and well-spoken."

"So I felt when we met Fox," I said. "If we go, I would like to see if they could accept better practices for preventing the small pox among them."

"Fox will try to pave the way for that there, but traditions are there for a reason, and they are hard to change. They have an enviable closeness of community."

"If you were a trader, we could get them implements to make their lives easier. They have a treasure to trade in ginseng, a most miraculous herb that probably saved my life on the trail. I blush to tell you that I could not stay alert in the first months of my pregnancy. At times, Gwyn had to carry me, well, almost. I missed your strong arms."

"Oh, is that all you missed?" he said, sticking out his lower lip in an exaggerated pout.

"Well...," I said, raising one brow.

"Aww, just my weak little woman," he teased. "Just my little baby carrier! Ouw! Don't hit me, woman!" And we were off in gales of laughter, this time as muffled as we could make them.

*****

Finally, finally! We were at the settlement, for it could hardly be called a town, of Wilmington. From the river, the main view was of the docks and shipyard. We pulled into the wharf and tied up the canoe. Three Deer stayed with me while James and Gwyn went up some steps to inquire about a ship to Philadelphia. This time we were in luck, as there was a ship standing off in the harbor that could take us as passengers.

We rowed immediately to the ship, climbed the shaky ladder to board her, and were welcomed by Captain Rogers, a tall rangy man with squinted eyes.

"There is only one cabin available, I'm afraid, but it might do for the ladies," he said. "There is a berth amongst the other passengers for the gentleman." He bowed slightly toward James.

"That will be sufficient," James said. "What provisions should we lay on for journey?"

"We have very little fresh fruit, so you might wish to procure more. I will show you to the cabin so that you may see what else you require. We will be here two more days, but sail with the tide on Wednesday morning. Today you may use the lighter to go to town for supplies, if you wish."

"That's good," said James.

Well, we were back on a ship. This voyage would never take us too far from land, for which I was grateful. Thank goodness I didn't have the morning sickness that many women suffered, nor was I prone to seasickness. I was out of the ginseng that had helped me on the trail, though, and I still felt languid at times. This afternoon was one of those times. James insisted that I stay aboard while he and Gwyn traveled on the lighter, a barge-like vessel made for hauling goods between ships or between ships and shore. They would arrange for us to stay in an inn, if one was available.

He paid Three Deer, and I think generously, as the normally quiet Indian was exuberant in his thanks. Then James and Gwyn set off with the lighter and I, having requested that hammocks be hung in our cabin, went there to rest.

CHAPTER 92

July 1752
Gwyn

EVER THE GENTLEMAN, JAMES helped me onto the lighter. It seemed to move slowly, after our experience in the swift canoe.

I didn't know how to make use of the time with James as we crept along. We first compared notes on our list and felt we had remembered what was needed.

James cleared his throat. "I'm sorry you didn't find your mother. I can't imagine what you must have felt when David told you that you all had been tricked."

"It was a horrible time, but perhaps the worst for David, having just lost his wife," I said.

"Ardath said you had premonitions that she wasn't there," he said.

I looked up at him. We sat close together on a small bench that was the only seat for passengers. "Thank you for not doubting me, for not doubting that I sometimes see things."

"Oh, no, I don't doubt that for a moment! My family has an estate in Wales at Glenmorgan. Some of my happiest times as a child were spent there. I have great respect for the Welsh people, and I know for a fact that our nursemaid could see around corners and sometimes into the future as well. Unfortunately, she warned my older brothers never to go to sea or they would be in great danger. When my mother got wind of that, poor Elen was gone from our lives in a wink."

"Oh, dear. Did your brothers ever go to sea?"

"Oh, no, I think they remember and respect Elen as I do. They are complete landlubbers." He showed those very white teeth.

"You have a sister as well, I believe," I said.

"Yes, the best person in the whole family! Luckily, she doesn't take after our mother." He looked quite serious.

"Is your mother so awful, then?" I asked, half-teasing.

"Little sister, she is thoroughly awful!" He shook his head. "Poor Elizabeth writes to me often, in desperation. I wish I could get her out of there, but they want to marry her off to some old goat with a fortune." He sighed, a heartfelt sound.

"Oh, I'm sorry to bring up such a hard subject," I said.

He shifted a bit on the seat. "Gwyn, I shouldn't ask, I guess, but have you had any premonitions about the baby?"

"Only that I know you and Ardath are very strong and likely to have a strong child," I said. "But anyone could see that."

He smiled, nodded. "Thank you. It will be good to get back to Philadelphia and plan our futures. Have you thought ahead to what yours may look like?"

"You mean will I marry Gregory, don't you?" I asked.

"Never fool with a seer," he said. "It is none of my business, though."

"My future is a mystery to me, honestly, except that I would like to learn more from Ibrahim, grow to be a good healer like him," I said.

"One thing I can see. You will be very successful in whatever you do!" he said.

We felt a bump as the lighter hit the dock. The lighter deck was loaded with water barrels and crates for shore goods. We wound our way through them. The burly seaman helped James and me up the ladder, then tied the boat in with a huge hawser.

"Sir, if you could, be back in two hours," he said.

"Yes, of course," James said.

We first secured rooms in the inn for two nights. It wasn't hard to find the general store, not far from the dock and, in fact, almost next door to the inn.

It was a very ordinary day, in a very ordinary little town, but something felt very strange to me. "James, I believe I need something to drink," I said, sitting down on the bench outside the store.

"Of course. Do you want me to stay with you?" he asked with great concern.

"No, just a drink, please," I said. I had never felt such a strange overweening weakness before. James went inside quickly. That was when I saw the ghost coming down the street.

The ghost looked like Alex, hobbled around like him, but had white hair curling out from his broad-brimmed hat. He was dressed like a merchant, not a seaman, and he held the arm of a woman of color almost as brown as he.

I rose in a dream, calling out to him. "Alex, Alex!" the ghost looked up the street at me and smiled. It was Alex's mouth, no mistaking that. What was happening to me?

The ghost hurried up to me, took my arm. "Ma'am, are you all right? Do I know you?" he asked, puzzled. It was Alex's voice!

"Alex?" I asked.

"Yes, ma'am," he said, tilting his head in the old way and removing his hat. We stared at each other.

At that moment, James emerged with a bottle in his hand. "Good God Almighty!" he said.

"Do I know you also?" he asked James. He shaded his eyes with his hand. Suddenly, I realized that Alex couldn't see us very well as the sun shone behind us.

"Alex, it is Major James and Gwyn Rhys from the ship!" James said.

"From the *Gracious Anne*? But I saw her go down! I saw everyone die."

"No. We didn't go down. The ship grounded on an island in the storm. All left aboard survived and sailed into Philadelphia eventually," James said. "But how are *you* here?" he asked.

"Oh my! Oh dear! Unbelievable! A very long story, but I found the longboat," Alex said, white beneath his tan. He hugged James unashamedly and turned to take me in his arms soon thereafter. Our bodies shook. It was shock to us all!

Alex drew a deep breath and turned to his companion. "And…and please allow me to introduce my wife, Marta."

Marta smiled a huge smile for us. "Friends of Alex, gives me pleasure!" she said, holding out her hand.

"You made it to Philadelphia, a miracle!" Alex said. He looked around. "Ardath too?" he asked.

"Yes, Ardath too. She is my wife now," said James.

"Oh, yes, well, congratulations! How eventful our lives have been!" Suddenly, Alex said, "Oh my! But she doesn't know, does she?"

"Who, Ardath?" I asked.

Marta grabbed Alex's arm. "Look!" Along the dusty street came another ghost.

My heart squeezed in my chest. It looked like Mother hurrying along, with a small boy in tow, calling, "Alex, whoever is this?"

Time stopped then. It restarted violently. I had to gulp a breath. This was no ghost, but our true, real mother. I ran to her. "Mother! We never gave up!" I cried, holding her to my breast, panting with the enormity of it, my vision blurring with tears.

She held me back for a moment, staring into my face. "Oh, my Gwyn, this must be heaven! To see you again, a grown woman, but still my precious girl! But…how?" Tears poured down her cheeks, anointing us both with happiness.

James stood by, clearing his throat and wiping his eyes as if dust had got in them.

Alex wrung his hands, a pained expression on his face. "Oh, dear, so sorry, really was sure, oh dear," he said.

"No apology, Alex. This is the happiest moment of my life! You must be happy too!" said Mother, grinning her broadest.

"And so I am," he said, looking every inch of it.

"Mother, this is Major James. He was a large part of the effort to save the ship, including both Ardath and me!" I said.

"Major, thank you! Oh, my girls!" Mother said.

"Madam, I have the honor of being married to your daughter Ardath."

"Married, oh, yes, I see," she said, shaking her head as if to clear confusion. I still clung to her as if my life depended upon it.

Marta said, "What do you think, Dougie?"

"Of course, Dougie," said Mother, smiles beaming from her face. She drew the little boy from behind her skirts. He stared at us with wide eyes.

"Dougie?" I asked.

"Oh, there is so much to tell, Gwyn. Dougie is my adopted son."

I looked down at the jolly little chap. What a story Mother must have! I thought. All of us did! Suddenly, I had a brother.

He had the most angelic, rosy face, with curly brown hair bleached almost to blond, and clear blue eyes that strangely reminded me of James's.

"Dougie, here is your sister Gwyn," said Mother.

He reached for me with a giggle. I knelt in the dirt street, and soon he was in my arms. Showing himself to be a very beloved child, he melted into my breast as if he had always known me. I turned to show him to James, who had a most peculiar expression on his face. Another ghost? But I soon forgot my curiosity, jiggling Dougie up and down to his delight.

"I thought I had lost all my family!" exclaimed Mother. "I am a rich, rich woman! But where is Ardath?"

James replied, "Ardath is resting on the ship." He looked at me as if I should be the bearer of news.

"Mother, Ardath is with child. Now you can deliver her!" I didn't say, "And I don't have to."

I had thought her smile could not get brighter. "But she is all right, Gwyn?"

"Oh, yes, fine!" I said.

"I'm afraid I must sit down," said Mother in a weak voice.

"Please, let us adjourn to our house," said Alex.

"I must return to the ship and tell Ardath the happy news," said James. Alex pointed at the house on the far end of the street. James bowed and walked the other way.

When we arrived at the house, we retired to the shade of the garden trees. The temperature was soaring. I would never get used to these Southern Lowlands. That thought called to mind David. What if I had stayed with him? Well, I wouldn't be here with Mother, Alex, and my new brother. Present circumstance seemed to confirm that I had made the right choice!

We sat silent for a moment while Marta left to bring us ale. Then everyone began to talk at once, so that no one could be heard.

"All hands!" Alex called with a smile. "I think we should first explain what we are all doing here and make at least a preliminary plan for the immediate future. Gwyn, you start."

"Mother, we have been looking for you. We sent out notices in Wales and in most parts of America. Uncle Thomas's son, David, heard that you were near him in Anson County, North Carolina. We had settled in Philadelphia but came down the Wagon Road, hoping to find you. When we got to David's, we found that we had been tricked. You had never really been seen there. Major James joined us at David's, but he needs to report to his commander in Philadelphia, so we have booked passage on a ship that sails in several days. You must join us with Dougie, and we can all go to the home we have made there," I said, running out of breath.

"Good nutshell of it, Gwyn!" said Alex. "But I must know briefly how the ship survived."

"Well, it wasn't a short or easy trip. The storm pushed us far to the north. We came aground on a rocky island. After the ship was repaired, Ardath was able to guide us westward using the tools you had taught her. Eventually, with some help from the navy, we were able to limp into Philadelphia."

"My word! I don't know how you did it. Later, there must be a full accounting of it. There weren't any sailors alive on the deck when I was swept into the water. By God's mercy, I crawled into the longboat and survived. I truly believed I saw the ship go down!" He fell silent.

"Mother, how are you here?" I asked.

"Mine is a long story too. But suffice it to say that I was abducted when coming home from delivering a baby. I traveled a long way tied to a wagon.

Then I was forced to deliver Dougie, but the woman in charge wanted my abductors to kill Dougie and me. I talked those two ruffians into selling us into slavery instead. In short, we were brought by slave ship to Jamaica, where I had the good fortune to be given as a gift to Alex."

"Dios Mio!" said Marta. "No one could make up stories more fantasticos!"

Alex said, "Marta is right. Yet it happened… Gwyn, your mother and Dougie have become part of our family, but now that you are here, I believe they must go with you to Philadelphia. Marta and I must stay here to get our ship built. Then we will be merchant seamen," he said, squeezing Marta's arm affectionately.

"What do you say, Mother? Will you go with us?"

At that moment, James peered around the frame of the house. "Ah, good, the right house," he said. He reached behind him to lead out and steady Ardath, red of eye from weeping, tears still rolling down her cheeks. She rushed to Mother, clinging as I had clung, as if there were no one else in the world.

"I hardly dared believe," Ardath sobbed. "Oh, Mother, I have failed you! I am not always kind, and I didn't protect Gwyn as I should have, and now I am being weak and womanish!"

"Ardath, my beloved daughter, it is not weak to have strong feelings about those you love. Obviously, Gwyn is fine, and so are you," Mother soothed. She held Ardath at arm's length to look at her. Her mouth pursed in mischief. "What is this I hear, that you will make me a grandmother?"

She and Ardath embraced again. Then, of course, the brief version of everyone's story had to be repeated. It still amazed us all.

Later, when our hearts had stopped racing and we could breathe more easily, we sat in smaller groups in Alex's little house. Ardath was answering Alex's questions about "the miracle" of how we had managed to salvage the ship, while James sat nearby to add details at times. He moved to the floor where Dougie was playing with his little feet. He seemed very drawn to Dougie. I hoped his first child would be a boy.

I could not be far from Mother, of course, and sat near her in a chair. She looked at me, tilting her head. "Dear Gwyn, I'm so sorry you had to endure the pain of losing both your father and me, and the hard trip down the road to

North Carolina, only to be met with disappointment."

"Thank you, Mother. It does seem a hard life we have seen since we lost you, and not only our own, but so many others."

"Gwyn, you are such a good heart. You feel everyone's pain and wish to ease it, don't you?"

"Yes, I know that can't be, but I do wish it." I smiled, feeling wistful. "Perhaps that is what makes me so determined to study with our doctor friend, Ibrahim, when we return to Philadelphia. Wait until you meet him. He is such a kind man and so well versed in the medicine of the Moors. It is a much-better physic than practiced by the English. He needs a midwife to help him, and I don't know enough yet to do so. I want to learn more from you, of course, because you are greatly esteemed as both midwife *and* healer."

She smiled at me. "I believe we can learn from each other. I am eager to know more about the plants you have been studying here and to tell you about the ones I found in Jamaica. This Ibrahim sounds quite impressive as well. And beyond gaining knowledge, there is a passion in you to heal. It was there when you were a tiny thing, bringing home injured animals. Together, even though we can't help everyone, we can do much good."

"I believe we *can* do some good." I beamed at my mother, who deeply understood so much of importance in life.

Ardath and James had gone outside. I was suddenly glad that it was her place to be with him, not mine.

Alex excused himself to find Marta. "May I take Dougie with me?" he asked.

"Of course, he should be outside," Mother replied.

Alex swung Dougie into his arms, and out they went, accompanied by Dougie's infectious giggles.

"I wonder whether Ardath will join us in our healing practice," she said when we were alone.

"Perhaps, but Ardath also shows great skill and interest in starting and running business enterprises. You'll see when we get to Philadelphia all the things she has established. She is good at making money multiply."

"Money? We have never had that!"

"But we do now. Father had some silver saved to make his way in the New World, and then there is the gold the slave trader was carrying."

"Silver? Gold?" she said, her brow creased in curiosity and amazement.

I told her the stories of how we had come to have these things until I thought her jaw would drop in surprise.

"It seems I shouldn't have worried about how you and Ardath would take care of yourselves!" Mother said.

"Well, we always had help of one kind or another. James has loaned us his strength, for example."

"He seems a very able man."

"Yes, he is. You should have seen how magnificent he was on the ship." I blushed to think of my feelings for him.

Mother understood, I think, without me telling her any more. "According to Ardath, I believe you have left behind two men who love you, as you came in search of me."

"I have wanted so badly to talk to you about them. Gregory in Philadelphia and then David. Both want to marry me, or at least I *think* Gregory still does. I don't know what to do."

"What do you feel when you are with each of them?"

"Gregory is a little older. He's clever and funny. He makes me feel safe and loved. His was my first kiss."

"But?" she said, with a very slight smile.

"But David is a passionate man. What I feel with him is different. I feel his ardor and my own. His children are precious and need a mother badly."

"But?" Mother said again.

"I have *you* now, and Philadelphia feels like home. I hardly know him, and I don't know if I could live in such isolation on that frontier."

"But?"

"But, he excites such feelings in me!"

"He has shown you a side of yourself you didn't see before," she said.

"Yes, that's it! I felt like a full woman with him, but maybe that was just happening anyway."

"You are still so young and have much of your life to explore yet. Perhaps now is not the time to make a decision between two men, both of whom you love in different ways. I think confusion is just natural."

She reached to curl some of my hair behind my ear. "I reared you girls to seek knowledge of the whole world, including yourselves. Now your world has widened and your knowledge needs time to widen too. Although, I must say that you have had experiences of which others your age, or *any* age, couldn't even conceive."

We laughed. I felt such a sense of relief. My worries slid off my shoulders. How I had missed her guidance and love! We linked arms and I laid my head upon her shoulder. I could wait and learn. That seemed the best plan indeed.

We stood, as Alex and Marta reentered the room with Dougie close behind. "James says the ship must leave in three days' time," Alex said to Mother. "Suddenly, we are to part after all we have experienced together. We will miss you without end, but I am happy for you, dear Carys. I do require a promise from you that you will visit us and bring Dougie to play with our son or daughter. Also, who knows? Maybe our ship will sail someday into Philadelphia harbor!"

"You know how much Dougie and I love you both," said my mother. "Rest assured we will keep in touch and will long to see you again."

"I am sorry you must go, Carys, my dear friend," said Marta. "Will you stay with us until you must leave? We will help you get your things together and enjoy time with Dougie too."

"Is that all right with you?" she asked me.

"Of course. We are not far away, at the inn," I said.

At that moment, James and Ardath joined us, Ardath immediately making for Mother to hold her as I did. Dougie pulled up on her skirts and stood swaying and laughing.

"As much as I hate to leave you," Mother said to Alex and Marta, "I must go with my children. In the old world or the new, wherever my children are, that is my home."

Historical Note

While inspired by a true family story, this is a work of fiction. I have tried to place historical figures in their correct times and places. However, I must apologize to the courageous Moravian Brethren for placing their settlement in North Carolina several years before they actually reached there. The wagon train that the sisters meet up with in the book is fictitious. Ben Franklin and Susanna Wright may not have met until the year 1753.

ACKNOWLEDMENTS

MANY THANKS TO MY Grove Writers' Group colleagues, who helped me through the years with their excellent advice and steered me away from the potholes I might have fallen into.

Thanks also to my friends Bonnie Mastro, Peggy Brooks, and Sandra Smith, who read through the entire manuscript and gave important feedback.

Most of all, I thank my husband for his encouragement and perseverance. He got me to the places I needed for research, whether they were Philadelphia, the Wagon Road, or the Welsh manor house and castle of the Rice/Rhys family. His generosity and love strengthen my foundation.

ABOUT THE AUTHOR

SUSAN POSEY LOVES SEARCHING in the woods for wild plants, studying family history, and writing, now that she has retired from her practice of psychotherapy.

Research in Wales, where she found the Rhys/Reese/Rice family castle ruins and manor house, was a delight. She also traveled the Great Wagon Road from Philadelphia to Bethania, North Carolina. Unlike the sisters in the book (her many times great aunts), she had bridges to cross all those rivers.

She lives in the Western North Carolina mountains with her family.

CPSIA information can be obtained
at www.ICGtesting.com
Printed in the USA
LVHW031932110720
660354LV00001B/26

9 781645 444633